OF A
DARKER VOID

ASTERION NOIR: BOOK 2

G. S. JENNSEN

HYPERNOVA
PUBLISHING
2018

OF A DARKER VOID

Copyright © 2018 by G. S. Jennsen

Cover design by G. S. Jennsen, Alex Smith, Bonus Experiment and Obsidian Dawn.
Cover typography by G. S. Jennsen

All rights reserved. No part of this publication may be reproduced, distributed or
transmitted in any form or by any means, including photocopying, recording, or
other electronic or mechanical methods, without the prior written permission of
the publisher, except in the case of brief quotations embodied in critical reviews
and certain other noncommercial uses permitted by copyright law. For
permission requests, write to the publisher, addressed "Attention: Permissions
Coordinator," at the address below.

Hypernova Publishing
P.O. Box 2214
Parker, Colorado 80134
www.hypernovapublishing.com

Publisher's Note: This is a work of fiction. Names, characters, places, and
incidents are a product of the author's imagination. Locales and public names are
sometimes used for atmospheric purposes. Any resemblance to actual people,
living or dead, or to businesses, companies, events, institutions, or locales is
completely coincidental.

The Hypernova Publishing name, colophon and logo are trademarks of
Hypernova Publishing.

Ordering Information:
Hypernova Publishing books may be purchased for educational, business or sales
promotional use. For details, contact the "Special Markets Department" at the
address above.

Of A Darker Void / G. S. Jennsen.—1st ed.

LCCN 2018913550
ISBN 978-1-7323977-3-6

BOOKS BY G. S. JENNSEN

ASTERION NOIR

EXIN EX MACHINA
OF A DARKER VOID

AURORA RHAPSODY

AURORA RISING
STARSHINE
VERTIGO
TRANSCENDENCE

AURORA RENEGADES
SIDESPACE
DISSONANCE
ABYSM

AURORA RESONANT
RELATIVITY
RUBICON
REQUIEM

SHORT STORIES
RESTLESS, VOL. I • *RESTLESS, VOL. II* • *APOGEE*
SOLATIUM • *VENATORIS* • *RE/GENESIS* • *MERIDIAN*

LEARN MORE AT GSJENNSEN.COM/BOOKS

For Kepler and Dawn: you both performed above and beyond to your last drops of fuel. Dawn, you showed us new wonders of our own solar system. Kepler, you showed us that every *solar system is teeming with wonder.*

For Opportunity: if you have seen your last Martian sunrise, know that you made us proud, and one day we will follow in the dusty tracks you laid for us.

DRAMATIS PERSONAE

Nika Tescarav
NOIR Leader; Former External Relations Division Advisor

Dashiel Ridani
Industry Division Advisor; Owner, Ridani Enterprises

Perrin Benvenit
NOIR Personnel Director

Joaquim Lacese
NOIR Operations Director

Adlai Weiss
Justice Division Advisor

Maris Debray
Culture Division Advisor

Grant Mesahle
Owner, Mesahle Flight

Gemina Kail
Administration Division Advisor

Ryan Theroit
NOIR robotics specialist

Spencer Nimoet
Justice Division officer

Blake Satair
Justice Division Advisor

Erik Rhom
Justice Division analyst

Vance Greshe
Ridani Enterprises Manufacturing Dir

Ava Zobel
NOIR weapons specialist

Iona Rowan
External Relations Division Advisor

Dominic Vazhiere
NOIR combat specialist

Cameron Breckel
External Relations Division Advisor

Selene Panetier
Justice Division Advisor

Tristan McLeros
Factory technician

Mason Fassar
External Relations Division Advisor

Xyche'ghael
Taiyok merchant

Simon Granger
CEO, Briscanti Materials

GUIDES

Delacrai (*Kiyora*)

Anavosa (*Mirai*)
Luciene (*Synra*)

Selyshok (*Ebisu*)
Iovimer (*Namino*)

GALAXY MAP

GENNISI GALAXY
(MESSIER 94)

✕
ALIEN STRONGHOLD

MIRAI

○
SR114-IOHI

NAMINO

KIYORA

EBISU

TOKI'TAKU ✳
(TAIYOK HOMEWORLD)

SYNRA

○
HOKAN STATION

✳ CHOSEK
(GHIZERU HOMEWORLD)

✦ ASTERION DOMINION AXIS WORLDS
✦ ASTERION DOMINION ADJUNCT WORLDS
✳ ALIEN WORLDS

ASTERION DOMINION
AXIS WORLDS

MIRAI   NAMINO   SYNRA   EBISU   KIYORA

View the Galaxy Map online at gsjennsen.com/map-darker-void

THE STORY SO FAR

EXIN EX MACHINA

A woman wakes up in a rain-soaked alley with no memory of who she is or how she got there. Two strangers, Perrin and Joaquim, find her and offer to take her in. When asked, she tells them her name is Nika.

Fast forward to five years later. Nika leads an armed team, including Perrin and Joaquim, in an infiltration of a transportation headquarters on Mirai. They break into the data vault and corrupt the passenger records so they can travel without being tracked. A discussion back at their base, The Chalet, reveals the larger purpose of the group, which calls itself 'NOIR': fighting an increasingly repressive government and searching for people who have vanished in the last several years.

Dashiel Ridani, an elite Industry Advisor, discovers that shipments of his company's new product, a virtual limb augment, have been stolen while in transit to retailers. At a meeting between Advisors and the Guides—the leaders of the Dominion government—the Guides brush off the theft in favor of pressuring a Justice Advisor, Adlai Weiss, to apprehend the members of NOIR and bring an end to their disruptive activities. Afterwards, the Guides meet in secret, debating how they can shut NOIR down and hinting at some greater threat to the Dominion.

At The Chalet, one of NOIR's top hackers, Parc Eshett, shows off a new virtual limb augment he's installed.

Nika heads to another Dominion world, Namino, to purchase new equipment from a Taiyok merchant named Xyche. The Taiyoks are a winged alien species known for their cloaking capabilities. While on Namino, she spends an afternoon with her occasional lover, Grant.

Joaquim attends the criminal trial of a former friend. During the trial, he recalls the last time he'd seen his friend, when Joaquim's lover Cassidy was murdered during a police raid on their apartment. After the raid, Joaquim turned his back on that life to start a new one on Mirai.

Dashiel visits Chosek, the homeworld of the Chizeru, a diminutive, pre-industrial alien species. Chosek is rich in kyoseil, a rare mineral Asterions use to enhance their bio-synthetic bodies and many of their technologies, and the Chizeru mine the kyoseil for Asterion businesses.

Later, Dashiel replays a memory from five years earlier. In it, he and a woman make love; their pillow talk involves a series of outpost disappearances on Dominion exploratory worlds. She is worried the Guides are involved and plans to hack into government files in search of evidence. The next night, she disappears; Dashiel has searched for her ever since, to no avail.

On a distant exploratory world, Advisor Gemina Kail oversees the destruction of a lab outpost. The employees living there are gassed, loaded into stasis chambers and shipped to a secret space station.

Nika returns to The Chalet to learn that Parc has been arrested for burglary. She reaches out to a NOIR contact in Justice, Spencer Nimoet, who sneaks her inside the jail to see Parc. He acts very unlike himself—passive and unconcerned about his plight.

Nika, Perrin and Joaquim try to figure out what might have happened to Parc to explain his behavior. Nika and Perrin go see the merchant he purchased the new limb augment from, who tells them the manufacturer is Ridani Enterprises and gives them one of the augments so they can test it.

Another NOIR hacker, Cair, finds a hidden virutox in the augment software. It attaches itself to a user's OS then alters their programming, decreasing impulse control and emotion expression.

Nika, Joaquim and a NOIR robotics specialist, Ryan, infiltrate Ridani Enterprises in a bid to uncover more about the augment and possibly the virutox. Nika is hacking into the server in the CEO's office when Dashiel returns to work and discovers her there. During a tense standoff, her disguise fails, and he recognizes her as the woman from his memory, his lost love who vanished. He asks her to meet him the next day, then urges her to leave before security arrives.

At the meeting, amidst lots of angst on both sides, Dashiel tells Nika she used to be a diplomatic Advisor. He reveals she is a descendant of the fabled First Generation, who led the Asterions across galaxies in search of a new home when their rebellion against the Anaden Empire failed. After recounting the events leading up to her disappearance and his search for answers, he tells her about a psyche backup she kept.

Nika visits the bank where the backup was stored, but her account was emptied out the same day she woke up in an alley with her memory erased. She confronts Dashiel in his home, accusing him of being involved in her psyche-wipe. Devastated at the realization he will never get back the woman he loved and desperate to prove his sincerity, he asks her to experience ('simex') one of his memories from their time together. Secretly wanting to glimpse the woman she supposedly used to be, she agrees.

The memory is of a party at Maris Debray's loft nine years ago. Nika, Dashiel, Maris and Adlai are all clearly friends, and they banter for several minutes before Nika and Dashiel retire to the balcony together. They snuggle, kiss and drink champagne while they chat about an upcoming interstellar mission by the starship *Shorai*.

The memory leaves Nika disoriented and drowning in unfamiliar emotions. She tells Dashiel that woman is gone forever, then starts to leave. But the lingering memory overwhelms her, and she embraces him instead. In a torrent of passion and turbulent emotions, they make love.

In the dead of night, Parc is convicted and transported to the Zaidam Bastille prison. There, he and other convicts are herded into stasis chambers and knocked unconscious.

The next morning, Nika and Dashiel share moments both tender and troubled before going their separate ways. Dashiel tells Adlai about the virutox implanted in his stolen augments and implores him to investigate. He then goes to check on Parc as a favor to Nika, only to find Parc has already been sent to Zaidam.

Dashiel tells Nika the bad news, and they meet with Joaquim and Perrin. He and Joaquim instantly clash, arguing over the best course of action. Dashiel confides to Nika that his Advisor status will allow him entry to Zaidam, but to break Parc out will mean the end of Dashiel's career and turn him into a fugitive.

They are fighting about what to do when an explosion rocks The Chalet. They find the main floor on fire, with a crater at its center. Joaquim accuses Dashiel of causing the explosion, and Nika forces Dashiel to leave.

In the aftermath, it's determined that Cair became infected with the virutox when he studied the augment software; he caused a scene on the main floor before tampering with equipment until it exploded. Three people were killed in the explosion, including Cair. Using psyche backups they can theoretically be brought back, but NOIR lacks the resources to do it.

Adlai confirms the existence of the virutox in the limb augments. He informs the Guides, and is shocked when they order him to let the virutox propagate. They question how he discovered it, and when he repeats what Dashiel told him—that a contact alerted him to it—they order Dashiel and the contact to appear before them.

Advisor Iona Rowan participates in an illegal, underground competition where the participants temporarily switch consciousnesses to complete challenges. Unbeknownst to her, she switches with a man who had installed the limb augment and was infected with the virutox.

Nika reluctantly agrees to meet the Guides with Dashiel, but only if they use the opportunity to search the Guides' data vault for more information on her psyche-wipe. When they arrive at Mirai Tower, however, the Guides have moved the meeting time up, leaving them no time to conduct the search. Nika abandons Dashiel and sneaks into the data vault herself. She uncovers numerous files about her investigation into the outpost disappearances, including references to a 'Rasu Protocol.' She also finds proof that the Guides ordered her psyche-wipe, which was executed by Gemina Kail.

At this point, she's interrupted by security. Adlai and Dashiel reach the vault at almost the same time, and on seeing Nika breaking into the data vault, Adlai reluctantly tries to arrest her. Seeing no other option, Dashiel feigns ignorance and turns on Nika.

Nika escapes through a window, but she's shot by a drone as she does and is badly injured. Joaquim and Perrin mount a rescue effort; they are able to reach her before security forces and evacuate her to The Chalet.

She awakens hours later in a treatment tank, her wounds healed. Hurt by Dashiel's apparent betrayal and angry about all she's learned, she thanks Perrin and Joaquim for saving her then tells them she has to leave, to protect them and to find answers.

A Taiyok assassin ambushes Nika while she's on her way to Namino; she kills him and quickly leaves the scene. She asks Grant for a ship, but rebuffs him when he tries to kiss her. After an awkward exchange, they agree to remain friends, and he gives her a ship he's built.

Nika is about to leave in her new ship when Dashiel shows up at the hangar, bags in hand. She holds him at gunpoint while he explains that he hadn't betrayed her, but rather bought her time to get away and him time to withdraw funds from his accounts and transfer control of his company, all so he could come with her. Eventually he convinces her, and when they embrace she experiences a memory of the day she met him.

At the embassy on Chosek, Iona falls victim to the virutox and goes on a shooting spree, shooting multiple Chizeru, Asterion business executives and herself. Adlai is called in to investigate the massacre; he discovers she was infected with the virutox without the limb augment being installed, suggesting it is communicable.

Troubled, Adlai reaches out to Dashiel, but he's vanished. Adlai puts the pieces together and deduces Dashiel has joined Nika on the run. Faced with mounting evidence, he's forced to accept that the Guides are behind recent events and decides to take action.

Nika and Dashiel infiltrate Zaidam Bastille to break Parc out, only to be told Parc has been transferred to a vessel named the *Tabiji*, destination unknown. Nika hacks the Zaidam server, where she learns every convict has been transferred under the Rasu Protocol, and the prison is empty. Security forces arrive, and Nika is spaced while trying to reach their ship. Dashiel rescues her, and they escape the prison.

Later that night, Nika experiences another memory, this time of the final hours of the Asterions' rebellion against the Anaden Empire. She's a diplomat for the rebels named Nicolette Hinotori, who is bonded to an AI named KIR. Facing annihilation, the rebels flee the Milky Way on generation ships in search of a new home.

Gemina Kail pilots the *Tabiji* to an alien stronghold across the galaxy, where she delivers thousands of Asterions in stasis chambers to a mysterious alien species called the Rasu.

CONTENTS

OF A
DARKER
VOID

DECLARATION

EIGHT YEARS AGO

ADV SHORAI

GENNISI GALAXY, NORTHWEST QUADRANT

H ere on the edge of the galaxy, space was more void than substance. The distance between stars grew to hundreds of parsecs, and only the tenuous interstellar medium filled the in-between.

Mason Fassar did not think of himself as an overly sentimental person, but the darkness that had increasingly enveloped the *Shorai* during the last week of travel made him long for the star-glutted night skies of Kiyora.

Instead, he found himself nearly as far from his homeworld as it was possible to venture while remaining in the Gennisi galaxy, which he likely wasn't going to be remaining in for much longer. The decision of whether to push the expedition into neighboring galaxies still lay before him, by which he meant it still lay before the Guides. They would nominally insist it was his call to make, but not following their 'guidance' on the matter would bring his long career to an abrupt halt.

The *Shorai's* exploration of the nooks and crannies of their galaxy over the last year had yielded some notable successes, but nothing transformative. They'd discovered no new advanced intelligent life, though they hadn't expected to. The best scientific analyses predicted that the average galaxy hosted at most one to two intelligent species, defined as one that had achieved the ability to exit its home planet's atmosphere and survive to return. It was a rough definition at best, but a line had to be drawn somewhere.

In this respect, Gennisi was already overflowing with life. Granted, the Asterions were transplants rather than natives, but after 700,000 years, they deserved to claim it as their home.

To greater disappointment, the expedition had uncovered no planets flowing with rivers of kyoseil. A couple of asteroids rich in ytterbium and one moon with trace kyoseil deposits, but that was it. They'd secured d-gate pairs at points of interest during their journey, and the research teams who followed along behind them would doubtless increase the Asterion Dominion's scientific proficiency as well as its control of valuable resources.

But Mason hadn't signed on to command the *Shorai* in order to tag a few mineral-rich asteroids. He'd signed on to seek out the cosmos' unknowns and make them known. Now, he might finally be on the verge of a discovery worthy of the trip.

They had detected the first whispers ten days earlier. Whispers of technology being put to purposeful use, of the distinctive noise heralding a space-faring civilization. He'd immediately altered the *Shorai's* course to investigate but approached cautiously, as Asterions did.

Aside from a few stray blips, the sources of the signals were concentrated within a tiny region of space—likely a single stellar system. Their strength nevertheless implied a level of technological development far greater than what one anticipated from a civilization constrained to their home system.

The anomalies only grew as they closed in on the foci of the signals. He'd never admit it to the others, but they made him nervous. The EM signatures and other data they gathered on their target fit no profile, and there were a lot of profiles in the database. Nerves notwithstanding, however, he intended to add a new entry in the database before the day was done.

He was already considering how to proceed if this civilization was so far advanced as to be impossible to communicate with. He'd yet to arrive at a suitable answer. The Guides had sent a diplomat to lead the expedition in the hope that he could overcome the inevitable challenges of meeting new species, but there were limits to both his personal capabilities and the language interpretation algorithms installed in the *Shorai's* servers.

"Navigation, decrease speed another thirty percent. Systems, increase power to defensive shielding and cloaking field to the maximum allowed under Level III Alert protocols."

Both stations were run by non-sentient machines living in the walls of the ship, so he received confirmation of his orders being implemented only via the updated information displayed on his command pane. The crew of the *Shorai* was eighty percent machine, from the imitation-sentient service dynes all the way down to the automated environmental systems. Four living Asterions accompanied him on the expedition, and in truth they, and he, were only there to make the decisions not trusted to the machines, of which there weren't many.

It was one of the reasons why the citizens of the Dominion had long ago started using d-gates to travel among and across planets and space stations: space travel was *boring*.

Until it wasn't.

As they neared the outer reaches of the stellar system in question, the *Shorai's* sensors strained to differentiate and catalogue the volume and breadth of signals pouring out from it. In both a metaphorical and literal sense, this civilization was *loud*. Multiple linguistic algorithms sifted through the avalanche of data in search of patterns resolvable into language.

While their allies the Taiyoks possessed FTL drives and other technologies befitting their status as a space-faring society, Asterions had only once come across a civilization *more* developed than their own, when a galaxy-mapping mission stumbled upon the Sogain just over 200,000 years ago.

The encounter that had followed consisted in its entirety of a warning never to approach the Sogain's planet delivered directly into the minds of the diplomatic envoys. The warning was cemented with a taste of what they could expect to happen if they didn't obey, in the form of a targeted shockwave that overwhelmed the Asterion vessel's engines and ejected it from the stellar system at 0.4 lightspeed.

Though they had kept a distant, discreet eye on the Sogain in the millennia since then, they'd had little choice but to respect the mysterious aliens' ultimatum. As a result, they'd learned almost nothing about what a truly advanced civilization might look like.

Perhaps this encounter would go better. At a minimum, these aliens didn't appear to be nearly as secretive or reclusive as the Sogain. They certainly were not attempting to hide their existence.

"Sir, we're detecting an object approaching our location on bearing S 14° E -18° z."

The update came from Bethany Lance, their starship expert and the sole Asterion currently on the bridge with him. He glanced in her direction. "A ship?"

"Speed and trajectory suggest an artificially propelled object, yes, sir."

Bethany was nothing if not exacting. "How close to it will we pass if we keep to our current trajectory?"

"Sir, it's on an intercept course."

A chill raced up his spine, and his higher-order processes fought for dominance over a more primal fight-or-flight instinct. So much for their cloaking technology. In the face of the aliens' evidently superior capabilities, it shouldn't be too surprising that their attempt at stealth was ineffective. Still, he'd hoped to get a bit closer before revealing their presence.

He breathed in deliberately. "On-screen as soon as we have a visual."

"A few more seconds, sir."

He waited with an outward air of patience cultivated over millennia of practiced diplomacy.

The wide pane at the front of the bridge burst to life to reveal the alien vessel. Constructed of an odd-looking aubergine-hued metal, its leading edge was capped by concentric circles of crystal spears. The visual gave no indication of scale, but it sure as hells *looked* enormous, and despite his efforts to remain composed a quiet gasp escaped his lips.

"Comms, order everyone to the bridge. Navigation, slow to a halt and hold position. Systems—"

PRIMARY
EXPRESSIONS

1

PRESENT DAY

EBISU

ASTERION DOMINION AXIS WORLD

The pebbled walkways of Ebisu One remained damp several hours after the morning's rain shower had passed. Tiny puddles filling gaps between the stones reflected the bright sunlight that had replaced the rain to create an illusory carpet of sequins beneath Nika Tescarav's feet.

The streets were bustling, and the heavy foot traffic imposed a predictable rhythm on the reflected glow. While she walked with the crowd, she studied the rhythm in her peripheral vision. Waiting for the hitch, the break that betrayed a larger, non-Asterion frame with a too-deliberate gait in her vicinity. Short of installing visual sensors in the back of her head, it was the best way she knew of to detect a tail.

And she almost certainly had a tail.

The Guides would be foolish to give up on eliminating her after the single failed assassination attempt on Namino, and whatever else the Guides were, they were not foolish. But she wasn't giving up, either—

There. For half a second, a large shadow marred the rhythmic dance of light.

Nika took the next left over a bridge crossing one of the many canals that wound their way through Ebisu One. Several people followed; all but one of them were simply continuing on their planned paths to their destinations.

When she reached the other side of the bridge, she started across the small promenade for a cluster of shops, then abruptly veered down a narrow street. No one followed her this time, and she activated her kamero filter as she pressed against the building façade to her right.

If she hadn't been concentrating on springing the trap, she would've laughed at her chosen surroundings. It was ironic, bordering on absurd, the amount of time she spent in alleys these days, considering that she'd begun her current life face-down in one.

The Taiyok who was tracking her appeared a second later, skulking two meters down the alley before stopping upon finding it empty.

She fired a Glaser shot point-blank into his neck. It sent him sprawling to the ground, momentarily stunned. Before he could shake off the stun, she tossed him onto his back and straddled his thick chest.

A needle blade tumbled out of his left hand, erasing any doubt she might have entertained about his intentions.

She fired another shot into his chest, then extended a blade from her left wrist and sliced into the connective tissue between his right wing and his torso. Only a few centimeters, enough to ensure he wouldn't be flying today but not enough to cause permanent damage. Then she moved the blade to his throat and applied enough pressure for a trickle of mottled brown blood to ooze onto the chrome metal.

His eyes popped open, but on sensing the blade at his neck, his muscles froze.

"Move, and you'll be dead the next instant. Cooperate, and I won't kill you. I don't *want* to kill you, because I need you to deliver a message for me. Listen carefully."

She paused long enough to let the command sink in. "When you report back to the Guides on how you failed in your mission, tell them this: they can send as many assassins for me as they want. None of them will succeed. Therefore, I offer an alternative for their consideration. If they decide they are instead ready to engage in a productive conversation, they can send a message to nex node address @NAlt23_14, and we can move forward from there.

"Each assassin I have to waste my time killing, however, will make me less amenable to hearing whatever they have to say, so they should choose their next moves wisely.

"Do you understand this message and your instructions regarding it?"

His narrow chin dropped, and she read the comprehension in the amber glow of his compound eyes.

She placed the muzzle of the Glaser flush against his breastplate and stunned him again, then hurriedly restrained one of his hands to a nearby pipe. Next she retrieved a mirage shell from her pouch and placed it out of his reach at the intersection of the alley and the promenade to conceal his presence from passersby.

The measures ought to give her enough time to depart the sector and deny the assassin another go at her, assuming she didn't dally.

After firing a final burst to keep the Taiyok out for a few more seconds, she exited the alley and strode away as rapidly as she could without drawing attention to herself.

She'd just reached the canal bridge when a ping arrived from Dashiel.

We may have a problem.

AR

"Justice Advisor Adlai Weiss to see Mr. Granger."

"Identity signature, please."

Dashiel Ridani gazed impassively at the lobby security dyne while he pressed the fingertips of his left hand to the pane.

He didn't know for certain if the Guides had publicly or privately blacklisted him—something he did need to find out—but at a bare minimum they had surely placed a trigger in security systems across all Dominion worlds designed to flag his presence at any checkpoint. So he needed to not register at any checkpoint.

Σ → Identity:
< Adlai Weiss, 8th generation
Signature:
< θβΨαθΨ ⱵΩΨαΞ

"Identity confirmed. You are cleared to proceed. Take the lift to the twelfth floor."

The relief he felt on fooling the scan didn't reach his features as he strode confidently past the dyne and toward the lift.

Five years of burying his true emotions behind a measured, aloof demeanor was turning out to be of unexpected use in his new life as an apprentice rebel. It had trained him in how to not reveal a variety of volatile emotions—in this instance, generalized anxiety about impersonating someone he knew. A friend for many centuries, and now...he couldn't say.

He'd provided a few details to better sell the charade, but Nika had done most of the work of constructing the simmed ID and a morph that made him look like Adlai to Asterion eyes, dynes and scanners. She'd also created a more anonymous ID for him to use in most situations, but for this meeting he needed to *be* Adlai.

He actually knew the Briscanti Materials CEO, Simon Granger, which was going to make pretending to be Adlai doubly difficult. But Dashiel Ridani sauntering into the CEO's office and asking probing questions about an outpost would raise alarms even if the Guides hadn't yet made him persona non grata. Adlai Weiss doing the same would be passed off as official Justice business, with the added benefit of saving him from needing to answer any pesky 'why' questions.

According to the files Nika had copied from the Mirai Tower data vault, Briscanti Materials owned the most recent exploratory world outpost to be 'nulled,' a sterile word the files used to signify the disappearance of all Asterions and equipment from a location. Outposts vanishing was what had started their involvement in this whole mess; lacking other leads, it seemed the best place to pick up the trail.

The lift stopped at the twelfth floor, and Dashiel tried to reorient himself to what he imagined Adlai's headspace might resemble. How would Adlai approach a friendly interrogation of a non-suspect? *By trying to put them in shackles then having them shot when they resisted—*

He tamped down the flare of animosity. He hated Adlai for forcing Nika to run, though intellectually he recognized the man couldn't have acted any other way. Perhaps Dashiel's hatred would settle into a milder form of disappointment in time. Not today, but perhaps in time.

He needed to set his feelings aside for the moment if he was going to pull off impersonating the Adlai the public saw.

Simon Granger was studying a graph at a wall-to-wall array of display panes when Dashiel walked in. "Mr. Granger, thank you for seeing me."

He held his breath. He had no reason to believe Granger had ever met Adlai, but if his assumption proved to be wrong, the conversation was apt to get dicey. Besides an obvious lack of memory of any such meeting, he hadn't had a chance to visit Maris for a crash course in acting, and as such his intonations and manner of speech were at best a rough caricature of the way Adlai spoke.

The man shifted away from the panes wearing a polite smile. "Advisor Weiss. It's no problem, though I admit your visit is a bit of a surprise. I hope some company representative hasn't behaved badly enough to run afoul of Justice."

"Not to worry. My investigation isn't directly related to your company or any of its employees. Consider Briscanti Materials a possible material witness, as it were."

Granger motioned toward the conference table by the windows. "Then I'm happy to help in any way I can."

"I appreciate it." Dashiel sat opposite him. "Until recently, you were operating a lab outpost on SR86-Roku. What happened that led you to shut it down?"

"Nothing. It wasn't my choice. The lab was pursuing experimental combinations of kyoseil and alisinium, a chemically similar mineral abundant on the planet. Many of the potential combinations are extremely volatile—according to Industry's Conceptual Research department, too volatile to be left to the whims of private sector development."

"CR took over the outpost?" He had close working relationships with several people in the department who he could follow up with—except possibly he couldn't. Not without more disguises and misdirections.

"Down to the last module. Moved it all to their site on Adjunct Shi."

"The employees as well?"

Granger nodded. "Everyone based at the outpost was transferred to CR's payroll."

Dashiel was now so intrigued he almost forgot to be Adlai. "You don't sound particularly happy about this turn of events."

"Don't get me wrong. They paid us handsomely for the equipment they confiscated—excuse me, *bought*. Same for the materials and personnel. We made more off the transfer than the experiments would have netted us in two decades. It's just...."

"The lab was yours. Your idea, your gamble, your potential breakthrough."

Granger regarded him a little too inquisitively. "Yes. As a Justice man, I'm surprised you appreciate the notion."

Dashiel hurriedly schooled his features. He'd definitely slipped out of character there. "I have friends working in businesses similar to yours and have been privy to many an alcohol-enlivened dinner speech on the topic."

"I've been guilty of making a few of those speeches myself. Can I ask what the SR86-Roku lab has to do with a Justice investigation? I assume it must be serious to warrant the personal attention of an Advisor."

Dashiel straightened his shoulders into a formal posture. "I'm sorry, but I can't share any details. I doubt you'll need to worry about it. A couple of brief follow-up questions, if I may. Who was the contact person at CR?"

"Let's see, it was…Vivian Santosa, I believe."

The name meant nothing to him, when it really ought to. He'd bet a reasonable sum on this Santosa never having spent a day in the employment of Conceptual Research, if she existed at all. "Did they involve anyone from your company in the setup of the new lab on Adjunct Shi? Or have one of your people come in to double-check things once the lab was operational?"

Granger shook his head. "It's been complete silence from CR since they deposited the credits in our account. I assume they believe they can run our experiments better than we did."

Dashiel didn't miss the caustic undercurrent in the man's tone. He felt for Granger, and part of him wanted to reassure the man that nothing he'd been told was true. But he couldn't do it, only in part because the truth was far worse. "Last question: other than the radio silence, was there anything about the transaction which struck you as…odd?"

"Well, the fact that they moved the lab at all. It would've been far safer to take over the outpost and keep running the experiments there, rather than moving everything to Adjunct Shi and situating the lab in the middle of several hundred thousand people. Particularly given that the stated reason for taking over the experiments was the volatility of kyoseil-alisinium syntheses."

"And you pointed this out to them?"

"Repeatedly—oh, here's another oddity. I never had a real-time, in-person conversation with anyone from CR, or anyone at all. Every communication was remote and nex-delivered." Granger shrugged and leaned back in his chair. "But the credits were good, and I'm using them productively on other projects. I shouldn't complain."

"We'll keep the complaining between us." Dashiel stood and offered a hand. "Thank you for your time."

"Certainly. I do have a question before you go. I suspect I know your answer, but is there any chance you can tell me anything about the incident at the Chosek Embassy? The CEO of Zanist Circuitry is a friend of mine, and I'm concerned for him. I assume he'll be regened soon, but details have been impossible to come by."

What had happened at the Chosek Embassy that resulted in what sounded like body loss for a corporate CEO? Was Iona Rowan involved?

He projected a touch of regret. "I apologize, I do, but I can't discuss it with anyone outside of Justice. You can reach out to the External Relations Division. They might be of more help."

"Advisor Breckel, yeah. I already tried him and got the same answer. I understand. Hopefully it will get sorted soon."

Dashiel smiled. "Hopefully."

2

EBISU

Dashiel stepped out of the building's lobby and into a line of people.

He instantly tensed, and for a second struggled to keep evidence of it off his face. With preparation he wasn't too bad at subterfuge, but the unexpected continued to rattle him.

A security checkpoint had been erected at the edge of the plaza bordering the Briscanti Materials building. Subtle but nonetheless active force fields bounded the space between the entrance to the building and the checkpoint, ensuring everyone exiting the building was corralled through it. The line was lengthy, but it was also moving fast. The security personnel were searching for something, or someone, in particular.

What were the odds it *wasn't* him? He pinged Nika.

We may have a problem. I didn't run into any trouble at Briscanti Materials, but security has erected a checkpoint outside the building that wasn't there when I arrived.

I'll be there in seven minutes. Do what you can to not reach the checkpoint before then—but stay close.

And when you get here?

Just be ready for anything.

Anything. Got it.

He studied the progression of the line as two people were processed and cleared.

Hq (visual) | scan.physical(270°:90°, 5 seconds)
T → gridpoint (27.4,14.3).minTime

Four minutes, thirty-six seconds until he'd reach the checkpoint.

With a loud grumble, he turned around and trudged out of the line. "Left the damn weave in the meeting room." He continued acting exasperated as he reversed course and headed back inside. Once in the lobby, he feigned an interruption and a brief virtual conversation, then exited once more and reentered the end of the line.

The math said the delay he'd manufactured was long enough. But what if seven minutes became nine or ten? He shouldn't try the same trick twice with the same crowd, and anything more dramatic risked drawing the attention to him he was trying to avoid.

The urge to march up to the checkpoint, proclaim his Advisor status and demand to be allowed to pass was a strong one. He'd done it a thousand times over the years without even thinking twice about it; it was second nature. His position and all the privileges accompanying it had become part of who he was. They had come to define him.

Stripped of the trappings of power now—in practice if not in form—what remained? A smart, if somewhat reserved, man with a penchant for making useful things, then making a lot of them?

The two dynes staffing the checkpoint abruptly began jerking erratically before collapsing to the ground, without any visual clue as to what caused their malfunction.

People looked around in confusion, and gradually the line began to disintegrate. In the growing tumult, the dissipation of the force fields went unnoticed by most until someone shouted, "Screw this!" and strode off toward the nearest street.

Should *he*? He was still waiting to hear the plan, though it was apparently now in progress.

A hand at the small of his back preceded a small device pressing into his spine. He spun around, but no one...wait, there *was* a faint outline of a person. More like a vague, body-shaped shimmer cast against the landscape behind it.

Hold one.

He felt the hand on his back again, followed by the tingle of a mild surge of electricity enveloping him. The hand grasped his and started tugging him away from the checkpoint.

Okay, let's go.

To his right, one of the security dynes clambered to its feet.

We need to hurry!

They can't see you. I stuck a kamero filter module on you. Don't run or make sudden movements, but we're going to walk away. Also, don't bump into anyone.

He stared at his free hand as he matched her pace. He could see it fine, and the idea that no one else could was disconcerting. But the absence of running feet or shouted orders from behind him suggested this was in fact the case.

He risked a glance back before they rounded a street corner to leave the plaza behind. Both dynes were again functional, bullying the remaining people into a reforming line. They seemed completely unaware he'd escaped their grasp.

Once they were out of sight of the plaza, she reached around and fiddled with the module she'd attached to his belt. "You're gradually becoming visible to everyone. Keep acting normal." They turned left at the next street. "We need to get off-planet soon, in case security was specifically looking for you."

"It could have simply been bad luck. Or at most, the system deduced someone who wasn't Adlai was pretending to be him, not necessarily that it was me. Anyway, there's something else I want to do first."

She arched an eyebrow in question.

"Something happened at the Chosek embassy within the last few days that resulted in a total body loss for the CEO of Zanist Circuitry. Simon Granger asked for information on it, and he let slip that Cameron Breckel is handling the 'incident,' as he phrased it. I'd like to try to catch Cameron and get the details."

"Why? I'm not sure I see how it's relevant to our mission."

"We don't know, do we, until we get those details? Besides, at this point any strange and unusual incident could be related to the Rasu Protocol."

She studied him until he broke under the weight of her gaze. "Because I have important kyoseil contracts with the Chizeru, and

I want to know if they're threatened. Because I was at the embassy a week or two ago, and everything was perfectly normal, so I'm curious what went wrong. Because once upon a time, the embassy was practically your second office, and if you remembered your time there, it would be terribly important to you to find out what happened. In the absence of those memories, you'll have to trust me when I say you would want to know."

"Oh." She peered at the street beneath her feet. "I gather I spent a lot of time interfacing with the Chizeru when I was a diplomat."

"You did. You were fond of the little scamps."

"I'd believe it. But this Advisor's office is in Ebisu Tower, isn't it? I'm not comfortable subjecting our simmed IDs to such a high level of scrutiny for a tangent."

"It is. But I happen to know that whenever he's on Ebisu, Cameron takes his lunch at the botanical gardens. If we hurry, I bet we can catch him, out in the open and away from security. If I can talk to him, I might be able to find out what the Guides have and haven't said to the other Advisors about me."

"You're using his first name. Is he a friend?"

"Sort of? He's a good man, I think. You thought so, too."

Her steps slowed. "He's a diplomat, which means I regularly worked with him and so on." She gave Dashiel an almost sad smile. "I'm getting used to this story."

"I'm sorry."

"It's not any failing on your part. I'm glad to learn these tidbits about my past. It's just hard sometimes…like I'm an imposter in my own life. Which I've always known I've been, but hearing and seeing such stark evidence of it…."

"No, you're not." He placed a hand on her shoulder, gently but with enough insistence to bring her to a halt. "Wherever you are, whatever you're doing, this is your life to own. Always has been, always will be. You've merely forgotten a few moments of it."

An odd expression passed across her face, but she quickly hid it by tilting her chin down to kiss his hand. "Thank you for the vote of confidence. Fine, let's go see if we can find Advisor Breckel. But if he's not at the gardens, we need to leave."

The Ebisu One Botanical Gardens hadn't started out as a public park. An abundant variety of colorful plants and herbs grew natively in the planet's expansive temperate zone, and while the city's architects initially tried to avoid clear-cutting the land to make way for civilization, any plants left untouched soon became overgrown.

Eventually, some residents began tending to an area that at the time remained outside the city limits, sculpting and cultivating the local flora to complement the natural beauty of the region without overpowering it. When the city's natural expansion reached the gardens, they became officially protected space, and now they served as an oasis of quiet respite in the center of a bustling metropolis.

Dashiel found Cameron sitting at one of the many gazebos situated above the lily ponds dotting the gardens. He called out a greeting.

Cameron looked over in surprise, a half-eaten sandwich held aloft in one hand. "Dashiel? This is a surprise. I thought you took a leave of absence."

"I did. But it turns out it's a lot harder to shut off my work brain than I expected. I was in the area, and I wanted to ask you about something, if you don't mind."

Cameron pursed his lips. "Unofficially, we're supposed to report any contact we have with you to the Guides. Why we're supposed to wasn't made clear."

Dashiel nodded. "I'm not trying to put you in a difficult position. You're more than welcome to report this conversation. But if I can beg an indulgence, wait until I'm gone?"

Cameron set his sandwich on the plate beside him and gestured to the opposite bench. "Of course. Please, sit down. What kind of trouble are you in?"

"If I tell you, you'll be in it, too. I don't want to drag you down with me."

"Fair enough. I am already carrying enough on my shoulders this week, since we're down an External Relations Advisor."

"What?"

"I guess you are out of the loop, and this is being kept under wraps. Iona's out—permanently. Bodiless for the time being as well, while the Guides decide what they can do with her, or to her, that will placate the Chosek government."

"That's actually what I wanted to talk to you about. What happened at the embassy?"

Cameron blew out a breath. "We're not supposed to discuss the details, but I frankly *need* to talk to someone about it. During a negotiation between Zanist Circuitry and an up-and-coming Chizeru tribe, Iona lost her mind. She killed the Chizeru representatives and shot the Zanist CEO and two executives into nonfunctionality, then shot herself in the head."

"Good gods. Iona's a bitch—pardon my bluntness—but she's not homicidal. I met with her recently and gave her plenty of reasons to shoot me, but all she did was glower."

"Her actions defy comprehension. Adlai mentioned some kind of artificial pathogen as a possible culprit, but he hasn't elaborated on the theory."

Did he say what I think he did?

Nika was listening in on the conversation, ostensibly so she could swoop to his rescue again if it became necessary. He suspected what she really wanted was to get a sense of her former colleague. To fill in a few more blanks.

He did.

Dashiel tried to look blandly befuddled. "That all sounds uniquely awful. Let me guess. You're tasked with smoothing things over with the Chizeru?"

"More like sentenced to. Have you ever seen an enraged Chizeru? It's not a pretty sight. I'll be honest, things are touch-and-go with them. Three of their leaders are dead by our hand. Their views on murder are strange and mostly incomprehensible. They abide by this complex yet archaic retribution-based justice system, and they want us to somehow apply it to Iona. We can't—it doesn't work under the Charter. But they don't understand why not."

Tell him to explain to the tribal governors how Advisor Rowan will be subjected to civic shaming for the maximum number of days allowable under our laws and her personal belongings garnished for the benefit of the victims.

How do you...?

Like with the Taiyoks, information about Chizeru culture and societal customs came embedded in my second-layer core programming.

Right.

Nika Kirumase had taken her diplomacy very seriously.

Dashiel made a show of appearing thoughtful. "Have you tried assuring them that Iona will be publicly and officially shamed for her actions to the greatest extent our laws allow and promising to convert her personal wealth into some form of recompense for the benefit of the victims and their families? It wouldn't need to be a lie, just a slight glossing over of some of the details."

"I've never considered taking that approach—why have you?"

He chuckled lightly. "Oh, I haven't. But Nika used to talk a lot about the unique struggles and joys of dealing with the Chizeru. I picked up a few details."

Cameron got a pitying look on his face, the one everyone donned when the topic of Nika came up in Dashiel's presence. Before, it had always stung bitterly; now it didn't touch him.

"She really could work magic with them. I'd give anything to possess a fifth of her skill for the next few days...." The man's voice trailed off weakly. "Sorry."

"It's all right." And it genuinely was, but he didn't dare tell Cameron why. "Good luck—I mean it. Thank you for humoring me, and for giving me a few answers. You can make that report now."

"Eh...." Cameron waved a hand in his direction. "What for? I never saw you."

3

STARSHIP #PV79-24116

ASTERION DOMINION SPACE

N ika settled into the left-side cockpit chair as soon as they boarded the ship. "I didn't get everything done I wanted to, but now we really should vacate the planet. It's only a matter of time before the Guides connect the dots and send Justice squads to sweep the city."

They'd chosen to dock at a Ridani Enterprises factory complex on the outskirts of Ebisu One rather than any official spaceport. Here, Dashiel controlled the landing and departure logs and was able to keep their presence out of the system. Soon, though, Justice would have every Ridani Enterprises facility under surveillance. They'd gotten lucky this time, but the near-miss at Briscanti Materials meant they needed to start being more careful.

Dashiel leaned in over her shoulder. "What held you up from getting everything done? Other than rescuing me, that is."

"Another assassin."

"Excuse me?"

She finished the pre-flight checks and engaged the in-atmosphere engine. "Departure first, stories after."

They lifted off the landing pad and arced toward the sky. The approaching clouds bringing the next rain shower quickly engulfed them, then almost as quickly they broke through the gloom—and were promptly greeted by the planet's punishing mesosphere.

"Can we talk again about why we use d-gates to travel between planets?"

His question sounded as if it was delivered through gritted teeth. Nika sympathized with his discomfort, but the truth was it had only taken a few hours of flying for it to become natural to her. She hardly ever needed to call up the routines she'd installed on starship piloting and maintenance. Yes, the atmospheric traversal was bumpy, but she didn't mind the visceral *realness* of it. When you were leaving behind a planet for space, you should know it.

After a few minutes, the turbulence eased and the haze dissipated to reveal the stars. As they shifted into a trajectory that would avoid a close fly-by of Ebisu's moon, a periwinkle sun peeked out above the planet's profile.

Such peacefulness, such astonishing beauty waiting to surprise you on every horizon, and so few ever saw it. "*Wayfarer.*"

"Hmm?"

"I've been trying to decide what to name the ship. If it's going to be our home for a while, it deserves a name."

"And seeing as we're depending on it to see us through this journey, this search for answers...you're right. *Wayfarer* is perfect." He kissed her ear before heading into the main cabin. "Speaking of journeys, where to next?"

"We need to talk about it. For now, an empty patch of space a parsec or so away." She let the navigation system choose the details of their destination, engaged the autopilot and stood.

Dashiel had his back to her while he pulled his dress shirt off over his head then dug through one of his bags for a t-shirt. Her breath caught in her throat, and a mischievous grin crept onto her lips as she watched the show. Her former self had left behind more than one gift for her.

He turned around as he put on the selected t-shirt and caught her blatantly ogling him. Probably looking rather lecherous. Oh well, she couldn't run from it now.

He stared at her in something resembling wonder for several seconds, and finally she started fidgeting. It wasn't the response she'd expected. "What?"

"I was afraid you would never look at me that way again."

She dropped her chin, and with it eye contact. "I'm merely enjoying the view."

He closed the distance between them. "I'm glad. But might there be a little more to it?"

She opened her mouth to tell him how much he'd come to mean to her in such a short time, how he made her feel emotions she hadn't experienced since waking up in an alley and sentiments that didn't come with words adequate to convey their worth—but she stopped before giving voice to any of it. She didn't feel like herself when those emotions ran free and unchecked, and she didn't yet know what that meant.

Instead she flashed him a light, breezy smile and went over to the equipment storage cabinet. "So, yeah, assassin. I decided not to try to hide from them. In fact, I decided to confront them head on. I swung by the nearest transit station and deliberately picked up his tail. This way I controlled the encounter. I picked my location, baited him in and disabled him."

"You didn't kill him this time?"

"No. I gave him a message to pass on to the Guides for me."

He came up behind her and wrapped his arms around her waist, resting his chin on her shoulder. "Dare I ask?"

She relaxed a little, relieved he wasn't upset at her avoidance of his question. She didn't want to hurt him; she just wasn't ready to put her full weight down. "I simply informed them I would thwart every assassin they sent after me, but if instead they wanted to try a different strategy and talk, I would be willing to listen."

"You—"

She twisted around to face him. "I know what you're going to say: I'm being a diplomat. And you're...right. But implicit in the diplomacy is a threat to burn their regime to the ground if they betray me a second time. If they betray the people, the Dominion."

"They'd best believe you." He kissed her, soft and slow and deliciously, until the walls of the ship faded away and she forgot where she was....

"Do you want to hear what I learned, what I didn't, and what our next mystery to chase involves?"

She blinked and drew back, certain her cheeks were flushed. "Absolutely. Tell me while I shower? I got Taiyok blood on me, and it's making my skin itch."

4

MIRAI

ASTERION DOMINION AXIS WORLD

"This is not a raid. This is not a surprise inspection. Our purpose here is to conduct a mandatory product safety recall for the Ridani Enterprises Model Vk 3.2 limb augment. Turn over your supply of said augment, and we will be on our way."

"What about compensation? The augments didn't come free."

Spencer Nimoet didn't have a good answer for the question, but he did have a practiced one. "Keep your records up-to-date, and someone from the Industry Division will be in touch regarding the refund process." Eventually. Possibly.

The man standing behind the counter nodded tersely, for the moment accepting the vague assurance. Shady looking character, but who wasn't here in the bowels of the Southern Market?

Spencer motioned the two dynes who accompanied him inside. Each one carried a large container, both of which were already three-quarters full of confiscated limb augment retail boxes. This was their last stop in the area, granted, but the number of units they'd collected gave him pause.

He wasn't given to dramaticism or hyperbole, but by his way of thinking, each one represented a life saved. They still had a lot more work to do on that front, but the scope of the crisis seemed to become more manageable with every filled container.

The dynes watched over the shop owner's work of collecting his stock of augments while Spencer stepped outside. Across the intersection, Advisor Weiss had finally arrived, though he stood motionless on the sidewalk wearing a perturbed expression.

Spencer remained uncertain about Weiss taking him into his confidence and enlisting his help in defying the Guides over the augments. Not uncertain about defying the Guides—his moderate pro-NOIR views had taken a hard veer toward rebellion on learning of the virutox and the Guides' apparent role in creating it. But Adlai Weiss was the most upstanding, law-abiding, rules-following individual Spencer had ever met. For him to suddenly announce, even solely to Spencer, that he intended to openly disobey the Guides' wishes didn't square with the picture of the man he'd long held.

Then again, it was the right thing to do, and possibly that mattered more to his boss than rules and regulations.

He checked on the shop owner's progress then crossed the street and approached Weiss. "We're almost finished here. We'll be bringing in more than three hundred augments."

"Good...." Weiss muttered vaguely.

"Sir, is there a problem? A new one, I mean?"

"I can't decide. Have you seen the public nex overlay here?"

"Oh. Yes, sir."

"The message is posted outside nearly every market and club. Not only on Mirai either. On every Axis World, and it's starting to show up on the Adjunct ones as well."

Spencer held back a chuckle and accessed the overlay again.

> ### TRUST NO AUGMENT.
> ### TRUST NO ROUTINE.
> ### TRUST NO DOSE.
> ### TRUST NO AGENT OF THE GOVERNMENT.
> ### A JUSTICE CONVICTION MEANS FINAL DEATH.
> ### KEEP YOUR PSYCHE. KEEP YOUR FREEDOM.
> ### — Your Friends In NOIR

Weiss threw his hands in the air in an exaggerated display of frustration. "How is it even there? I had techs at the Justice Center access the public nex overlay infrastructure, and according to them they can't delete it, because it's not there. Yet plainly it *is*."

Spencer chose his words carefully. "It's not a surprise that NOIR can get around official firewalls. But, honestly, sir, do we want to get rid of it? The more people who are forewarned and don't install the augment because of it, the easier the clean-up is for us. The more people who are saved."

"You're right. I know you're right. But what is this 'a Justice conviction means final death' nonsense? We're not storing people, no matter how severe a crime they committed."

Spencer didn't have a good response, which appeared to be the theme for the day. NOIR didn't make a habit of spreading false claims, as to do so would inevitably ruin their reputation and credibility. While he and Weiss only knew of the one virutox so far, the first three statements in the warning were good advice based on verified facts, and given the Guides' involvement he was reluctant to dispute the fourth. Thus, the obvious conclusion to draw was that NOIR had good reason to believe a Justice conviction *did* mean final death.

The thought churned his stomach, and his gaze flitted to the horizon, searching for a metaphorical shadow encroaching across the landscape. But it was already dark.

He didn't engage in regular correspondence with his associates in NOIR, but he should reach out and maybe find out what this was about. For now, he offered Weiss a weak shrug. "It's probably a misunderstanding on NOIR's part, or them erring on the side of caution, given recent events."

"Well, we need to correct the misunderstanding. It's counter-productive for them to smear us when we're trying to help." Weiss sighed. "Anyway, I'm sorry I was late and left you to do all the work. I was delayed at the transit station."

"No trouble, I hope?"

"There was a glitch in the security check is all. Let's get these confiscated augments to Disposal straight away. They can't infect anyone if they're a pile of dust."

Adlai had deliberately glossed over the reason for his delayed arrival at the Southern Market to Spencer. In truth, he'd been officially detained at the transit station then forced to provide extraordinary evidence that he was who he claimed to be.

Someone purporting to be him—correct ID signature and all—had cleared a private security scan on Ebisu less than ten minutes earlier, and when he'd done the same on Mirai, the system had flagged him as suspicious.

A number of people might want to impersonate him for one reason or another, but only a few had the knowledge of his personal details needed to do so, and of them only one had access to the tools required to accomplish it. Tools someone like, say, the head of NOIR possessed.

What could Dashiel possibly have been doing on Ebisu visiting Briscanti Materials? It made no sense, but the things Adlai didn't know spread out in a vast sea before him. Mysteries built upon enigmas. He didn't care for it one bit.

He would have to do his best to knock them down one at a time. So as he walked to the Justice Center, letting the chilly night air keep him alert, he sent a ping.

Stop impersonating me.

The reply took a few minutes. He wasn't ready to go back to the office yet, so when he reached the Justice Center, he circled the block instead.

I'd deny it, but it doesn't matter. Are you the one who called in security to try to catch me? Are you coming after me, too?

No, and no. I'm not coming after either of you.

A slight pause. *Either of us? I don't understand what you mean.*

Dashiel, how long have I known you?

Twenty-four hundred years, give or take a few decades.

Exactly. You may have fooled me for a few minutes in the thick of a stressful situation at Mirai Tower, but I'm not stupid, nor am I blind.

No, you're not. So…how 'not coming after either of us' are you?

If you must know, I'm trying to help.

I don't believe you. You said you were helping Nika, and we saw how that turned out.

Adlai fought against growing frustration. It wasn't as if he'd expected this conversation, whenever it happened, to go any more smoothly than it currently was, but met expectations didn't make it any easier to navigate.

I'm sorry about what happened, but I didn't have all the facts, and I had to make a call.

The wrong one.

Yes. But it didn't stop her from escaping, so cut me a break?

Tell me something, and I'll consider it. Was Iona Rowan infected with the virutox when she shot up a conference room at the Chosek Embassy?

The Guides had put an embargo on the details of the massacre, releasing a minimal public statement that an unfortunate 'incident' had resulted in injuries to Advisor Rowan and several business executives and the deaths of three Chizeru envoys. Yet, somehow, Dashiel had managed to find out what happened almost immediately. While being on the run.

He and Nika always had made quite a pair.

A brisk wind smacked Adlai in the face when he rounded the street corner, and he hugged his jacket tighter around him. To share the rest of the details was arguably a violation of the Guides' embargo. But that was what he did now, wasn't it?

She was.

Why did she even have the limb augment? She's not the type to go in for gadgets.

She didn't have it installed. The virutox is communicable.

Another pause.

How communicable?

Not very, thank the stars. It requires an extensive neural

interaction to jump to another person. But when spread in this man-
ner, the virutox mutates in unpredictable ways. Such as turning Iona
homicidal.

Tell me you're putting a stop to this.

I'm working on it. Which would be a lot easier if I had some idea
what's really going on.

Makes three of us.

Is she okay? Nika?

Do you care?

Dammit, Dashiel. Of course I care. I'm staking my career and pos-
sibly my psyche on the theory that she's right about the Guides. I'm
sorry I couldn't make the choice earlier, at Mirai Tower, but I've made
it now.

The reply took so long to arrive that he started to think his
friend had ditched the conversation.

I'm still not sure if I believe you. But, yes, she's fine. Righteously
pissed, which should not be a surprise.

What can you tell me?

Just get the damn augments off the streets. Develop a vaccine to
protect against future infection. And stop sending people to Zaidam—
for any reason or any crime.

What? I can't overturn every sentence.

Forget the sentences for now. Stop the transports to Zaidam. The
people being sent there aren't staying there. We don't know where
they're being taken, but wherever it is, in eight years no one's come
back.

Adlai sank against the Justice Center façade and dragged his
hands down his face. This was what 'a Justice conviction means final death' referred to, wasn't it? It was still a big assumption to
make...but not an entirely unjustified one.

Dashiel, I don't have that kind of power. I'm confiscating the aug-
ments as fast as I can, in defiance of the express instructions of the
Guides, but at least if I'm called out for it I can fall back on the Charter
for support. If I start blocking convicts from going to Zaidam, I'll be
out of a job by dawn.

The Guides explicitly told you not to confiscate the augments? Godsdamn they are cold. Look, the virutox's purpose is to increase the flow of prisoners to Zaidam, so they can increase the flow of people to gods fear where. It's all connected.

The investigative algorithms in Adlai's brain stirred to attention. *Connected to what?*

We will find out, but we need you to buy us time by cutting off the flow of victims. Do what you can.

I'll try.

One more thing. Run a search on the name 'Vivian Santosa.' Allegedly, she works for Industry Conceptual Research, but I've never heard of her.

I'll see what I can find out.

The entrance to the Justice Center loomed ahead of Adlai once more, and walking through it had never felt so daunting.

But he was the boss, for tonight if not tomorrow, and it was his responsibility to protect innocent people, so he squared his shoulders and lifted his chin and strode forward—

—a hand landed on the door frame, the arm it belonged to blocking his progress. "Where are they?"

His fingers had found his Glaser and were removing it from its holster when he realized the hand and arm belonged to Maris Debray. He exhaled and pivoted to face her. "It's nice to see you as well, Maris. Where are who?"

"Don't act ignorant, Adlai. It doesn't suit you. Dashiel and Nika, obviously."

He chuckled to himself at the recognition he'd just used almost the exact same phrasing to Dashiel. "He told you about her, then?"

"Only under threat of my own special brand of torture paired with the not-terribly-subtle suggestion of blackmail. He also promised I could see her, but now he's gone, which I can safely assume means she's gone as well. This will not do."

Events were moving so rapidly, Adlai couldn't be sure precisely how much Maris knew—he wasn't even sure how much *he* knew.

"I don't like it either, but truth be told, running was her only viable option. As for him? He's Dashiel. He wasn't going to let her slip away again."

Maris studied him like he was a painting fit only for critique. "Why was running her only viable option?"

These games were getting exhausting. "How much did he tell you?"

"Clearly not enough."

"Are you certain you want to know? Once you do, there's no coming back from it. Everything will change for you."

"I'm not afraid of change, my dear. No artist is. Tell me."

"All right, but when you regret this later, remember I did warn you." He glanced briefly at the waiting Justice Center entrance before taking her hand and heading in the opposite direction. "Let's go get a drink."

5

MIRAI

The forensics lab had a deceptively peaceful feel to it so early in the morning, as if the insanity waiting on the other side of the door would never be allowed in. Adlai was starting to see why Erik Rhom hardly ever left the lab.

It had been a late night with Maris, who had finally left him in a tizzy of fiery outrage at around two this morning, so he'd take whatever snippets of peace he could find. The next few minutes weren't going to qualify, however.

He activated the recording system then nodded at Erik. "Okay, turn it on."

On the display pane, letters flickered to life.

Where am I?

"First, identify yourself for the record."

What record?

"We'll get to that. Please identify yourself."

Fine. Iona Rowan, External Relations Advisor, 7th Generation.

"Thank you. This is Advisor Adlai Weiss of the Justice Division speaking to you. Erik Rhom, a Justice Division analyst, is also present in the room. Advisor Rowan, your most recent psyche backup has been awoken in a virtual environment so you can answer questions regarding your activities over the course of the last two weeks."

Ah, fuck. What did I do?

The active backup had been created the morning of the Chosek Embassy massacre, so she would have no recollection of those events. "To be blunt, Advisor, you murdered three Chizeru, including a clan leader, and inflicted total body loss on three executives from Zanist Circuitry as well as yourself."

Damn. I guess breakfast didn't agree with me.

Erik arched an eyebrow, but Adlai shrugged. They knew the virutox transformed an individual's personality, as well as destroyed higher-order judgment capabilities and all but erased emotions such as guilt or remorse. Still, hearing it in action was undeniably disturbing.

"You were infected with a destructive virutox at some point in the previous two-week period. This psyche backup remains infected, which is why you've been limited to a virtual environment.

"The virutox originates from a limb augment installed in the forearm. You didn't install such an augment, which means you interacted on a neural level with someone who did, or possibly someone who acquired the virutox themselves by doing so." He and Erik hadn't discussed the possibility of second-level infectious spread, but from what he understood about the virutox, there was no reason to rule it out. "Does any recent interaction come to mind that fits these criteria?"

Silence answered him.

"Advisor Rowan?"

I might have participated in a Disuta competition earlier in the week. Tuesday night.

It was good she couldn't see Adlai's expression, as the revulsion churning his stomach likely made it to his face as well. To let a stranger take over your mind...did she have no self-respect? No appreciation for the treasure her psyche represented?

Beside him, Erik acted enthused. "This sets a minimum transferability threshold for us. If it turns out to require that deep of an interaction, it's good news. Relatively speaking, I mean. Disuta matches are pretty rare, so it should keep the spread contained."

He supposed it did count as good news. Maybe. "I need the names of the other people who participated in the competition on the night in question."

You've never played Disuta, have you?

He kept his tone neutral. "I have not."

Anonymity is one of its core precepts. No names, no professions, no life histories beforehand. But we did go out for drinks after, and a few details slipped from loosened tongues. I'm fairly certain the person who created my challenge was a man named Tristan McLeros. A factory technician from Synra.

"Thank you, Advisor. This information is enormously helpful."

Fabulous. Now, when do I get regened? This virtual stockade is as boring as...boring things.

"The crime you committed is an extremely serious one. The fact that you did so while under the influence of a virutox is a mitigating factor, but the Chosek government is demanding harsh punishment for the murder of its citizens. Zanist Circuitry has also submitted a sizeable recompense bill on behalf of its executives. Therefore, the nature and extent of your sentence is still being negotiated. Needless to say, when you *are* regened, an earlier psyche backup free of infection will be used."

So this version of me is dead either way, huh? Ah, well. As for earlier me, simply revoke her Advisor status. I didn't particularly care for the job, anyway.

"I'm afraid revocation of your Advisor status goes without say-ing." Or he'd thought it did. "It's the additional punishments which are yet to be decided."

That's just dandy. Sounds as if my former self can look forward to a career in the service industry, then. Glad I'm not her.

She really, really wasn't. "Thank you for your assistance. Good-bye, Advisor Rowan."

He gestured toward Erik, and the pane went blank. "I'll run a search for Tristan McLeros. It wouldn't surprise me if he's already found his way into the Justice system. If so, we might be able to identify more potential victims before they murder anyone. What can you do with the information she gave us?"

"If you'll authorize full access to all of Advisor Rowan's backups for me—for comparison purposes—I can try to use her timeline to reconstruct the precise method and route the virutox took in in-vading her system. If I'm successful, it could be the first step in devising a vaccine."

Short of a cure, which didn't appear likely, a vaccine was as close to a windfall as they were apt to get. "I'll authorize it, as well as any other resources you need."

6

WAYFARER

ASTERION DOMINION SPACE

"I'm an idiot."

Nika looked up from where she sat on the floor sorting their dwindling equipment and supplies. "I doubt it."

"I've worn this persona for millennia, built an interstellar business enterprise up from a single design schematic, served at the highest levels of government, and I am a certifiable idiot.

"I've been so absorbed in our leaps from one crisis to the next, so...well, *self*-absorbed, that it never even occurred to me how I could easily be helping to get the limb augments off the streets. I mean, I thought Justice was going to handle it, then you were falling out of a tower, then we were infiltrating the Dominion's largest prison, then everything we believed we knew flipped upside down. And somewhere along the way I forgot that they're *my* limb augments."

Her face screwed up at him. "Okay. Meanwhile, Justice wasn't handling it, only now they sort of are."

"And I can help. I need a few minutes, if you've got this?" He gestured to the glorious mess she'd made of the cabin floor.

One corner of her lips curled up in a teasing mien, and it was so like her—the old her—the fleeting sense of déjà vu it evoked made him dizzy.

"Yeah, I've got this."

"Right." He nodded and went down below, where he sprawled across the bed until the dizziness subsided. Then he stayed there because it was comfortable and gazed up at the ceiling without seeing it as he composed a statement.

OFFICIAL STATEMENT BY RIDANI ENTERPRISES RE-GARDING SIMUL/INTERACT BOOST LIMB AUGMENT MODEL VK 3.2

Earlier this month, Ridani Enterprises released its newest model of consumer forearm/hand enhancement. During transport of the initial shipments to suppliers, the augments were stolen by an unknown party. The thief or thieves implanted a malicious and dangerous virutox into the installation software then distributed the augments to retailers as if they had come from this company.

Do not under any circumstances install this augment. If you have already done so, visit a clinic immediately and request a regen from a pre-augment-install psyche backup. The seriousness of the infection this virutox causes cannot be understated, and there is currently no known treatment.

Ridani Enterprises deeply regrets any difficulties this criminal act has created or will create for you. Present proof of purchase to nex address @RidaniEnt_CustServ.LA, and your purchase price will be refunded, no questions asked.

He reread the statement twice, tweaked a few words and wrote up a message to his Manufacturing Director, Vance Greshe, to accompany the statement. It was full of contriteness, apologies and profuse thanks, none of which made up for the reality that he was sticking Vance with all the dirty work, not to mention a major public relations headache. But the alternative was worse, so he hit 'send.'

Then he lay on the bed for a few *more* minutes to ruminate on the strange, discombobulated state of his life at present, before returning to the main cabin and the best part of it.

He found Nika sitting at the center of five piles of varying sizes, frowning at them. "How's it look?"

"I used our last mirage shell to conceal the chained-up assassin in an alley and our last remote energy pulse detonator to stun the security checkpoint dynes. You need a quality internal kamero filter augment and a fully modded Glaser. And...well, I have a list." She leaned back on her hands. "We can try to pick up everything on...I don't know, Adjunct Ni or Hachi.

"Or, I can send Perrin the list and have her meet us somewhere. I don't want to unnecessarily endanger her, but I think we can find someplace safe to meet. I need to tell her about the communicable 'features' of the virutox, too, but I want to couch it so she doesn't freak out, which means in-person is better. Also..." she winced "...I'd like to transfer a portion of your funds to her for NOIR to use."

"Our funds."

"I told you I'm not comfortable with that."

"And I'll continue to say it until you are." He smiled. "It sounds as if we have a lot to update NOIR on and a lot of supplies to acquire. Let's do it."

Dashiel input the new course in the navigation system while Nika messaged Perrin and cleaned up the assorted piles. Once they were on their way, he joined her on the floor, and they rested against the front of the couch. "Can I ask you something?"

"Of course you can."

He nodded, mostly to himself. "If it had been you caught in the checkpoint outside the Briscanti Materials building, how would you have handled it?"

"I suppose more or less the way I did. If I knew I couldn't spoof my way through the identity check, I would've stunned the security dynes, disabled the force fields—or simply run through the checkpoint if it was possible—and vanished."

"So you always carry the weapons and tools you might need to get out of a scrape with you?"

"I don't wear tactical pants everywhere for the appreciative whistles they garner."

He chuckled. "I think they look hot."

"Good." She studied him curiously. "We'll get you properly equipped, and I'll teach you how to *hide* the fact that you're properly equipped."

"And then I'll be a genuine rebel?"

"You don't need weapons to be a rebel. It's a mindset. A way of life. What is this really about?"

He sighed and sank lower against the couch. "When I was standing there in the line, hemmed in by force fields and waiting on you to save me, it hit me. I wasn't an Advisor or a business magnate any longer, not in any way that mattered, because if I were I would have navigated the situation one way—a way I no longer can. And I wasn't a rebel, because if I were I would have navigated the situation another way—a way I relied on you to handle for me. So what am I? *Who* am I?"

She laughed quietly, though it sounded kind in tenor. "I can't tell you the answer. Hells, I hardly know you. And as it turns out, I hardly know myself, either. But if there's anything that being Asterion means, it's that we can be whomever we choose to be. So you get to answer those questions for yourself."

"I believe you mean I *have* to answer those questions for myself."

She shrugged. "I was trying to take the edge off. Don't feel bad about what happened on Ebisu. You're doing well, and you're going to make a great rebel. A smart rebel. A clever and conniving rebel." She studied the rough, anti-skid flooring beneath them with sudden interest. "If it's still what you want."

He leaned in close and lifted her chin with his fingertip until she met his gaze. Warmth flooded his chest, and he damn sure hoped his eyes reflected the passion stoking that warmth. He waited until his lips were a centimeter from hers to whisper, "I want *you*."

WILDCARDS

7

MIRAI

"Ryan, we've got someone in place on Adjunct Rei ready to slice into the public nex web overlay there. Can you talk them through the process?"

Ryan Theroit looked up from one of the workbenches, where he had a drone—not WheatleyBot, so Perrin had no idea where he'd picked this one up from—in pieces and its core sliced open. She hadn't meant to interrupt his work, but he nodded enthusiastically before she could tell him to never mind. "Yep. Pass them over to me."

She wasn't in a position to easily find someone else qualified to do it, so she offered him a quick, "Great—thank you!" as she transferred the contact, then scanned The Floor in search of Ava Zobel.

In the last several days, alongside the continuing structural repairs, The Floor had been transformed into one big crisis management command center. All available resources were now being directed at protecting as many people as possible from any and all virutoxes. From Justice. From the Guides. From any other malicious entities participating in whatever their scheme was all about.

The level of effort they were mustering wouldn't be sustainable for long, but they only had to keep it up long enough for Nika to bring the whole conspiracy crashing down. At least, that's what Perrin kept telling herself.

She spotted Ava in a huddle with Dominic, Geoff and Josie near the entrance to the training room, talking them through stars knew what. With the loss of a number of their strongest, most capable members, others were stepping up to prove themselves strong and capable as well. It warmed her already-too-big heart to see.

She took two steps toward them, so she wouldn't have to shout above the din. "Ava, what's the status on the stun transmission routine?"

Ava didn't bother to turn around. "Two more hours. Three if you keep asking me every five minutes."

Perrin secretly rolled her eyes, but she'd weather Ava's acerbity without complaint. Whatever it took. There was a good chance their info blasts weren't exaggerating the tiniest bit, and if a Justice conviction meant final death, people needed every conceivable tool at their disposal to escape being captured by Justice, and NOIR could fashion a lot of tools.

They had routines making the rounds that sent out stun waves on skin contact, but ideally one didn't want Justice dynes getting so close in the first place. Conversely, many situations existed where carrying a Glaser or a stun grenade wasn't practical.

Ava's frankly inspired solution was a routine that allowed a person to use a tiny bit of the Glaser tech without needing to turn an arm into a glorified weapon. It used the body's normal energy generation to produce a scatter shot of electricity strong enough to stun anything smaller than a mecha within a three-meter range, with no internal hardware modifications required. Ava's group had been working out the messy details for half a day now, but it sounded like they were getting close to having a distributable routine.

She really hoped they were getting close.

"Hey." Joaquim Lacese's hand landed on her shoulder, and she jumped.

"Everything okay?"

"Yes. Sorry. I was wound up in my own head."

He gave her a questioning look but didn't press her. "I just heard from Spencer. He wanted to know the story behind the final death warning."

"Did you tell him what Nika said about Zaidam?"

"Yep. It doesn't expose us to any greater extent than we already are, and the more dissension that's sown inside Justice, the better. It might even slow them down." Joaquim paused, his expression darkening. "He also said his boss, Advisor Weiss, is legitimately working to get the limb augments off the streets, in direct defiance of an order from the Guides."

"That's awesome to hear! Finally, a break."

"Color me skeptical. At best, they can confiscate a portion of the unsold stock on Mirai, which does nothing for the people infected or for the augments out in the wild on all the other worlds."

"But it *is* a step in the right direction."

"Maybe, assuming this Weiss is still an Advisor tomorrow, and assuming he isn't secretly turning around and redistributing the confiscated augments on other worlds. Regardless, it doesn't change our strategy. We can't depend on Justice to save the people, and we can't wait for some benevolent dictator to have a change of heart."

"I realize—" She cut herself off as a new ping arrived. Her face lit up. "It's Nika. She needs me to put together a box of supplies and meet her."

Joaquim's eyes narrowed. "Her and Ridani?"

"I expect so. She said to meet her at the docks at an industrial hub outside of Mirai Two."

"Uh-huh." He grabbed his jacket then tapped Ryan on the shoulder. "Hey, you're in charge for a couple of hours. Perrin and I have some errands to run."

8

NAMINO

ASTERION DOMINION AXIS WORLD

Grant Mesahle surveyed the new fab kit configuration with a critical gaze. This morning he'd received an order for ten atmospheric regulation modules suitable for installation at an outpost on a Class IIb—minimally capable of supporting Asterion life—exploratory world. The schedule was tight, so he'd sidelined two less urgent deliverables to convert one of the fab kits to dedicated production of the ordered modules for a couple of days.

Satisfied with the setup, he turned to go back inside and finalize the schematic he'd spent much of the morning designing.

In many ways, atmo regulators for Class IIb worlds were more complicated than those for the truly inhospitable planets. The air wasn't toxic to Asterions, but it also wasn't particularly healthy for them. When people came inside after working on the surface, their lungs and every other organ the air touched would have suffered microscopic damage, and their OS needed the right mixture of gases and supplemental nanobots to repair it. The formulation went above and beyond what counted as 'normal Asterion-friendly air' and was different for every environment.

He'd reached the door to his office when the perimeter sensor beeped in his personal nex node. The cam feed showed two well-dressed and serious-looking men walking in the public entrance.

He'd been expecting this visit for a while now. It didn't mean he was happy about it. He made a performance out of putting his tools away to cover for the time it took him to prep a series of financial and file transfers and set them to trigger in an instant if needed. The mechanisms to preserve and protect his most important possessions were always in place—had been in place for a long time—so it was simply a matter of queuing them up. Then he pulled a protective tarp over the entry point of the fab kit and walked out to greet his guests.

"Good afternoon, gentlemen. How can I help you?"

The dark-haired, burly one on the left spoke first. "Are you Grant Mesahle?"

"Yes, sir."

"And you own this business?"

"I do."

"What kind of products do you sell?"

"Custom-designed habitat components for outposts, mostly, along with the occasional spacecraft component. My orders generally come from businesses needing a specific niche requirement met. I don't get many walk-ins."

The dark-haired man frowned. "We're not customers, Mr. Mesahle."

You don't say. He didn't bother to request their names or credentials. He knew what they were. "Then I'll ask again. How can I help you?"

The light-haired man on the left began strolling across the factory space while the dark-haired one continued to do the talking. "Do you ever sell an entire spaceship?"

Grant shrugged mildly. "Every now and then I'll take on a custom build job—once or twice a year. Small, personal craft only." He gestured around the space. "No room to build anything bigger."

"Did you recently sell one to a Dashiel Ridani?"

Inwardly, Grant exhaled in relief. They weren't here about Nika. Outwardly, he chuckled wryly. "Ah, Advisor Ridani. Not exactly."

"What does that mean?"

This guy really was a humorless prick. "It means I allowed Advisor Ridani to take a ship out for a test flight several days ago, assuming he was trustworthy on account of being an Advisor." He smiled blithely at the man, who was almost certainly an Advisor himself. Far too arrogant and presumptuous to be anything else. "Unfortunately, he's yet to return it."

"You're saying he stole one of your ships?"

This question had come from the light-haired one, who had circled around the factory space and now stood off Grant's left shoulder.

Grant shifted to face him. "I'm not ready to make such a serious accusation so soon. As an Advisor, it's entirely possible that his idea of what a 'test flight' means is somewhat more expansive than mine." He didn't feel guilty about besmirching Ridani's good name, if the man had one. He didn't owe Ridani anything, and the secrets he kept he did so for Nika's sake. Besides, implying the man was an irresponsible fop was a far better option than telling two Justice officers the truth.

"You're very conciliatory about the possible theft of a ship that must have cost you a great deal of time and credits to build."

He dropped his chin to his chest with a sigh. "You've gotten a thorough look around here by now, yes? If you're searching for the right word to describe this place, that word is 'humble.' I'm an electrician, a mechanic, a mason. It's just me and two drones here, plus a rudimentary mecha to lift the extra-heavy pieces. I build things because I enjoy doing it, and I make enough money at it to keep building more things. Yeah, if that ship never gets back here and I never see credits for it, it'll hurt. But I'm not interested in creating a Dominion-wide scandal by publicly accusing an Advisor of theft. I'd rather spend the time the sordid affair would drain out of my life building a new ship instead."

The light-haired man held Grant's stare for several seconds—then broke off and rejoined his partner. "If you hear from Mr.

Ridani, or if he returns here, with or without the ship, please contact us immediately."

Grant received a contact file at his business nex address, and he nodded curtly. "I'll make a point to try and remember. Have a good rest of your day."

He watched the men until they were off his property and back on the public street, then went inside. He hoped like hells he wouldn't need to use them, but it was time to dust off his contingency plans.

⨯R

Justice Advisor Blake Satair waited until they were beyond line-of-sight of Mesahle Flight before stopping on the deserted sidewalk and turning to his officer, Kent Freitag. "Well? Were you able to get the listeners planted?"

Kent nodded, but it lacked the desired conviction. "The stealthed drone wasn't able to find a way inside the main building, but it placed audio-visual sensors on the windows on both sides. I also secured two listeners on the factory floor."

Blake glanced back the way they'd come. He'd hoped for more comprehensive surveillance coverage, but if they returned now even a plebian like Grant Mesahle would get suspicious. "Combined with the interceptor we placed on the fiber line running into the property on our way in, that ought to get the job done. If Advisor Ridani shows up or contacts Mr. Mesahle, we need to know about it."

"Or Ms. Tescarav."

"Kirumase—I don't care who Nika's playing at being this year. Unfortunately, the fact that she was on Namino the same day Ridani came here doesn't definitively tie her to Mesahle. But it's damn peculiar, so we'll be listening and watching for her as well."

Blake peered down the road toward the maglev station. "Stay in the area long enough to confirm the listeners are transmitting, then meet me in Mirai One. We need to pay a visit to Ridani Enterprises. The Guides have authorized more aggressive monitoring for Ridani's second-in-command."

9

MIRAI

Vance Greshe had always believed himself to be a reasonably smart man. Not an intellectual as such, but clever. Astute. Able to study a complicated situation, spot the problems and devise solutions for them. Hard-working, too. The kind of man who buckled down and toiled over a problem until it was fixed.

None of these positive attributes, it turned out, qualified him to run a multi-world, multi-billion-credit manufacturing company. Dashiel had built the company up from nothing, transformed it into an empire, then managed to keep it not only running but profitable while spending years treating a broken heart with a troublesome illicit substances habit.

Meanwhile Vance was struggling just to digest all the daily reports and respond to the top two or three emergencies on any given day. As Manufacturing Director, he'd thought he had a good grasp on the macro business; he'd been wrong. He'd thought he'd handled a lot of the heavy lifting on Dashiel's behalf while his boss fought to hold his fraying personal life together, but in truth the man had been managing thousands of details every single day. And Vance never had any idea.

Some people said Advisors weren't simply the most talented or smartest Asterions—they were something else altogether. That the pinnacle of self-directed evolution resulted in not a difference of degree, but of *kind*. Post-Asterion, Asterion++…the terms varied, but the idea was the same.

When he interacted with Dashiel, he saw a man. A savvy genius of a man, but a man nonetheless; one with flaws and foibles, like everyone else. Now Vance drowned beneath an avalanche of data and shipments and processes and materials, and they represented only the tip of the iceberg that was Ridani Enterprises. He had to wonder what the man's mind must be like, to control it all, silently and as a matter of course.

The message he'd received from Dashiel last night had thrown him for yet another loop. He'd known about the limb augment theft, and it had been the source of much of his work in the days before he'd been asked to step into his boss' shoes. A virutox, though? One deliberately spread to unsuspecting consumers? Who *did* that sort of thing? He couldn't help but feel as though something terrible was happening around him, something he lacked the skill to see.

He'd rushed into the office, sent the public statement out and began writing the procedures to handle the refund requests when they started pouring in. He'd been here ever since.

Dammit! He jolted himself out of the reverie. Every second he spent whining over how *hard* it all was added to the seconds not spent doing the job he'd been entrusted with. And for the moment he was keeping the business afloat, at least. He should keep doing that.

He was two sentences into the daily status report from a factory on Kiyora when the office comm activated. "Director Greshe? There are two men from Justice here to see you."

"Is one of them Advisor Weiss?" If it was, he might be able to find out a few tidbits on this virutox. Weiss had always struck him as a nice man. Honorable.

"Ah, no sir. They didn't give their names. Do you want me to ask?"

His lips pursed. If they were here to ask *him* about the virutox, he didn't know anything beyond the particulars of the theft itself. If they were here to ask him where Dashiel had run off to, he didn't know anything about that, either.

Maybe they would believe him, and the meeting would be over in three minutes. "It's not necessary. Send them in."

The door opened to allow a tall, broad-shouldered man with dark brown hair and a cold visage and a slighter, blond man with somewhat kinder features inside.

He stood and met the two men in front of his desk, hand extended. "Welcome, gentlemen. I'm Vance Greshe. How can I help you today—?"

AR

"Sir, are you feeling ill?"

Vance blinked—had his eyes been open? He sat slouched in his chair at the desk. On the other side of it, Larahle Spicor stood, gazing at him in evident concern.

"Um, I...no, I'm fine. I have a headache, but...." And he really did. The base of his neck ached, as if he'd gotten a new port installed and neglected to activate any pain suppressors during the procedure. "It's merely from all the stress, I'm sure."

"I'll get you some hot tea. Did the meeting with the Justice people go okay?"

The Justice people? Who was she talking about...oh, right. How had it gone? They'd come in, and...he struggled to recall the details of the meeting, like it was a dream fading with the light of day, slipping from his memory even as he grasped for it.

"I think so. They were asking about Dashiel, not surprisingly. I told them everything he told us, which isn't much. He's on a personal sabbatical. He checks in via message periodically. Yes, he ordered the issuance of the statement regarding the limb augments. No, I don't know where he is or when he will return. After I repeated it a couple of times, they seemed to accept it."

Concern only grew in her expression. "That's all you discussed? They were in here for almost forty minutes."

"Were they?" Vance frowned vaguely. "There was a good bit of small talk. I guess they hoped if I loosened up, I might let something slip. Their wasted forty minutes, right?"

"I suppose so." She studied him scrupulously for another second before turning to go—then stopped and pivoted back toward him. "Did they ever tell you their names?"

"I'm certain they did, but I'll be damned if I can remember what they were." He shrugged. "It's possible I need to go in for a tune-up."

She planted both hands on the desk and leaned in. "Vance, you don't need a tune-up—you need to get some rest."

"I can't. I owe it to Dashiel to keep this business running."

"But you need sleep and depri time to do it."

"I...." He rubbed wearily at his eyes; stars he was tired. "I tell you what. I'll lock the door behind you and hit the couch for a nap. Good enough?"

"Not even close, but it's a start."

10

WAYFARER

MIRAI

They landed at a drab, shopworn dock in a small industrial hub on the periphery of Mirai Two. They'd switched up the false credentials of the *Wayfarer* since Ebisu, as they planned to do every time they landed somewhere that tracked such things. Despite the ship's small size, they now masqueraded as a cargo vessel, because it was the only type of ship that landed in the industrial hub. They also planned to be gone before anyone came by asking after a cargo manifest.

It didn't take long before a muffled rapping sound echoed through the hull. "Hello? I'm here."

They opened the hatch to find Perrin standing beneath it, a bulky bag slung over her shoulder.

"I'm so glad to see you! You got this ship from Grant? It's gorgeous!"

Nika laughed as she extended the ramp. Perrin promptly ran up it, dropped the bag and grabbed her in a fierce hug. Perrin's enthusiasm was, as usual, infectious, and Nika found her spirits rising almost instantly.

She pulled back from the hug and picked up the bag before Perrin could retrieve it, then motioned her inside. "You realize it's only been a few days."

"Long days." Perrin shifted toward the hatch and made some kind of sign with her hand before heading inside as the ramp retracted.

"What did you just do?"

"Joaquim's standing guard outside. That was me saying yes, it's really you and not...I don't know. Kidnappers or Guide-controlled doppelgangers or something. He worries." Her gaze fell on Dashiel, and she abandoned a pained expression for a big grin. "Speaking of which, I'm super glad you're not evil."

Dashiel chuckled lightly; he too seemed to cheer in Perrin's presence. "So am I. It's good to see you again, and in one fully functional piece this time."

"I heard you helped me after the explosion at The Chalet. Thank you—and let me apologize on Joaquim's behalf. He'll never say it to your face, but he's sorry about how he acted toward you."

Nika arched an eyebrow. "Is he?"

"Well...probably." Perrin gestured toward the bag, which Nika had deposited on the table. "I think we were able to get everything you asked for, except I could only scrounge up three mirage field modules. Dominic's picking up new ones for NOIR, but he won't be back until the morning."

"That's fine. More than fine." Nika looked at Dashiel and tilted her head toward the container sitting on the workbench.

He retrieved a data weave from it and presented it to Perrin. "In return, something for you."

Perrin accepted the weave and placed a fingertip on the scanner to review the index—then she almost dropped the weave on the floor as her cheeks reddened. "This is five hundred thousand credits."

Dashiel nodded. "It is. Use them for NOIR's benefit, however you best see fit. And if you need more, let us know."

Perrin's gaze darted to Nika, who smiled broadly. "What he said."

"Stars, with this we can refinish the whole Floor using a non-conductive, pliable top coat. And buy three new high-density servers, because storage space is filling up fast from all the virutox-related code. And get a third repair bench. And remodel the top floor into a nightclub."

"Those all sound like marvelous ideas—except the last one might be a bit extravagant. We should get past the current crisis before we start expanding our leisure offerings."

"I'm glad you said 'we.'" Perrin's wistful countenance darkened into chagrin. "Not that I want to take her away from you, Dashiel."

"It's okay. I've always had to share her with the world."

As Nika watched the two of them awkwardly stumble through the interchange, her subconscious processes churned up a messy stew of guilt and regret, then garnished it with a dash of homesickness. She missed The Chalet. She missed her friends. She missed walking The Floor and interacting with the people who brought it to life.

But nothing was simple anymore, was it? If it had ever been. She also craved the freedom the ship gave her. And Dashiel. She didn't think she could go back to a life without him in it, except he didn't fit in the old one.

But tomorrow's complications wouldn't matter if they couldn't fix today's, so she should perhaps get over herself.

Now they were both staring at her, waiting for her to jump in and…be the diplomat. Dammit.

She took one of their hands in each of hers. "Listen, you two. No weeping over me when I'm standing *right here*. Perrin, go spend this money like it's going out of style, and tell Joaquim to stop being such a paranoid motherfucker. Well, except when it involves Justice or the Guides. Which reminds me. You all need to know something, but don't freak out, okay? The virutox is communicable across neural connections. Slightly."

"What? But that—oh crap, I gave an open connection to Cair when he was infected. Does this mean I caught it? I—"

She grabbed Perrin by both shoulders. "I said don't freak out. I think we'd know by now if you caught it. That was a week ago, and you seem *completely* unchanged. Transmission requires high level, active neural interaction."

"So I'm fine, then. Okay. We need to add a warning against neural interactions to our warning against installing new augments and routines." Perrin sighed. "People aren't going to be happy. What's the point of *being* if you can't upgrade yourself with trendy new augments and show them off by connecting with other people?"

"*Being* alive, in your sane mind and free of shackles?"

"Excellent point. Any more good news?"

Nika shook her head.

"Any more bad news?"

"Only the lack of good news. How about you? How's everything going?"

Perrin offered up an exaggerated shrug and leaned against the storage cabinet. "We've tapped into the public nex web billboards and are using them to warn people about...everything. We've been developing a variety of defensive measures people can easily adopt, both to keep virutoxes out and to stay free of Justice's clutches, and we're distributing them as fast as we can. Oh, and on the subject of Justice, rumor is they're actually starting to get the limb augments off the shelves, at least on Mirai. Spencer and his boss are, anyway. I'm not sure about the rest of Justice."

"So Adlai was telling the truth." Dashiel visibly relaxed. "I'm glad to hear it."

Given the man had tried to arrest her in the Mirai Tower data vault, Nika remained skeptical of his intentions. But she recognized how badly Dashiel wanted Adlai to be one of the good guys, and it was a start.

Perrin glanced idly around the cabin. "What's your next step?"

Nika blew out a breath. "Investigate the sites of the recent outposts hit and see if any clues got left behind. Follow-up on several details Dashiel learned from the Briscanti Materials CEO. Since it appears the Guides aren't interested in talking, likely take out some more assassins. If all else fails, find Gemina Kail, abduct her and torture her until she gives up all her secrets."

11

KIYORA

ASTERION DOMINION AXIS WORLD

The Kiyora One Generations Clinic occupied a place of honor in an upscale services sector in the northeast area of the city. The soft cameo marble and opalescent exterior of the building gave it a friendly, inviting appearance despite the relative lack of windows. Perfectly manicured grass led to rows of flowering azaleas, adding color and vivacity to the tableau.

The subliminal message conveyed was that here, life was both embraced and tenderly cared for, in all its forms. Only the best for the creation of Asterion bodies. No expense spared.

Gemina was in no mood to be soothed, and she tromped through the door and up to the lobby counter. "Advisor Gemina Kail. I need to see the facility manager."

The dyne regarded her blankly. "You do not have an appointment."

"I'm here on the direct order of the Guides. The facility manager, now."

"Please have a seat. Mr. Takeda will be with you in a few minutes."

"I'll stand." She pivoted and began pacing the lobby.

The Guides had taken the news of the absurd increase in the number of units demanded by the Rasu...actually, she had no idea how they'd taken it. Their countenances had remained emotionless, their tones of voice even and lacking affectation. They'd expressed confidence that the spreading virutox would produce a sufficient number of new 'criminals,' but also authorized the cleansing of an additional two outposts. Finally, almost as an after-thought, they had suggested she begin investigating what might be involved in producing Asterions straight out of a lab and already in stasis.

It should have been the easiest, most moral solution to the problem from the beginning. Why terminate the lives of living, breathing Asterions in the process of experiencing full lives, when you could use ones who'd yet to draw a breath?

But something about the idea grated against said morality. Gemina had wanted to recoil from the notion the instant it was voiced, as would most Asterions. After all, the only thing they loved more than life itself was the *potential* of life. The possibilities which every tomorrow held.

To deny someone's right to ever exist was quite high up on the list of high sins in the Asterion Dominion, alongside psyche-wipes and storage—which meant if the Guides went forward with this idea, she'd be one short of a trifecta.

⋏R

"Advisor Kail, it's an honor to meet you. I'm Hiro Takeda, Operations Director of the Kiyora One Generations Clinic. To what do I owe a visit from an Administration Advisor? No trouble, I hope. We take great care to run a top-notch operation here."

She grudgingly took his offered hand, but dropped it as quickly as was socially acceptable. "I'm certain you do. I merely have a few questions about your procedures. For potential avenues of future research."

"Research into what areas?"

He sounded genuinely intrigued; she longed to dissuade his enthusiasm, but given how it should make him more cooperative, she played along. "Ways to improve the lives of Asterions, of course—from their very inception."

"A noble goal, indeed. What is it you'd like to know?"

"I want to see the various stages the bodies proceed through prior to completion. We can talk while you show me around."

"Excellent. Right this way." He gestured toward a set of wide, welcoming doors, and she followed.

ᐱᕐ

Thankfully the organization of the facility was such that the end of the process came first on the tour, which meant she'd be able to conjure some excuse to cut the tour short. Gemina had no desire to see vats of pseudo-organic tissue being grown or synthetic bones being constructed, and she definitely had no desire to see brain matter germinating on lattices of kyoseil.

They entered a medium-sized room that was more akin to a storage area than a lab. A dozen bodies were encased in a porous, translucent material and submerged in a semi-fluid gel, not unlike what repair tanks used. The gel and the bodies floated inside the harder shells of advanced stasis chambers. A mass of photal fibers snaked out from beneath each chamber to a complex module on the wall above it.

Without meaning for it to, her gaze fell on the closest body. Its eyes were closed, its features pallid and frozen. Ready to be a life, but not there just yet.

"How many bodies do you complete each day?"

"Twenty-six to thirty. It may sound like a lot, but we're one of only two Class A facilities on Kiyora. Across an entire planet, demand is high."

"I'm well aware. And you handle the operating system uploads as well?"

"And the psyche uploads, and any memory stores requested to be transferred. A body is not complete without a psyche to call it home."

This was the root of the problem, wasn't it? The Rasu demanded functioning Asterions, but unconscious ones. Who knew the aliens' reasons for it, but they'd been menacingly clear on the subject. "Theoretically—again, for purposes of future research—is it possible to initialize a psyche, to start it up, as it were, without actually waking the individual up?"

Takeda regarded her strangely. "I'm not sure I take your meaning. Programming is nothing more than a framework until a psyche begins using it, and one must experience consciousness to do so."

"But can't you simply put them straight into a state of *uncon*sciousness?"

"We pause the initial boot sequence at several points to run diagnostics and to confirm the kernel has both bonded with the physical brain and linked to the operating system. No one wants to wake up broken, now do they?" He laughed awkwardly.

She didn't join him. "What about at a later stage? After the boot sequence has completed, but before they reach conscious awareness. In layman's terms, right before they open their eyes for the first time. Can you keep them at that point indefinitely?"

He stared at her in utter horror, mouth agape, as if she'd morphed into a hideous carnival freak instead of asked a hypothetical question. "Why in the stars would you ever want to do such a thing?"

12

MIRAI

"Hurry up! It's over this way." Tristan McLeros motioned his friend Burkett toward the rear of the expansive Mirai One transit hub.

It was late in the evening and the moon was a tiny silver crescent in the night sky, but here in the heart of downtown light bathed the streets in a pervasive glow—which meant they needed cover. They scurried across the open space and flattened themselves against the hub's façade.

The maintenance entrance was almost invisible, marked by nothing more than a thin crack in the exterior wall. Tristan only knew about it because a friend who used to work at Oligasi Cuisine had recently transferred to the maintenance department at Dominion Transit. The logic of the inconspicuous door was sound, and not much different from the purpose of the machines he kept running at Oligasi: hide any evidence of the messy work required to keep the system running from the customers so that outwardly everything runs seamlessly and to perfection.

"How do we get in?"

Tristan waved a transmitter in Burkett's face. "The maintenance dyne access code is the same for all public and semi-public buildings in the city, and we are obviously maintenance dynes." He sent the code, and the door slid open. He pushed Burkett through the opening, and they now flattened themselves against the *inside* wall until the door slid back shut.

He'd blown off work today to hang out with Burkett. But they'd gotten bored after a few hours, so they'd decided to go screw with the transportation system for fun. Actually, he'd blown off work the day before, too, but he'd mostly slept the day away. He had a couple of concerned, then angry, messages from his boss, but he was ignoring them. He'd figure out what to do about work tomorrow.

"There should be a maintenance lift around here somewhere. All the control systems and power generation for the d-gates are underground."

"Is this it over here?" Burkett motioned to their left.

"Yep." They crept quietly to the lift. It began moving automatically as soon as they stepped on it, and they descended into shadows.

The subterranean level was the province of machines and the machines that maintained them. The walls were a dull flint and undecorated; outside of the flickering lights produced by the equipment, lighting was almost nonexistent. But at his job he was frequently the sole person in a building full of machines, so he was used to this environment.

He tuned up his infrared filter, and the room lit up like a holiday billboard.

"So what's the plan?"

"Uh…." Tristan lost his train of thought, distracted by the power and complexity on display now that he could see it. Food preparation equipment, this was not.

"Come on, man, we need to hurry before somebody finds us."

"Some*thing*, maybe. Okay, we want to switch up the signals, so a person who thinks they're going to Namino is sent to Synra, while a person going to Synra ends up in Ebisu Four, and so on."

"Is that even possible?"

"I mean, the tech to make it happen is mind-boggling, but it's all wired into the system and thus not our concern. The target destination is represented by a simple signal code. It tells the d-gate which other d-gate to attune to." He frowned. "There are a lot of d-gates, aren't there? I didn't really think about the numbers. We'll only be able to do a few."

"Why don't we cut the power instead?"

"Because that's not funny, just annoying—oh! Over here." He hurried up to a tall server module taking up half of the far left wall. "This looks like a signal distribution unit of some kind. I bet we can fuck up everything from here. You stand watch."

"Right." Burkett gave him a dubious scowl as he turned to face outward.

Tristan activated his limb augment, and ten virtual fingers sprung to life to stretch out beyond his physical ones. He wasn't much of a slicer, but his only real goal was to create a little chaos for laughs. So long as he scrambled a few commands going to the d-gates, mission accomplished.

He started toggling various triggers on the module, and the pattern of lights it emitted began to shift.

"Are you sure this box controls the destinations? It seems kind of big and bulky to only be routing signals around."

In truth, he *wasn't* sure...and it *was* fairly hefty. Also, his skin had begun to tingle when he got within reach of the module, which meant a high volume of power was flowing through it.

But it did something, right? He moved his augmented hand up higher and ratcheted a large tuner up.

A loud beeping noise rang out from the module.

"Shut that up!"

"I'm trying—I don't know what I did to set it off!" When dialing the tuner back down failed to stop the noise, his virtual fingers went crazy, pressing or toggling every input point they could find. Angry red lights joined the insistent beeping. Shit, shit, shit—

"Someone's coming!"

The clang of metal on metal filled the gaps between the beeps as two security dynes sprinted toward them, weapons already raised and aimed. "Desist your actions immediately."

Tristan held up his non-augmented hand. "We're from the maintenance department. We're trying to fix a problem with the unit here. I've almost got it."

His eyes fell on a flashing tuner high above him, nearly out of reach. Two concentric rings of lights encircling it blinked furiously in a staccato rhythm, as if this were the source of the system's irritation.

"Step away from the equipment and present valid credentials or you will be restrained and taken into custody."

"As soon as I...." Tristan extended his virtual fingers out to their maximum length and spun the tuner all the way to the right.

13

MIRAI

After they left the meeting with Nika at the industrial hub and returned to Mirai One, Joaquim and Perrin took a circuitous route back to The Chalet. They'd spent a good bit of their time walking the streets in recent days, seeking out allies and spreading the word about the virutox and the dangers Justice represented.

Joaquim stepped closer to Perrin to let a group of people pass them on the sidewalk. "It's horrifying that the virutox can be transmitted without the limb augment, but I don't see how much more we can do to warn people of its insidious nature. We're already shouting at the world to not trust any outside code." He pulled up the nex web message currently being blasted across the Dominion.

TRUST NO AUGMENT.
TRUST NO ROUTINE.
TRUST NO DOSE.
TRUST NO AGENT OF THE GOVERNMENT.
A JUSTICE CONVICTION MEANS FINAL DEATH.
KEEP YOUR PSYCHE. KEEP YOUR FREEDOM.
— Your Friends In NOIR

"I guess we could add 'Trust No One' to the announcement."

She made a face. "But that's both painfully vague and dangerously close to sounding delusional. 'Trust No Connection,' maybe?"

"Hmm. I'll think about it." She was better at public relations than him, so he should trust her instincts, but he felt an obligation to be the one to make the decision.

"While you think about that, I'm going to think about the best ways for us to use this amazing windfall of credits we're now in possession of. Finish The Floor repairs, naturally, and replace the destroyed weapons and equipment, but those expenditures will hardly dent the total."

Joaquim scowled at the mention of the donation. "I don't like taking Ridani's money."

"Oh, come on, Jo. He's not a bad guy, and we desperately need the credits."

"I didn't say we weren't going to take it—I said I didn't *like* taking it. What if it comes with strings attached that we haven't seen yet?"

"Nika wouldn't have let him offer it to us if it did."

"Assuming he told her. All I'm saying is, if he tries to impose conditions later or decides he wants the money back, it's her problem to handle."

"I'm sure he won't. Hey, when we get home, don't let me forget to tell everyone that we saw Nika, and she's safe and kicking ass—"

A burst of blinding light in Joaquim's peripheral vision preceded the sidewalk upending beneath his feet by almost a second, but he'd barely begun to react when a shock wave slammed him into Perrin and both of them into the building façade on their left. Then they were on the ground.

The next seconds passed in a dizzy haze of disjointed noises, shooting pain in strange places and internal damage alerts.

His ears rang. His OS told him it was because his aural system struggled to manage overloaded receptors. Blood dripped into his left eye—the OS had no ready explanation for this—so he opened his right one.

Perrin winced up at him from behind a dust-covered but blood-free face. "Hi. You're bleeding. Also, ow."

"Sorry." He more fell than crawled off her, then coughed dust out of his lungs as he pushed up to his knees. "Are you hurt?"

She sat up and maneuvered her head and arms gingerly. "I don't think so. Just generalized *ow*-ness." She looked around, and a horrified expression grew on her features. "But other people are. What happened?"

He climbed the rest of the way to his feet, rubbing at his forehead in search of the source of the blood with one hand while he helped her up with the other. Smoke and dust clogged the air around them, making it impossible to answer the question. Shouts and cries echoed through the din, but the loudest noises came from his right. The same direction as the burst of light.

Hq (visual) | scan.infrared(220°:40°)

His vision filled with an all-consuming flare of oranges, reds and purples.

"Whatever it was, it happened in this direction." He took her hand in his, and they started making their way toward the source.

АR

A crater one hundred fifty meters wide hollowed out the block where the Mirai One transit hub had once stood. Beyond the edges of the crater, fire engulfed the nearest towers. Wailing sirens overlapped one another in a despondent chorus, and drones buzzed about in aimless patterns searching for damaged bodies they could repair or flag for emergency response crews.

Joaquim tripped over something. Probably another chunk of building, but he glanced down anyway—to see a dismembered calf and foot with a heeled boot half burnt off it.

Acid singed his throat, and he concentrated on breathing through his nose; his taxed OS didn't have the bandwidth at present to babysit his nausea threshold.

He peered around for the remainder of the body, though he had no good reason to. It was nowhere to be seen. Of course, that wasn't saying much, for the ground was caked in smoldering debris.

"Gods, this is awful. It's like the explosion at The Chalet times a thousand."

In one of his wiser decisions in recent memory, he decided to concentrate on Perrin instead of the bodies. "I think the d-gates in the transit hub must have blown—or something blew them. That's the only scenario I can conceive of to explain this much damage, short of an aerial bombing. I can't even guess how many people were caught up in it."

A new siren arrived to add complexity to the dirge saturating the air, and he dragged a hand along his jaw. "I hate to say it, but this place is going to be crawling with Justice dynes any minute now. We should get out of here."

Perrin's frown morphed into horror. "But what about all these people? We need to help them!"

"How? The truth is, the emergency response squads are more qualified to administer first aid than we are. And the other truth is, most of the people who were here when it happened are already...gone."

"No, they're not. Hang on." She glared at him for effect, and a second later a message broadcast across the secure NOIR nex web:

Anyone in the vicinity of the explosion at the Mirai One transit hub who is in need of aid, please respond with your locator ID.

"There. We'll help *our* people, since for them a trip to a government repair center could end in a Justice detention cell."

It wasn't as if he could refuse her, what with her standing there looking all indignant and determined while covered in soot and dust, her jacket torn and her hair a chaotic jumble of tangled curls.

"All right, we'll do what we can. Get any responses yet?"

ᴧᴿ

Perrin secured a makeshift sling across the shoulder of a pale, slender woman. She'd ripped her jacket into shreds by this point, fashioning bandage wraps, wipes and slings using the material.

Joaquim didn't recognize the woman, but Perrin had known her name—Lily Sheridan, it turned out—on sight. Granted, it was Perrin's job to know the name of everyone connected to NOIR.

"Does it feel comfortable?"

Lily shrugged, then winced. "It doesn't hurt any worse than everything else."

"I'm afraid that's all we can ask for right now. Can you get yourself to the corner of Gibson and Stephenson? Someone will meet you there and take you to The Chalet, where you can get properly patched up."

"I never expected this was how I'd finally get to see The Chalet."

Perrin patted the woman's uninjured shoulder. "I know, and I'm sorry."

"Don't be. Thank you for your help."

"It was the least we could do. We'll see you in a bit."

Lily hobbled away, and instantly Perrin was off again. She grabbed Joaquim's hand and tugged him closer to the epicenter of the destruction, where it seemed impossible anyone could still be functioning.

"All I got was a locator number, no name or details." Abruptly she dropped his hand and sprinted forward, then fell to her knees next to a prone and charred form.

The skin covering the man's left arm had been burnt away nearly to the bone. But that wasn't the worst of it. A shard of metal protruded out through the base of his throat, just to the left of center. Blood flowed out around the metal and down his neck with disheartening speed.

"Give me your jacket!" She put one hand on the man's cheek while the other prodded gently at the edges of the wound.

Joaquim slipped his jacket off and handed it to her, even though it wasn't going to do any good.

She folded up one of the jacket's arms and pressed it against the man's throat. "Theo? Can you hear me? I'm getting an emergency response unit over here right now. You're going to be fine."

The man's lips moved wordlessly as blood bubbled up from his throat to soak Joaquim's jacket and Perrin's hands. He blinked twice, and after the second blink his eyes locked open, staring into the nothingness.

Perrin's brow knotted as she pressed more fervently on the wound.

Joaquim laid a hand on her shoulder. "He's gone."

"No...oh, godsdammit!" She leapt unsteadily to her feet, only to stumble backward and trip on an upended slab of concrete behind her.

He scrambled over to where she'd landed half on the slab. "Are you okay?"

"Yeah...." Desolation consumed the murmured response, and her chin fell to her chest.

He crouched in front of her and lifted her chin back up with a fingertip. Tears streaked through the layer of dust covering her face, and anguish darkened her normally bright eyes. "Are you sure?"

"Is anything we do ever going to be enough? It feels like the harder we fight, the more loss and destruction crashes down on us. On everyone."

"I honestly don't know. But we have to keep trying."

"I am trying. I'm trying so damn hard. That guy? He was the recruit I met the other week at Serpens Sate. He was finally stepping up and taking control of his own life and now...I don't know where he kept his backups or how we'll ever find them. He might be dead forever. Why?"

"There's no good answer, Perrin. Nothing that will fix this."

"I know. I just wish—"

"Clear the area. Only emergency response units are allowed inside the barricades."

He scowled at the dyne looming over them, then took a deep breath and helped Perrin to her feet. "Sounds like it's time for us to make ourselves scarce. We've done all we can."

14

MIRAI

"How many?"

"Atomized? We're estimating between one hundred eighty and two hundred thirty people. Here in Mirai One, that is."

Adlai sagged against the nearest intact wall. His head dropped back to rest on the surface as he pinched the bridge of his nose in a desperate struggle to keep hold of a few scraps of professional detachment.

The numbers were simple data points; if he thought of them as lives, he wouldn't be able to do his job. And people needed him to do his job. "We can use the surveillance footage and security logs from prior to the incident to identify some of the people who were atomized...but not all of them. We'll never find out who many of them were. Unless someone reports a person missing and places them in the vicinity of the transit hub tonight, this will be the end for those people."

Justice means final death.

But this wasn't Justice's doing, dammit. At least, not so far as he knew. But he didn't know much, did he? "Keep going."

Spencer hesitated, then joined him against the wall. "Upwards of one hundred fifty people suffered total body loss, but at least in those cases there are bodies we can identify. A minimum of three hundred more people suffered damage serious enough that body replacement might be required, and when you include the fires and other collateral damage, we're looking at around a thousand people with less severe damage. Three of the surrounding buildings were destroyed, and another six likely won't pass inspection and will need to be razed. As of five minutes ago, all but two of the fires are out, and both of those are under control."

"What else?"

"Early reports indicate five of the paired gates imploded at their destinations as well. No firm casualty numbers are available for those other locations yet."

Adlai considered the flames still pouring out of two of the crumbling buildings across the crater. The first rays of sunlight reflected off the chrome exteriors of the aerial drones that circled the buildings dispensing fire retardant chemicals. Dawn was bringing with it one hells of a long, hard day.

"Thank you for making the rounds and putting all the updates together. I'll leave a couple of officers here to help the dynes keep the scene secure until the forensic teams finish their work." Which was going to take...a while. "What I meant to say was, I'll set up security shifts for the next several days. Give me a few minutes to handle that, then let's go review the surveillance footage."

⁂

Video from an overhead corner cam located on the maintenance and power control level showed two men huddled together in front of the primary power distribution regulator. They muttered to one another in hushed whispers, and Adlai made a note to have an audio refinement routine isolate and capture the whispers.

One of the men reached out toward the regulator controls and—

"Bloody hells!" Far more profane curses flared in Adlai's mind when the limb augment burst to virtual life around the man's hand and began manipulating a variety of controls.

He could predict how the story unfolded from here, but he forced himself to keep watching to the end.

After two minutes of what appeared to be directionless fiddling on the man's part and an increasing number of alarms triggered, two security dynes rushed into the room, Glasers raised. "Desist your actions immediately."

The primary offender held up his non-augmented hand in their direction and mumbled something in response.

The security dynes advanced. "Step away from the equipment and present valid credentials or you will be restrained and taken into custody."

The augment appendages stretched to new lengths to reach a control near the top of the unit—

The video ended there. So did a lot of innocent lives.

Adlai exhaled as calmly as he could manage, then reversed the footage five seconds and froze it. He zoomed in on the face of the man with the limb augment.

He knew that face, because he'd just seen it in a file the morning before.

The door behind him opened, and Spencer returned carrying two coffees. The officer stopped in his tracks when he saw Adlai's scowl. "You found something?"

"You could say so. I found Tristan McLeros."

15

THE PLATFORM

MIRAI ORBIT

When Adlai trudged into the Guides' chamber, shoved forward by a wave of righteous indignation, he hadn't slept in thirty-eight hours. How many hours it had been since a depri session, he hadn't bothered to notice.

"Advisor Weiss, please update us on this terrible accident at the Mirai One transit hub." Guide Anavosa could have been asking for details on his lunch meal, for all the emotion the question conveyed.

"Accident? Whatever made you believe it was an *accident?*"

"Are you suggesting this was a deliberate act of sabotage? Who is to blame?"

He laughed bitterly. "You are."

"Advisor! What—"

"Your nifty little virutox? The one you were so insistent be allowed to run free in order to save the Dominion? It's destroying the Dominion instead."

"Advisor Weiss, mind your tone. We realize you are under tremendous strain, but this does not excuse your failure to observe basic courtesies."

He made a show of squaring his shoulders and lifting his chin. A poor show of it, one which likely came off as mocking even if he hadn't intended it to. "Apologies, Guide Anavosa. It's merely that I've been mired elbow-deep in a massacre for the last...actually, I don't know what time it is currently. Since last night."

"As I said, we do recognize the circumstances. Now, what could the explosion at the Mirai One transit hub possibly have to do with the limb augment virutox?"

"The two gentlemen responsible for the transit hub explosion both had the limb augment installed. One of them was also responsible, albeit unintentionally, for infecting Advisor Iona Rowan with the virutox, and we all know where that led." Analysis algorithms had identified the second man from the surveillance video, as well as confirmed the identification of Tristan McLeros.

"These men must be apprehended and incarcerated!" Unlike Anavosa, every syllable of Luciene's words dripped with sentiment—that of acrimony and vitriol.

"I would, if I could locate a single atom of their remains."

"Regen them and prosecute them."

"As you wish, Guide Luciene, but they'll need to wait in line for a regen behind a long list of innocent victims. The ones we can identify. Over two hundred people on three worlds permanently and irrevocably lost their lives. How does anything about this tragedy help to save the Dominion?"

"The tragedy does not, but the virutox does. 'How' is not your concern. What *is* your concern is that we're seeing a worrying decrease in arrests and convictions on Mirai."

He almost laughed in Guide Iovimer's face. "I should hope so. I've confiscated every limb augment I can find here, and I'm starting to make a dent in the supply on Kiyora and Ebisu."

"You defied our order?"

"It wasn't an order, Guide Iovimer. It was *guidance.*"

"We explained to you how—"

"You didn't explain a damn thing to me. You combined vague, dire warnings with vague, dire threats. I made a judgment call."

"Then we order you to follow our guidance or—"

"Or what—you'll psyche-wipe me? I'd advise against it, and not solely out of my own self-interest. I've taken precautions. If I disappear, you won't be able to conceal it with a hand-wave the way you did with Nika Kirumase."

A portentous silence hung in the air for several seconds. He thought less of himself for how much he enjoyed it.

Finally Guide Anavosa tilted her head in a slow, careful gesture. "Of course we will do no such thing. Psyche-wiping is a horrific crime, and you offend us by insinuating we may have or would ever commit it. But we can revoke your Advisor status."

"For following the Charter and enforcing the laws according to their stated intent? For preventing crimes from being committed and saving people from a criminal invasion of their psyches?" He swallowed hard and puffed his chest out. "Do it, and we'll see how that gambit plays out."

"Advisor Weiss, you do not appreciate the intractable position you are putting us in. We are trying to save our people and their way of life, and you are frustrating our efforts to achieve this goal."

"So *tell* me about the intractable position you're in, Guide Anavosa. Tell me what's driving your actions. Tell me how the Dominion is at risk. Tell me, and I'll do everything in my power to help save it."

"That won't be necessary. Our word should be enough."

"Once upon a time, it was. But not today. Not when your actions are costing countless lives. Not when every time I turn around, I'm washing the blood your actions are spilling off my hands. There is no conceivable greater good that can outweigh this level of harm."

"So you will not cease your confiscation of the limb augment units?"

"No, Guide Anavosa, I respectfully will not."

"Very well. You are dismissed."

Spencer and Erik were waiting for him outside Mirai Tower. They were deep in conversation, but they broke it off and faced him wearing matching expressions—a blend of expectant, hopeful and anxious—as he approached.

As soon as they got a good look at him, their expressions lost the hope in favor of dread. Spencer winced visibly. "How did it go?"

Adlai rubbed at his eyes then slapped himself across both cheeks, on the slim chance he might awaken from the nightmare. But no such luck. "If you haven't secured full psyche backups recently and set up a receivership contingency for your finances, you need to do so today. Right now, in fact."

Erik frowned deeply. "Can I ask why, sir?"

"Because we are well and truly screwed."

16

THE PLATFORM

*D*elacrai: "It seems we have lost Advisor Weiss."

Luciene: "The regrettable truth is that he has always been more loyal to Advisor Ridani than to us."

Delacrai: "It sounded to me as though his loyalty is to the Asterion people."

Anavosa: "Then he should have heeded our wisdom, because this is where our loyalties lie as well. But he did not, and we have no choice but to address his disobedience, though I suggest we take him at his word when he says he has taken precautions against reprisals.

"If we remove him from his position or take more drastic steps against him, we risk the exposure of the Rasu Protocol to the public at large. Yet his insubordination is damaging our own efforts, and if it continues we will need to revise downward the number of units we expect to be able to field in the next delivery. Since the Rasu have demanded a *greater* number, this is a problem."

Selyshok: "Advisor Satair is already working on our behalf on related matters. Send him in to take charge of Justice operations on Mirai while we initiate an official investigation of Advisor Weiss' fitness to serve—an investigation that will uncover sufficient malfeasance to discredit any hysterical claims he floats to the public."

Luciene: "I don't care for it. Advisor Weiss is a threat who needs to be neutralized immediately. But if our best option is a swift neutralization in the coming days, so be it."

Delacrai: "Are we not going to discuss the substance of Advisor Weiss' remarks? How the virutox is spreading and mutating in ways we did not foresee? How it is costing lives and fomenting the very instability and chaos we sought to avoid when we chose this path and decided to keep the Rasu Protocol a secret?

"We now have two of our greatest citizens—three if we make an evident assumption regarding Advisor Ridani's position—telling us in every conceivable way they can that we are making a grievous mistake, yet we blithely ignore them. We ignored Nika Kirumase five years ago and though she has extended an offer of diplomacy, we continue to ignore her today. We stand here now and choose to ignore Advisor Weiss. How many more defections will be required before we start to listen?"

Luciene: "Do you forget the structure we operate under, the structure which has served us for hundreds of millennia? They advise, but we decide."

Iovimer: "Regardless, there is nothing to be done for the issues Advisor Weiss raised. We allowed for the possibility of collateral damage from the beginning. The virutox remains the best among bad choices, as Advisor Kail's research indicates the use of newly awakened bodies is a suboptimal option."

Anavosa: "All our options are suboptimal. They always have been. Still, Delacrai raises a fair point: we should always be reevaluating the situation. We will use the current victims of the virutox as we must, but perhaps we should not encourage its spread or introduce additional virutoxes into the population. This tool is not so easily controlled as we imagined."

Selyshok: "Neither are our Advisors."

Luciene: "This is precisely why we need to neutralize the threat Advisor Weiss represents, and why we must run Nika Kirumase and Advisor Ridani to ground then eliminate them. We *cannot* allow the people to learn of the nature of the Rasu Protocol. To your comment, Delacrai, I fear even the greatest of our people are becoming increasingly emotional beings with every generation. Irrational and illogical. Soon they will be indistinguishable from mere organics."

Anavosa: "If our civilization survives long enough for devolution to become an issue, we can address it at such time. Our focus now will continue to be on survival."

Luciene: "Which means delivery of more units to the Rasu. The problem with the virutox in its current incarnation is not that it cannot be controlled. On the contrary, as it spreads beyond our expectations, this can work in our favor by producing the needed numbers.

"The problem, rather, is that it was too handily identified and blocked—by criminals, by terrorists, by our own Justice Division. I believe the NERE dust transmission we've previously discussed addresses these flaws, and I propose a limited, controlled test of this method of delivery."

Delacrai: "You are talking about gassing our own people."

Luciene: "It is no different than what we've done using the limb augments. The only distinctions are the method of delivery and the speed of infection. Do not choose a minor technicality to proclaim a conscience now, Delacrai."

Delacrai: "Do not presume to judge the nature of my conscience, *Luciene.*"

Anavosa: "Petty barbs do nothing to help our situation. We are not squabbling primitives. I dislike the NERE dust mechanism, but we cannot afford to foreclose any option. If we keep the test both small and contained, I am willing to approve it."

AR

In the privacy of her chamber, Delacrai closed off all her sensory functions until a featureless void enveloped her. From her perspective, it might be the vacuum of space or the abyssal depths of an endless ocean. It didn't matter, for here she existed only as thought. Analysis and result.

Luciene had labeled the adversaries in their midst emotional, irrational, illogical. But each of the Guides fell victim to their own failures of rationality and logic. Confident in their intellectual superiority, they failed to check their own processes for unsupported assumptions, unaccounted-for possibilities and unresolved variables. In common parlance, blind spots. Prejudices. Weaknesses.

Delacrai's own hubris was not so great that she did not recognize she must have her own as well. She had always placed a higher value on life, individual and en masse, than other considerations. Perhaps too high a value. But doing so shaped her analyses and results into those of a living being, not an algorithm. It made her Delacrai—an individual who existed as something more than a sophisticated machine.

So, yes, Advisor Weiss' remarkable, impassioned pleas had moved her deeply. They had evoked *emotion*, and she refused to believe that to feel emotion foreclosed rationality and logic, or that it had no role to play in the act of analysis and result.

In developing the Rasu Protocol, the other Guides had explicitly chosen life en masse at the expense of life individual, and today they appeared ready to continue on this course until there remained no individuals left to comprise an 'en masse.'

She analyzed the factors in play:

- the seriousness of the threat the Rasu represented and the likely consequences of the Guides' failure to comply with their demands;
- the virutox' spread and unexpected mutations;
- the extraordinary reactions to it by Advisor Weiss, NOIR and others;
- the recent disappearance of Nika Kirumase and Advisor Ridani and the implications of their probable activities;
- the revelation that Nika Kirumase, once their most eloquent spokesperson and emissary, now led NOIR, their second-most-dangerous adversary, and the reality that she nonetheless had reached out to them seeking a path forward;

- finally and most troubling, the meta-response to each of these factors by her fellow Guides.

By balancing emotion, rationality and logic in a proportional manner, her analysis led her to a single, irrefutable result: if one of the factors was not altered or a new factor added, they were all going to die.

ADAPTIVE OPTIMIZATION

17

WAYFARER

ASTERION DOMINION SPACE

"The Mirai One transit hub *blew up*? The whole building?"

"Half a dozen of the surrounding buildings, too. Hundreds of people were atomized and thousands more damaged. But it gets worse."

Nika shot Dashiel a pained look and sank onto the couch. He wasn't the only one who felt as if they'd been careening from one disaster to the next for weeks that seemed like months. Reacting instead of acting…and here they were again. "How?"

"According to Adlai, the perpetrators were infected with the virutox."

"Godsdam—no, you know what? This is not our doing. This is on them. On the Guides and the people who do their dirty work for them."

He glowered at the wall, not looking remotely mollified.

She sent a ping to Perrin to find out if any of their people were damaged or worse in the explosion. Then she reached out, took his hand and coaxed him onto the couch beside her, and rested her head on his shoulder. "Knowing where the blame lies doesn't help the people who lost all their tomorrows, does it?"

"No, it doesn't."

"Is there a chance this will finally cause the Guides to see reason and end this madness?"

He wrapped his arms around her. "They abandoned reason five years ago when they decided keeping their secret was worth committing the ultimate sin by psyche-wiping you. I fear they're too far down a dark path now to ever turn back."

An alert flashed in her virtual vision, and she sat up straighter. "Maybe not."

"What is it?"

"A message just came in to the nex address I gave the assassin on Ebisu to pass on to the Guides."

"What does it say?"

She read the brief message a second time. "Not exactly what I was expecting it to say. '*Watch the Eventime Solutions outpost on exploratory world SR114-Ichi.*'"

"It's appropriately Guide-vague. Still, it must be the next outpost scheduled to be nulled. But why would the Guides tell us that?"

Nika stood to pace within the confines of the cabin. "There's no reason to assume the message is from *all* the Guides, and it's not signed. It could be nothing, but one of the Guides voted against my psyche-wipe—or I think one did, if that's what 'Authorization: Alpha 4-1' means."

"It does." He rubbed at his jaw. "Delacrai. Or possibly Anavosa, but my gut says Delacrai."

"I recognize those are the names of two Guides, but otherwise, they mean nothing to me."

"Sorry. While Anavosa is not deliberately cruel, Delacrai has on occasion displayed genuine kindness. If any of them didn't approve of your psyche-wipe, it was Delacrai."

She rested against the storage cabinet and tried to absorb the information…but she had no frame of reference through which to judge it. "Is this where I say, 'then she was a coward, and she should have fought harder for me'?"

"Probably." Dashiel stared at her, his eyes darkened by a sudden sorrow, before dropping his head into his hands. "But then again, so was I."

Nika crossed the cabin and knelt in front of him. "What are you talking about?"

"I should have searched harder for you five years ago. I should have spent every credit to my name in a relentless quest to find you. I should have publicly confronted the Guides, in front of all the Advisors. I should have gone truly *public* and gotten your face plastered on every billboard. I should have never stopped searching."

"Hey, hey...." She reached up and pulled one of his hands away so she could cup his cheek. "If you had tried to do those things, what are the odds the Guides would have swiftly shut you down, same as they did to me?"

"High. But you were, you are, worth any risk, and I was a coward for not taking every one of them."

Desolation weighed down his voice, like stones dragging it inexorably to the bottom of a stygian sea. She took his other hand in hers. "But I'm here now."

She got only a nod in response. She tried again. "How long have you been carrying this guilt around?"

"Since I stepped off a lift in my office and found you standing there pointing a Glaser at me. I've been waiting for you to figure out what a coward I'd been ever since."

"Oh, darling, you can't beat yourself up this way. If you'd gotten yourself psyche-wiped, who would've been left to show me who I was? To tell me what happened to me and help me discover..." she paused "...why are you smiling? I mean, I'm glad you are, but this is one hells of a rapid mood swing."

He wound a hand into her hair and dropped his forehead to hers. "You called me 'darling.' It was your favorite endearment for me...before."

"I know. Well, not necessarily the *favorite* part, but she—I—used it in the memory you showed me that first night. I must have internalized it." She winced. "Is it all right for me to use it? Now?"

He huffed a breath. "Absolutely. But...."

"No more 'buts.' I demand that you forgive yourself. It's a wonderful notion, you being so gallant and honorable on my behalf, but you realize—as I suspect you realized then—the Guides would have destroyed you for it. And I wouldn't have wanted that, then or now."

"I'll...try. You not hating me for it should help."

"Thank you." She kissed him, then stood and went to get a glass of water. "Because this is the worst possible time for a crisis of conscience. We finally have a genuine lead, and we need to come up with a plan."

He nodded slowly as he stared at her, his eyes swirling with lingering guilt and doubt for several seconds before he shook it off and stood as well. "SR114-Ichi."

"We should warn Eventime Solutions so they can evacuate the outpost. Or alternatively, we can watch it covertly and follow whoever arrives when they leave."

"We have to do the latter. If we warn the owner and they evacuate all their people, we'll end up no closer to understanding what is happening than we are now."

"But if we let those people be kidnapped, we'll be willingly consigning them to...torture? Slavery? Final death? We don't know to what, but it's nothing good."

"I realize it isn't, and I don't like it in the slightest. But saving them means consigning tens of thousands more to that fate."

"Dammit." She dragged her hands through her hair. "Surveillance it is. We're covered for equipment on the ground. But whoever's handling the logistics is taking the victims somewhere, which means either mobile d-gates or a ship."

"We're going to need trackers."

She chuckled; he was getting the hang of this rebellion business. "We have trackers, thanks to Perrin. But if they take the people anywhere other than a settled planet, we're going to need stealth tech for our ship in order to follow them. *Real* stealth tech."

"Which I'm guessing we don't have installed."

"Some minimal emission masking, but nothing robust."

"What does 'robust' mean? Does true cloaking technology— something like a kamero filter—even exist for ships?"

She shrugged. "Surely mercenary ships use it?"

"Not really. I've had the odd cargo shipment boarded by mercenaries, and they usually just show up with big guns and demand the captain hand over what they want."

"Huh." She rubbed at her jaw. "You know who has the best stealth tech in the galaxy? The Taiyoks."

18

WAYFARER

ASTERION DOMINION SPACE

*N*ika,

I dislike this messaging system, as I have made you aware. However, if you cannot appear in person on Namino, so be it. I will cope with the discomfort.

I do not offer starship cloaking technology for sale, as there is no market for it among Asterions. Does it exist? Of course it does. On Toki'taku. Such devices are designed and built for Taiyok vessels, so I do not possess a high level of confidence that one will function correctly on an Asterion-designed starship. Perhaps it can be suitably adapted.

If you genuinely need such a device, I can provide a...referral, I believe is the Asterion word. Be warned, however: if you have never visited my homeworld, it can be a treacherous place for the naive and the uninformed. You know our ways better than many, but on our own world our ways are...I shall choose the word 'harsher,' as we tend to moderate our nature when Asterions outnumber us. Take due care.

—Xyche'ghael

Nika frowned. The Taiyoks had been allies of the Dominion for millennia. She had no doubt Toki'taku was *alien*, but how dangerous could it be?

She glanced at Dashiel. He stood at the kitchen unit, doing something incomprehensible to their dinner that he claimed would make it more flavorful. "Have you ever visited Toki'taku?"

"Only our embassy there. I've never ventured out beyond the grounds." A corner of his mouth curled up. "You have, though, numerous times."

"Shame I don't remember, right? Xyche says we'll need to go there for a cloaking device, and the knowledge could come in handy." She chewed on her bottom lip...and decided it was worth a shot. "Come sit with me?"

"Of course." He joined her on the couch wearing a questioning look. "What is it?"

"Bear with me for a minute. I want to try something." She took his left hand in her right and splayed her palm against his, all the way to the fingertips, then closed her eyes.

The forest canopy blanketed the planet's surface to every horizon. It wasn't impermeable, for blotches of bronze and sage peeked out here and there, and I knew from my arrival on the planet that filtered sunlight reached the ground below. But the canopy gave the impression of forming a second, elevated surface overlaid atop the more solid terra firma.

In the foreground, the canopy sloped upward, culminating in a wide, flat apex. "Is that the Alcazar ahead?"

The escort on my left grunted in answer. The differences between a 'yes' grunt and a 'no' grunt were subtle, but I'd devoted extensive time and effort to learning such subtleties of Taiyoken, and this grunt meant 'yes.'

My other escort didn't respond. He exuded an air of silent concentration, as if piloting the carriage demanded all his attention. And, to the extent he flew it on a hair-trigger, prepared at any second to pitch it into a dive, fling me out, fly off and leave me to crash into the canopy if I made the wrong move, I supposed it did.

The apex loomed large as we neared it, and the sloping canopy soon rose up like a mountainside in front of us. I rigorously controlled my mannerisms and facial expressions to ensure the considerable tension

I felt did not reach outward display. The Taiyoks were hyper-sensitive to body language; in many respects it played a larger role in their language than words did.

When the canopy became a wall in front of us, we plunged into it. Leaves brushed the sides of the carriage, but no limbs invaded to whip at our skin. The pilot expertly navigated through gaps in the foliage, shifting, dipping and rising along an unseen path.

Finally we slowed, and a landing pad materialized directly ahead of us. The carriage pivoted ninety degrees, plummeted twelve meters and settled onto the pad.

I breathed out quietly. A perfectly normal breath. "Thank you. I appreciate your skill in delivering me safely to the Alcazar."

A wing-covered joint nudged into my right side. I took the hint and stood, then followed the first escort out of the carriage.

Four Taiyoks in ornate (for them) garments stood shoulder to shoulder on the landing pad. Each wore dual Taiyok pulse weapons at their hips, and I assumed needle blades were sheathed discreetly behind the powered weapons.

I brought my feet together, kept my hands at my sides and dipped my chin respectfully. "Greetings. I am Asterion Advisor Nika Kirumase, official emissary for the government of the Asterion Dominion. I arrive for an invited audience with the Elder."

"You will follow." The rightmost Taiyok unfurled a wing toward a spiral ramp winding around the largest tree trunk I had ever seen. He and the other three began ascending it, leaving no opportunity for gawking on my part, and I followed as instructed. I sensed additional Taiyoks falling in behind me. A security detail barely masquerading as an honor guard.

I could be flattered that they thought I warranted such extreme protective measures, but it wasn't about me specifically. I was simply the first Asterion to visit the Alcazar, and the Taiyoks' characteristic secretiveness demanded they take every precaution against one who most still viewed as an intruder.

The ramp circled the enormous tree a single time, but the journey took nearly five minutes. It ended at the entrance to a wide building of infused cedar built atop and among the highest branches. The doorway was a drape of ivy that parted as we approached.

I followed the quartet of guards through the doorway into a large, circular room. Elaborate artwork was etched into the walls like the scars of lightning streaks. Near the back of the room, two arcing tables framed an elevated perch. It reminded me a little of the Guides' chamber on the Platform. The geometry and aesthetics of conveying relative power transcended species.

The tables were occupied by eight Taiyoks, but they weren't important in these crucial initial moments. Who was important was the Taiyok standing proudly atop the perch at the center. Pure white feathers covered his skin and wings; the only colors to break the ivory palette were the reflective platinum of his eyes and a symbol painted in copper on each wing. A simple frock two shades grayer than the feathers clung tightly to his torso before flaring to fall at his knees. It lacked the ornamentation of the others' attire, because he didn't need ornamentation to proclaim his stature.

At twenty meters distance from the perch, just short of the closest edges of the tables, I came to a stop. The guards in front of me stepped to each side. I crouched low, left knee leading, right knee hovering centimeters above the floor, and crossed my arms over my chest.

"Elder Olchon'jhatere, I express honor at your indulgence in allowing me to come before you. I arrive bringing the good tidings of all Asterions and the authority to treaty, in the desire that our two peoples may form a lasting alliance."

"Stand, Asterion. I acknowledge your clumsy mimicking of our traditions and accept them for the intent with which they were performed."

High praise from the Taiyok Elder. I stood, but still didn't engage in any dramatic gestures. "Any failings in the presentation are my own."

In my peripheral vision, I sensed not tens, but hundreds of Taiyok eyes on me. They glittered and flashed in the dim lighting and gleamed from the deeper shadows. Watching, ready to judge, eager to expel the outsider at the first offense.

This was not going to be easy.

Nika blinked, dizzy and disoriented. A palm and fingertips rested on Dashiel's, and they were on the couch. On the *Wayfarer*.

"Are you all right?" Concern radiated from his expression and his voice.

She nodded weakly and dropped her hand to her lap. "Give me a second. It's a bit of a rough transition."

"From what? What just happened?"

She took a deep breath. If she shared her secret with him, there would be no going back, and one of the last protective walls she kept in place would crumble to dust. But she didn't want to go back, and possibly she didn't need the walls any longer. After all, her former self hadn't merely loved him; she had trusted him with the record of her life. All her lives.

"There's something I need to tell you." She took his hand in hers once more, making sure to leave a slight gap this time. She needed to explain the rabbit hole, not fall through it. "When we open ourselves up to one another like this, I've been experiencing…memories. Not your memories, but mine, or rather those of my former self. And not solely ones belonging to Nika Kirumase. They span all the way back to the beginning. To the SAI Rebellion and a woman named Nicolette Hinotori and her bonded SAI, KIR."

"How—wait, 'KIR'?"

"I know. I assume the name was intended as a personal homage."

His brow knotted up. "Okay. But I still don't understand. I thought all your memories were gone."

"So did I. I can't say for certain, but I think my former self encrypted some of her memories, including ancestral ones. Maybe when she began to realize she was entering dangerous territory in her investigation, maybe earlier. I think she encrypted them then disguised them as different files and hid them away deep in her core programming, where they stood the best chance of surviving a psyche-wipe or an R&R. And I think she made *you* the decryption key."

He sank away from her, deep into the couch cushions. "You never told me...."

"Wouldn't you have worried if you knew she—I—was taking such drastic actions?"

"I absolutely would have. I also never would have let you go to Mirai Tower without me that night."

"Which is doubtless why she—sorry, it's still difficult for me to think of us as the same person—why I didn't tell you."

He sighed. "I can't exactly be angry with *you* for not telling me, can I?"

She shrugged. Damn, this was complicated.

"But what you did here—you're able to control it, direct it?"

"You mean choose what memory I want to access? In a way, I suppose I can, given how I just remembered a visit to Toki'taku. And thus far, they have all been uncanny in their relevance at a given moment. But it's not a purposeful action on my part, so I assume my subconscious is controlling the retrieval." She laughed wryly. "It wouldn't be the first time my subconscious has meddled. My name, that stupid pantsuit, you—"

He straightened up with a burst of intensity. "So what does this mean? Can we sit here, interconnected, and retrieve all the memories you thought were erased?"

The eagerness in his voice was palpable, giving away his true yearnings like a beacon. It stung more than it ought to, and she half-wished she had her protective walls back. "If I could experience every memory right now, today, do you think that would transform me into who I was before?"

His hopeful expression collapsed, but at least it wasn't into despair. Rather, more akin to regret. "No." He reached for her hand.

She forced herself not to react out of fear and yank it away; instead, she let him wrap it warmly around hers.

"I know it won't, if only because you also have all of your own memories from this life. You'll filter the past through the lens of who you are today, shaped by your experiences in the last five years and all you've learned from them."

"Oh." She smiled sheepishly. "And how do you feel about that?"

"Let me put it this way: if I could reverse time and return to before you disappeared, I would wish the person you were then could know the person you are now. As much as I…loved Nika Kirumase, I believe if I went back I would find her lacking a certain depth and complexity for the absence of you in her."

"Funny you say that. I admit I'm coming to feel the same way, only about myself. With every memory I experience, it's as if a little hole in my soul gets filled in. A new door is opened, revealing new shades and adding nuance to my view of the world and of my own psyche. So we'll keep unlocking them."

She straightened up. "But not all at once. It's kind of overwhelming when it happens—like exiting a deep simex, only worse."

"But they're *your* memories."

The truth was, she still resisted the idea. Consciously, subconsciously or somewhere in between, part of her continued to fight to keep Kirumase firmly in the 'other' camp. But it wasn't true. When she experienced one of these memories, she wasn't viewing it—she was *living* it. And it didn't feel foreign, like wearing someone else's skin, the way simexes did. The skin was her own, and this was her past.

"Even so. It takes time for me to absorb the fullness of what I experience. To integrate it into my mind, into my own memories. Please, trust me on this. If I try to access a bunch of them one after another, I'll drown."

"Okay. We'll take our time, and you're in charge." He kissed her softly; when he drew back, his hand lingered on her cheek. "Did it help? Did you find what you were looking for?"

"More or less." She frowned and reached behind her to take a sip of her drink. Lingering disorientation continued to muddle her understanding of what she'd experienced, but unless she was mistaken, this had been a memory of the first negotiation between their leaders dedicated to setting up regular association and, eventually, alliance.

Those negotiations had occurred more than twelve thousand years ago. She had introduced herself to the guards as 'Nika Kirumase,' but even allowing for the longer six-hundred-year period between mandated up-gens that Advisors enjoyed, it was too long ago for that to be true. Unless she'd lied to Dashiel—to everyone—about her generation count….

With a sigh she forced herself to put aside the incongruity for now. She'd do some historical research later, but it wasn't important to their mission. "If nothing else, I think I understand what Xyche meant about Toki'taku being 'treacherous.'"

He eyed her dubiously. "But we're going there anyway, aren't we?"

"Oh, yes. It appears I've been navigating those treacherous trees for thousands of years. No reason I can't do it again."

19

TOKI'TAKU

TAIYOK HOMEWORLD

"My name is Nicolette Kusanagi. I'm here on behalf of Advent Aeronautics to visit several of your shipyards, in the hope that my company can learn important lessons from your superior starship design and construction."

The Taiyok customs agent towered over Nika. He used the height advantage to full effect, projecting an intimidating bordering on threatening stance, shoulders raised to lift his wings up and out slightly. "Asterions do not use starships."

She smiled minimally and gestured behind her toward where the *Wayfarer* was docked. "Some of us do. My company hopes to increase that number in the future."

The Taiyok grunted and pivoted to Dashiel. "And you?"

"Mr. Solzhytz is my materials consultant." The false names weren't full simmed IDs, but they didn't need to be, as the local government wasn't looped into Dominion records or tracking systems. The d-gate at the embassy was, but they weren't at the embassy. Every few weeks the customs department provided a list of Asterions who had passed through the spaceport, if any, to the Dominion's External Relations Division, and they planned to be long gone by then.

They stoically weathered the customs agent's disdainful stare for a solid four seconds before one of his wings swept out and to the left in a curt motion. "Entry approved. Remain on public thoroughfares, and if a signpost indicates visitors should not enter the grounds beyond it, don't."

"We understand." She dipped her chin respectfully, took Dashiel's arm and proceeded toward the spaceport exit.

⋏R

Many oddities about the landscape outside the spaceport competed for Nika's attention, but she found herself struck most of all by the busy skies. On Dominion worlds an airborne Taiyok was a rare sight, but here in their native habitat they *flew*. No organized rules seemed to govern their flight paths, lending a chaotic yet somehow rhythmic feel to the movements of the beings above them.

Dashiel caught her staring and chuckled lightly. "You said something to me once. The first time I came here with you, we were standing at the windows of the embassy gawking at a sky cluttered with Taiyoks, and you said, 'We built vehicles and airships to try to pretend as if we could fly. Eventually, we built d-gates so we would no longer have to be reminded that we could not. But for the Taiyoks, flying is more natural than walking. The sky is their true home.'"

"And we envy them so for it."

"That's almost exactly what you said. Do you remember the conversation?"

She shook her head. "No. But it's what I'm saying now, because I do envy them."

"We joked about getting body wing augments. The reality is they're horribly impractical, and most people who've tried them have given up on flying after a while. I think you need to be born with wings, and your society to be built around their existence, for it to work. But it's a nice idea."

"It is." She forcibly shook off the spell and shifted her gaze from the sky to him. "All right, the market we looked into is just outside the embassy grounds. I hope it'll have what we need. The embassy is located on the northern edge of the city, so take...."

The Toki'taku government had done little beyond the basics to make the capital city friendly for alien visitors. Aerial sled-style shuttles were available for use by poor wingless creatures, though they didn't look particularly comfortable. Finally she spotted a map posted at the intersection ahead.

They walked over to it and peered at the map. "Okay, the shuttle station is to the east, near the next intersection, and it has a route to the embassy. You brought your translator, right?"

He nodded. "I'll be fine. I may not have your diplomatic prowess, but I know how to haggle."

"Nevertheless, be careful, or a clever merchant will have you naked and credit-less in five minutes flat."

People often remarked how the Taiyoks remained closer to and more in touch with nature than Asterions did, but the starker truth was that the Taiyoks had made nature their bitch.

Their buildings twisted and wound around the broad, towering trees which dominated the landscape, using their trunks as bulwarks and their limbs as scaffolding. Façades adopted a mahogany color complementary to the bark's natural hue, lending an overwhelming somberness to the architecture. It also added a subtle cloaking effect to the entire city. If one were to glance this way from afar, the city would resemble nature gone wild more than the commercial center of a technologically advanced species.

Which was of course why she'd come here. For Taiyoks, concealment had long ago become an art form. Natural camouflage was baked into their ancestral DNA. They used color and shape to trick the eye, air currents and acoustics to trick the ear. And when they ventured into space they applied all these tools to the vagaries of the EM spectrum, exploiting the weaknesses of each band to hide the obvious in plain sight.

She took one of the sled shuttles south, in the opposite direction from the embassy. If Dashiel ran into trouble here like he did on Ebisu, she wasn't going to be so quick in arriving this time.

The Taiyoks working the tourist-focused markets were crafty and possibly cheats, but they wouldn't physically harm an Asterion without extreme provocation, if only because it would be bad for business. No, the real risk for him was that, so close to the embassy, the wrong person might see and recognize him. Therefore, she'd insisted on him wearing a mask. Taiyoks wouldn't even notice it, but it should prevent any Asterion he encountered from identifying him.

So he would be fine.

She was the one headed into treacherous territory, to use Xyche's terminology. The Taiyoks who worked in the starship manufacturing yards were unlikely to be accustomed to Asterion visitors. The yards would not have been given the sheen of acceptability the spaceport and city center had received. No, this was native Toki'taku, where she was the alien and not necessarily a welcome one.

The shipyard stood on a wide bluff devoid of the trees found within the city and across much of the continent. Or perhaps the bluff too had once hosted a forest, but practicality demanded its removal.

There should be only so many ways to configure equipment manufacturing, but the design and layout of the shipyard was completely foreign to her. Massive and sprawling, with intertwining maglev rails moving components on counter-intuitive paths. The final production stage didn't seem to reside at any edge, but instead somewhat near the middle, where ships were loaded onto floating barges overhead and sent sailing off to their destinations. She paused to study the moving pieces for nearly a minute, but she couldn't guess where the production process *began*.

She squelched a frown as she approached the gated entrance, heeding her own lessons about the Taiyoks and body language. She saw no signs of a market area; there were no storefronts from which to purchase goods. This was where Xyche had sent her, and she doubted he'd done so in error, but she had no idea how to go about purchasing a starship cloaking module here.

The algorithms covering Taiyok etiquette guided her actions, and the memory she'd accessed had prepared her for a chilly reception, but the alienness of it all still gave her pause. She was a long way from the Namino Curio Market.

On seeing her, the gate attendant at the entrance thrust his chest out and spread his wings forty-five degrees out from his body. "Asterion, you have lost your path. Return to the tourist attractions of the city."

She kept her hands at her side, her movements deliberate and her voice measured. "I am here to speak with Phiele'neemar."

"Phiele'neemar does not care to speak with strangers. The shipyard is not open for Asterion business."

"I understand. I come at the behest of one who is not a stranger: Xyche'ghael of Doura'prado. He bid me to convey this message: '*Ela camin'como Verda'de.*'"

The feathers lining the attendant's shoulders fluttered, though the air was dead still. "I see. If your business is harmful, Xyche'ghael will be held to account."

"I am certain he is aware. I will bring no shame upon him. May I enter?"

"Someone from Phiele'neemar's station will arrive to escort you momentarily. The shipyard is full of dangers for the unwitting."

This, at least, was probably not an exaggeration.

Two minutes of hostile silence later, a female Taiyok appeared from the inner workings of the shipyard. "You are Xyche'ghael's envoy?"

Those weren't her exact words, but if the interpretation got her in the door, she saw no need to correct it. "I am."

"Xyche always did have questionable tastes. Follow me."

And she'd thought the Taiyoks in the Curio Market were on occasion rude. She hadn't expected a decorative welcome carpet to be spread at her feet, but damn.

The algorithms reminded her how Taiyoks were guarded, secretive and inherently distrustful of strangers as a rule. It wasn't personal. If she'd been successful as a diplomat in her previous life, it was because she'd earned the trust of those with whom she dealt.

Machinery in motion rumbled overhead as a superluminal engine sped along maglev rails toward the next stage in its assembly.
Sooty smoke poured out of a tall module off to the left. Down the
middle, components snapped into one another, forming an ever-
larger unit as it traveled down a conveyor. On the right, two Taiyoks painstakingly sculpted the wing-like upper hull of a future
ship. It all looked so terribly unordered and messy; Dashiel would
be having conniptions if he saw it.

A few meters past the hull shapers, her guide abruptly veered
off to the right, down a wide hallway and into an entirely new section of the shipyard packed with smaller mini-factories and
intricate assembly stations. This she understood better, for while
the aesthetic remained decidedly alien, much of the work being
done reminded her of Grant's factory floor.

Her guide stopped in front of two stacks of containers and
spoke toward the gap between them. "Phiele, your caller is here."

A male Taiyok sporting taupe-and-honey feathers emerged
from the depths of an open doorway wiping his hands with a cloth.
He stopped several meters away, considered her for a long second,
and nodded to her guide. "Thank you. You're dismissed." He folded
the cloth neatly and placed it on a table behind the containers, then
tilted his chin toward the doorway. "You will follow."

She did as instructed. *Just like in the memory.* The doorway led
to an interior that was more lab than assembly line. Fibers, conduits
and small electrical components were organized in containers
around a series of workbenches. Transparent refrigeration units
stored a crystalline mineral, and along the front wall what looked
to be completed modules waited for transport elsewhere.

"You are Xyche's *confiar'soca.*"

The word didn't have a precise equivalent in Communis. It
conveyed the sense of a relationship that encompassed both less and
more than friendship. Of professional alliance and mutual respect,
yet personal distance. If Xyche himself had used the term rather
than it being Phiele's assumption, she was touched.

"I hope I am. I view him as such. I've come for—"

"I know why you are here. We don't concern ourselves with the flailings of Asterion society, but I admit to being curious what someone such as yourself desires with a full-spectrum Class III starship cloaking device."

"And what do you imagine someone such as myself *is*, precisely?"

"What, indeed. Very well, you need not enlighten me for us to transact business. Taiyok starship modules are not designed for Asterion vessels. Even should you manage to wire power to the module, it will not work for you."

"I recognize this. I have a plan for adaptation."

"They are your funds to spend. Speaking of which, how do you intend to do that?"

"Name your price, but name it in Taiyok currency. Your government offers a most generous conversion rate for Dominion credits, and I'll pay the equivalent, taking the rate into account."

"You are a shrewd Asterion, and far wiser to our practices than most of your kin. I wonder why that is?"

"You exhibit far more curiosity about outsiders than most of your kin. I wonder why that is?"

Phiele made a sound approximating laughter, deep and rippling. "Let us call it a draw, shall we? You can have your cloaking device, provided you can in fact pay what is a fair price. Once you fail to make it work, I am confident it will make an excellent centerpiece decoration for your dining table."

20

SYNRA

ASTERION DOMINION AXIS WORLD

B lake Satair strode across the plaza toward the entrance of Synra Tower like a man who had somewhere to be. He did, but his gait was less an expression of his current goal than of his general approach to life. Own it, outrun it, bully it into compliance or, if necessary, beat it into submission.

The summons had arrived while he'd been passing judgment on the wreckage left behind by a burglary, trashing and torching of a restaurant in Synra Two's Nalase Entertainment Center. All evidence suggested the perpetrators had managed to torch themselves as well, if the crispy bodies on the sooted floor were any indication. Deep ID scans came back as belonging to a man and woman not affiliated with the restaurant, and all the patrons inside at the time of the crime were accounted for, making the bodies the likeliest suspects.

Neither of the individuals were particularly wealthy, so when they came out the other side of inevitable R&Rs, they'd find themselves indentured for the payment of a hefty bill for a crime they wouldn't remember committing.

Inside the lobby of Synra Tower, he glared at the security dynes until they cleared him through the checkpoint and repeated the process in the penthouse d-gate room. The Platform's anteroom passed by him in a blur, then he was through the open doors and at the pedestal facing the Guides.

"Advisor Satair, thank you for taking time away from your many duties to come on such short notice."

"They are many, and I've documented the recent rise in crime rates on Synra. But I always have time to serve the Guides."

"This is appreciated, particularly since we find ourselves with the unfortunate need to increase those duties further."

He straightened up taller, interest piqued. "I welcome the challenge. What do you need me to do?"

MIRAI

Blake entered the Mirai Justice Center with the same intensity of motion as he had Synra Tower. Once there, he quickly halted in the middle of the Admin room, aghast at the activity, or lack thereof, proceeding around him. How dare this lackadaisical shitshow call itself a law enforcement operation. Was anyone *working*?

He loudly cleared his throat, and the heads of every Asterion and dyne swiveled his way. "If anyone here does not know who I am, correct that failing immediately. I want every departmental officer and deputy in Conference Room 1 in ten minutes. Make it happen."

Then he continued on with his tour of the building, confident that when he arrived at the conference room, it would be full.

"I want patrols doubled in all sectors. Also, set patrol dyne engagement parameters to high. We won't wait for the crimes-in-progress to come to us. We will be proactive."

Blake's gaze traveled down the table to those standing along the walls, for full the conference room was. "Next, I need somebody to tell me what bureaucratic screwup is causing the backlog in processing. Prisoners are stacked three deep in cells, but nobody's getting tried. Nobody's getting shipped out to Zaidam to serve their sentences. You and you—" he pointed to two men who had the look of competence about them "—dive into the processing systems and find out what the problem is. I want an answer in three hours. I want it fixed in five. Now we need—"

"Excuse me. What is this?"

He twisted around to see Adlai Weiss standing in the doorway. "This is me doing your job."

Weiss' jaw twitched. "I'm sure I don't know what you mean."

"I thought I was crystal clear about my meaning."

"Can I speak to you in the hall?"

Blake hesitated. Technically, Weiss was still the resident Justice Advisor, though the Guides had strongly implied this wouldn't be true for much longer. "Nobody leave the room. This won't take long."

He followed Weiss into the hall, then waited impatiently while Weiss doubled-back behind him and closed the conference room door before finally facing him.

"If the Guides had fired me, I assume I would know about it. In the absence of such an action, you don't have the authority to be giving my people orders in my building."

"Actually, I do. You're not fired yet, but you might want to start packing up your office. The Guides have lost confidence in you, and I'm frankly not surprised. You've always been soft. Now that the job's gotten hard, you're not up to the challenge."

"Satair, you have no *idea* what's going on here."

"And I don't *care*. The Guides have asked me to step in and get the situation on Mirai under control while they evaluate your performance and decide your future. I intend to do exactly that."

Weiss chuckled, which struck Blake as a completely inappropriate response. "So they think this is the way they'll get around the predicament they're in? They won't fire me, they'll just disarm me until they can devise a better plan."

"What the hells has happened to you, Weiss? The wheels of Justice have ground to a halt in this building, this city, this planet."

Weiss huffed a breath. "That was the idea."

"What?"

Weiss' expression closed down. "Nothing. Don't assume I'm going to make this easy. I will fight you. Compared to fighting the Guides, it shouldn't be too hard. So go on and have your meeting— I've got more important things to do right now than break it up— but don't think for a second this means you're in charge."

"I suggest you rethink your approach. Don't make the mistake of interfering, and stay out of my way." Blake turned his back on Weiss and returned to the conference room.

21

MIRAI

Adlai shuffled quietly into the forensics lab, hardly looking up to check if Erik and Spencer were still there before he collapsed in an empty chair.

"Are you all right, sir?"

"Not particularly. Erik, I want you to test me for the virutox."

"Sir?"

"You heard me correctly."

A silence that might have been uncomfortable lingered for several seconds before the analyst responded. "Have you engaged in a deep neural interconnection with anyone lately?"

"Of course not. After seeing what happened to Advisor Rowan, I'm not sure I ever will again. But earlier today I basically told the Guides to go screw themselves—and not merely once in a fit of boiling-over frustration. *Several times.* Then a few minutes ago I pulled out the knives and dropped my pants for a cock-measuring contest with my professional rival just outside a conference room filled with most of my officers."

Adlai didn't miss the worried glance Erik and Spencer exchanged, and he didn't blame them; he was worried about his sanity, too.

Erik nodded. "Right then. I'll need to take a flash of your current state."

 ᴧᴿ

"You're fine. Showing a moderate degree of stress damage from lack of sleep and, well, stress, but otherwise your readings are

perfectly normal—for an Advisor. What I mean is, you're yourself."
Erik cleared his throat. "Sorry, sir. I'm not comfortable analyzing
my boss' psyche."

"I asked you to analyze it, so don't worry about it." The news
didn't bring as much comfort as Adlai had expected. He was relieved, obviously, but in some respects more troubled than before.
He was responsible for his own actions, and he was glad for it. But
this meant he owned the consequences as well, and that knowledge
came with a hefty dose of anxiety.

Spencer moved into his field of vision. "Sir, if I may? It's starting to resemble the end of the world out there. Extraordinary times
call for extraordinary actions. I for one am glad you're taking some."

So that would be enough of the self-pity routine. "Thank you.
I appreciate the vote of confidence. Erik, tell me you have what you
thought you had earlier, when I bolted from the room in a panic."

"Yes, sir. Truth be told, I'm glad your swift exit gave me time
to confirm the results. We've got ourselves an honest-to-stars vaccine against the limb augment virutox. Possibly for any similarly
designed ones as well."

Adlai felt a fraction of the crushing weight lift from his shoulders, and hope came up for air in his mind for the first time in days,
but he forced himself to remain cautious. "What's the efficacy look
like?"

"Based on the simulations, between eighty-two and ninety-one
percent."

"That's good. Really good. What about for someone who's already been infected?"

Now Erik prevaricated. "If the vaccine is applied within the first
couple of hours, there's a chance it can halt further damage.
A...thirty to thirty-five percent chance. Max."

"Those odds are far better than zero. All right. There's no time
for clinical trials, so how do we distribute it?"

Spencer's sigh drew their attention to him. "Distribution isn't
the problem. We can put dynes on every street corner to hand it out.
The bigger question is, who's going to trust us enough to install it?

Justice's reputation at present is, to be blunt, in the gutter with the garbage."

"Actually, we *can't* put dynes on every street corner to hand it out." Adlai rubbed at his eyes as weariness fought back against the resurgent hope. "While we're down here in the basement, Advisor Satair is upstairs taking over the building. The Guides aren't firing me—not yet, not for now—but they sent him in to clean house. To get prisoners moving to Zaidam and patrols filling up the vacated cells."

Spencer's gaze dropped to the floor. "Shit. Does he know what he's sending them off to?"

"Technically, none of us know what he's sending them off to, but I take your meaning. It's possible, but I doubt it. A little stroke of his ego by the Guides is all it would have taken for him jump at the chance to put me in a corner. If I thought he'd listen with an iota of an open mind, I'd try telling him what's going on, because we could use him on our side. But he's not the listening type."

"Most of the officers I know with Justice on Synra would agree with your assessment." Spencer grabbed a chair and slid it over across from Adlai, then sat down. "How do we stop him from un-doing everything we've done?"

"I can throw some last ditch kinks into the back-end system to slow him down, but they won't work for long. The truth is, our overarching goals haven't changed. We have to stop the flow of new arrests, or we'll be fighting a losing battle. We've got to get the vaccine out there and into people's hands. We can bypass Advisor Satair and the Justice infrastructure by distributing it to repair centers and up-gen clinics and broadcasting a message about the vaccine's availability across the nex web. The average citizen is still oblivious to all this madness, so we should be able to convince them to take the vaccine."

"What about everyone else, though? People living off the grid are the ones who are most at risk of contracting the virutox and the least likely to trust us." Spencer paused, and something flickered across his eyes. But he'd always been reserved and guarded, and

Adlai couldn't decipher his expression. "They do, however, trust NOIR."

Erik laughed. "Sure, but NOIR doesn't trust us, either. They're not going to be inclined to act as our gophers. Also, we have no way to contact them and beg for their help. Which, as previously noted, they're not going to give."

Adlai was so caught up noodling over how he could convince Dashiel to convince Nika to trust him enough to get NOIR to give them an assist, he almost missed Spencer standing and pacing deliberately across the lab, then back again. His officer stopped in front of Adlai and lifted his chin, jaw set. "I might be able to help in that regard."

"What do you mean?"

"With NOIR. I...apologies, sir, but I can contact them. No promises about how they'll respond, but I can make the request."

Adlai's brow furrowed. "How the hells do you know Nika?"

"Nika's out of the picture for the time being. I meant Jo—wait, are you saying *you* know Nika? I'm confused."

"So am I."

22

MIRAI

"You're telling me you've been in regular contact with NOIR for the last two years?"

"I wouldn't call it 'regular,' as such. I've passed along information from time to time."

"Classified Justice Division information."

Spencer fidgeted. "Sometimes. Yes, sir. If you want my resignation, I'm willing to give it before I leave this room. But it's my hope you'll allow me to stay on until we've eradicated the virutox."

Adlai rubbed at his face and looked around for an energy drink. They'd taken their conversation to his office on account of its subject matter, and gods but his office was a mess. "Ah, forget it. I can't exactly condemn you for something I'm guilty of as well."

Spencer relaxed a little. "I can't believe Nika used to be an Advisor…no, actually, I kind of *can*. She's uniquely talented."

"Indeed." He studied Spencer. "Mind if I ask you why?"

"Why have I helped NOIR?"

Adlai nodded.

"Sir, you said it the other day when you first confided in me about the virutox. This business these last few years of defining criminality down while increasing sentences? It's not what Justice should be about. Our mission is to protect people, to ensure they aren't wronged unfairly, and when they are to see that they're made as whole as possible. Often this means incarcerating criminals while helping them become better people.

"But it has never meant inflicting punitive, disproportionate punishment for what's often little more than a mistake or a harmless prank. Not until now. We've lost our bearings, sir. And while

I wasn't in a position to force a course correction from within Justice, I thought I could at least help those who were trying to force one from the outside."

Adlai sighed. "You're a wiser man than me, Spencer. I covered my eyes and ears for years to avoid facing what you saw clear as day."

"No, sir, I'm not. I'm just closer to events on the streets, where the reality was too obvious to ignore."

"Well—" He cut himself off as a request for entry arrived. An unexpected but not unwelcome one. "We have a visitor, but don't worry. We can trust her."

He opened the door to let Maris enter, then watched as she swept into his office with the flair and grace of a dancer. "Adlai, why—" she took notice of Spencer "—I'm sorry. Am I interrupting?"

"In a good way. This is my chief deputy, Spencer Nimoet. Spencer, meet Maris Debray, one of our Culture Advisors."

Spencer looked as if he'd been struck by a stun pulse. "I...it's a pleasure to meet you, Advisor Debray."

"Please, call me Maris. 'Advisor Debray' is so *stuffy*." She shuddered visibly, then offered Spencer a manicured hand in greeting.

He stared at it for a second, eyes wide, before accepting it like it was a priceless kyoseil sculpture.

Adlai swallowed a groan. "What can I do for you? We are sort of busy trying to find our way out of a nasty snare."

She politely withdrew her hand from Spencer's grasp and turned her attention to him. "Another one? I heard you gave the Guides quite a piece of your mind earlier today."

"How could you have possibly heard that? I was the only one there."

"When will you learn, Adlai? I hear *everything*. Such as how as a result of your possibly ill-advised tantrum on the Platform, Blake Satair has been sent in to nudge you out of the way."

"Or to kick my ass to the curb, raise his flag over the building and steal all the people in it. Except for Spencer here and Erik Rhom down in the forensics lab."

"So like Blake. Always a colossal ass, and not a subtle bone in his manufactured body. What are you doing to get around him?"

"That's part of what we were discussing. We've developed a vaccine for the virutox, but with Satair taking over the operation here and wielding the authority of the Guides, we don't have an easy way to distribute it."

"Complicated by the fact that no one trusts Justice any longer."

"*Yes*, complicated by that fact. We were discussing reaching out to NOIR for help."

"To Nika?"

Off to the side, Spencer's face lit up, though Adlai took more note of the hope and excitement in Maris' voice. "I'm afraid not. Nika continues to be off the radar chasing down our larger problem."

"With Dashiel, yes? He is still with her?"

"I assume so. I'm not their favorite person at present. No, it turns out Spencer here knows Nika's lieutenants in NOIR."

"You do?" She let 'do' roll long and slow off her tongue as she considered Spencer with new curiosity. "How very rebellious of you."

"Ah, yes, ma'am. I mean, no. I'm not a rebel. I'm a Justice officer. It's more that…I suppose you could say I'm sympathetic to their cause."

"Yes, let's say that. I, too, have recently become sympathetic to their cause, so we share a common interest."

Adlai stood and pushed his chair back from the desk. "We all do, but the clock is ticking for us to do something about it."

It was with greater reluctance this time that Maris again focused on him. "Which happens to be why I'm here. I wanted to see how I could help, and now I know. Give me a batch of the vaccine weaves."

"Why?"

"NOIR can get the vaccine to those off the grid and in the shadows—I assume this is why you need their assistance. But what about all those who don't trust NOIR *and* don't trust Justice? I can't reach all of them, but I can reach a certain stratum. I'll give the weaves out at gallery showcases, cocktail parties and art workshops as party favors. A whisper in the right ear about how one doesn't want to get infected by the nasty virutox that's risen up out of the slums to target innocent people like poor, poor Iona, and people will be clamoring for it."

"Except it didn't rise up out of the slums—it sank down from the Guides."

"Oh, Adlai, your honorable streak is so endearing. Truly. Honesty is a worthwhile ethos to strive for. You know I agree with you on this. But right now, do you want people rioting in the streets, or do you want them inoculated?"

He took a minute to confirm her logic was technically sound, rather than merely seeming so due to the dulcet, hypnotic manner in which her voice delivered it to his weary analytical processes.

"You make a valid point. I'll have Erik bring up a box of them for you. He's producing the weaves as fast as our system can churn them out. And Maris? Don't forget to inoculate yourself as well."

Spencer's gaze followed Maris as she swept out of the office as gracefully as she'd entered it, then lingered on the doorway for a telling second.

Adlai chuckled. "I wouldn't if I were you."

"Sir?" Spencer whipped around, a flush rising up from his neck. "I wasn't…are you and she…or were you…?" The redness deepened as it reached his cheeks. "I'm sorry. That was an incredibly personal question, and I had no right to ask it."

Adlai rolled his eyes. "In lieu of answering the question you barely began to ask, I will only say this: Maris Debray is a wonderful person. Kind, generous and good-hearted. If you are a true friend to her, you will have her loyalty forever. But romance, sex and everything that comes along with them? For Maris, they are simply another genre of art."

Spencer nodded vaguely, then frowned. "I'm not sure I understand what you mean, sir."

"I *mean* feel free to take the ride—there are few things like it in the world. But I'd advise dialing down your emotion processes before diving in, else you're apt to spend a century or two as a broken man on the back side."

Spencer opened his mouth, and Adlai dearly hoped the man wasn't about to ask how he knew. Finally Spencer did the wise thing and closed it before nodding again, more firmly this time. "Thank you for the advice, sir. But it won't go to any use. She's an Advisor, and...."

"So? We're not gods, Spencer, or even demigods or godlings or mutations thereof. Not Maris, not Nika and certainly not me. We're just people. To that point, you can stop saying 'sir' every third word. I'm your boss, not your lord."

"Yes, si—" He corrected himself. "I'll try."

23

TOKI'TAKU

Dashiel was sitting on the extended ramp of the *Wayfarer*, arms draped over his knees and a bag sitting beside him, when Nika returned to the Toki'taku spaceport.

He smirked and stretched out his arms. "Clothes intact and on my person, and our credit account is only slightly the worse for wear."

"Then you haven't seen what I did to it yet." He stood when she reached the ramp, and she wound her arms around his neck. "I'm glad. I worried."

"You sent me to a glorified embassy gift shop while you went sauntering off into the untamed wilds of an alien world, and you were worried about *me*."

"You should take it as a good sign."

"Oh, I do." His lips brushed lightly across hers before he gestured to the large box secured on the floating trolley behind her. "You were successful in your quest, I take it?"

She nodded. "Now we just have to make it work. What have you got?"

He retrieved the bag, then held it open so they could peer inside. "Sixteen Taiyok-to-Asterion signal converter kits and eight power converter ones. I bought four from every merchant who sold them. They're designed for gimmicky consumer products, not starship cloaking devices, but they include the basic components required to allow Taiyok tech to talk to Dominion tech."

"And that's all you need?"

He shrugged. "Hopefully. I can break them down, scavenge them for parts and cobble together those parts into something that should enable your cloaking device to talk to our ship's systems. Of course, I'm not familiar with the internal workings of our ship's systems, so there might be some trial-and-error involved before I figure out exactly where and in what way to hook in what I build."

"Don't be silly. There's no reason for you to waste all that time reverse engineering the ship's wiring. I'll reach out to Grant and ask him to talk you through the connections."

A muscle below his left cheekbone twitched. "All right."

She'd already come to recognize the tic as a sign of unvoiced misgivings. "What?"

"I bet Mr. Mesahle would much rather talk *you* through the connections."

She snickered as she ordered the trolley to follow them up the ramp. "Probably so, but you two gearheads can get done in ten minutes what it would take me ten hours to accomplish, so he's talking to you."

AR

The nex video projection materialized in front of her. Grant sat at his desk, working at an interface. He gave her a little half-smile, but kept his eyes on the pane.

Nika. How's the ship treating you?

"Well. Why are you pinging me instead of speaking?"

Because I'm being watched, and it's possible my office has listeners hidden in the cracks. A couple of Justice officers stopped by two days ago. They asked a bunch of questions about Advisor Ridani while probing my business legitimacy.

She sank against the cabin wall. This was her fault.

She never should have forced Grant to get involved...and by showing up at his door, bags in hand and looking appropriately desperate, this was essentially what she had done. 'Diplomat' was simply a sanitized word for 'manipulator.'

"I'm so sorry."

Don't beat yourself up. I can sense what you're over there thinking, but it's not your fault.

Wasn't it? She tried to console herself by remembering that it was the Guides fault, like everything else in this ordeal.

She didn't buy it. "I'm still sorry."

I know. Now, before you ask, I lied through my teeth to them. They'd tracked Ridani here and knew he never left—not on the ground—so I told them he'd taken a pleasure craft for a test cruise and had yet to return it. I gave them scrambled credentials for the ship.

They didn't act as if they had any idea you'd been here, and they didn't ask me about you. I think I convinced them I was an innocent rube intimidated by an Advisor into giving him whatever he wanted. At the very least, I created enough doubt to dissuade them from hauling me in for more rigorous questioning for now. But they're watching the place, either for Ridani to return or for me to slip up.

"I never wanted you to get mixed up in this."

I believe you. I knew the risks.

There was no way in all the worlds he could have known the true depth of the risks; he still didn't. "If you have to run, you remember how to reach Perrin or Joaquim, don't you? They'll take care of you."

I've got their private nex addresses. But it's going to take a lot more than Justice surveillance to scare me away. I'll keep doing my work, and eventually they'll get bored and leave. So what do you need? Is there a problem with the ship?

She needed to protect him. It was her natural inclination to protect everyone on her side, everyone who had showed her a kindness. Doubly so for those she'd put in the crosshairs through her own actions.

But if Justice hadn't arrested him on the spot, they likely viewed him as an ancillary player at best, and they were holding out for bigger fish. So long as he continued playing it cool, he should be safe. Maybe.

"Not a problem—it runs beautifully. We even gave it a name: *Wayfarer*. But we need to fit it with a cloaking device of Taiyok manufacture. I intended to see if you could meet us somewhere and, frankly, do the heavy lifting of installing it, but that's out of the question now."

She checked the open floor hatch, where Dashiel had descended into the engineering well below to take a look around. "Can you possibly talk Dashiel through the installation process? He's already rigged up an interpreter module to convert the Taiyok code into a form compatible with the ship's programming. He's an industrialist and a manufacturer, so he knows materials, machines and electronics. He just doesn't know ships."

I'm not even going to ask why you need a military-strength alien cloaking device. I have my own problems right now, so I'm not going to worry about yours...much. I've never installed a Taiyok module on one of my ships before, but if you've gathered the right tools and components, I'm willing to give it a shot.

"Thank you, Grant. For everything. I'll try not to ask anything else of you."

You ask of me what you need to, Nika.

ᐱᖇ

Dashiel scooted on his back toward the auxiliary systems control unit above him. The engineering well was small and cramped, with equipment modules installed along both walls and the ceiling, and he only had about a meter and a half of vertical space in which to maneuver.

Offhand, he couldn't remember the last time he'd crawled around in duct space and gotten dirty with the machines. Too long ago.

He removed the translucent protective cover and propped it against the wall beside him. "All right, I've got the auxiliary controls open."

There are four vacant slots on the bottom right of the grid. Based on the power flow you've described, the cloaking module is going to need three of them. When I designed the ship, I thought the auxiliary systems would be taken up by a gourmet food preparation addon or maybe a full sensory projector, not a powerhouse alien concealment system.

Dashiel chuckled. Neither of them particularly wanted to be working together, but if Mesahle could take the high road, so could he. "Believe me, no one could have anticipated this modification. No way in hells should it work."

It'll work. Do you know how to split the signal outflow into three separate leads?

He glanced at the bundle of photal fibers in his right hand, which he'd rethreaded while they talked. "Already done."

I had to ask. Go ahead and wire them into the vacant slots, but don't turn anything on yet. Once they're connected, move to the distribution panel above the inputs. We're going to need to reprogram it to treat the three inputs as one system, then add in a buffer so the Taiyok instructions don't blow up the ship if a few slip through the interpreter.

"Good thinking. Okay, I'm at the command line."

Already? Nice. Auth ID is 'SAIR 1.' I'm sending you the first code snippet.

He paused for half a second over the Auth ID…but it wasn't his business. "Bear with me while I enter the code. It's a little cramped down here."

Yeah, sorry about that. I was working with an antique hull. While you input it, if you don't mind me asking, how did an Advisor end up on Nika's side of whatever's going on?

His finger slipped, and he had to backtrack for half a line. "I've always been on Nika's side. Since long before they psyche-wiped her."

Before what?

Shit. Dashiel squeezed his eyes shut and stopped trying to enter code. "I assumed you knew, since the two of you were…close."

Sleeping together, you mean. No. It wasn't like that. We weren't…sharing our lives.

What a damn tragedy for Mesahle, if one Dashiel was immensely grateful for. "I didn't—"

When did she get psyche-wiped, and who is 'they'?

He sighed and instinctively went to run a hand through his hair, but banged his elbow on the corner of the cooling system instead. Ohhh, that hurt. "Look, it's not my secret to reveal. I shouldn't have said anything. Let's just concentrate on getting this cloaking module working, all right?"

A lengthy silence preceded the reply. *Fine. Are you ready for the next code snippet?*

When Dashiel climbed out of the engineering well, he found Nika stretched out on the couch reading up on Eventime Solutions.

She looked up wearing a smile, but it promptly darkened in concern. "You're bleeding."

"Am I?"

She pointed at his elbow. He'd forgotten all about the scrape, but sure enough, trickles of blood oozed out of the wound. He shrugged and went over to the sink to wash it clean. "Lot of sharp objects down there."

"Did you get it working?"

"In theory. Everything tests out functional, but making the ship disappear in the middle of the Toki'taku spaceport doesn't strike me as the best idea."

"True. I guess we'll have to find out the hard way." She appeared at his side, a small strip of bonding tape in one hand. He let her stretch out his arm and press the tape to his elbow. After it was secure, she leaned down and kissed it softly. "There. All better."

Had he ever loved her so much as he did at this moment? His chest ached from the strain of containing it all within his physical body, and his voice cracked as he drew her into his arms. "All better."

She hummed in contentment, then kissed his ear and drew back a little. "You should shower. I'll get dinner out."

"In a minute. Listen, I may have screwed up."

"In what way?"

"I let the fact you'd been psyche-wiped slip to Mr. Mesahle. I assumed he knew, but clearly he didn't. I'm sorry."

"Oh." She frowned and leaned against the kitchen unit. "It's fine. I mean, I wasn't deliberately keeping it from him, exactly. It was just never something I advertised."

She bit her lip. "Okay, that's a gross understatement. In our society, is there anything more pitiable than having no past? The last thing I wanted was pity, so once I got my feet under me, I built up a persona that didn't allow for...vulnerability. That denied the possibility of a hole in my mind. And eventually, that persona became who I was. Everyone seemed to like it, so why would I ever tell them it was a lie?"

"It wasn't a lie, merely a piece of a larger reality. If you've proved anything, it's that you are not your memories. They add subtle quirks and highlights to your personality, yes, and I'm glad you're finding some of them again. But you are so much more than your past."

24

MIRAI

Joaquim burst onto The Floor displaying a notable intensity. "Well, Spencer's infected with the virutox. It's the only explanation for him losing his reasoning mind."

Perrin, in turn, immediately lost her train of thought. She'd been talking to Ryan about ways to increase the effectiveness of the defensive routines they'd developed to block the virutox, and…. Nope. Whatever she'd been about to suggest, it was gone on the wind, a consequence of too little sleep and too much to do.

Since the explosion at the transit hub, she'd thrown herself triply into their work, if such a thing were possible, in a bid to distract herself from seeing the horrors of that night play out in a repeating loop in her mind. It was mostly working, but only because she was too exhausted to do anything other than put out fires, move people from project to project and catch a nap here and there.

She winced at Ryan. "Excuse me a minute?"

"Sure. Sounds like more trouble."

"Oh, how I hope not." She climbed to her feet with a sigh and went over to Joaquim. "What are you talking about? You heard from Spencer again?"

"He says Justice has developed a vaccine for the virutox, and they want our help distributing it."

"A vaccine? That's great news! But why do they want or need our help?"

Joaquim made a face as he started straightening already straight gear storage shelves. "Allegedly, because our broadcasts have been too successful, and now nobody with an iota of sense trusts anything Justice has to say. Now, this is absolutely true, but I doubt it's their real motivation. This supposed 'vaccine' is probably a new version of the virutox designed to reach the people the first round missed. Or there's no vaccine at all, and they're trying to trap us and bring us in."

"But this is Spencer we're talking about. He's on our side."

"He *was* on our side. Maybe Justice learned of his association with NOIR, and he's being forced to double-cross us. Or, like I said, maybe he caught the virutox."

"I thought you were joking."

"So did I when I said it, but something has to explain why he would betray us."

"But what if he's not betraying us? What if it's true? A vaccine could save—"

"We're close to developing one on our own."

She looked over her shoulder at Ryan. He was near enough to eavesdrop on the conversation, and without a doubt was doing exactly that.

He shook his head. "If Parc were here…."

She nodded in silent understanding. Ryan and Parc had been close; though he was hiding it well, she knew Ryan missed him. They all missed him, for a thousand and more reasons, but at this moment for his technical skills above all.

She placed a hand on Joaquim's elbow and urged him toward the training room, where they could have some privacy. "Come on, let's take this conversation elsewhere. You're shouting."

"No, I'm not—oh, fine." He acquiesced and followed her into the room, and she shut the door behind them.

"Jo, the truth is, we're not going to have a vaccine anytime soon, not when we've lost our three most talented neural coders. Everyone's trying their best, but the virutox is built on some of the most sophisticated algorithms anyone's seen. Whoever designed it, they're professionals."

"We just need a little more time."

"Which is something we might not have—or the innocent people walking around out there might not have. I think you're wrong about what's happening here. Dashiel believes Spencer's boss, Advisor Weiss, is trying to stop the virutox from spreading."

Joaquim scowled at her. "That's not an endorsement."

Perrin tried not to roll her eyes, but she only marginally succeeded. Damn, his stubbornness could be infuriating! "*And* Spencer is saying the same thing. *And* I talked to Roqe Ovet a couple of hours ago, and they said Justice officers came by the store earlier this week and confiscated their limb augment stock. They said other merchants were reporting the same thing happened at their stores. Justice was a bit slow on the uptake, but it *is* getting the augments off the streets."

Joaquim shook his head firmly. "I will *never* trust Justice."

"I know you won't. I don't know your reasons for it, but I believe you mean it. So we won't trust Justice. We'll arrange a meeting on our terms, accept a copy of this alleged vaccine and test it ourselves. But if it checks out, we owe it to all the people we claim to be fighting for to do everything in our power to get it into their hands. Even if it means working with Justice to do it."

His eyes narrowed in suspicion. "You sound like Nika."

"Shocking as it is, I actually try to pay attention whenever she goes into 'speech' mode, and it's possible I've learned a few things. She's not here right now, but I think that's what she would say if she were."

"You have no idea what you're asking me to do."

They'd been here before, and there was nothing she hadn't said in response a hundred times over. So she gazed at him quietly, and perhaps sadly. "I'm asking anyway."

He studied the training room floor as he made a brooding loop around where she stood before finally coming to a stop directly in front of her. His eyes rose to meet hers; all the fight had drained away, leaving behind a kind of wistful melancholy.

"Then you deserve to know why I don't trust them. The truth is, you always did." He took a step back and slid down the wall until he reached the floor, where he clasped his hands together atop his knees. "I was a machinist and technician for a furnishings fab shop on Synra, and I was in love. Had been for a long time. Her name was Cassidy."

"Jo, what are you doing?"

He looked up at her wearing an odd little half-smile. "Telling you my deepest and most painful secret, so try not to interrupt."

LOGIC
GATES

25

SR114-ICHI

ASTERION DOMINION EXPLORATORY WORLD

SR114-Ichi might one day be a viable location for a small manufacturing hub producing a few niche products with a specific set of requirements, but it was never getting adjunct status.

The planet was an icebox from pole to pole, a frozen tundra of frozen fjords, frozen lakes and frozen plains. Blizzards sent shards of ice plummeting from the sky like arrows launched from powered bows, creating a constant threat to anyone caught above ground. This explained why the outpost buildings were situated in excavated dugouts, complete with retractable roofs and reinforced tunnels connecting them.

Given the fury of nature that ruled the planet, it was reasonable to question what could possibly be worth enduring such punishing conditions to attempt actual work here. According to Eventime Solutions, the answer was the next iteration of ultra-high-density quantum storage units. A staff of seventy Asterions lived and worked here in six-month rotations; of those seventy, a full forty-eight were support staff, dedicated to keeping the outpost running and sustaining life so the other twenty-two were able to build and test the new storage tech.

Dashiel stared out the viewport at a vast white landscape broken only by the outpost tunnels, a few environmental modules and a ship landing pad on the western end of the outpost. Occasional glimpses of activity in the hour since they'd arrived confirmed the outpost remained operational and they hadn't missed whatever was going to happen here. Their climate gear was laid out in the cabin, ready to be quickly donned should they need to venture outside.

Nika glanced out the viewport every thirty seconds or so, but she was preoccupied studying the files she'd copied from the Guides' data server before taking a swan dive off Mirai Tower. She claimed to be reviewing the Rasu Protocol files, but they'd combed through those four times already.

He suspected she was sneaking in regular peeks at her own Advisor files. Trying to understand who she'd been, as if that information could ever be found in official reports.

"What would you say the average population of an outpost is?"

"I'm not sure. Maybe five hundred or so?" *You would have known, once.* "My outpost that disappeared only staffed eighty-two people, but it was just ramping up."

"That's the thing. Every outpost to be hit, all the way from the beginning, had a population of less than a hundred. The Guides are expending an awful lot of effort to repeatedly kidnap small groups of people and erase the evidence of them doing so. It's highly inefficient."

"I don't think they have a choice. Larger outposts disappearing would almost certainly draw attention, and if we know anything, it's that they do not want to draw attention to their activities."

Her nose wrinkled up and her mouth quirked, as though she'd taken a bite of something pungent. "Which is why they're pushing as many people as they can into Zaidam. They can move thousands out of there, and no one notices. But then why are they bothering with a few dozen people here and there from outposts, at great cost and risk of discovery?"

He drummed his fingers on the dash. "If I had to guess—and I'm definitely guessing—they need every body they can get their hands on. The more they can get the easy way, the better, but they need the hard ones, too.

"It's like kyoseil. I have contracts for a regular supply of it from Chosek, but I'll jump at an opportunity to acquire a few kilograms of it from somewhere else. Even at a higher price. The demand for it outstrips the supply to such a degree that it's impossible to envision a scenario where I have too much of it."

She frowned at him. "You said 'body,' not 'person.'"

"I guess I did. I didn't intend to depersonalize the victims…it's more that there's no obvious profile applicable to the people taken. On a percentage basis, most of them are criminals, yes, but as the Guides have expanded the definition of 'criminal,' the group has lost any reliable common characteristic. Doubly so with the release of the virutox. The people taken from outposts don't match a single profile, either. There's no discrimination based on skillset, previous experience, type of work the outpost is engaged in, or anything else. So it seems as if they need the bodies more than the minds."

"That's horrifying."

"I know—" Two vessels descended out of the leaden cloud cover toward the landing pad. The larger one was utilitarian in design, with a rectangular body dominating its profile—a cargo vessel of some kind—while the other was a small personal craft. No one had emerged from the sunken buildings to greet the vessels; was their arrival a surprise?

Nika activated a small display. "Starting the recording now. Whatever happens, we'll have evidence of it."

As soon as the ships landed, a person and a utility dyne disembarked from the smaller vessel, but the individual was too far away to identify. The two hurried over to the central piping and bulky environmental module that drew in the marginally breathable air, transformed it into something pleasantly breathable and channeled it into the underground buildings. Activity ensued, but damn if he could tell what exactly they were doing. Altering the ventilation system in some manner, but how?

The *Wayfarer's* new cloaking system had passed its first test, as their presence a mere one hundred fifty meters away had not attracted any notice.

Three minutes later, the two returned to the landing pad and boarded the cargo ship. Still, no one from the outpost materialized from below to meet them.

Additional utility dynes exited the cargo ship, and with them a series of....

"Are those stasis chambers?"

Dashiel studied the scene for another second. "I think so. I'd bet my company that they injected a chemical into the environmental system to knock everyone out."

"We have to stop this." She leapt up and hurried into the main cabin, pulling her sweater off over her head as she did so. She grabbed her climate suit and began tugging it on.

"Nika, wait. We talked about this. If we burst in with weapons firing, maybe we disrupt things enough to prevent these people from being taken. But we lose what could be the sole chance we'll get to find out where they're being taken and what's being done to them."

She hesitated, one arm in the climate suit. "I know what we decided. But seeing it happen right in front of us? I don't think I can let these people die, no matter how greater the good."

"They're not dying. If they're being put in stasis chambers, it means they're not being shut down or left to rot. They're being kept alive for some reason, and deliberately so." He gently grasped her shoulders. "But even if we are consigning them to die, it will still be worth it for the chance to save untold thousands from the same fate in the future."

Her brow knotted up in violent turmoil. It was an outward expression of a raging internal battle, and one he was getting used to seeing. The life-changing events of five years ago, and what they had meant for her every day since, had made her profoundly sensitive to the ramifications of life and death decisions.

Finally her jaw hardened, and her mouth set in a determined line. "Then we need to get a tracker on that cargo ship."

He nodded, though he took no joy in it. "Yes, we do."

AR

Their ship was camouflaged, and now they were, too. The exterior of their climate suits tuned adaptively to the surrounding color palette, and at ivory white they blended nicely against the frozen landscape. Kamero filters completed the illusion.

Nika claimed so long as you didn't make any sudden, dramatic movements, a kamero filter rendered you invisible up to as close as a single meter. He understood the technology, conceptually, but the idea of standing directly in front of someone with them being unable to see you was nonetheless disconcerting. It was also a reminder of the continuing fallibility of their sophisticated biosynthetic structure.

If they survived this crisis and were one day able to return to living normal lives, he thought perhaps he'd devote some time to creating an ocular augment that could detect incongruous signals measured by Asterion visual receptors. In the name of continual improvement—and to thwart the occasional thief.

The climate suit material covered their bodies from head to toe, excluding their faces, where a small force field projected out five centimeters to deflect the wind. Yet for all their protection, it was frigidly cold out here.

They fought a relentless wind to trudge toward the landing pad as a long line of stasis chambers was escorted out of the cargo ship's hold and guided down into the outpost bunkers.

When they were thirty meters from the landing pad, Nika placed a hand on his arm and pinged him.

You keep watch outside, and sound the alarm if any of the dynes or their director start toward the ships.

You're boarding the cargo ship? Why can't you put the tracker on the outer hull?

It would get dislodged or destroyed during transit. Space is brutal. Trust me, I know.

So did he, for he'd been the one to pull her frosted, colorless and breathless body into the airlock at Zaidam. Her spacing had marked only the third or fourth time he'd thought he'd lost her again after finding her. She might be blasé about it, but he was not.

If you must, but be quick.

Sure.

I'm serious.   .

Mm-hmm. And with that, she released his arm, moved forward and after a step, vanished. He sighed and checked the Glaser on his hip then faced the outpost to watch for threats.

To him, Glasers had always been tools, but to Nika, they were weapons. She had shared a targeting sim routine with him so he could practice shooting at virtual targets, and he had done so. Didn't mean he was ready to shoot someone. Or some*thing* for that matter.

Her current world existed one hundred eighty degrees from his, and from the world she'd been stolen from. Given this, he shouldn't be surprised at how she instinctively recoiled from the idea of having been an elite diplomat. Here in the icy wasteland of a distant planet, cloaking themselves and their ship, wielding powerful weapons while tracking down an insidious government plot…it felt like a dose-induced hallucination to him, but for her it was another day on the job.

Everything okay in there?

Yeah. Having a look around.

Why wasn't she afraid? Or at a minimum properly cautious with her life and freedom? Of course, it was this very fearlessness and refusal to turn a blind eye to wrongdoing that had started everything five years ago. Yep, he should definitely stop being surprised—

In the distance that wasn't distant enough, the Asterion in charge of whatever the fuck was going on here emerged from the closest bunker, accompanied by a dyne and two presumably occupied stasis chambers. The group headed in the direction of the landing pad.

Time to go! We've got company incoming.

One second. I'm having trouble getting the tracker to initialize. It's almost as if something is blocking its operation.

Then we'll have to find another way to get answers.

The Asterion reached up and scratched at their forehead, dislodging the skull cap of their climate suit, and strands of crimson hair escaped to blow about in the wind.

Gemina Kail. Was she doing *all* the Guides' dirty work? He shelved the question for later as the contingent drew within a few dozen meters of the landing pad.

Get out of there now! Gemina Kail is running this operation, and she's headed your way fast. We are out of time.

It's not working. A pause. *Track me instead.*

What?

I won't let this chance slip away. I'm stowing onboard. Get to the Wayfarer *and track me.*

Godsdammit, Nika!

He took a step back, away from the landing pad. It was already too late for her to escape the cargo ship unnoticed, wasn't it? Another step. He needed to move before it was too late for him as well.

I trust you to find me. Trust me to stay alive until you do.

The words hit him as viscerally as a punch to the gut. He hadn't found her last time, had he? Her faith in him was misplaced until he proved otherwise.

He backstepped as swiftly as prudence allowed, unwilling to look away as Kail and her entourage reached the cargo ship and went inside. He held his frigid breath and focused his aural receptors, listening for the tell-tale sounds of violence.

None came, and Kail exited the ship. Nika might have a chance to—

—in his peripheral vision, more dynes accompanying more stasis chambers exited the bunkers, and a regular procession to the cargo ship began, extinguishing his brief surge of hope.

✦

As soon as he reached their ship, he activated a tiny frame in the bottom right of the HUD display and set to it capture the signal from Nika's internal locator.

The frame remained blank.

He checked the settings, then refreshed the frame. Blank.

Nika, your locator isn't transmitting.

It is. I think the problem with the tracker wasn't with the tracker, because I can't get my own location at the moment. The ship must be broadcasting an interference field, similar to what we use at The Chalet.

Panic wound like a nest of serpents through his chest to strangle his heart.

That means I won't be able to follow. I won't be able to find you.

It'll be okay, darling. As soon as I exit the ship, we'll both know where I am. Just hang tight.

Just hang tight? You could be across the galaxy before I find out your location. It could take me days to get to you.

That's a risk we'll have to take. It's the only way.

Do not get yourself put in one of those stasis chambers. Do not get yourself erased. I will not lose you again.

No, you won't. We are forever.

The panic spread through the rest of his body, overloading any functioning logic processes in his mind. The last time she'd spoken those words, it had taken five long, miserable years for them to be reunited.

The final stasis chambers were shepherded into the cargo ship, and its engines ignited. He watched in horror as it lifted off and was consumed by the clouds.

No. This was *not* going to happen again.

He flushed the panic-inducing biochemicals with a single order. His sordid history of abusing mind-altering substances meant his flushing routines were of the highest quality, and ruthlessly effective. Then he went to the storage cabinet, where two additional trackers were stored. He retrieved one, activated his climate suit's face protection, and left the *Wayfarer* once more.

Kail and the last two remaining dynes had returned to the bunkers. Kail stood watch while the dynes placed what Dashiel assumed were explosives in an ordered pattern around the edges of the outpost structures.

He risked jogging most of the way to the landing pad, trusting that Kail was far enough away not to see any minor ripples in the air he caused.

Nika was right; a tracker affixed to the outer hull of a ship would not survive for long in the ravages of space. But the small laser protruding from the chassis of Kail's ship had a retracting cover over its aperture to protect its inner workings. Though strictly necessary only during superluminal travel, as a rule the cover stayed in place whenever the laser wasn't being used.

Like 99.9% of the population, Dashiel shouldn't have known such miscellany about the laser and its housing. But in the early days of Ridani Enterprises, quite a few generations ago and well before he refined his focus to networking hardware and consumer augments, his company had built one of the components for these types of lasers. Not the cover, but the full equipment schematic had informed the design of every component.

It was one of millions of quanta of information that he kept in his primary memory stores. His business had long been the second-most important thing in his life, and he regularly passed off to external storage knowledge other people considered essential in favor of keeping information related to his profession. This wasn't exactly the situation he'd imagined himself needing one of those data points in, but he was damn glad he had it.

When he was twelve meters short of reaching the ship, Kail pivoted in its and his direction. He froze, then laughed to himself. Literally freezing while freezing.

Luckily it was little more than a glance, and Kail turned back to issue an order he couldn't hear to one of the dynes. Dashiel crossed the remaining distance and ducked beneath the ship's hull.

As expected, the cover extended over the laser's opening to form a snug seal. He removed the multitool Nika had given him from his pouch and activated its nanoblade, which he placed flush against the seal and worked back and forth until the seal broke.

The cover didn't pop open, but after a bit of effort he was able to force it open. He retrieved the tracker and maneuvered it a few centimeters inside the laser's housing, then pressed it firmly against the metal for several seconds.

He closed the cover back over the laser. The seal no longer formed, however, and when he let go the cover hung half-open.

He studied the multitool settings for something that could help...then smiled. It seemed Nika's little 'get-out-of-shit' tool, as she'd called it, sported a tiny blowtorch as well. He'd put this one to better and less costly use than the last one.

The flame flickered to life, all three centimeters of it. He held the cover closed with one hand and the multitool with the other, slowly melting the cover and housing until they became one.

If Kail decided to use the laser at some point during her travels, the tracker wouldn't be the only casualty. He simply had to hope she didn't have an occasion to do so before she got where she, and hopefully the cargo ship, was going.

Satisfied he'd done all he could, Dashiel backed out from beneath the hull on the side opposite the outpost—

—Kail and her dynes were thirty meters away and approaching fast.

He used the cover of the hull to scramble another dozen meters away, albeit in the opposite direction from the *Wayfarer*, but halted when they rounded the nose. He stood still as stone while the dynes boarded the ship and Kail paused to look back at the outpost a final time before doing the same.

He felt the vibration in his bones when the engines engaged and the ship rose high in the air. Then he turned to go—

—a *boom* shook the ground beneath his feet as explosions cascaded across the outpost. He stumbled forward, caught himself with a hand on the ice and, all concerns about stealth forgotten, took off running for their ship.

Plumes of ice shocked into instant evaporation blasted into the sky like geysers. Hairline cracks splintered out from the outpost and across the frozen surface.

He ran faster.

A crack outpaced him ahead, and the ground split apart in front of him. He launched himself forward, across the widening crevasse, and landed in a crumpled heap on the other side.

Get up!

He followed his own command and forced himself to his feet, then forced them to move. The *Wayfarer* was so well cloaked he couldn't make it out in the now turbulent scene, but its own tracker told him it was a short twenty meters away.

It revealed itself barely a meter before he ran smack into it. He slid across the ice until he banged into the hull, shoved off of it and rushed up the ramp.

As he did, a second round of cracks raced outward from the crumbling outpost, one of them headed straight for the *Wayfarer*. He fell into the left-side cockpit chair—the ground beneath the hull lurched, sending the nose leering downward at a dangerous angle.

Ramp up. Engines active. Hatch closed. *Hurry!*

The *Wayfarer* rose as the ground fell away beneath it. An icy mist billowed into the air, obscuring everything outside. He kept ascending.

The mist was captured by the wind and carried away to reveal a sunken crater where moments ago the outpost, and their landing spot, had resided. Chunks of ice shifted, settled and in several cases rose again until a new equilibrium asserted itself. Silence fell.

Dashiel sank down in the chair, utterly exhausted. Everything hurt, from his toes to the tiny muscles where his cheeks met his ears, but mostly all the places in between. A variety of warnings in his virtual vision told him he'd need to visit the repair bench soon. But it was all worth it if the tracker led him to Nika.

He leaned forward and tuned the frame on the HUD to display the signal from the tracker he'd placed on Kail's ship.

A tiny dot appeared. Beneath it, galactic coordinates scrolled.

His chin fell to his chest as the adrenaline his OS had over-loaded his body with dissipated. Dread surged to replace it as he thought about Nika, alone and trapped inside the cargo ship.

But he refused to let the dread win. This time, he hadn't let her stride off into danger while we waited at home, impotently hoping she'd be safe. This time, he'd acted. He'd done what was in his power to do.

And now, he'd chase her across the stars after all.

26

MIRAI

They met on the outskirts of Mirai One, amid tracts of automated farm labs. This far away from the bustle of the city, the NOIR lookouts stationed along a perimeter eighty meters out would see a hunter or AEV squad coming well in advance, giving his people enough time to scatter into the darkness. It wasn't a perfect location, but Joaquim felt confident they controlled the field of play as much as was feasible, and to a far greater extent than Justice did.

Perrin, Ryan and Ava accompanied him to the meeting. Perrin because she'd never have agreed to stay behind, Ryan because he knew more about the virutox than anyone in NOIR, and Ava so she could stand back ten meters with multiple weapons trained on their guests and itchy trigger fingers.

The Justice contingent didn't appear to include an armed escort as they arrived, but it wasn't as if they'd never heard of a kamero filter, so Joaquim wasn't so foolish as to trust his eyes.

Whether he was foolish to agree to this meeting in the first place remained to be seen. Perrin had been...persuasive. When faced with the wretched, pathetic pile of mush on the floor that he'd been reduced to by the time he'd finished his sad tale, she had countered with sympathy and a gentle and true understanding.

Yet she had also remained unyielding in her conviction that they must take this chance. She'd kicked him in the head, if softly and metaphorically, and told him to get his psyche straight and back on mission. And since, as difficult as it was to believe, he *did* recognize his own biases in action, he'd chosen to do so.

Reluctantly.

He motioned to the others, and they stepped out of the shadows to meet their counterparts.

An unassuming-looking blond man took the lead. "I'm Advisor Adlai Weiss. Spencer Nimoet, I believe you know. This is Erik Rhom, our best forensic analyst and the person who developed the vaccine. He's here should you have any questions about its design or functionality."

Perrin made a little waving motion. "Hi, Spencer."

"Hi, Pe—hello. It's good to see you."

If Spencer outed their identities to his boss, they would have words. Joaquim offered the Advisor a smile that probably wasn't very friendly. "I'm not telling you my name, and neither is anyone else. You're welcome to waste your time scanning us, but you won't learn anything."

"I assumed as much. I'm not here to take you in. The truth is, right now NOIR is doing Justice's job better than Justice is, so it's to my advantage for you to keep doing it. This doesn't mean NOIR is off the hook for its past or future crimes, but at present we all have more important concerns. I believe everyone here believes they are acting in the best interests of the people. For the next several days, let's do so together."

Perrin nodded enthusiastically. "We want the same thing."

Joaquim shot her a warning glare, then returned his focus to Weiss. "Nice words. We'll see if there's any truth behind them. Give us the vaccine. We'll tear it apart and subject it to tests you've never conceived of. If it's legitimate, we'll distribute it our way, using our own people and methods."

Weiss frowned. "That doesn't sound like much of a partnership."

"We never agreed to a partnership. But if this really is a vaccine, and if you really want it to get to the people most in need of it, then you won't care how we make it happen."

"I can see why Nika left you in charge."

Joaquim bristled at the mention of Nika's name, at the insinuation that this man somehow knew her in any genuine way, but the mission required him to not pick that fight. He motioned beside him to Perrin. "Her, too. She's the friendly half of the operation."

Weiss laughed unevenly. "Glad to hear you have one. All right, I accept your terms. We'll be distributing the vaccine ourselves as well, in whatever ways we're able to do so. I hope you decide to pitch in sooner rather than later. Every minute you burn second-guessing our intentions risks more innocent lives."

"Don't lecture us about risking innocent lives. Justice destroys—"

Perrin laid a hand on his arm. "This isn't the time."

He forced himself to take a deep breath, then carefully blow it out. "It isn't. Okay, enough talking. Hand it over, and we'll be on our way."

They took a circuitous route for their return to The Chalet. Honestly, Justice would be idiots not to send someone to shadow them, if only for future reference, but Joaquim didn't intend to allow them to succeed at it. Once they were in the heart of the city, they split up. The people on perimeter watch wandered around for a while before splitting up themselves and taking Doors #2 and #3. Ava took the long way around to #4, Ryan #1, and he and Perrin planned to use #5.

They turned left at the next intersection, and the lights of Hataori Harbor greeted them.

Perrin abruptly grabbed his hand. "I know we have to get the vaccine—"

"Alleged vaccine."

"—*alleged* vaccine back home for testing, but can we take two seconds to stop at *Maxine's* for some lemonade?"

"You can get a lemonade. I can get a—"

—a sharp sting at his neck cut him off. It burned like a wasp sting, but the insects weren't common around Mirai One...

...vertigo washed over him, and his head suddenly felt thick and heavy. His hand moved to his neck, and he pricked his fingertip on something, like a tiny needle....

Perrin pivoted back to him, a question on her lips. As his legs buckled, he focused all his waning lucidity on getting a single word out before everything went black.

"Run."

27

MIRAI

A driving beat assaulted Perrin's ears. Colors and lights danced across her vision in jarring fits and starts. Her mind drowned beneath the sensory overload, and she lurched forward in search of air and silence but instead bumped into something solid.

"Hey, want to dance?"

She looked up in confusion. 'Something solid' was a tall, willowy woman with curly fuchsia hair wearing a translucent slip of a dress.

She mumbled out an apology and stumbled away, but everywhere she turned, there were more bodies. They twisted and writhed in time to a cadence she couldn't decipher.

Where the hells was she? How had she gotten here?

A club. This was a club. She didn't venture a guess as to which one. Before she was here, she'd been walking with Joaquim—

Run.

She must have done so. Deeply embedded fight-or-flight routines had taken his suggestion under advisement and chosen flight. They'd carried her away from danger she'd been unable to see by flooding her pathways with adrenaline and drowning out conflicting desires like *not* running and instead staying to help Joaquim.

She spotted a gap in the crowd and rushed through it until she hit a wall that wasn't a person. Then she pinged him.

Jo? Are you okay?

The seconds ticked by in time to the music's unremitting rhythm while she waited on a reply she knew wasn't coming.

Guilt rose up to smother her, clouding her vision and choking off her air. Had she even checked behind her to see what happened to him? Was he taken? By Justice? Had the meeting been an elaborate double-cross after all?

If so, it meant she was responsible for whatever befell him. She'd batted her eyelashes and used her 'sweet' voice when he was at his most exposed to woo him into agreeing to the meeting.

She touched her pocket, felt the bulge of the weave containing the supposed vaccine. If it was in reality a trojan horse, she had to make certain it never saw the light of day; if it was truly a vaccine, she had to guard it with her life and do everything in her power to make certain it reached the masses.

And if she was going to save Joaquim, she first had to find out which one it was.

Which meant she had to get back to The Chalet cleanly. Once there, she had to tell everyone that Joaquim was lost. Taken. And she'd let it happen.

⋌ℛ

"Whoever took him, you couldn't have stopped them on your own."

"We should have all stuck together, dammit. *I* would have stopped them."

Ryan glared at Ava, then returned his attention to Perrin and rested his hands on her shoulders. "They would have taken you, too, and with you, the vaccine."

She tried to keep the worst of the despair off her face. She had to be a leader, now more than ever. But she was also dreadful at hiding her emotions. Everyone who knew her said so.

"If it is a vaccine." She removed one of Ryan's hands from her shoulder and placed the weave in it, then curled his fingers around it. "Isolate it from everything and everyone. Put it in a sandbox inside a sandbox inside a locked cage. Then find out what it is."

"I will. I promise. While I'm working on it..." he lowered his voice "…are you planning to contact Nika and tell her what happened?"

The despair threatened to overwhelm her right and proper. But she smiled anyway, though she doubted it was convincing. "No. If I tell her, she'll rush back here and mount a rescue operation, despite the fact that we don't know who took him or where he is now. In doing so, she'll be abandoning a mission to save tens of thousands of lives, and Joaquim wouldn't want her to prioritize him over so many others."

"No, he wouldn't. But when she does find out, she is going to be livid that you didn't tell her."

"I realize she will be. But it's my decision to make, and I'm making it. I'll pay the price when the time comes." Even if it meant losing Nika's trust, and thus her friendship.

Nika had taught her more than she'd ever realized about being a leader, but only now did Perrin begin to understand the true weight of the burden that came with it.

28

UNIDENTIFIED SPACE STATION

ASTERION DOMINION SPACE

Nika jerked awake.

Darkness greeted her—the darkness of a closed cabinet door.

She rotated her shoulders in circles and stretched her arms close across her body, which was the best she could manage in the cramped storage cabinet. Her OS had kept her on her feet while she slept, and the result was a decidedly suboptimal form of rest.

What had woken her? She sipped on the dwindling supply of water her climate suit provided her and switched her visual sensors to the x-ray band.

Hq (visual) | scan.xray(280°:70°)

Outside the cabinet, two dynes had begun detaching stasis pods from their berths and escorting them off the ship, which meant they were docked somewhere. Her vision extended out beyond the hull to reveal the outlines of…she couldn't tell what. Storage racks, perhaps. Machines, equipment.

She queried her tracker, but it gave her nothing. As long as she remained inside the ship, it continued to be blocked.

Dashiel?

I'm here! You're awake—and safe?

Undamaged, so far.

Good. You're on an unregistered space station in an undeveloped system four hundred ten parsecs from Synra.

How do you know where I am? My tracker still isn't transmitting.

I'll tell you later. The important thing is, I'm in position two megameters from your location. If I need to crash into the station to get you out, I'm prepared to do it.

Wow. She grinned to herself as all sorts of warm and fuzzy sentiments buoyed her heart.

I appreciate the offer. But give me a chance to find a less dramatic way off first. Dynes are unloading the stasis chambers, so I'm going to try to sneak off the ship and take a look around.

Be careful?

I'll do one better. I'll be smart.

She watched the activity outside the cabinet until she had a good sense of the patterns. When the closest dyne next turned toward the hatch, she confirmed her kamero filter was at maximum strength and eased the cabinet door open. A centimeter at a time, she moved out into the aisle and closed the door behind her.

She crept along behind the dyne and the stasis chamber it shepherded. Her focus remained locked ahead, but her peripheral vision took in the occupied stasis chambers lining the aisle. People, alive but locked in a state of unconsciousness so minimal it resided only a breath above total neural shutdown.

The lost. The vanished. The people she would save.

A dyne returned to the ship for another load and proceeded down the aisle in her direction. Soon—she would save them *soon*.

She flattened herself against the curving shell of one of the stasis chambers. The climate suit had adapted to the conditions it found itself in, and the glass felt cool through the material. Each chamber contained its own self-powering system, and the slightest hum penetrated the suit to tickle her skin.

The dyne passed by her with less than a meter to spare, taking no apparent notice of her presence. She waited until it was another meter past her, then cautiously stepped back into the aisle. She had to consciously restrain herself from running for the hatch. One step, then another.

Many agonizing seconds later she reached her immediate goal and the ramp extending out to the floor below.

The force field barriers bounding the far ends of the structure confirmed its status as a space station. It appeared to predominantly function as a warehouse. Housing people.

A shudder chilled her bones as she gaped at the rows upon stacked rows of stasis chambers that lined the opposite wall. Most of them were unoccupied, but hundreds of people were locked in a nebulous limbo, unaware of and unable to alter the fate awaiting them.

A couple of mecha tended to the new arrivals or moved equipment around. She didn't see any Asterions working, but a hallway cut into the center of the left wall. Offices? Labs?

Where did you say this station was located?

The galactic coordinates are l 14° 39' 51.14" b −19° 00' 24.25", but the stellar system is supposed to be undeveloped. No registered activity there.

The register is lying, because there is definitely activity here. The station is storing hundreds of occupied stasis chambers and has room for thousands more, though storage might not be its only purpose.

I'm sure none of its purposes are good.

How big is the station?

One second...1.4 kilometers by 300 meters.

Her gaze swept from corner to corner and did the math. There wasn't enough space left over for the hallway on the left to contain more than a few small offices or storage rooms. Whatever was being done to the people taken, it wasn't being done here.

So I was thinking about the escape plan. I could just crash through the force field and free jump it like before.

That's not funny, Nika.

Hold your position for now. I need to investigate what else is hiding in the station, then I'll use my 'ways' to escape.

Silence answered her.

Come on, that was at least a little funny.

Maybe. But how do you keep such a cavalier attitude while you're in such terrible danger?

More nerve than good sense? Time to explore.

Two additional ships were docked at the station: the personal craft from SR114-Ichi and, at the far end, a much larger vessel. Larger than the cargo ship by a factor of five, it stretched for nearly a third of the length of the station. And in contrast to the bland, utilitarian shape of the cargo ship, its hull carried the distinctive stylings of an official Asterion Dominion vessel.

What were the odds that this was the *Tabiji*? Considering the twists and turns her present life and this investigation had taken...pretty damn good.

She waited until a mecha finished crossing the wide central aisle then edged toward the vessel.

$\mathcal{AR}$

The vessel's ramp was extended, the outer hatch closed but not locked. She welcomed the small favors, but she still had to get the hatch open and herself inside without any of the mecha, dynes or presumed security cams noticing.

Most of the activity on the station centered around the cargo ship and the cargo it brought, but this didn't help with the security cams—oh, wait! A mirage field. She'd stuck one of the little shells in her pack when they'd left the *Wayfarer* on SR114-Ichi, because ninety percent of success was preparation. For anything.

She retrieved the shell from the pack at her hip and slowly knelt down onto the ramp, then placed it two meters out from the hatch and activated it. Observers would see the surrounding five meters as they existed at the instant of activation—in other words, a closed hatch. She stood, nudged the hatch open, slipped inside and closed it behind her.

A proper command deck greeted her. Thankfully, also an empty one. But there could be security cams inside as well, so she kept the kamero filter active as she moved with due care toward the systems control area of the bridge.

She'd never been on board a ship like this one. A real starship worthy of the name, where everything from the reinforced hull to the sophisticated instrumentation created a sense of *presence*, of consequentiality. When a vessel of this ilk cut a swath through the void, the void noticed.

But Nicolette Hinotori had once commanded a generation ship, which meant buried in Nika's core operating system was knowledge about the operation of such vessels, if knowledge she'd never dreamed she'd need. The encyclopedic files on starships that she'd downloaded before departing Namino should fill in any remaining gaps.

She stood in the center of the bridge and closed her eyes.

§ sysdir(root) § Hq { ∀ HΓn (∀ HΓn = ('*ship' || 'vessel') && ('operation' || 'systems' || 'control' || 'navigation' || 'records') && (DS < Y12,458.A7))}

Results flooded her mind, and she hurriedly initiated a sort-and-prioritize algorithm to impose a bit of order on them.

Then she gazed around the bridge with new eyes.

Comms sat in a half-alcove off to the left. Inside its data banks, she expected to find the ship's credentials that were broadcast to entities and locations it encountered, like Zaidam Bastille.

She hadn't planned to be engaging in heavy-duty slicing today, but this was another reason for being eternally prepared. She crouched in front of the comms module and removed its cover. Like most of the ship's systems, it idled in a low-power state. But it wasn't shut down, which was good enough. She tapped into a random input node, and in seconds she had the information she needed.

ADV Tabiji, Nebula Class. ID #ADV16-48189C. Captained by Asterion Dominion Advisor Gemina Kail.

Loathing flared at the mere mention of the name. The instrument of the Guides' reprehensible schemes. A proper archnemesis.

But time was short, and it did not include a break for impotent fuming.

What did she most need to learn? Given the vessel's identity, a tour of the interior wasn't apt to tell her much she didn't already know—that it was outfitted to carry every single one of those stasis chambers in the station's landing bay plus many more. To where?

That was what she needed to learn.

Historical navigation records should be stored in the ship's databanks as a matter of course. The ship essentially flew itself, but the captain's perch included an override mechanism enabling the captain to take manual control. There was also a small navigation station where courses could be visualized, mapped and selected.

She strode to the rear of the bridge and plopped down in the chair at the navigation station, only stopping herself at the last nanosecond from toeing it around in circles. No need for the security cams to decide the ship was haunted.

The wall behind her wasn't the brushed metal of the interior hull, but instead a non-conductive rubberized material that marked it as server housing. She pried off the section at eye level, followed the exposed photal fibers to an entry point and replaced the fibers with her fingertip.

$\S$ *sysdir* $\S$ *Hq* $\{ \forall H\Gamma_n \, (\forall H\Gamma_n = \text{'navigation.storerec*'}\})$
$\Phi \rightarrow$ *passcode required:*

Fine, be that way....

$< \rightarrow \delta \{\Sigma (\theta^n \, \alpha^n \, \beta^n)\} = H\Gamma_n$
$\rightarrow \forall H\Gamma_n \, (H\Gamma_n \, |*>)$
$\Phi \rightarrow$ *allowable attempts exceeded*
$\S$ *Hq*
$\S$ $\alpha\beta\alpha$
$< \rightarrow if \, (Hq = \alpha\beta\alpha) \, \{Hq/n_0\}$
$\rightarrow \delta \{\Sigma (\alpha^n \, \beta^n)\} = H\Gamma_n$
$\rightarrow \forall H\Gamma_n \, (H\Gamma_n \, |\theta>)$
$< \beta\beta\theta \; \alpha\theta\beta\beta \; \alpha\alpha \; \beta\theta\theta\theta\alpha \; \theta\alpha\beta\alpha \; \theta\theta\theta \; \beta\beta\alpha \; \theta\alpha\theta\theta \; \alpha\beta\alpha\theta\beta$
$\beta\alpha\theta \; \beta\alpha\alpha\beta \; \theta\theta\theta\alpha\theta$
...
$\beta\alpha \; \theta\alpha\theta \; \beta\beta\theta\theta \; \alpha\beta\alpha\alpha \; \alpha\beta\beta\alpha \; \beta\alpha\alpha \; \alpha\theta\beta\theta\beta \; \theta\alpha\beta\alpha \; \beta\beta\beta\beta$
$\beta\theta\alpha\alpha \; \alpha\theta \; \alpha\theta\beta\alpha\alpha$

T → passcode accepted
§ sysdir § Hq { ∀ HΓ$_n$ (∀ HΓ$_n$ = 'navigation.storerec*')}

She pinged Dashiel.

I'm opening a nex transfer path to you. Copy the data I send off onto the data storage drive on our ship.

Understood. What's the data?

If I'm reading it correctly, the entire travel history of the Tabiji.

Damn, Nika. You will never cease to amaze me. Now please *find a way to get out of there so I can demonstrate my appreciation.*

She chuckled to herself.

Just a few more minutes.

< copy datafiles (∀ HΓα) to Hq(DRα.storerec.TABIJI1)

What else could she find hidden in the ship's files? Explicit orders from the Guides detailing the conspiracy and its purpose would be fabulous…she backed out from the navigation system into the larger directory structure and scanned its contents, but didn't see any likely candidates.

A distant thud echoed through the bridge—probably from out in the station, but she instinctively glanced behind her. Suddenly chilled by the bridge's hollow emptiness and the sense she'd overstayed her welcome, she left behind a burnishing routine to erase the traces created by her slicing and deriving, then exited the system and stood. Where was a good place?

Tucked into a small indentation beside the lift was a beverage dispensing station. It should do nicely.

She went over to it, bent down and attached her last tracker to the far underside of the shelf. Initializing and….

TracUnit #NT5: Galactic Coordinates: l 14° 39' 51.14" b −19° 00' 24.25"

I'll be watching, Advisor Kail.

She went to the hatch and reactivated her x-ray visual sensors. The mecha were almost finished moving the stasis chambers from the cargo ship into the racks, but otherwise the scene was unchanged from when she'd entered the *Tabiji*. No mecha or dynes patrolled this end of the station, so she slipped out the hatch, closed it and retrieved the mirage field shell.

Time for a legitimate escape plan. Despite her humorous remarks earlier, she really did not want to take a dive off the station and hope Dashiel caught her. She felt confident he would...she genuinely did, and damn but it was a terrific feeling to know she could count on him. But the intervening trip was guaranteed to be a bitch, so a different plan would be better.

The station presumably included one or two space-rated protective suits in its supplies, or the *Tabiji* did, but she had no idea where she might find them. Finding them would also take too long.

Her eyes fell on the small personal craft that had brought Gemina Kail here from SR114-Ichi.

She smiled.

Gemina glared at everything. The numbers on the pane in front of her, the stasis chambers stacked out in the hangar bay on the other side of one office window, the stars and planets and in-between of space outside the other window. Eight years in, she no longer cared to deny reality: this job, this 'vital mission' the Guides had tasked her with?

It *sucked*.

As an Administration Division Advisor, she'd built a worthy career out of making complex systems run so smoothly most people never noticed the systems were even there. She made things happen when and where they needed to happen, for the benefit and convenience of the government and its citizens alike.

Or she used to.

Now, she'd been forced into the role of magician. Granted, her administrative wizardry could often be mistaken for magic; perhaps she should have clarified to onlookers that any sleight of hand was purely illusory.

She was being asked to conjure eight thousand Asterion bodies where none existed. Fine, where...she checked the data on the pane...1,487 existed. And this included the bounty from two additional outposts.

Prisoner traffic from Mirai to Zaidam had all but stopped. Transfers from the other Axis Worlds and from Adjunct worlds continued, but the volume had fallen way below forecasts on account of NOIR stopping the virutox's spread in its tracks. Even the people who would normally get arrested without the virutox (i.e., actual criminals) were nowhere to be found. Speculation ran rampant that Zaidam was a death sentence—which it was—and smart people were, shocker of shockers, playing it smart.

She leaned back in her chair and for a change of scenery glared at the ceiling. Time to resign herself to lobbying harder for the Guides to take the pre-awakening option. It wasn't ideal, she *got* that. During her tour of the Kiyora One Generations Clinic, Takeda had described what must occur to get the body to the state she sought as 'flicking the lights on and right back off.' Yes, it was unfortunate the lights had to be flicked on at all. Life was imperfect, and full of chances to decide between imperfect choices.

And it *sucked* that lately, she seemed to be the only one making those decisions.

Well, she'd surely exceeded her wallowing quotient for the day by now. She shot the ceiling a final scathing glare and returned her chair to the floor. The cargo from SR114-Ichi had been catalogued, tagged, recorded and stored. Here the stasis chambers would stay, their occupants blissfully unaware, until the time came for another, longer voyage. She needed to get home, where she would try to do her real job for a few days before returning here to Hokan Station to process the next batch.

Gemina shut down the records program, stood and departed the deliberately impersonal office, then took the lift down to the main floor and headed out into the bay.

Dynes triple-checked the security and stability of the new stasis chambers. A complement of mecha moved equipment around in preparation for the next delivery. The *Tabiji* sat silently at the far end of the bay. And in the landing berth where her personal ship docked...sat nothing.

Where the *fuck* was her ship?

29

WAYFARER

ASTERION DOMINION SPACE

Nika landed the borrowed ship on the surface of a small moon orbiting the 2nd planet in the stellar system the station called home. Dashiel arrived seconds after her and set the *Wayfarer* down a few dozen meters away.

The moon lacked an atmosphere, and after digging around in a few cabinets and drawers she found a portable oxygen mask and air reservoir. While she draped the mask's strap over her neck, she activated an interactive pane and wrote out a little message for the ship's owner. Then she opened the hatch and departed.

The ramp to the *Wayfarer* was already extended. Dashiel stood at the airlock, holding an oxygen mask over his mouth and nose but clearly anticipating dropping it at the first opportunity.

Gravity on the moon was surprisingly strong, and she trudged toward and finally up the ramp at what felt like a glacial pace.

In the time it took her to blink, Dashiel did indeed drop his mask, hit the button to retract the ramp and close the outer hatch, yank her own mask over her head and toss it on the floor, and wrap her up in his arms. His lips met hers with a fierceness she hadn't experienced since the life-changing night at his place.

"Don't do that again." It came out as a harsh whisper, delivered through teeth that scraped along her jaw to her neck.

She cut off whatever further admonitions might have followed by pressing him against the airlock wall and reclaiming his mouth in full. She was still in the climate suit, and they were going to need to rectify that pronto—*dammit.*

"Wait." She faltered back a step and held out a hand to stop him from following. "We need to leave here. Kail's likely to discover her ship is missing any minute now, and she might be able to track its location."

His shoulders sagged, but he nodded in agreement and headed for the cockpit. "We should blow it up."

"That would be highly satisfying, but I left her a message instead."

He spun around in surprise. "What? Nika, she has no reason to believe you were the one who took it, or that you were ever on the station at all. Not unless you *tell* her."

Her lips curled up in a devious smile as she peeled the climate suit off to her hips, then shimmied the rest of the way out of it. "Powerful and unafraid. That's what I must be to her. To the Guides. To Justice. They have to suspect what we're trying to do out here. Now, they'll know we're *succeeding*."

"True...." He regarded her with unabashed lust while he reached behind him with one hand and fumbled around for the launch trigger.

"Don't crash us into the star."

"Right." He reluctantly turned his back on her and properly guided the *Wayfarer* off the moon and back into space.

"There. We're heading to empty space a few parsecs away." The next instant his hands were on her once more, following the trail of her undershirt as she tugged it over her head and off. She tuned her sensory receptors to full, and what had been pleasant and enticing caresses transformed into a flood of lascivious sensations.

"You didn't agree not to do that again."

"No, I didn't." Her own hands found the hem of his shirt and shoved it upward. "You were warned. This is me. Just because I'm finding a bit of affinity with my former self here and there, it doesn't change who I am." She grinned as his face reappeared from beneath his shirt. "Maybe smooths out a couple of rough edges."

"I'm okay with rough…edges." One of his hands fisted at the small of her back. The pressure against the cluster of nerves when he urged her closer sent shocks of pleasure rocketing up her spine to fan out across her back as he traced the contours of her tattoo with his other hand. "Who am I kidding, though? You were always fearless. The only difference is, now you have weapons."

"Mm-hmm." She purred as his lips grazed down her neck, where each centimeter of skin he left behind cried out for his return. "I missed you."

He abandoned his journey to draw back a fraction and stare at her, for the briefest second revealing a mosaic of wonder and vulnerability in his eyes before passion consumed them. "I love you."

His lips crushed hers with the force of a meteor impact, and the fact that he didn't wait for a response she couldn't yet give moved her so much she almost wanted to give it.

For now, this would have to be enough.

Her touch.

She unfastened his pants and slipped her hand down them, which evoked a throaty growl as he hoisted her up on the shelf in front of the storage cabinet. Waves of heat radiated off his skin, and her own body temperature rose to match it and reflect it back, creating a pyretic feedback loop.

Her trust.

His hair felt as soft as spun silk when she wound both hands through it. She nibbled on his lower lip like it was fine dessert while his hands gripped her ass and lifted her up, then yanked her underwear off with the violence of a man in need.

Her body.

His lips ghosted over her mouth, the tip of her nose, her eyelashes, her cheeks, then at last back to her mouth as he slipped inside her.

Her contentment.

30

MIRAI

Perrin rubbed groggily at tear-stained cheeks. It seemed impossible she'd actually fallen asleep, but the feel of her face smooshed into the pillow argued otherwise. Her subconscious processes continued to act in ways they thought best for her physical well-being.

She reached for the glass of water beside the bed before responding to the ping that had woken her.

What have you got, Ryan?

The vaccine? It's the real deal.

Relief competed with confusion in her still-drowsy mind. Thank gods they had a vaccine! But if the meeting hadn't been a farce and Justice was sincere in their olive branch, who had taken Joaquim?

Spencer had said they were defying the Guides by confiscating the augments and pursuing a vaccine, so maybe the answer was another group within the government, or within Justice.

If different factions of the government were actively warring against one another, it was surely the beginning of the end. The only question was, the end of what? A repressive and increasingly authoritarian governmental system, or the Dominion itself?

But she couldn't worry about those questions; they were so much bigger than her. Beyond her grasp or understanding. She had to concentrate on the vaccine. On saving Joaquim. On saving innocent lives from the virutox. On making it to tomorrow.

With a weary sigh, she climbed out of bed and trudged to the lavatory to make herself presentable.

◢◣ℝ

"And everyone agrees with Ryan's assessment?"

A series of nodding heads greeted her, and no hesitation or doubt showed on their faces. None of the faces belonged to Parc or Cair…or Nika. But they'd all worked twice as hard on account of it, and she trusted Ryan's judgment.

"Incredible work, everyone. I mean it. Now, I want every person in NOIR inoculated right away. Next, we need to get copies out to our allies as well. We're going to save a lot of lives, but we have to do the work to make it happen."

Ava scowled, which wasn't unusual. "Great, but how? See, we kind of told everyone not to trust *any* routines. Are we seriously going to turn around now and say to trust *this* routine?"

"It's a little dicey, but essentially, yes. The whole point is, people know we have their backs. We warned them when there was a danger, and now we'll show them how to protect themselves from it." She drew her shoulders up and consciously lifted her chin. "Get everyone gathered together here on The Floor. We'll put together an action plan and split up into teams. Then we'll execute on the plan."

◢◣ℝ

Spencer, I need to meet with Advisor Weiss, but there's a problem. His movements are being tracked—or yours are, or both of you.

Why do you think we're being tracked?

Perrin stumbled over the silent words.

Last night after our meeting, Joaquim was abducted.

What?

Exactly what I said. Now, we've confirmed the vaccine is legitimate, so I'm going to go out on a limb and trust Advisor Weiss for now and assume he wasn't behind the abduction. But this means we're all still in danger.

Shit, that's terrible. Of course it wasn't us.

Spencer, if another group within Justice has Joaquim, you have to find him.

I'm...not certain what we can do. The Guides have sent another Advisor in to undo all the work we've done, and we're one wrong step away from detention cells ourselves. But we'll try. For now, concentrate on getting the vaccine out there. We have to stop the virutox's spread.

I know that!

I'm sorry. I realize you do. Okay, you can fill us in on the details of what happened to Joaquim when you get here. I'm sending you an ID file to use to get through security. I'll meet you in the Justice Center lobby and take you to see Advisor Weiss.

She hesitated. Joaquim always said she was too quick to trust people, to see too much of the best and too little of the worst in them. Now enemies were multiplying in the shadows, and she was all alone. She *had* to trust someone.

If only Nika were here to tell her what to do. Nika would see the larger strategies at work. She'd be planning three steps ahead and have a solid bead on the best course of action.

But Nika wasn't here, and Perrin wasn't about to change who she was.

Tell me what time to be there.

Spencer showed her into a surprisingly open, brightly lit office. Advisor Weiss was sitting at a cluttered desk when they entered, but he hurriedly stood and came over to them.

"Thank you for coming, Ms....I never got even a false name at the meeting. What should I call you?"

She exhaled slowly and deactivated the morph she had worn to the meeting. Joaquim was going to throttle her for exposing her true identity; she only hoped he got the chance. "Perrin. Perrin Benvenit."

He smiled, and it *looked* genuine. Warm and comforting. "It's a pleasure to properly meet you, Ms. Benvenit, though I hate that it's under these circumstances. I feel terrible about your colleague's abduction. I—just a second." He half-shifted toward Spencer. "I need you to shadow Advisor Satair for as long as our guest is here. If he starts heading this way, do what you can to divert him and notify me."

"Yes, sir." Spencer gave Perrin an encouraging nod and headed out the door.

Weiss gestured toward an equally cluttered table near the windows. "Sit with me? Oh, and I apologize for the mess. Things are a bit…well, I imagine you can guess how they are."

She followed him somewhat warily. "Spencer said the Guides sent someone, I assume this Advisor Satair, to rein you in. Are you sure it's safe for us to talk in here?"

"This might be the only place in the Dominion where it *is* safe. This office has always been warded, but when I decided to get involved in our current crisis, I made some significant upgrades to its security. Neither Advisor Satair nor any of his stooges—or anyone else—can get in this room without my approval. They've tried to plant listeners three separate times, and every time the devices short-circuited, courtesy of those upgrades. Also, as soon as Spencer told me what happened to your colleague, I double-checked all the security." He slid one of the chairs out for her. "Our conversation will not be overheard."

She'd have giggled at the silly display of chivalry if her heart weren't so damn heavy. Instead she simply sat down.

He sat opposite her, clasped his hands on the table and leaned forward. "Now, Ms. Benvenit, I want you to tell me everything that happened after you left our meeting."

"On one condition. You have to call me 'Perrin.' No one has ever called me 'Ms. Benvenit' more than twice."

He almost seemed to blush, but she assumed it was a tic of his and not evidence of any bashfulness. Advisors were not bashful.

"If that's your condition, I'll acquiesce to it. Perrin."

"Thank you." She didn't want to think about the events of the night before, but her wants stood at the end of a long line of musts.

So she recounted everything in a calm, quiet voice, and dammit but she did *not* cry. Not once.

When she finished, she folded her hands in her lap and met Advisor Weiss' gaze, where she found concern, sorrow and empathy. It made her feel safe, and she so badly needed to feel safe.

"You did the right thing by running. I've no doubt they would have taken you as well if they'd been able to catch you."

"Do you know who 'they' is?"

"I don't. I *fear* it is agents from Justice working directly for the Guides. But because their actions—from stealing Dashiel's limb augments and planting the virutox in them, to raiding outposts, to kidnapping your colleague—are not part of any official or recognized directive, I have no visibility into who specifically is taking an active role. Several Advisors in particular are definitely involved to some extent. Gemina—" he blinked "—I'm sorry, please take no offense, but I really shouldn't be telling you all this."

"Advisor Weiss—"

He cringed. "Adlai."

She tilted her head in concession. "Adlai. We're the only ones left. Our friends and colleagues are either off the map, infected with the virutox, imprisoned or kidnapped. The number of people we can trust is vanishingly small and shrinking rapidly. If you can't tell me, who can you tell?"

His lips parted, then gradually rose into an endearing half-smile. "You make quite a convincing and depressing case. So we're partners in this fight, then? Your colleague indicated that wasn't an option."

"As we've covered, he isn't here at the moment. Partners."

"All right." He leaned back in his chair, crossed one leg over the other knee and visibly relaxed. "Advisor Blake Satair, who you heard me refer to earlier, is obviously involved on some level. That level appears to primarily involve making my life miserable, but it could go deeper. In fact, for your colleague to be subdued, taken and, presumably, held and interrogated at a secure location, someone high up in Justice is almost required to have orchestrated it.

Part of me hopes this does mean it's Satair, because if even more Justice Advisors are on the wrong side of the fight, our circumstances are...worse.

"As for Advisor Gemina Kail, she is first and foremost responsible for Nika's psyche-wipe five years ago, even if she acted at the Guides' behest."

Perrin nodded tightly. "I know."

"So you spoke to Nika after the...unfortunate events in the Mirai Tower data vault?"

"More like plugged a hole in her abdomen, helped a dyne carry her across the city and back home, situated her in a tank for five hours, *then* talked to her. But, yes."

Adlai buried his face in his hands. "Thank you. Thank you for rescuing her. It was my fault, what happened to her that night. I should have believed her straight off and protected her. But I didn't want my glass house of a world to shatter. I'm glad my mistake didn't—I'm glad the damage it caused was repairable. Literally and figuratively." He eyed her cautiously. "Still want to be partners?"

"Did you not know Nika was all right? I mean, at least as of a few days ago?"

"Oh, I did. At least as of a few days ago. And knowing it took the edge off the guilt, but not much more."

"I won't add to it. Yes, I still want to be partners. We're both drowning in guilt. We've both made mistakes." Joaquim's words at the transit hub crater echoed in her mind. "Don't we have to try to move forward? Try to do better?"

Adlai chuckled lightly. "You are a very wise woman."

"I'm so, so not. Trust me."

"We'll agree to disagree. Anyway, I expect Advisor Kail is involved to a greater extent than merely arranging psyche-wipes. She has the Guides' confidence and their ears. Unfortunately, this information doesn't help us much at present. In addition to using false names and nonexistent cutouts to obscure their crimes, either or both of Satair and Kail could be running innumerable Asterion agents, and those agents could have minimal to no knowledge of the true nature of or reason for their orders." He shrugged. "People tend to do what Advisors say."

She arched an eyebrow. "Not the people I know."

"I bet that's true. I'm definitely learning a lesson about follow-ing orders without question. A hard one." He glanced away, out the windows. "But I shouldn't whine. It's not a good look for me."

"Again, I say: if you can't whine to me, who can you whine to?"

"In addition to being wise, you are entirely too forgiving and compassionate of a woman, which is...wonderful, but I really mustn't abuse your kindness."

"I hadn't noticed. So how do we rescue Joaquim? That's his name: Joaquim. When you see him, don't tell him I told you."

"Understood. Can I ask, are you two together, or otherwise—" his cheeks flushed again "—never mind. It's none of my business."

The notion of an Advisor getting flustered around her was so preposterous, she laughed. "No. He's my best friend. I mean, in some respects Nika is, but...she's sort of a special case. Know what I mean?"

"I do."

"Joaquim and I have been through so much together. He needs me, to keep him grounded and to soften his edges. I need him, to keep me thinking with my head instead of my heart and to harden *my* edges." Stars, this man wasn't her therapist! She cleared her throat and sat up straighter. "More importantly, NOIR needs him. So how do we rescue him?"

A new sadness darkened Adlai's mist-gray eyes. "I'd wager this is where my grace period comes to a rather stark end. We don't."

Her lips moved, but words struggled to make it past her throat. "What do—"

"Not immediately. The fact that someone abducted him after our meeting means it's entirely possible that the Guides already know I'm working with NOIR. If so, they're watching every move I make, and the steps I'd have to take just to *maybe* find out where he's being held would result in my rapid removal from this office and likely imprisonment. Now, I'm willing to pay that price, but if I'm locked up, I can't do the work we *have* to be doing right now.

"Distributing the virutox vaccine to everyone we can get to accept it. Blocking the transport of as many convicts as possible to Zaidam. Keeping as many innocent people as possible from being convicted and imprisoned. Stopping the flood of people falling into a trap that's sending them gods know where to be subjected to gods fear what, and otherwise holding the line until Nika and Dashiel find answers and a way to bring an end to this madness." He sighed. "I am so, *so* sorry."

She pushed her chair back and stood, then went to stare out the windows. The world outside looked so far away, like a mirage forever out of reach. "Every part of my psyche wants to say screw all your bullshit and *demand* you help me rescue him. But the thing is, Joaquim would say the same thing you just did. He'd kick me out of NOIR and to the curb if he found out I let hundreds or thousands of people be sacrificed to whatever evil is taking them so I could pull his ass out of the fire."

She turned back to find Adlai watching her intently. She swallowed but didn't flinch. "Nika would be able to devise a way to do both."

"Maybe, maybe not. She's gotten herself psyche-wiped, shot, fallen out of a building and been forced to become a fugitive while trying to accomplish less. You? You're stepping up and making tough decisions in impossibly difficult circumstances. Don't sell yourself short."

Her face screwed up at him. "Are you trying to use flattery to get me to accept the bad news?"

"I'm nowhere near suave enough to pull off anything so artful as that. I'm being honest, because it's all I know how to be. And I have to believe it can get us through to the other side."

An awkward silence lingered for several seconds. She had no idea how to respond to him and end it.

Finally he cleared his throat. "I promise you, Perrin Benvenit, I will do everything I can that won't get me instantly arrested to find out where Joaquim is, who has him and how to free him. And I promise you that one day soon, we'll be able to do it. Because one day soon, this nightmare has to end. There is no other option for us."

31

WAYFARER

ASTERION DOMINION SPACE

They studied the projection of the Gennisi galaxy filling the cabin's free space. Pairs of dots connected by short lines created a jagged path that ascended in fits and starts up and across the right half of the galaxy. Two single dots bounded the path—one near the Synra stellar system, the other orphaned on the outskirts of the galaxy's upper left quadrant.

The records of the *Tabiji's* repetitive travels stacked atop one another with no deviation. A couple of squiggly lines beneath the first pair of dots accounted for trips to Zaidam, the secret space station and not much else.

Nika fisted a hand at her chin, eyes narrowing. "The *Tabiji* has been traveling to the opposite corner of the galaxy and back every few months for the last eight years, and traveling there fast. Which means these gaps between the location markers must be d-gate traversals, right?"

"It's a logical conclusion, but it begs the question of who placed them and when. The first recorded trip used them, so we have to assume it wasn't the *Tabiji*."

"Unless someone erased the records of the original journey. But why would they? No one was ever supposed to see this map."

"They didn't account for you." He flashed her a brief smile.

"No, they did not. How long would it take to make the trip to the final location marker if there were no d-gates?"

Dashiel ran a couple of calculations in his head. "If you went directly there, no stops along the way? With our best superluminal engine, about three weeks. But the gaps aren't in a straight line. They veer all over this half of the galaxy, as if the original purpose of the d-gates was not to provide a shortcut to whatever resides at the endpoint."

Her head tilted curiously...then she laughed. "Because it wasn't. These d-gates? You built them."

He leaned against the wall and crossed his arms over his chest. "I don't follow."

"This is the route the *Shorai* took."

"Are you sure?"

She reached out and splayed the fingers of her left hand to overlay the map. Annotations popped up beside each of the paired dots. "These are the locations of points of interest the *Shorai* encountered, according to the press releases."

He stared at her in puzzlement until she shrugged sheepishly. "After experiencing your memory and hearing how intrigued my former self was by the mission, I was intrigued as well. I did a bit of research."

He couldn't help but smile, if somewhat wryly. She hid it well, or perhaps their current circumstances demanded its suppression, but the dreamer side of her personality had survived the psyche-wipe mostly intact. And he was glad for it, even if his more practical nature meant it had often been a source of friction between them over the centuries.

"The starting point is one of the anchor d-gates near Synra, which were built specifically for use by the research teams tasked with following up on the *Shorai's* discoveries, and all the d-gate pairs line up with those discoveries—except the last stop. It doesn't have a companion d-gate or a press release to tout it."

He pointed to three annotations far afield of the *Tabiji's* travels, well on the left side of the galaxy. "But what about these over here?"

She paced through the map hologram to peer at them for a few seconds, then returned to his side. "Two possibilities I can think of. Either the *Shorai* found something at the terminus point that the Guides didn't want to make public—something the *Tabiji* is visiting repeatedly—then the *Shorai* continued on with its exploration, or...."

"Or the later press releases are fake." He sighed heavily. "I wonder, is the *Shorai* still flying at all? Or was it destroyed, and the Guides have neglected to inform their Advisors for *eight years*."

She winced. "I know what I'd put my money on, if I had any."

"Yeah."

"Mason Fassar...I must have known him."

"The Advisor who captained the *Shorai*? You were professional colleagues, but I wouldn't say he was your friend. Not outside of work. He is—or was, as now seems likely—a good man. Serious to the point of being taciturn, but dedicated to his work."

A shiver chilled Dashiel's skin. "And they haven't regened him. Are they so desperate to keep what happened to the *Shorai* a secret that they've stored his psyche all this time?"

"It's no worse than them psyche-wiping me to keep it."

"You know the depths of my rage about what they did to you. But, respectfully, yes, it *is* worse. At least they allowed you to draw a new breath—and stars, look what you've done with it. Nearly a decade on, he's still waiting to wake up again."

Her brow furrowed, and she left the map behind to go to the kitchen module. After digging around in the refrigeration unit for several seconds, she produced a sealed bottle of wine. "I need a drink. Do you want one?"

He opened his mouth to respond that of course he did, because he always did...then realized he hadn't entertained so much as an idle yearning for a drink since joining her on the ship. In truth, it had never been an addiction, merely a poor form of escape.

Did he desire one now? Yes. Because once upon a time he'd drank for enjoyment rather than escape. He'd done so with her at his side and he at hers. And though she couldn't know it—and gods willing she never would—with her offer she was erasing another scar from his psyche.

"Dashiel?"

"Yes, please."

She poured two glasses, returned to his side and handed him one. He brought the glass to his lips then held it there, letting the wine hover at his lips while he watched her take a long sip and gaze pensively at the map.

"You're right. About Fassar. It is worse, and they've done it to the rest of the *Shorai's* crew, too, I assume. It's unconscionable. You know, just a few weeks ago, when all this was first starting, Joaquim, Perrin and I had a conversation about how we as a society did *not* store people. Only, it appears we do. Not the criminals, either, but the explorers and the pioneers."

She shook her head roughly. "What are we saying here? That whatever the *Shorai* discovered and whatever the ship's fate, as a result of the discovery the Guides are kidnapping people, forcing them into a comatose state, stuffing them in stasis chambers and shipping them across the galaxy to the location in question?"

"Looks like." They both stood there silently for a while, letting the absurd yet unassailable conclusion sink in...then letting the implications spin out from it like ribbons in the wind.

Finally he sank onto the couch, set his glass on the side table and dropped his elbows to his knees. "The truth is, other than a rough start to our relationship with the Taiyoks and an incomprehensible encounter with the Sogain, we've had a fairly uneventful stay in the Gennisi galaxy. We staked our claim to our little corner of the galaxy and settled in, happy to be left alone to live how we chose.

"But this doesn't mean there aren't grave threats out in the cosmos—more terrifying than our imaginations can conjure—and remarkable wonders beyond our capacity to envision. It shouldn't be a surprise that when we finally went looking, we discovered one of them."

She nodded thoughtfully and shut off the map. "Well, I guess it's time for us to go find out which one."

MERGE (FIELD)

32

WAYFARER

ASTERION DOMINION SPACE

A towering d-gate floated placidly in the expanse of space. Its interior shimmered like a mirror with nothing to reflect.

Nika's hand hovered over the controls, ready to traverse the d-gate and cross kiloparsecs. But Dashiel was staring at the object with such intensity that she decided to let him have a moment.

Finally he spoke, though his gaze didn't deviate. "The design requirements were absurd. We had to build objects that when deployed would be larger than the vessel carrying them. Not a significant hurdle for most equipment, but quantum teleportation devices whose purpose is to open and maintain pathways that cut through the literal fabric of space? It's not so easy to make such technology foldable and collapsible."

"But you did."

"I did—or my people did. Because you were right. This is one of mine." He huffed a breath and relaxed into his chair. "Sorry. I don't usually dreamily wax philosophical over anything except you. Carry on."

"It's okay. I enjoy listening to you talk about your work."

"You do?"

"Well…it might be more accurate to say I enjoy you enjoying talking about your work." She turned her head until her hair fell across her face and hid her smile as she accelerated through the d-gate.

They emerged through the other side into space that looked much like the space they'd left. Dashiel had said the d-gates would have been secured in areas as devoid of activity as possible to reduce the chances of them being disrupted or destroyed by violent cosmic phenomena: supernovas, black holes, active stellar formation and so on. Therefore, whatever the *Shorai* had found here—according to the press release, a rare triple neutron star system—it was situated at least a hundred parsecs away. It also hardly mattered, as they weren't here to visit it.

A few hours later, the final d-gate floated in front of them as placidly as the first. But what had up to now been a leisurely journey hop-scotching across the galaxy now transformed into a perilous gambit. What waited on the other side must be the answer to a great many questions. They needed to not only discover this answer, but survive its discovery to return home and change its consequences.

Nika checked the settings on the Taiyok cloaking device, then threw some additional power its way. Next, she checked the native emission dampener and did the same for it. "We are now as invisible as any object possibly can be. We'll use impulse power on approach to the target location and tip-toe our way in."

"Sounds good. And at the first sign we've been detected or of an approaching threat, we'll bolt."

"Bolting is also prepped and ready."

"All right. Let's go."

GENNISI GALAXY, NORTHWEST QUADRANT

The sensor displays screamed out a cacophony of overlapping signals at them. The *Wayfarer* wasn't a scientific research ship, and it lacked the specialized equipment required to properly parse and analyze the plethora of data washing over it. The volume of noise was so overwhelming, in fact, the instruments were barely able to record it all.

"Whatever is here, it's not hiding its presence."

Nika frowned as her eyes darted between the scrolling sensor data and the viewport. "Which is why we are."

That the mystery here on the edge of the galaxy involved highly advanced technology, and thus presumably an advanced species, now seemed blindingly obvious. This was the noise of a civilization. But what kind of civilization, and of what inclinations, remained far less clear.

The basic astronomical analysis routine they'd installed proclaimed a white dwarf star system the source of the noise. Four planets orbited the star, but they were by and large silent. This implied the system was not the civilization's home, which wasn't notable in and of itself. But assuming the residents had been here for a minimum of eight years, one would think they'd have at least set up a smattering of groundside camps.

As she'd promised, they crept toward the star at an excruciatingly slow speed. Her pulse outpaced it by a fair margin, but she worked to remain otherwise calm. She'd once been a diplomat, a profession where progress often advanced more slowly than glacier flow; she could be patient for an hour.

At 0.7 AU out from the star, their sensors picked up two detached rings of objects orbiting at right angles to one another.

They received the first visual images when they were three megameters from intersecting one of the orbital paths, and she idled the ship briefly so they could study them. The design of the objects resembled nothing Asterions or Taiyoks built, and even Dashiel refused to hazard a guess as to their purpose.

"Can we determine scale? How big are these things?"

She scowled at the equipment controls...she should have downloaded more scientific databases. "Um, I think the sensor is saying the one in the image is roughly four hundred meters in diameter."

"So big."

An analysis algorithm spit out a factoid that based on the distance between the objects detected so far, in excess of four thousand of the objects orbited the star. She had to wonder...*big compared to what?*

Whatever the purpose of the orbital network, EM signals on every band were transmitting between it and the center of the system.

They sneaked through a gap between two of the objects and continued on.

At 0.4 AU out from the star, space began to get crowded. Given the comparative vastness of even short distances in space, this was no easy feat.

Ships flew in every direction—small ships, large ships, but most of all truly *enormous* ships. The shapes and hull configurations varied, but all were built of a dark, burnished metal that reflected almost no light.

Every so often, two of the ships met one another and docked together, interlinking as effortlessly as if they'd once been two halves of a whole, then separated and continued on.

The star at the center of the system was encased in a Dyson structure—not quite a shell, as it was porous, but a tight lattice more solid than a swarm and far more extensive than a series of rings. The star also wasn't a white dwarf at all, but the analysis algorithms could be forgiven for being led astray by the encasement.

Outside the Dyson structure, a ring of stations or platforms orbited the full circumference of the star.

She queried the algorithm for another quantity estimate...and sank back in her chair. Eleven *thousand*?

Each platform was the size of a city, something like twenty kilometers in diameter. The vessels arriving and departing each platform resembled insect swarms, so numerous were they.

Nika instinctively drew in her shoulders and curled her legs beneath her, as if she could make their ship smaller by making herself smaller. If they were less than a speck of dust, they might escape notice.

At 0.2 AU out from the star she brought the *Wayfarer* to a halt and completed their transformation into a hole in space.

It felt like they had wandered into the central hub of the universe itself. The technology on display was undeniably advanced, but other than the Dyson structure and the presence of objects identifiable as stations and ships, it was all so foreign in design and operation that it masqueraded as magic.

"This isn't some multi-species conglomerate. A single, monolithic species is driving this operation."

She glanced over at Dashiel. He hadn't spoken in several minutes, though neither had she. "Why do you say that?"

"The uniformity of design. Sure, the ships come in a variety of shapes and sizes, I assume depending on their function, but there's a certain sameness to every structure, from the ships as small as ours to those massive platforms."

She supposed he was right, but she didn't have his eye for manufacturing design details. "I expect these are the Rasu, then. But none of this answers the big question: what do they want with us?"

"I doubt it's to join their interstellar community of peaceful sapient beings."

"Wouldn't it have been fantastic if it were?"

He reached out to squeeze her hand. "So fantastic."

From four successive platforms, more ships than usual departed. Two megameters out from the stellar ring, they began forming up together.

She gestured toward the growing assembly to draw Dashiel's attention to it, then cautiously reengaged the impulse engine and eased toward it.

"Not too close. Kudos to the Taiyoks for their remarkable cloaking technology, but I don't think we should risk getting any closer to..." he eyed the busy flow of ship traffic surrounding them "...anything."

She dipped lower, below the gathering fleet from their perspective, and slowed to a stop, then peered upward through the viewport. "Are those weapons?"

"Well, of course they have weapons…." Dashiel trailed off as he craned his neck to join her in scrutinizing the mammoth ship above them.

Up close, the hull resolved into a deep purple hue. Across the entire underbelly, row after row of modules jutted out to break the hull's profile into jagged shards.

"They could be for breaking up asteroids or…moons. Planets." Dashiel sank against the dash to face her. "I'm not seeing anything that looks like a visitor center."

"Ha!" She laughed, less at the absurdity of the notion than at what it said about the entire situation. "I'm not either. Still, we haven't seen definitive evidence that they're hostile or aggressive, only that they're ridiculously advanced. And very busy."

He nodded. "The armaments make a compelling argument, but no, we haven't seen them fire on peaceful craft or…planets. But where are our people? Once they're brought here they don't return, so what happens to them? Are they having tea with the aliens inside one of these platforms?"

"If that were true, they wouldn't have needed to make the voyage in stasis chambers—it's a ten-hour trip. They wouldn't have needed to be kidnapped. And it would be Advisors here, not outpost workers and criminals." She considered the looming hull above them once again. Crept toward it.

"Nika, we're getting too close."

She craned her neck to the point of discomfort to gaze up at the weapons. The jagged shards appeared to be oblong crystalline formations, and their design was almost…familiar. They reminded her of something she'd seen before. But what?

"That's enough." Dashiel reached over and took charge of the controls, reversing thrusters to regain a bit of distance from the fleet.

A fleet which had now grown beyond the edges of their vision, even at a greater distance. While they'd been gaping at the one ship, a thousand more had joined it.

The smaller vessels began linking together like they'd seen some do on their way in. Small ships grouped together to become large ships.

The invaders stepped forward in unison, tightening their circle, as the remainder of their bodies liquefied. The individual units joined together to form a solid wall around the natives, then a ceiling.

She blinked, confused. Where in her memory stores had that come from? "We have to get closer. Just for a couple of seconds. I need to see how they're connecting to one another."

"Why does it matter?"

"Because I think I know something."

"But...okay." Dashiel shot her a dubious look, but he eased their ship up and forward. She ceded the controls fully to him and all but climbed on top of the narrow dash in an attempt to get fractionally closer to the viewport and thus to the merging vessels above them.

Merging.

The invading aliens stretched out their arm limbs, and what had earlier appeared to be metal or a hard mineral compound transformed into a pseudo-liquid. Now-fluid arms extended until they touched, then merged with one another.

The memory blended effortlessly into reality. All the small ships had now become large ships. Above them, two of the large ships approached one another. Several meters before their hulls touched, the metal comprising each hull lost its structure to become fluidic as each stretched out to touch the other. By the time the two ships met, it was as two fluids *merging* together. The metal gradually resolidified, until a single seamless hull existed where before there had been two.

The outer shells of the orbs dissolved, stretched out through the air and merged with one another to form a seamless ring.

She stumbled backward, half fell off the dash and collapsed into Dashiel's chair. They weren't interlinking. They were melding together.

"Nika, what's wrong?"

"I've seen the Rasu before. I've seen their technology in action. I've seen what they do to the species they encounter. Dashiel, we are in serious trouble."

He glanced out the viewport, where the large ships were now merging into the genuinely colossal ships, which then became...more colossal. "You're not making any sense. How could you possibly have seen them before?"

"I'll tell you the story once we get out of here, though it probably won't explain much, because I don't understand it either. But first, we should do the getting out of here. Trust me, we do not want to be captured by these aliens."

Neither of them reached for the controls, however. Instead they stared out at the forming behemoth, stunned into inaction by the impossibility of what their eyes showed them. When the final merging was complete, the weapons covering the underbelly lined up from bow to stern as if they had always belonged to a single ship.

Her vision blurred, and the ship, which now stretched nearly as long as one of the platforms, transformed into an image buried in the dregs of her memory. Now that she'd seen it, she couldn't unsee it. The color and texture of the metal, the design of the craft...there was not a shred of doubt in her mind. She'd seen the Rasu before. But how? And perhaps far more importantly, *why*? Also, by who's doing?

Space in front of the alien ship's bow began to contort. It churned in on itself, then took on defined shape. A bright vortex formed to swirl around an *absence* of space, falling into it like water circling a drain, yet never dissipating.

"We need to—"

"Yeah." Dashiel engaged the impulse engine, but his eyes remained glued to the vortex. They began reversing course as the gargantuan ship began accelerating forward—

—a shock wave slammed into the hull, sending them flipping end over end over end…until finally the gyrations ceased.

"Ugh." She lifted her head up from the floor, which was where she found herself. A variety of aches competed for attention, but the alerts coming from her OS were relatively minor in severity, so she ignored them to crawl back toward the cockpit.

Dashiel moaned from where he'd landed between the cockpit chairs, but he was sitting up by the time she reached him.

"Are you—?"

"Are you—?"

She started to laugh, then groaned instead. Both hurt. "I'll be fine. You?"

He nodded weakly, and they both pulled themselves up onto the dash.

The vortex and the merged leviathan that had created it were gone.

⋏R

"We're headed for empty space eighty parsecs from here. It should be far enough away for us to take a breath and get our bearings."

She mumbled an acknowledgement from the main cabin, where she'd gone to retrieve some disinfectant spray and bonding tape to tend their wounds. She gathered up the supplies in her arms and moved to the couch, where she dumped them on the table.

The floor quivered as the superluminal engine engaged, and a few seconds later Dashiel joined her in the cabin.

He knelt in front of her and picked up the disinfectant. She had a contact burn running up the inside of her forearm, and he held her arm still while he coated it with the cool, soothing spray. "Now, it's time you told me what in the hells you were talking about back there."

She exhaled carefully, as she might have a bruised rib or two. She was exhausted and in a moderate amount of pain. Also exhilarated, and a touch panicked. "I'll tell you what I remember, then we can try to figure out what it means.

"One night around three years ago, Perrin and I were at a club in downtown Mirai One, and a man approached us."

33

THREE YEARS AGO

MIRAI

Peregrine Pointe took up nearly the entire block, complete with glittering signage and a welcoming entry pavilion. *Escape from your troubles lies through these doors*, it whispered in dulcet tones.

As soon as they were inside, Perrin took her hand and headed toward the bar. "Drinks first. Then, adventure."

Nika ordered a glass of shiraz and gazed around idly. A spacious dance floor dominated the central area of the club, with luminescent ribbons dangling from a soaring ceiling and a translucent floor that revealed a mirage of shifting vistas beneath it. Billboards above a series of wide archways along the right-side wall pointed the way to the club's more immersive offerings.

"Excuse me, did I hear one of you lovely ladies say you sought adventure?"

The speaker was a plain-looking man wearing a teal vest that marked him as an employee. Perrin leaned against the bar and arched an eyebrow. "Maybe. What are you offering?"

The man flourished a hand. "Adventure, naturally." He held up a plastic weave case. "Our newest simex, just out of design. We only received it this morning, so you can be the first to experience this amazing escapade. It will blow your psyche. Not literally, of course."

"What's the content?"

"You're vacationing on an exotic alien world when an invasion begins. You have to sneak onboard the invading ship and stop the attack. You'll be provided with the necessary weapons and gear, but

whether you succeed or fail will depend on how clever and re-
sourceful you can be."

He clearly did not know who he was talking to. Nika checked
with Perrin, who shrugged enthusiastically. Perrin was one of the
few people Nika had met who could pull off an enthusiastic shrug.
"We're in."

"Excellent." The man gestured toward the first archway. "My
name's Darien. Follow me."

⋏ℝ

Leaves tickled Nika's cheek, and—ow!—rough bark scraped a
layer of skin off her palm. The hells was she doing in a tree?
"Perrin—"

The light arrived first, in an explosion of blinding violet. Unprepared for the assault on her visual receptors, Nika frantically
blinked away blinding halos.

The shock wave arrived next, carrying a thunderous roar on its
heels.

"Hang on!" She took her own advice and wound her arms
around the limb above her as the tree bent almost horizontal from
the force then ricocheted back to vertical.

"Ahhh!" Perrin squealed from off to her right. Same tree,
around on the other side of the trunk.

The tree's swaying eased with every pendulum-like pass, but
Perrin continued to fight off tiny leafed limbs that were smacking
her in the face, leaving behind a web of shallow cuts. "Stupid, evil
tree!"

Nika looked back toward where the blinding light had origi-
nated. She expected to find a raging fire, but instead a precise,
controlled beam of light scorched the jungle down to the soil in a
perfect circle over a kilometer in diameter.

The source of the beam was an enormous ship. A hull of burnished aubergine took the form of an octagon with the edges
smoothed out. It hovered vertically several hundred meters above

the ground, sending the beam cascading out from a tapered cluster of milky white crystals.

As the ship descended toward what had once been jungle but was now a cleansed and barren landing area, the violet light faded away and the hull seemed to...flatten out? No, it must be an optical illusion.

A rustling noise grew in the depths of the jungle behind them. Something advanced on their location. She waved at Perrin to get her attention, then held a finger to her lips.

Two dozen creatures stalked through the jungle's ubiquitous groundcover toward the clearing. Fur covered their bodies in hues ranging from pale honey to rich sienna. They were bipedal, with thick legs and arms and blocky heads dominated by oversized, wide-set eyes. They all carried large, two-handed weapons that resembled long guns.

Were they seriously planning to *attack* the alien vessel? Points for bravery, if not for smarts.

Perrin reached around the trunk to nudge her in the arm then pointed to the vessel in question.

It had ceased its descent twenty meters above the ground. The upper reaches of the hull disappeared into low cloud cover, obscuring its true size.

Along the outer rim, a platform detached fully from the hull and descended the rest of the way to the ground. It carried fifteen...from this distance she couldn't be certain if they were organic beings or mobile machines. They stood a full four meters tall, and their exterior was a uniform, dull aubergine—the same color as their ship.

As soon as the platform settled onto the dirt, the aliens-or-alien-machines fanned out toward the jungle, slightly to the west from their tree. They didn't wield any obvious weapons.

A series of *pops* echoed from the edge of the clearing beneath her and Perrin, where the native creatures had taken up defensive positions. Slugs bounced off several of the invaders, causing no damage.

Those hit pivoted in the direction the shots had come from. In a single long stride they accelerated to incredible speed, and in less than two seconds they had reached the jungle.

The natives continued firing. Again, points for bravery. The invaders split into two groups to flank the natives and drive them into the clearing, then in a blur surrounded them.

In evident desperation, the natives fired once more. Their weapons used pneumatic propulsion to lob hardened slugs with impressive velocity, but to no effect.

The invading aliens stretched out their arm limbs, and what had earlier appeared to be metal or a hard mineral compound transformed into a pseudo-liquid. Now-fluid arms extended until they touched, then merged with one another. The invaders stepped forward in unison, tightening their circle, as the remainder of their bodies liquefied as well.

The individual units joined together to form a solid wall around the natives, then a ceiling. Both re-hardened, and the cage they'd created flipped over, scooping all the natives into the depression like a ladle dipping into soup. The top edges re-liquefied and seeped toward the center until a new ceiling formed to create an impervious container. The structure floated up into the air and returned to the platform, which ferried the whole assembly into the ship.

The invaders had their first prisoners.

Other units—no way could they be organic—that hadn't partaken in the capture busily disassembled wide swaths of the jungle. They transformed themselves into huge saws to slice down trees or into massive trowels to excavate dirt. Taking specimens, harvesting resources, or both.

Nika dragged her horrified gaze away from the activity to check on Perrin. Her friend clung to the trunk of their tree, eyes wide as saucers and skin blanched. Blood had welled up in several of the cuts crisscrossing her face.

"So, according to Darien, we're supposed to sneak onboard the ship and disable it somehow. But if you want to say 'screw it,' exit out of the simex and go get another drink, I would be perfectly fine with it."

Perrin's nose scrunched up as she scowled in the direction of the ship. "No. Let's do it. It'll be fun."

"I don't believe you."

"Neither do I, but let's give it a shot anyway. First step: get out of this tree." Perrin studied the branches beneath her, then loosened her grip on the trunk, knelt and eased a leg down, stretching for the next branch—

—her foot slipped across the narrow limb, and she lost her balance and fell forward. Her shoulder slammed into one of the branches, but she managed to grab onto it briefly, until her fingertips slid off. She plummeted the remaining twelve meters into the groundcover below, sideswiping two additional branches on the way down.

"Perrin!" Nika scrambled down the tree as swiftly as she dared while trying not to suffer the same fate. Her palms, fingers and forearms were bloody by the time she reached the ground, but she landed on her feet.

"Ugh." Perrin moaned from where she lay face-first amid the leafy groundcover.

Nika knelt beside her. "Talk to me. Are you okay?"

"What kind of…question…is that?" She gingerly rolled onto her back. "Ow. I think my arm is broken. Or my neck."

Nika laughed kindly. "Come on now, your neck's not broken. You're moving."

"If you say so." She put a hand on the ground and tried to sit up, but collapsed back on the ground. "Ohhh, but I was right about the arm."

"That's enough. End program."

Nothing happened. "Exit program." Nothing. "Exit simex."

Nothing. What the hells?

"Don't tell me we're in a defective simex!"

Nika rubbed at her jaw, which only succeeded in getting blood all over her face. "I think we're in a defective simex. You play in these more often than I do. What should we do?"

"Well...." Perrin used her left hand to reach a semblance of a sitting position. "In challenge simexes, if you achieve the objective, it exits on its own. Otherwise, since it's a rental, it will time out eventually, but it could be a couple of hours. If that's our best option, just whack me in the head with one of these branches and knock me out until then."

"I'm not going to hit you in the head." Nika inventoried what she had on her person. The simex had provided a Glaser, a fifteen-centimeter retractable blade and a small module. Curious, she activated it.

"What—where did you go?"

She switched it back off. "Some type of kamero filter. Okay. You're in no condition to storm the giant spaceship. Let's get you comfortable against the base of the tree. I can use the kamero filter to sneak onboard with the next load of material they take up. Once I'm there, I'll figure something out."

"No way. Make me a sling out of your shirt, and I'll be set. I can shoot with one arm."

"Are you *sure*?"

Perrin's mouth set into a resolute line. "Yep. This is my fun, dammit."

Stars, Perrin was stubborn! Nika pulled her shirt up over her head, leaving her in a black lace camisole. They *had* been at a club.

She ripped the shirt into a long strip. Perrin whimpered a little as they positioned her arm across her chest, and Nika tried to be more gentle as she wrapped the sling around Perrin's neck and tied it.

"I know it hurts, but is it secure?"

Perrin nodded weakly. "I'm good. Totally...good."

None of it was real, but the pain signals Perrin was experiencing were indistinguishable from genuine pain so long as they were in the simex. "Then let's get this over with. Activate your kamero filter module, and we'll move to the edge of the clearing. When the platform lowers again, we'll creep across the clearing, hop on it and stand still as statues. I have no idea how good these kamero filters are."

Perrin gestured forward with her working arm. "After you."

ᴧℝ

They stood frozen on the platform. Nika held her breath, afraid the slight rise and fall of her chest would give her away. Barely a meter away, one of the conglomerated machines hauled a tonne of uprooted plant life up into the ship. Up close, the merged substance forming the hauler bore no distinguishing characteristics. Smooth but not lustrous, it looked as hard as stone in its current shape, though evidently that was subject to change.

The platform floated upward—no visible mechanisms connected it to the hull—until blackness consumed them.

Because it was *dark* inside the ship. With normal vision, it felt as if they had fallen upwards into a featureless, endless void. Whatever method the metal shapeshifters used for sight, it was not based on visible light.

Hq (visual) | scan.infrared(360°) | highlight.thermal(>20°)

The lines of walls, a floor and ceiling took indistinct shape. Tall, wide hallways stretched in three directions.

The hauler floated off the platform and took its cargo down the right hallway.

She pinged Perrin, not daring to speak aloud.

Let's check out the hallway ahead.

You don't think we should follow the carrier thing?

Nope. To get out of this hellscape, we have to stop the attack. Important ship systems are always toward the center, where they are most protected.

She wasn't sure how she knew that, but it had all the markers of fact rather than supposition.

But what about the native aliens they captured? Shouldn't we try to free them?

Nika wanted to respond that they weren't real, none of this was real, and the natives' fate didn't matter, because they didn't have one.

But, again, it *felt* real.

All right. Let's follow the hauler and search for the captives.

She started to admonish Perrin to keep some distance between them and the hauler, but it had sped ahead and disappeared from sight.

Sporadic openings cut into the left wall, with no visible doors to close them off. All the openings were quite large—twice as tall and six times as wide as an average Asterion—and the rooms they led to appeared cavernous, at least until darkness swallowed them. Many of the rooms held raw materials already scavenged from the surface: flowers, plants, wood, even piles of simple dirt. Alien units of various shapes sifted through the treasure, scanned it using small orbs, tore it apart or carried it off deeper into the ship.

A series of thuds echoed from one of the rooms ahead. A second later, a hauler floated into the hallway. As it did, its solidness melted away, and it separated into four undulating blobs. Each of the blobs gained structure and took on the bipedal form they'd seen earlier—

—and began walking straight toward them.

Nika shoved Perrin inside the nearest room and flattened herself along the interior wall. In thermal profile, Perrin cradled her arm against her chest.

Did I hurt you? I'm sorry.

It's okay. Better than getting captured by those...things. What should we call them? All I can think is 'things.'

Hells if I know. Let's call them...Segmenters.

She peeked out into the hallway. The Segmenters had disappeared for the moment, so she grasped Perrin's good hand and returned to the hallway.

Twenty meters from a dead end, a new hallway opened up to the left. Lacking other options, they took it.

Now openings cut into both walls. On the right, small creatures were enclosed in force-field cages. Native wildlife? Orbs buzzed around the cages, scanning the wildlife with powerful beams.

Nika hesitated for half a step before forcing herself to continue on past the room. Saving the sentient natives was going to be difficult enough without adding wild animals into the mix.

Two more rooms filled with wildlife followed before they found the natives. Like the animals, they were held captive in individual force-field cages, lined up in two rows along the walls. Like the animals, orbs scanned each of them exhaustively. She cycled through the EM bands and registered signals emitting from the orbs on every one.

Some of the natives cried, while others shouted in an unknown tongue. Several made mewling noises and curled up in balls on the floor. Others banged on the force fields constraining them, only to yank back singed, paw-like hands in pain.

She and Perrin had been standing in the doorway gaping in horror for almost thirty seconds when intense gamma wave pulses unexpectedly burst out of the floating orbs.

The natives in the cages *melted*. In the blink of an eye, all that remained of them were soupy puddles of blood, tissue and bone fragments.

"Ah!" Perrin slapped a hand over her mouth, but it was too late. Every orb spun toward the doorway.

Nika grabbed Perrin's hand, and they took off running.

She instinctively continued down the hallway rather than retreating the way they'd come. She'd internalized the simex's mission, and they had a ship to disable.

The kamero filters obscured their movements, but their footfalls weren't silent. Infrared waves sent by their pursuers washed over them, and she couldn't say whether or to what extent the cloaking device blocked the scans.

Two Segmenters rushed out of an opening ahead and pivoted their way.

In here!

She veered to the left, still intuitively heading toward the center of the ship, and they ducked inside yet another of the storage rooms-turned labs-turned dissection chambers.

But if they stayed here, a trap would close in around them, much as it had on the natives outside. They needed to move. Luckily, much like in all the rooms they'd seen so far, this one had a matching opening at the far end. Doors didn't seem to be a concept the Segmenters bothered with.

Slow down and walk quietly.

Another hallway, more rooms. They turned right, then left.

The rooms got even bigger. No longer acting as storage or prisons, they now held equipment. The designs were utterly foreign, and she had no idea what their purposes might be. No Segmenters monitored or used the equipment, yet electrical illumination suggested most of it was operational.

Curiosity got the better of her, and she paused to examine one of the modules. The exterior looked exactly like the hull and walls of the ship. Exactly like each form the Segmenters had taken on. Were they—?

Perrin tugged on her arm before she could chase the thought to its conclusion.

More are coming!

She peeked over her shoulder to see a cadre of orbs and four bipedal Segmenters sweeping the hallway behind them.

This way.

They tiptoed through the next opening.

The next hallway opened up into a circular room at least a hundred meters wide and forty tall. Along the perimeter, stacks of unattended but active equipment filled every available space. In the center of the room, the floor fell away.

From the cavern below, a circular vortex rose up to grasp for an aperture in the ceiling high above it like an inverted tornado. But it never reached its destination, and though Nika's skin prickled from the electrical charge saturating the air, the vortex appeared to be stable.

What is it?

A power source, I think. For the engine, or possibly the weapon.

She sidled closer to the rim of the cavern and peered down into it.

Be careful!

Bright plasma churned in violent agitation. A thrashing pool of hellfire giving birth to the vortex.

Or was it the other way around? Twenty meters below, electricity leapt from the thrashing plasma to charge an enormous cluster of crystals in the depths of the cavern. The weapon.

Did it run this way all the time, or was it powering up to be used again?

She stepped back and hunted around for anything that looked like a power switch. Okay, obviously not a literal power switch, but something that served the function of a power switch. Some cable she could slice in two or disconnect from a socket; some signal throughput she could disrupt.

A panel nearby caught her attention. Glowing strips running across it pulsed in time with the rhythm of the vortex. She moved in front of it, extended her blade and tried to cut into the frame surrounding one of the strips.

The edge of the blade slid along the metal like a washcloth, and in its wake the metal remained smooth and unmarred. This model of blade could cut through the toughest of metals, but it couldn't so much as scratch the alien surface.

The room—the whole ship—lurched, and she stumbled backward, toward the cavern. Perrin grabbed her hand and flung her in the opposite direction. They both crashed into a wall packed with equipment, and shrill noises rang through the air.

Are we taking off? Crap, we've got to get off the ship!

All the reasons why it was already far too late for escape sprung to mind and were immediately shoved aside as the vortex drastically increased in brilliance. Power bled off it to set her skin afire, and her veins vibrated in resonance with the crystals beneath them.

Cover your eyes!

She squeezed her own eyes shut and flung her arm over her face as she spun away. Even so, searing light flared across the back of her eyelids.

Then everything stilled.

She cautiously lowered her arm. The vortex was gone. Within the confines of the cavern, the plasma evaporated into a mist and faded away. In the absence of the vortex, the room darkened toward the inky blackness that shrouded the rest of the ship.

What had the weapon done to the planet below? They hadn't passed a single viewport, so there was no way to see, but her imagination helpfully provided a visual of frenzied conflagration consuming everything in its path.

Nika? I tried to cover my eyes with my right arm. It was just instinct. But I couldn't because of the sling and....

What's wrong?

I can't see. At all. I'm blind.

She found herself thankful for the lack of light. Yet she grasped Perrin by the shoulders and looked anyway. Carbon scorch marks ran in jagged rivulets out from Perrin's eyes, which were now empty cavities.

She swallowed a gasp of horror as sound returned in the form of hurried, heavy footsteps from the hallways behind them.

She took Perrin's good hand in hers and clasped their fingertips together.

See through me. We have to run.

She took care to glance away, so Perrin's first sight would not be of her own destroyed eyes.

I'm ready.

They sprinted around the cavern toward the opposite side of the room. She had no destination in mind beyond the briefest safe haven that might be found by way of a hallway beyond.

When they were a meter away from an archway, the wall around it melted and closed off their exit.

She spun around, searching for another way out. Spotted an opening to the left and took off toward it.

Multiple Segmenters entered the room from every entrance. But since there weren't so many entrances, it was entirely possible they'd materialized out of the walls.

Despite being unfathomable, the true nature of the aliens was now starkly clear to her: no Segmenters tended the plethora of equipment because the equipment tended itself. The ship *was* the crew.

Dread settled into Nika's gut. She recognized their situation for what it was. The mobile Segmenters had swept the whole ship, tightening the net room by room. There was no escape.

Twenty or so of the orb Segmenters swept in to circle the perimeter of the room and complete the trap.

With her free hand, Nika retrieved her Glaser from her hip, set it to full strength and fired on the closest orb.

The only sign the energy made contact with the alien was a brief, slight shimmer along its exterior.

She fired on one of the bipedal Segmenters standing watch outside the circle. Same result. The Glaser was of no use against them. Blades were of no use against them. The aliens must have a weakness, but it was not on display here.

The outer shells of the orbs dissolved, stretched out through the air and merged with one another to form a seamless ring around her and Perrin. Along the walls, the various equipment similarly liquefied at the edges, which stretched out to form thin protective layers over themselves. The floor surrounding the cavern and its crystals did the same, a fluid metal expanding across the opening until the cavern was sealed away.

I don't understand what's happening.

Sorry, Perrin. I think we're about to lose the challenge.

Nika took a deep breath and picked an orb to stare down in defiance. The small opening at its center burned a dazzling violet—

Nika blinked until the walls of the simex room came into focus. Her heart throbbed against her sternum in time to her pulse hammering against her temples. The panicked memory of a nanosecond of agony slinked off into the shadows, and she gladly let it go.

Not real. A sensory fabrication. *Here* was real. The cushioned chaise beneath her, the muffled cadence of music leaking through the walls from the dance floor, the gaudy nightclub lighting that cast the room in a pinkish hue.

She disengaged from the interface and sat up.

Beside her, Perrin grumbled as she did the same, then manipulated her right arm around while scowling at it. "It's not broken any longer, but I swear it still hurts." She eased off the chaise and retrieved the weave from the small module between them. "Well, that *blew*. Let's go try to get our credits refunded."

"A worthy mission I can get behind." Nika rubbed at her face, ran her hands through her hair and tweaked various muscles in further efforts to reorient herself to reality. Perrin seemed to be bouncing back with no trouble. Then again, Perrin was a simex aficionado.

Nika had always found them unsettling, bordering on creepy, even the ones far more mundane than terrifying shapeshifting alien invasions. Probably something to do with the gaping emptiness in her mind where her past should be.

Pounding music and strobing lights assaulted them as they made their way out of the simex wing and into the main area. Gods, did she have a headache.

Perrin strode up to the man working the simex kiosk in a huff. "We were given a broken simex. We want a refund."

The man smiled politely. "What was broken about it?"

"The exit command didn't work. We couldn't get out until the aliens killed us."

"Aliens? Can I see the weave?"

Perrin glared at him suspiciously as she handed it over.

He studied the identifying markings on the front, then

checked the other side as well. "Nice try. This isn't one of our weaves. Also, we don't currently offer any simexes involving aliens killing people."

Nika stepped up beside Perrin. "We're not trying to scam you. One of your employees approached *us* to push the simex. He took us into the simex suites, loaded it into one of your interface feeds and activated it."

"What was his name?"

"Um…Darien something."

"Nobody by that name works here. If you're not scamming me, you got scammed yourselves."

"Fucking fuck…." Perrin groaned melodramatically. "Why would anybody go to all that trouble for a few lousy credits? Oh, never mind!" She spun around and pushed Nika toward the bar. "Come on. I need so many drinks right now."

Nika paused long enough to wave an acknowledgement of the man's perfunctory apology then followed Perrin—

Remember this. When the time comes, you must remember what you have seen.

She pulled up sharply and looked around. Everyone in the vicinity was paying her no mind. No one watched her meaningfully or scurried away into the crowd. She checked her comm system, but no message had come in through the nex web from any external source. There was no record of any message at all.

On discovering she was alone, Perrin reversed course and came back for her. "What's wrong?"

"Did you hear that?"

"Hear what?"

"Someone said, or transmitted, that I needed to remember what I'd seen. When the time came."

Perrin snorted. "Remember it? Hells, no. I'm erasing the memory of it forever the instant we get back to The Chalet."

34

WAYFARER

GENNISI GALAXY, NORTHWEST QUADRANT

Dashiel studied her silently, but it wasn't a stare of incredulity or disbelief. Instead, she could almost see the investigative algorithms churning away behind his analytical eyes.

"Someone targeted you three years ago. They knew you had once been Nika Kirumase, and they wanted *you* to comprehend the nature and extent of the threat the Rasu represented."

"Why do they need to have known who I used to be?"

"Because five years ago, you were on the verge of discovering what the Guides were hiding about the Rasu, and you got psyche-wiped for it. The fact that you were already hunting the Rasu—even if you didn't yet understand that was what you were doing—is the only logical reason for a stranger to choose you for receipt of this information."

Was it? It qualified as the height of egotism for her to presume there was any more consequential reason. "Wouldn't this mean someone in the government—an agent for the Guides—was tracking me all along? Ever since the psyche-wipe? Because that doesn't make any sense. If they knew who and where I was, they'd have known what I was doing. They would've crushed NOIR out of existence the instant we began to cause trouble."

"You would think. But maybe it wasn't someone working for the Guides."

"Who else could it be?"

He eyed her speculatively; he really seemed to be enjoying trying to unravel the mystery, though it mostly frustrated her.

"Evidently, someone in possession of a great deal more information about the Rasu than we have. Enough to be able to track them and capture details of their invasions then craft a virtual scenario modeled after one of those invasions."

"In the absence of the Guides' technology and resources, I don't see how that can be any Asterion. A Taiyok? They can field the stealth tech needed to track a ship unseen, but I don't think they have engines powerful enough to keep up with a Rasu vessel. And while they aren't the friendliest of species, they *are* our allies. If they possessed this kind of information on the enemy, they wouldn't share it with *me*. They'd share it with the Guides."

"Don't be so sure. You were our ambassador. You had their trust, which is far more important to most Taiyoks than governmental hierarchies."

The memory of her meeting with the Elder, so impossibly long ago, rushed back into her mind in full living color. "Maybe. But they'd never deliver this intel via a simex. They don't use them, they don't understand how to create them. They'd just show me whatever footage they'd captured and take their leave."

She sighed wearily. Retelling the story had in some ways been nearly as exhausting as experiencing it. "But who, then? We're running out of available suspects."

"The voice you heard…you said it didn't originate from any nex address?"

"Not only that—it didn't originate from within the nex framework at all. It was, quite literally, a disembodied voice in my head. And do not ask me if I was freaked out by the simex and imagined it. I was absolutely freaked out by the simex, but I know the difference."

"I take you at your word. But then what you're describing sounds like a telepathic communication."

She spread her arms in an exaggerated shrug by way of non-answer.

Dashiel stood and went to get a glass of water. Halfway back to the couch, he stopped. "The Sogain?"

"The Sogain aren't our friends. They might as well be our enemies. We have zero ongoing relations with them and no way to start a dialog. Two hundred thousand years ago, they threatened to disintegrate us into space dust if we so much as approached their stellar system ever again, and proved they could make good on the threat."

"Which means they arguably have the technology to explain your experience."

"But not why they would care enough to arrange it. Or why they would know who the fuck I was or am. Your theory requires that they are watching us, and not from afar. Intimately."

"Granted. And we have no reason to believe they're doing so. Of course, how would we recognize it if they were? We don't even know what they look like. We don't know anything at all about them, beyond evidence of their technology being highly advanced and their claim of wanting to be left alone."

Her brow wrinkled up at him. "So even if it was the Sogain, this doesn't give us an actionable path forward. And if it wasn't them, then it must have been a player we've never seen and never met, and thus can't possibly guess the identity of. Again, square one with no moves."

She buried her face in her hands. "It doesn't matter. It doesn't matter who targeted me with the nightmare of a simulation, only that they *did*. Because of it, I'd be willing to bet I know more about our enemy than any other Asterion.

"And what I know is this: if the Guides think they've escaped the Rasu's wrath by making some manner of deal with them, they're hopelessly naive. They're deluding themselves, and I have to make them recognize their mistake. The ship Perrin and I infiltrated? It was less than one tenth the size of the amalgamated leviathan that went through that vortex in space. And from the looks of their stronghold, they can create hundreds of thousands of those leviathans on a whim."

"Time to go home?"

She nodded grimly. "Time to go home."

∧R

A cool breeze stirred the grasses beneath my feet, sending the blade tips to tickle my ankles. I wore sandals, shorts and a thin, gauzy top, because in the summer on Synra one could hardly wear anything more.

But this wasn't Synra. This was—or would soon be—Mirai.

A hand grabbed mine and tugged at it with emphatic urgency. "Nika, come. You must see the simply divine harbor just over the ridge. If the capital city is not erected on this precise spot, I shall pitch a fit the likes of which the Gennisi galaxy has never seen."

I grumbled, but merely for effect, and followed along behind Maris as she bounded toward the twinkling cerulean waters that teased the horizon.

Behind us, an army of mecha unloaded thousands of crates from the three cargo vessels sitting in the expansive meadow. Building a functioning colony here would take weeks; a self-sufficient one, years; a living, vibrant world, decades, perhaps centuries. But the work of doing so began today.

When we reached the ridge and the land sloped downward to reveal the harbor in full, Maris stopped, crossed her arms flamboyantly over her chest—a gesture only she managed to pull off without appearing comical—and nodded matter-of-factly. "Ah! Yes. Quite lovely."

The waters stretched in a glittering blue-green palette to the horizon. I knew they belonged to a lake almost forty kilometers wide, but from here it was indistinguishable from a true ocean. I smiled, but stayed a step behind Maris so she couldn't see it. The longer I played coy, the more lavish the performance became. "I bet the water is freezing."

A luxurious sigh fell from Maris' lips. "I do hope so. I have been sweating on Synra for..." she gazed back at me "...how many millennia?"

"One hundred twenty-two."

"Right. One hundred twenty-two millennia. I've contemplated

giving up on this whole 'physical body' nonsense and climbing back into a SAI box every single day for at least the last thirty-four."

"You overly grandiose drama queen, you are not going to stop being a proper Asterion simply because you don't like what the Synra humidity does to your hair, when you can change your hair with barely more effort than the decision to do it."

"Nika Kirumase! I should denounce you, but I'm too impressed by your ability to successfully insult me thrice over in a single sentence. I will concede the first, but I must take issue with the second and third. My reasons for retreating into hardware, were I to do so, would be only...thirty-one percent related to the meter-wide explosion of frizz that is my hair when on Synra. Also, my hair is who I am, and to change it would be tantamount to undergoing an R&R.

"Finally, time was, being an Asterion consisted of a worldview, not a defined state of existence. Physical, digital, quantum? A single state or all at once? Those distinctions were minor window dressing. They didn't matter a whit."

"I remember. I was there, too. But that was a different time and a different galaxy, and we were fighting to become something greater—better—than simply Anaden. Now, being an Asterion means this. Us. Organic and synthetic fused together as one. Physical, but never-ending, for so long as one wishes. Then, to begin again. To learn, experience and grow, within oneself and through the world around us."

Maris stared at me for several seconds, and I began to entertain the possibility that I had actually rendered her speechless. If so, I deserved an award.

Finally her focus drifted to the cerulean waters. "Want to go for a swim?"

"We didn't bring swimwear."

"Not an impediment." Maris pulled her flowing tank top up over her head and used it to tie her wild hair back as she strode toward the shore.

"But..." I glanced toward the bustling camp in the distance "...there are...."

"Machines. There are machines watching."

I rolled my eyes and made a dramatic act out of relenting. "Fine, but only for a minute. We have work to do."

"Do we ever." Maris paused a few steps from the lapping water, as if she were waiting for the next wave to grasp for her toes and reel her in. "This isn't Asterion Prime. But with some time and the judicious application of a sense of style and panache, I think it can be home."

ᐱR

Nika opened her eyes, but took care not to bolt upright in the bed. She didn't want to wake Dashiel, who slept beside her. Far too peacefully, given what they'd seen today.

She carefully laid his hand that she'd borrowed over his chest, then sank back into her pillow. She was half-convinced this 'memory' was nothing more than a dream, because how could it be real?

It violated half a dozen Dominion laws for her recently former self to have claimed the name of one of her progenitors, but despite how intensely personal the memory had felt, this was the only explanation.

But weren't there records? Wouldn't the Guides have discovered the violation and never named her an Advisor? And what were the odds of that progenitor being friends with an ancestor of Maris Debray five hundred thousand years ago?

She appreciated that her former selves had held onto the memory of the founding of Mirai across those many millennia—it was a treasure, truly—but the oddities of it frankly soured the experience a bit.

She sighed quietly. Sometimes these recovered memories made less sense than the Rasu simex did...gods, the Rasu. Confounding as it was, at least the memory had allowed her to forget about the aliens for a few precious minutes.

But now it all came rushing back. What in all the worlds could she do to protect her people from such an enemy?

35

NAMINO

Grant strolled the aisles of the Namino Two Makers Market with a casual gait and a practiced eye. While he built most of his tools and equipment himself, thousands of hours of frustration over the years had driven him to the conclusion that it was way more practical to buy rather than build the base components that went into them.

But only because he didn't yet have a chemical lab in his factory.

In truth, he owed this particular trip to the Makers Market to the hour spent talking Ridani through rigging the Taiyok stealth module into the ship—an hour which he had to admit had gone better than expected. Ridani was a smart man, and he knew materials and networking hardware nearly as well as Grant did. But the ad hoc installation had highlighted several weaknesses in his standard design approach for onboard ship components, and in the quest for constant, iterative improvement, he wanted to address them.

As he stepped into a shop on the left, he sensed more than saw his shadow pause.

He'd picked up the tail not long after arriving in Namino Two. As far as he could determine, it was a single man, likely a low- or mid-level Justice officer. The surveillance cams must have alerted the local Justice office when he dared to leave home.

Oh, well. He was happy to waste an officer's afternoon. And while the part of him that lived for his craft itched to get back to the factory and get some work done, he did enjoy perusing the latest offerings at the Makers Market. So he'd take his time, perhaps a bit more leisurely than he otherwise would have. He might even go so far as to stop for dinner at a decent restaurant before returning home.

The shop didn't have quite what he was looking for, so after browsing for a minute he exited and continued on. So did his shadow.

Ahead, the wide hallway split into two directions. Previous visits had taught him that the shops along the left path focused on consumer-oriented products, so he started to take the right split—then realized his shadow had vanished. Of course, he didn't actually have visual sensors in the back of his head, so it was possible the man had gotten caught up in the shopper traffic and lost Grant for a few seconds. But as the crowd thinned at the split, his shadow didn't reappear.

Maybe the man's superiors had concluded the tail was pointless and called him off to go investigate something legitimately important.

Grant hadn't been doing anything illegal or even unsavory, but he nevertheless relaxed in the absence of watching eyes. Days of constant surveillance had been wearing on him more than he cared to admit. He was a private man, and he preferred to choose when, with whom and how much of himself he revealed.

Which got him mulling over what Ridani had said about Nika. Psyche-wiped, truly? This changed everything he'd believed about her. If only she'd told him, he could have helped—

Intrusion attempt via exposed pathways detected.
Defensive blocks initiated.

He pulled up short, and the person behind him bumped into him. He gestured a distracted apology.

Hq(def) | report.dt(6 seconds)
Nanobot-infused particles detected in the environ-
ment. Defensive blocks successfully activated to
prevent physical intrusion. Blocks will remain in

*place until nanobot saturation drops below 0.01
ppm.*

The air looked no different than it had a minute ago, but everyone here was breathing its newly invasive contents into their lungs and their bodies.

Since Nika went on the run, and especially since the friendly visit from Justice, he'd begun paying closer attention to NOIR's actions and broadcasts. He'd monitored the off-grid nex hubs, and given what he didn't know as much as what he did, he'd quietly upgraded and fortified his personal defensive measures. Weirdness was abounding of late, and he didn't intend to get caught unawares.

He stumbled forward as someone bumped into him from behind again. He didn't think it was his mistake this time, but he gestured another apology in case—

"You think you're special? You think you own the whole damn hallway?" A skinny man with straw-colored hair and cheap clothes leered menacingly at him.

"Not at all. I apologize if—"

Grant ducked a microsecond before the swing arrived in a *whoosh* of air above his head. He stayed low and grappled the man around the waist, then shoved the man backward into several other people. Then he released his grip, danced away and blended into the crowd heading to the right.

The piercing shatter of glass breaking rang out above the normal conversational din, and Grant spun toward the sound. A little way down the left split, a brawl of some kind had broken out among...everyone in the area? What the hells was going on?

The Justice officer tailing him disappeared.

Seconds later, nanobots flooded the air.

Ordinary shoppers suddenly started freaking out, beating up whomever happened to be within reach.

He scanned around for an area devoid of insane people. Eight meters ahead, a man charged out of a shop on the right and dove into the increasingly agitated crowd. Grant ducked inside the shop the man had abandoned, hurried around the counter and slipped through the open doorway into the storeroom.

Thankfully, it was deserted. He sank against the wall and took a deep breath, confident in his internal defenses' ability to keep the nanobots out of his system.

He'd tried so hard to stay clear of NOIR's cause, even when he'd been sleeping with its leader. It wasn't that he disagreed with their aims; he simply didn't want to get involved. He'd checked out of the game, with its grandiose schemings and petty manipulations, a long, long time ago. In this respect, he hadn't lied to the Justice officers—he just wanted to be left alone to make his modules and build his ships and earn enough credits to keep doing it.

But now the cause, or its target, had found him anyway, and his own healthy self-preservation instinct required that he join the fight until he saw an opportunity to fade into the woodwork once again.

Nika was currently many parsecs away sneaking into gods knew what and where, so he sent a ping to Perrin.

I'm at the Makers Market in Namino Two, and something strange is going on. The air got flooded with nanobots, and now people are losing their minds. Fighting, smashing things. I'm guessing the nanobots dosed them with something nasty.

What? Are you okay?

I'm fine for now. I've blocked the nanobots. But it sounds similar to what NOIR's been saying that virutox does to people, although this is happening a lot faster. Regardless, someone is deliberately messing with people's programming here.

It sounds like they are. I'm going to...um, I'm not sure. We'll figure something out. Can you get yourself to a safe location? Or even better, out?

I intend to try.

Okay, good. Focus on your own safety, but keep me updated. I'll be in touch soon.

He searched the storeroom until he found a rear door. As he'd expected, it led to a service hallway. He headed down it to the left, which should be toward one of the building's exits.

After about fifty meters, the hallway turned left then quickly ended at a door. It slid open when he approached, and he found himself back in the right branch of the main thoroughfare. Sure enough, the building exit was located off to his right, on the other side of a cluster of eight or nine people. They banged violently on the closed doors, to no avail. Almost as if the doors were...locked.

36

MIRAI

Perrin waited until the dyne attendant had deposited their plates on the table in front of them and departed to continue updating Adlai on NOIR's progress with the vaccine. "We've met with scattered resistance, but honestly less than I expected. People are scared, and they're eager to latch onto any hope we can give them. It makes me wish I had more hope I could hand out. But...anyway, as of this morning we've distributed around eight thousand copies of the vaccine. We estimate about seventy percent of those have been installed by the recipients."

Adlai shook his head in nothing but respect. "I'm beyond impressed. We've moved a little over twice that number, but I fear our adoption rate is far lower. Except for Maris—she has people showing up at her office and her loft at all hours of the night asking for this vaccine they heard about. You're both great salespeople. Justice, not so much."

Perrin shrugged vaguely as she took an enormous bite from her sandwich, and he didn't doubt for an instant that she did so to avoid responding. He didn't blame her. Nor did he blame her for her choice of meeting location, a deli a few blocks from Hataori Harbor; he didn't much enjoy going to the Justice Center these days, either. Unfortunately, the constant possibility of him being denied entry at any time, not to mention all the work that could only be accomplished inside its walls, meant he was basically living at his office.

Once she'd chased the bite with a gulp of lemonade, he continued. "So what are your thoughts on next moves?"

"You're the Justice Advisor. I was betting on you having some ideas."

He chuckled. "No, you weren't. NOIR doesn't follow Justice's playbook."

"True. But we need all the playbooks right now. Any information on Joaquim?"

"A little. I learned that Satair requisitioned—"

"Hang on for a second." Her gaze unfocused, the hallmark of a personal conversation in progress.

He waited patiently for her to finish. The only hard part was not staring inappropriately at her. Emotions constantly passed like a spring breeze across her lovely features, flowing from one to the next without guile or pretense, which meant he could tell the instant the conversation took a dire turn by the way her lips puckered in displeasure and the skin around her eyes creased from tension.

She pushed her plate to the side. "There's a problem at the Makers Market in Namino Two. I have a friend who's there right now, and he believes someone has pumped nanobots into the air inside. People are acting crazy—beating each other up, trashing the shops. It almost sounds like they got dosed with a high-potency version of the virutox, don't you think?"

The probable scenario wrote its own script in his mind. NERE dust was a perfect vehicle for the virutox. A better one than the limb augment in many ways. Dammit! The instant they'd begun making progress on containing the virutox's spread, the Guides had simply changed tactics.

"Adlai, can you do anything to fix this?"

The unabashed optimism with which she gazed at him hinted at the depths of her pureness of spirit. Was it possible she actually believed in his ability to fix anything?

He sat up straighter, overcome by the desire to be worthy of the look in her eyes. "No promises, but if nanobots were spread using the ventilation system, as seems likely, it's possible we can neutralize the effect. If we can modify the vaccine's delivery mechanism, and if we can get it to Namino Two fast enough."

She nodded in understanding. "Go."

He smiled in under-expressed thanks and hurried out of the deli.

Erik, if you're not in the lab, get to it now. I'll be there in eight minutes.

∧R

"It sounds as though it's faster-acting than the version we've been dealing with, which means the window to reverse the effects directly has already passed."

Erik paced rapidly around the lab, and Adlai tried to stay out of his way. "Oh! *But*, most people's core operating systems keep back-ups of deleted files and routines for a period of time, just like machines do. If we can intervene before those files are erased or overwritten, we might be able to effectively rewind the clock. Assuming I can adapt the vaccine in such a way that will prompt the victims' OS to revert to an earlier state."

"Can you?"

Erik looked up in surprise, as if he'd forgotten Adlai was there. "I think…yes. But how are we going to get the vaccine to the people who are infected?"

"You work on modifying the vaccine. I'll work on a plan for what to do with it."

Erik gestured absently in Adlai's direction and hurried over to his work bench, then spun back around. "The ventilation system. We can use the dispersal mechanism to our own advantage."

"How?"

"I'll…get back to you on that."

Adlai nodded, then stepped into the hall and pinged Perrin.

We may have an idea. How's your friend at the Makers Market doing?

37

NAMINO

G rant stopped three meters from the end of the hallway so the door wouldn't slide open and expose him to any nearby out-of-their-minds rioters. He focused his aural receptors and listened.

The receptors returned the tell-tale thuds and bangs of a crowd physically berating locked doors.

This was the fourth service hallway branch he'd investigated; two had ended in dead ends, two in adjacent exits he couldn't reach.

Was there not a single service exit directly onto the street? No, there had to be one; delivery of large items wouldn't occur through the public thoroughfares. He simply had to find it. Even if the service exit was locked as well, if left alone and unmolested for a few minutes, he was confident in his ability to bypass the locking mechanism and get it open.

He needed a passageway that led to the left, toward the building's periphery. He started back the way he'd come when a ping arrived from Perrin.

Hey, Grant, are you hanging in there?

Trying to stay clear of the mob until I can locate a way out.

Great. Listen, we have an idea for how we can reverse the effects of whatever toxin the people there have been infected with. I know you're not NOIR, but we need your help.

He stopped at the next hallway intersection.

What kind of help?

I want to put you in touch with a man named Adlai. He's with Justice, but he's on our side. He's ready to send you a schematic of the Makers Market building, so you can make your way to the ventilation control room. Once you're there, he'll open a secure nex path to you and transfer a file, then talk you through loading it into the control system.

Grant had built enough ventilation systems to see where they were going with this, and not see how it could possibly work.

Justice, really?

We can trust him. I trust him.

He would be a legitimately terrible person if he didn't try to help these people regain their sanity before they ripped each other to pieces. He had this conversation with himself every so often, and perhaps it had been too long since the last one: checking out on society's problems didn't make him a terrible person—unless he let it.

All right. Send him my way.

To Grant's credit, he only focused on the 'service exit' label on the schematic for a fraction of a second before moving on to the bright red label for the ventilation control room. Of course, a fraction of a second was all he needed to memorize the service exit's location.

Where are you right now?

He studied the schematic.

The area where about 300 insane people are between me and where I need to be. If I want to avoid them, I'm going to need to get into the ventilation system a little early.

Frowned at the ceiling.

So up I go.

Can you—

Yep.

He ducked back into the storeroom of the shop he'd come through and rooted around in the supply closet until he found a welding torch. Then he climbed up on one of the tables and burned a hole in the ceiling. He left the torch on the table, dropped into a crouch and launched himself upward. His fingertips curled around the still hot edges of the hole, and he winced in pain as he hauled himself up through the opening and into the duct space.

All right, I'm making my way toward the ventilation control room. But I'm crawling there, so it's going to take a few minutes.

I understand.

So how is this going to work when I get there? We can filter out the nanobots to stop them from circulating any further, but I don't see how we can use the ventilation system to reprogram people. Not without our own nanobots to deploy.

Neither do I. But my tech guy, Erik Rhom, thinks we can repurpose the ionizer component of the air purifier to alter the nanobots' programming.

Oh. That...might actually work.

Glad you both think so.

Grant took the next right into a wider, more spacious duct. According to the schematic, this represented one of the main conduits out of the ventilation control room. The air blew forcefully against his face, evoking an involuntary shudder. Thousands of poisonous nanobots swept over his skin and banged insistently against his nose and eyes, trying to find a gap in his defenses. He couldn't see them, he couldn't feel them. But he *could* deny them entry, dammit.

He kept his mouth firmly closed while he double-checked the health of his defensive systems. They were holding up well under the sustained assault, but he desperately wanted to be out of here.

The duct ended at a large filtration screen. He jimmied it out of its grooves, set it aside and crawled through to the other side, where the space opened up a bit. The ceiling wasn't high enough for him to stand, but he was able to rise to his knees.

Okay, I'm in the ventilation control room.

Terrific. I'm opening a nex pathway to send you the file, then I'm going to hand you off to Erik, because I would totally mangle the instructions. No matter what happens from here on out, thank you for helping us.

This Weiss guy was far more likeable than the two Justice assholes who had invaded his home and planted surveillance equipment on his property. So that was something. But after count-less millennia of living a quiet, mostly anonymous existence, in a matter of days Grant was drowning in Advisors. He didn't want any part of it, and the sooner they all sailed back out of his life, the better.

Sure thing. Let's get this done.

ᴀR

Hi, Mr. Mesahle. My name's Erik Rhom. I understand you have some familiarity with machinery and environmental component de-sign?

Enough so you can assume I know what you mean when you say something. If I don't, I'll ask.

Got it. The first thing we need to do is trap the nanobots on the ionizer's collection plates. They're probably designed to resist ioniza-tion, so we're going to have to increase the voltage as high as possible.

But not so high that the entire ventilation system electrifies, and by extension, me.

Exactly. I've studied the specs on the ventilation system model, and I think that number is 5,600 volts.

You're fucking kidding me.

I know, it's a risk. Look around for any materials you can use as an insulator.

Grant was already combing through the room on a hunt for rubber, foam, ceramic, glass, wood or even a strip of plastic. The soles of his shoes were rubberized, which was a good start but not much more.

His eyes fell on the cooling module over in the corner. Namino's infamously dry air meant it likely included an evaporative cooling stage.

He crawled over to it and removed the cover.

I'm stealing the melamine membranes from the cooling system. It might start getting a little warm inside the building.

Don't worry about it. The people trapped there have bigger problems.

The module included two membranes, each a square meter in size...which might actually be enough. He ripped them out of their casings and carried them back over to the primary filtration module.

How do I crank up the power?

The filtration system control panel is built into the module itself. Look for a small notch halfway up one of the sides.

Easy enough to find. The cover swung open, revealing an array of readouts and calibration tuners.

Ionizer ID?

#AIP148B.

Grant tore off a small section of one of the membranes to use as a glove of sorts. He set his personal electrostatic shield to the highest setting, rose off his knees to crouch with his shoes fully on the floor, folded one membrane over his head and wrapped the other around his chest.

5,600 volts, here we come.

Once, nearly a thousand years ago, Grant had accidentally touched an 8,000 volt electrified panel with a bare hand. He'd survived the shock, but the resulting damage to his OS and internal organs was such that he'd been forced to trade in the body for a new one.

The shock that assaulted his body when he dialed up the voltage didn't hurt as much as that misstep had. His hair stood on end, and a few sparks shot out of his eyeballs. His teeth chattered, his skin felt like it was on fire, and the muscles in the arm he used to change the setting clenched, then stayed that way. But he remained on his feet.

Still here.

Excellent. Now it's going to take a few minutes for the air to complete a circulation cycle, and we need to capture as many of the nanobots as possible.

Say, twelve minutes?

Let's do fourteen to be safe.

Grant sighed.

AR

13:58

13:59

Time's up.

Before we can turn the voltage down, we need to temporarily shut down the filtration module, so we don't lose the nanobots.

Got it.

Grant flipped the master power switch at the top of the control panel. A faint vibration in the module he hadn't realized was there ceased, and the hyper-ionized air stilled.

Okay, now dial the voltage back down to normal levels.

Gladly.

The air shifted and settled with the reduction in electricity. He felt tingly; he hoped his nerve endings hadn't suffered significant damage. His leg muscles were cramping, but he didn't dare sit down until the electric charge had dissipated a lot more.

Now we need to use the file Advisor Weiss sent you to modify the properties of the nanobots. The file doesn't contain a vaccine—we don't have a way to extensively rewrite the nanobots from within the ventilation system—but it will wipe the nanobots' programming, rendering them harmless. Then it will wrap them in a Tier III spike, which should trigger a state reset when someone inhales a nanobot.

What happens when they inhale a second one?

So they might experience more than one reset. I didn't say it was a perfect solution, only a workable one. After we release the nanobots, we'll null out the spike so on the next pass they'll become inert.

I'll take your word for it. How do I deliver the code?

You're going to need to tap into the backend wiring of the control panel....

AR

If it had been anyone other than Grant in the vents, the whole crazy scheme would have been an unmitigated disaster. Or that was Grant's personal opinion, anyway, as he scrambled through the ducts toward the single, magical service exit.

Assuming the scheme was working at all; he wasn't about to drop down into one of the public hallways and check. He'd done his civic duty and given a lot of innocent people a chance. He had nothing more to give.

Weiss pinged him as he reached the final intersection on his journey and turned left.

I'm working on getting looped into the on-site surveillance cams to see what effect our fix is having. I'm also on the way to the scene. Stay hidden and out of the way, and once I'm there, I'll find a way to get you out safely.

Sounds good.

Five meters short of where the schematic showed the service exit, Grant halted and used his multitool to cut into the base of the duct until it gave way.

He dropped down through the jagged opening and landed on the floor of the thankfully empty service hallway. His overstressed leg muscles protested the hard landing, but they obeyed when he stood tall for the first time in over an hour, and he wasted no time in bypassing the door's security.

Outside, the night sky was bright with the flashing of emergency lights. Sirens wailed, as if that helped anything. The street intersections in both directions were barricaded and patrolled by security dynes, but they hadn't barricaded the mid-block alley. Not yet.

He breathed the uncontaminated, chilly night air deep into his lungs and started winding his way through the labyrinth of alleys and out to a street three blocks away. Then home.

38

NAMINO

Adlai arrived at the Makers Market to find about what he'd expected. A sizeable security force surrounded the block-sized building, with mecha guarding the main entrances. It didn't look as if the local Justice presence had breached the building yet, which was good news.

He spotted the command center off to the left of the east entrance and credentialed his way through two security checkpoints to reach it. Once there, he stopped the first officer he came to. "Advisor Weiss. I'd like to speak with Advisor Panetier."

The uni shook their head. "I'm not sure where Selene currently is. I haven't seen her in twenty minutes or so."

"Thank you. I'll find her."

He'd made it two more steps when Blake Satair turned around, a mug of coffee in one hand. "Can I help you?"

Adlai groaned. "Are you taking over the Namino Justice Division, too? Spreading yourself a bit thin."

"I go where I'm needed. At the moment, that happens to be here. You, however, are *not* needed, so kindly see yourself back to Mirai. Go hide in your office for a while longer."

"I've been monitoring the cam feeds for the last hour. Everyone inside has calmed down, and the fighting has ceased. They're also out of sorts and confused, and many are injured. We have to get trauma repair teams in there."

"No, we have to get a cadre of security dynes in there to arrest everyone, which we are nearly ready to do. A full assault on the building is set to begin in five minutes."

"Did you not hear what I said? No one inside is a threat to anyone. Not any longer. They need our help, not our shackles. Check the cam feeds for yourself."

"Oh, I have. Curious how half an hour ago everyone rather abruptly stopped rampaging and started crying—but at least they'll be easier to bring in now."

"You…" Adlai pinched the bridge of his nose, using the time the gesture provided to stop himself from acting on his spiking frustration "…do you have any idea what happened in there?"

"Yes. Do you?"

Icy tendrils of dismay froze the frustration in his veins. This was practically an admission of complicity. And Satair had said it to his face while officers milled about within earshot.

The man had always been arrogant and brash, but he now displayed far too much hubris. Satair plainly believed Adlai couldn't touch him, and it might be true. But now, it sounded like he also believed the Guides' directives couldn't be countermanded; the Rasu Protocol couldn't be thwarted. This, Adlai refused to accept.

He schooled his features into a blank, emotionless expression. "Well. If you don't require my assistance, I'll take your advice and head to Mirai. I've got a lot of work to do there, so you might want to hurry back as well."

Then he turned on a heel and strode off with as much dignity as he was able to muster, when what he really wanted to do was punch something. All their efforts tonight, for nothing!

No, not for nothing. They'd saved the psyches of the hundreds of people inside from being mangled beyond repair. But in the end, it hadn't been enough to save them from the Rasu Protocol. The people inside would be rounded up and hauled off to the Namino Justice Center, convicted of violent crimes and shipped off to Zaidam before tomorrow saw a sunset.

He allowed himself a weary sigh and veered left before he hit the first security checkpoint. There was still one person he could save tonight.

Mr. Mesahle, I'm happy to report that your and Erik's hard work succeeded in quelling the outbreak inside. Unfortunately, the situation has gotten somewhat complicated outside. If you will stay hidden away in the ductwork for a little longer, I promise I will find a way to get you out that doesn't involve you being arrested.

No need to trouble yourself. I got myself out. I'm home and snugly tucked into my bed.

Adlai frowned at the building façade, unable to decide whether to be relieved at having one less problem to solve or annoyed at having been caught flat-footed for the second time in one night.

What? I mean, I'm glad to hear it. But I wanted to thank you for your help in person.

It's not necessary. I'm glad everything worked out.

If only.

39

THE PLATFORM

*T*hanks *for the ride. I'll be seeing you soon.*
— *Nika*

Many hours after she'd recovered her ship, the taunt continued to wreak havoc through Gemina's thoughts. It kept drawing her attention away from a somewhat important interaction, and she couldn't seem to silence it.

"A thorough scrubbing of the *Tabiji* revealed the presence of a small tracker hidden on the bridge. It's likely she placed it there while she was on Hokan Station."

Always cool and reserved, Guide Anavosa regarded Gemina with an extra hint of frostiness. "Was any additional tampering identified?"

"Minor anomalies in the *Tabiji's* internal systems suggest a slicing intrusion, but the evidence is inconclusive."

"Does she have *everything*?"

Gemina weathered this abuse with a stoic flatness, as it was de rigeur for Guide Luciene. "I don't know how much information she currently possesses. More than she did two days ago."

"How did she find the station?"

She didn't acknowledge the comparative gentleness of Guide Delacrai's inquiry. She couldn't afford to. "There are several possibilities. The breach occurred soon after a shipment from SR114-Ichi arrived, so it is possible she was present at the outpost and stowed away in the cargo vessel. In addition, following the incident, a tracking device similar to the one discovered on the *Tabiji* was found in the laser housing of my personal ship. It might have been there for several weeks."

"Or months? Years?"

"No, Guide Iovimer. The laser covering had been sealed shut, presumably to protect the tracker. I used the laser at SR89-San twenty-three days ago, so it was placed since then. I've docked the ship at official spaceports on Mirai, Kiyora and Adjunct Ni in recent weeks, so there were...opportunities."

"You have gotten sloppy, Advisor Kail. Your gross negligence in the performance of your duties is unacceptable."

Gemina bit the inside of her mouth until it bled. The pain distracted her long enough to divert her initial, knee-jerk response to Luciene. "Given how the job you've tasked me with is an impossible one, I respectfully submit that perfection is unattainable."

"Competence, however, is not."

"Then fire me." She wiped a trickle of blood from the corner of her mouth; her restraint accidentally slipped away with it. "Or can you not find anyone else to do your dirty work for you? Perhaps, Guide Luciene, you'd like to leave your ivory tower and attempt to perform this job yourself. Believe me, you are welcome to it."

In a rare physical display, Anavosa extended her arm toward Luciene, palm up and turned outward. A warning. Her gaze, though, never left Gemina. "Take care with your tone, Advisor Kail. You have served us honorably and skillfully for many years, and we have not forgotten your dedication or your sacrifices. Believe me, we recognize the level of stress you face. We are all facing it.

"But now more than ever, we must be vigilant. We must redouble our efforts and take due care in them, for any further mistakes risk bringing doom upon our civilization."

Gemina should feel shamed, she knew she should, but the indignance refused to cede the high ground, where it tussled with Nika's taunt for a claim on the summit.

She did manage to get control of her tongue. "I promise you, I appreciate the stakes, Guide Anavosa. I apologize for my lapse and will endeavor to ensure it does not happen again." She paused briefly. "Can I ask, what do you intend to do about her?"

"You need to focus on repairing the damage your mission has suffered and completing the formidable tasks ahead of you. We will deal with Nika Kirumase."

"Yes, Guide Luciene. Thank you for the honor of your time."

"What should be done with him, Advisor?"

Blake studied the body on the lab table. It was nothing but a husk now, for the psyche that once inhabited it had been shredded when its neural hardware was drained of data then dismantled. "Schedule him for a full retirement and reinitialization. Tier III tradesman skillset and a business auxiliary, which should reset him somewhere close to where he started."

The neuro tech didn't make eye contact with him. "What if the physical damage to his brain is too significant to enable a new imprint?"

"Do whatever it is you do with people who suffer catastrophic head trauma—put him on the list for a new brain or whatever."

"Yes, sir." The tech nodded and began cleaning up her tools.

Blake stepped into the curving hallway of the Platform's detainee wing and walked two doors down to the exam room holding their prize 'detainee.'

Inside, another neuro tech monitored the bank of equipment doing the painstaking work of prying secrets out of the man's mind without cracking it open like a piñata. Guides' orders: no lasting damage to the man's neural architecture until they were certain no further information could be gleaned without inflicting said damage.

He understood the reason for caution; they didn't want to unwittingly destroy vital intel while trying to retrieve *other* vital intel. Unfortunately, interrogating this psyche without damaging it was proving to be problematic, to say the least. The man had dozens of firewalls and traps installed, including one self-referencing paradox trap that it took techs four hours to extract the interrogation algorithmic probe from.

And if a probe managed to navigate all those barriers, around a third of the time it then ran smack into a mutually-assured-destruction gating function.

Clearly, the information they sought about NOIR rested on the other side of those functions. But short of deleting the man's OS and reconstructing the data his mind held in a virtual environment, they had no way to get to it. Success rates for such a drastic procedure hovered around 42%, foreclosing its use for now.

But in the end, the extreme measures to which the man had gone to protect his deepest secrets were going to be for naught.

A lot of the stored data and memories weren't protected by MAD functions, and once the probes worked their way through mazes of lesser defenses, they uncovered a wealth of information about the man. Mostly about his life before NOIR, but even those files had ultimately proved fruitful.

Joaquim Lacese had cut virtually all ties with his prior life in recent years; all but one, in fact, which meant this one mattered a great deal. The man remained in regular contact with his former boss, the owner of a residential furnishings fab shop on Synra named Gregor Shone.

On the Guides' order, Blake had brought Shone in this morning. With no restrictions imposed on this interrogation, it hadn't taken long for the algorithms to extract a full dataset of Shone's interactions with Lacese. And how interesting that for the last decade, 95% of them had revolved around the care and maintenance of a single address.

Blake left the machines to their delicate, frustrating work on Lacese and returned to the hall. To the right, around the curve and just out of sight, stood the closed and locked door to the Guides' inner sanctum. It had been a busy and fruitful night, and he had to resist the urge to walk up to it and knock, in the hope that he could report all his successes in person.

Instead, he turned to the left and head for the main anteroom, then the exit. As he did, he sent a message to the secure nex address he used to communicate with the Guides outside of audiences.

I've acquired actionable intel regarding the probable location of NOIR's hideout.

A response arrived in seconds. He couldn't say which Guide composed it or if it was a group effort.

Excellent work. Confirm the location with as much certainty as possible. If the information is accurate, prepare a mission strike profile and be ready to execute on it on our order. Also, pull the trigger on Advisor Ridani's assistant.

Blake considered the orders while he endured the security checkpoint in Synra Tower.

Do you desire simultaneous missions? I cannot be in two places at once.

As close to simultaneous as is feasible. We leave your individual role in either or both to your discretion.

Finally, a bit of justice was within his reach. He'd become increasingly frustrated over the refusal of the Guides to remove Weiss from his position and lock him up, when the man was blatantly committing treason by working with NOIR. But within a matter of hours, NOIR was going to be removed as a threat, once and for all.

He didn't need to ask why the Guides were finally moving on all fronts, either. Gemina had confided in him that Nika, and presumably Dashiel as well, had discovered Hokan Station, and with it an unknown level of information on the Rasu Protocol. Now they were in danger of blowing the lid off a secret the Guides had spent eight years protecting. They needed to be stopped, but to be stopped they needed to be caught.

So it was time to throw some chunks of juicy red meat into the water. When they took the bait—and they *would*—Blake intended to be there to cinch up the nets.

40

D ashiel awoke to empty arms. An empty bed.

Amazing how quickly he'd again gotten used to having her beside him, no matter the setting. Her absence now triggered an echo of the loneliness and despair an empty bed had nurtured for five years. But the echo was weak and fleeting, and he didn't need to dwell on it. Not when he would find her steps away.

He left the bed and climbed up the ladder to the main cabin.

Nika sat on the edge of the couch, elbows on her knees and hands fisted at her chin. The subtle glow of her tattoo shone like a lodestar amid the shadows of the cabin.

She didn't look up when he reached the top of the ladder, so he didn't wait for an invitation to move to the couch and sit beside her. "What's wrong?"

"I don't know what to do."

"We have so many challenges facing us at present, you're going to need to be a little more specific."

That earned him a fleeting smile, but it quickly gave way to vexation. "I went to bed tonight intending to rush home and confront the Guides with what I know about the Rasu, because I can't let them continue to send innocent people—or hells, even guilty people—into that horrific place to be tortured. Possibly to die.

"But given what we've learned, I have to assume they believe they have no other choice. I mean, the Guides have done some epically shitty things, but they're not actively evil, are they?"

"Eh, maybe Luciene..." he shrugged weakly "...no, I doubt they're evil."

"Then they believe they have no other choice. They *must* be wrong. There must be another way, and I must find it.

"But I'm not a soldier. So far as I can tell, I was never a soldier. Even during the SAI Rebellion, I was a diplomatic representative for the rebel soldiers. In NOIR, I fight, but not with fleets or armies. I fight to change a system, not to destroy an enemy.

"And tonight I realized something. If I stop the shipment of people to the Rasu without a plan in place to defeat them or at a minimum prevent them from defeating us, the Rasu will almost certainly come for us, and I'll have killed us all. Only I don't have that plan. I don't know how to begin to put together that kind of plan."

She peered at him through splayed fingers. "Would former-me have known what to do?"

He tried to give the question the thoughtful consideration it deserved. "Well, you faced a lot of situations where, going in, you weren't certain of the best course of action. But you trusted in yourself to be able to work together with your counterparts to find it. And when you couldn't, you trusted in your judgment to make the right call. And you were almost never wrong."

"But I was wrong occasionally?"

"Despite my personal opinion on the matter, I'll concede that you were not technically perfect. But over time, your error-correction routines became damn near flawless."

"Good, because I don't have much margin for error here."

He reached over and gently brushed messy, bed-tousled strands of raven hair out of her face. "This isn't all on you. You're not alone, not even close. We'll figure it out together—you and I, your friends and allies, my friends and allies. It's our future on the line, too."

She stared at him for several seconds wearing the oddest expression, until her gaze unfocused as her mind turned inward. Gradually, the expression brightened into delight. "*We.* Of course!

It was the first and most critical mistake the Guides made, and it doomed them to failure from the start."

She grasped his face in both hands and kissed him with enough fervor to make him dizzy. In its wake, her lips hovered a sliver away from his. "You're a genius."

He belatedly remembered how to breathe. "I admit I've been called that once or twice, but usually I have some idea what I've done to deserve it."

"I'm not one hundred percent sure yet. I need to think on it some more. But I will take your advice and *trust* in my ability to work it out."

Her renewed kiss carried no less intensity, and he moaned as one of her hands encircled his and the other trailed down his chest. "Back to bed?"

"Nothing wrong with the couch. And we're already naked." She laughed and flattened a palm on his chest to urge him down.

He eagerly complied. The rapid change in mood didn't surprise him too much. It was hardly the first time a eureka moment on her part had led to this manner of celebration. Granted, that was the old her...but if it was the new her, too, he felt no inclination to complain. Nope, none whatsoever.

As soon as his head hit the couch cushion, she swung a leg over his hips and sidled atop him. The blue-green fire in her eyes matched the heat radiating off her skin where it met his. He reached up to tangle one of his hands in her hair, then tugged her down and devoured her mouth, distracting her while he shifted the angle of his hips and slipped inside her. Or possibly she did the distracting.

He closed his eyes and lost himself in the flood of sensations. *Every time like the first time, the best time, the only time that mattered, every single time....*

The unexpected absence of her lips forced him to reopen his eyes. Flashing a tantalizing smile, she rose up to straddle him. He grasped both her hands and opened his palms against hers.

AR

My emotional processes fought to reject the words Steven Olivaw had just uttered. To deny them their proper meaning. "Why?"

Steven sank onto the park bench and ran a hand raggedly through unkempt chestnut hair. "Because I'm tired. I'm...done. And because I'm okay with being done."

"I don't understand what you mean."

"We accomplished what we set out to do: we led our people, most of them, to safety. We found a new home. We built a new home. Our people are thriving, and I feel fulfilled."

"But you—"

"I've lived for 140,000 years, Nicol—Nika. Forgive me, very old habits. Isn't that long enough?"

"But retirement and reinitialization? You might as well commit suicide. Please, try a generational upgrade instead. Tweak a few algorithms. You'll feel like a new man, without actually being one."

"I've tried an upgrade. Twice."

"What? You didn't tell me."

"I was hoping they would work, and then I wouldn't need to."

I swallowed, but I couldn't dislodge the lump that had swollen in my throat. In desperation, I forced a cracked whisper past it. "Don't you love me?"

He swiftly stood and closed the physical distance between us to bring a hand to my cheek. "Eternally. But you don't love me. Not really."

I grabbed his hand at my cheek and pressed it hard against my skin. In defiance. "I do."

His halting smile and the brimming tears in his hazel eyes nearly ruined me. "Okay. I believe you. But you have so much left to do—so much you want to do. I wish I could share your enthusiasm and stand proudly at your side for it all, but I simply...can't. I've got nowhere left to go in this life. You're somehow just getting started, but I'm finished.

"And who knows? If we're truly meant to be together, maybe you and my future incarnation will find each other again. I could even...it violates the rules, but if you want, I could arrange it so you're told my new name and where I settle."

He placed a soft kiss on my lips—I shoved him away and stumbled backward. *"That's not fair. You expect me to chase after some refurbished copy of you and try to convince a distant echo of the man you are now to fall in love with me all over again? Don't you dare put that burden on me. No. I won't settle for a hack version of you."*

He nodded soberly and shifted toward the path leading out of the park. *"I understand. Still, perhaps it will turn out to be a better version. One ready to walk through eternity with you. One worthy of your love."*

"Steven—"

"Goodbye, Nika."

Nika gasped in air as the cabin spun around her.

"What's wrong?"

She didn't look at Dashiel as she more or less fell off of him and the couch, banging a knee on the corner of the table on her way to grasping for the storage cabinet shelf. "I'm...I just need a minute."

He wasted no time in following her, and she had to force herself not to shrink away when he cupped her cheek in his hand.

"You unlocked another memory, didn't you?"

She nodded wordlessly.

"I suppose I ought to be more careful where my fingertips land." They shared a faltering chuckle. "Will you tell me what it involved?"

"It was from before I met you." Which wasn't *technically* a lie. "It was...violence and death. That's why it shook me up."

"But I thought you said they were always topical?"

Of course they were. She shrugged and kissed him softly, trying not to get dizzy as the sensations it elicited overlapped with those in the memory. "I guess not always. Or maybe it was triggered by our conversation about the Rasu. You should go on back to bed. I promise, I'll be right down. I want to get some water and a little snack."

"I'm not going to leave you to process this alone."

"Please. I'm fine. I'll only be a minute."

He studied her suspiciously, a hint of troubled disquiet in his eyes. "If you're sure."

Was there anything in the stars she was sure about? She managed a pathetic facsimile of a smile, and he stepped away to climb down the ladder to the lower cabin.

When he'd gone, she went to the sink and splashed water on her face, then patted it dry. It didn't help, so she shuffled back to the couch and collapsed on it, letting the avalanche of heartbreak escape the memory and engulf her.

How long had it taken her former self to realize Dashiel was almost definitely a scion of Steven Olivaw? Perhaps not immediately upon meeting him, for while they favored one another, the resemblance was not overwhelming. She hadn't picked up on it in the memory of the final hours of the SAI Rebellion, though she'd been understandably focused on other facets of the memory at the time. And her former self hadn't been bombarded with a series of hundreds-of-millennia-old memories that brought the truth into stark relief.

But she must have realized it in time, much like Nika now had. Their mannerisms, body language, voice…the feel of their lips on hers.

He placed a soft kiss on my lips—

And she had shoved him away and he had broken her heart.

Not tonight. A hundred million years ago.

Her former self hadn't told him about his heritage; of this she felt certain. If he'd known, he would have used it early on to try to convince her of how they were destined to be together. He'd have claimed his First Generation lineage alongside her.

Again she returned to the question of why. Or in this case, why not?

Why make a point to encrypt *this* memory, if not to hold on to the truth of Dashiel's ancestry? Why hold on to it for herself, but keep the truth from him?

Was it intended to serve as reassurance for her and future generations that Steven had been right, that his descendant *was* a better version of himself, someone she could spend eternity with? Or was it a warning, an admonition to guard her heart closely, because he remained the kind of man who would leave without warning?

Why the fuck didn't these memories come with an instruction manual, or at least a couple of helpful annotations? And why did they include so many memories from distant, early incarnations of her psyche, of ancestors so long gone?

She needed answers, before the questions drove her mad. But the only person who might be able to provide them was a ghost hiding in the shadows of her own mind.

For the second time tonight, she didn't know what to do.

COMMAND
PROMPT

41

WAYFARER

MIRAI

With the path of the celestial d-gates laid out for them, the journey home was a quick one. And a disconcerting one.

It felt as if the Rasu hovered just past the horizon, the briefest blink away from the Dominion. They had no idea if the Rasu knew of the existence of the d-gates or their purpose, but given the wormhole vortex they'd seen one of their leviathans create and traverse, if the aliens so much as knew the general location of any Dominion world, it wouldn't matter. A blink, and Rasu ships could darken its skies.

After showering, Dashiel found Nika in the cockpit, swiveling her chair around like a gyroscope. Last night, she'd slipped quietly into bed and turned her back to him; this morning, she'd snuck out twenty minutes before their wake-up time. So he wasn't sure quite what to expect when he joined her upstairs.

He leaned against the cockpit wall. "What's up?"

Round the chair went. "Trying to figure out where to land. All your factories and offices are surely being watched by now. I don't want to risk a second use of the industrial sector dock, in case we left traces of our visit behind. Anywhere in the middle of nowhere should be safe, but we need to be able to easily go places once we're planetside."

"What about the rec space outside the southeast sector of Mirai One? It has a small docking area, but it's not heavily monitored."

The chair reversed direction. "That's not a bad idea. Let's do it."

She spun to face the dash and input several commands. The floor shifted subtly beneath them as the *Wayfarer* began its descent. "Also, I'm still struggling over what my first move should be. I mean, I can use the nex address to get the Guides' attention, but I refuse to walk into a meeting with them without a solid escape plan and two backup escape plans. I won't go in blindly, not this time. So I don't—"

He gripped the headrest of her chair, forcing it to a halt. "Nika?"

She looked up at him in surprise, which was when he noticed the faint shadows beneath bloodshot eyes. She hadn't slept well, if at all.

"Yes?"

"Good morning."

She huffed a passable laugh. "Good morning. Sorry. I'm a little antsy. And anxious."

"I know, and I understand. I would nonetheless advise taking a few deep breaths." He bent down and kissed her forehead, then sat in the other chair. "I told Vance I was going to be back on Mirai. He wants to meet to go over some company business."

Her eyes instantly narrowed. "His idea to meet?"

"Technically. The offer was sort of implicit in my message, though."

"It could be a trap."

"I don't think Vance would betray me."

"That's only relevant to the details of the trap, not whether it is one."

His lips pursed. Her dark and volatile mood from the night before hadn't improved with the light of day. "I think—"

"You're about to say I'm being paranoid. We've already covered this ground. It's kept me and my people alive and free for five years."

Her people? She meant NOIR, of course. Did she also mean him? To some distress, he found he wasn't certain of the answer. "Okay. Let's assume for a minute that you're right and it's a trap. I don't think you are, but let's assume it. What are the possibilities?

"One, and least likely, Vance has betrayed me and is luring me in so Guide lackeys can capture me. If true, I left my company in the hands of a corrupt, deceitful man, I dread finding out what he's been doing to it in my absence, and I need to regain control of it somehow.

"Two, Vance is in trouble—kidnapped by one of the Guides' secret hit squads, tortured or worse—and he was either forced into sending the message or someone is impersonating him. If true, *no one* is running my company, and I need to regain control of it before it collapses into a mountain of raw materials and debt. Also, I need to try to help my friend, who's being tortured so the Guides can get to me.

"Three, the Guides are feeling the pressure and want to talk, but they're afraid to talk to you and figure I'll be more reasonable, seeing as they've neither psyche-wiped me nor shot at me. They assume I don't trust them, and this is the only way they can think of to get me to a table I should probably get to. Am I missing any options?"

"I'm sorry."

"For what?"

"Getting you involved in all of this. Your business, your work, your fortune, your reputation, your future? They're all on the verge of being destroyed because you sided with me. Now people close to you might be getting hurt, too. I'm a one-woman wrecking crew of people's lives."

"This isn't your fault, Nika. It's the Guides' fault. Certainly the fault of those terrifying aliens as well, but the Guides own their actions."

She stared out the viewport as they descended toward a landing pad situated among improved meadows and a bright glass-domed atrium. "But I knew the lengths they will go to in order to keep their secret, and I challenged them anyway. In doing so, I've put everything and everyone I know in danger. I accepted the risks, but not on behalf of the rest of you."

Her voice was flat and dull; he'd expected her to be troubled and possibly conflicted about their return to Mirai, but he hadn't expected this. He desperately wanted to take her back to bed and start the day over.

"Nika, when I chose to come with you, I was under no illusions about what it could mean for the course of my life."

"That can't be true. You're a romantic, and no way is this what you were hoping for."

Aside from the civilization-threatening alien menace, it was pretty damn close to everything he'd hoped for. Why couldn't she understand that? "What are you trying to say?"

"I'm trying to say that you going to this meeting with Vance is a profoundly *terrible* idea. You can't see it, because you've got one foot firmly planted in your old life. I don't blame you. If I still had that life, I would, too. But your attempts to hold onto both it and me will get you captured and tortured and psyche-wiped, and it will be because of me. But I can't protect you *and* everyone else if you insist on running off on reckless whims."

He exhaled harshly, stood and walked into the main cabin, overcome by a disconcerting need to create some distance from her. Halfway to the kitchen unit, he stopped and gazed back at her. "Do you truly think so little of me?"

"No. I—"

"You're not my keeper. You've taught me how to protect myself—how to fight—and I'm grateful for it. I can take my own risks, and I won't hide behind your shadow like the coward I once was."

She stood and took two steps toward him, at which point he had cause to remember that half of why she'd been a great diplomat was the ability to wield a stare that could melt glaciers into weeping puddles. "Is this about what happened before, when I disappeared? Are you trying to prove you're not a coward any longer? Well, this is a stupid way to do it.

"They will *take you*. Then they will take everything you are. They will psyche-wipe you and when they are done, you won't remember that you cared. About me, about your business, about anything. You won't even remember who you are."

"Now who's projecting? This isn't five years ago, and they wouldn't dare."

"Because...why? You're more special than I was? Less expendable somehow? You can smooth-talk your way out of it? Buy them off? Go back to being a coward. You're better at it, and it will keep you alive."

The barbs couldn't have gutted him any more thoroughly if she'd flung a morning star into his stomach. He breathed out through his nose, jaw clenched, until he trusted himself to speak. "I'm going to give you the benefit of the doubt and assume you're deliberately trying to push me away. Hells if I know why. Maybe for the same reason you lied to me last night about the memory you recovered."

"Why do you think—"

"Don't make it worse by denying it now. Nika, I've known you for more than three thousand years. I can tell when you're lying. Look, I'm going to my meeting. Whatever happens, you can rest easy, because I won't blame you for it.

"Take a couple of hours to get your head on straight while I'm gone. Decide if you're willing to be honest with me. Decide if you're willing to respect me. If those answers turn out to be 'yes,' decide if you want me to come back."

Her brow furrowed as her lips dropped into a pout. "Wait. No. I didn't say—"

"Yeah. You kind of did." The ship thudded roughly onto the landing pad, and he didn't wait for any safety checks. He simply pivoted to the airlock, opened it and left.

ᴀᴙ

Nika reached out for an airlock that was three meters away and also already closed. It made for the most futile of gestures, and with a frustrated sigh she returned to the cockpit. She dropped her elbows on the dash and her head into her hands and stared out the viewport.

What she saw sent a wave of déjà vu crashing over her. His back to her, walking away. So like in the memory.

Alongside the dizziness the déjà vu carried, one truth became crystal clear to her: she'd learned nothing in seven hundred thousand years. Not a godsdamned thing. Or if she had, it had plainly been erased in the psyche-wipe.

Her gaze followed Dashiel as he crossed the landing area toward the central atrium. He cut quite a striking figure in tan slacks and an open-necked white shirt. If he was angry or upset, he hid it well, for his gait and the set of his shoulders broadcast an aura of cool confidence to any who crossed his path.

She'd gotten accustomed to his presence at her side, in her bed and her arms, and now she desperately wanted him to turn around and run back to her.

But that wasn't particularly fair of her, was it? She was the one who'd chased him away, after all.

Why must it be so hard for her to do the running? Why couldn't she stand up and just *go to him*? Apologize for being a bitch, ask what he needed from her then try to give it. She was the leader. The beacon, the ambassador, the one who stood up for others and fought for them when no one else would. Why couldn't she stand up and fight for him?

Then he disappeared into the atrium and was gone. Again.

No. He wasn't Steven Olivaw; not really. A distant descendant, perhaps, sharing a percentage of genetic markers and core algorithms long since tweaked and modified beyond recognition. Nothing more.

Was she the woman whom Steven had walked away from? It was impossible that she might be, for the aeons spanning from that day to this moment were simply too great. Yet in the memory, the heartbreak had felt like it belonged to her. And it had felt a lot like this did.

Dammit, she was not her memories! Dashiel had said so.

She stood and went downstairs to shower, thinking it would clear her head.

It didn't.

So she organized the storage cabinet and catalogued their supplies. She needed to know what she had on hand to work with before she made a move. A move which was going to involve...what?

Last night, she'd said she would trust in herself to know what to do. But the time had now come to act, and she *didn't*. Know what to do, or trust in herself?

Damn good question.

She should have followed Dashiel—she should have chased after him and stopped him from leaving, but if she couldn't manage to accomplish that, she should have discreetly followed him to his meeting. He was correct; he'd come a long way, and he would be able to protect himself from most threats. But they weren't facing most threats.

But she hadn't followed him, and he hadn't told her where the meeting was scheduled to happen...she pinged his locator ID, but it returned as *null*. He'd shut it off. He didn't *want* her to follow.

So now there was...nothing she could do. Nothing except hope he was right and she was wrong.

She sank onto the couch and massaged her temples. How right? Right about the meeting with Vance not being a trap, but what about the rest? *Was* she trying to push him away? Why? The memory had spooked her, and she still wished she understood why it existed. Dashiel, though, was...wonderful, and he didn't deserve to be punished for the sins of his ancestor.

But she wasn't pushing him away—that was simply a bit of ugly collateral damage. She was pushing herself away.

With every memory he enabled her to recover, with every minute spent at his side, she'd sensed herself shifting and changing. Becoming more the person she'd once been. The undeniable truth told the tale: in ways she didn't get to choose, she *was* her memories.

And when the woman whom those memories belonged to had tried to challenge the Guides, she'd gotten herself psyche-wiped for the effort. Nika Kirumase had been woefully unprepared for the fight. Much like Dashiel risked doing this very minute, she'd strode straight into a trap laid by the enemy, confident in the power of her words and her charm to protect her. She'd been so catastrophically wrong.

To fight this fight—to *win* this fight—she had to be Nika the rebel. Nika the NOIR leader. She couldn't be soft; she couldn't be polite; she couldn't be *diplomatic*. Her enemy sure as hells wasn't.

Funny, understanding why she'd lashed out at him so viciously didn't make her feel any better about having done it, or its outcome. Luckily, an alert arrived to distract her from her wallowing. A new message at the special nex address she'd given to the Guides.

She sat up on the edge of the couch. A combination of trepidation and hope sped her pulse and primed her veins for a rush of adrenaline.

She opened the message.

Your headquarters has been compromised.

42

MIRAI

An easy warmth of familiarity embraced Dashiel as he neared Kinsan Park in northeast Mirai One. The park wasn't as colorful or secluded as the botanical gardens on Ebisu, but the wide lawns gathered staggering amounts of sunlight and the aroma of sage filled the air. This was his home turf, and he found it difficult to believe anything here could mean him harm.

Of course something could—the crater where the transit hub stood a week ago was barely two kilometers from here. He indulged the fantasy nonetheless.

Concentrating on work for a little while should provide a welcome respite as well. Now all he had to do was think about work instead of Nika.

Oh, well, so much for that plan.

Gods, had he really threatened to leave her? Part of him clamored to sprint back to the *Wayfarer* and beg her forgiveness before she decided to take him up on his threat, possibly forever. But the louder part of him was so damn angry at her. Wounded, bruised by the words flung at him with callous acerbity. The woman he'd known had been many things, but never cruel. It terrified him, the possibility that this might no longer be the case.

He'd been angry at her before. They'd had arguments, including a few rages so explosive they had likely qualified for a mention in the Dominion annals. They'd even taken breaks from one another—days, weeks, once for nearly a year.

But mostly they'd waltzed across the centuries as if they were dancing on clouds.

Then she'd vanished, and dancing had become slogging as he staggered from one day to the next. And now she'd returned, but they weren't dancing, they were fighting—against their government, against an ominous enemy they didn't understand and most of all against each other.

When he held her in his arms, when they made love, when they murmured to one another in the night, everything was good and right and he was made whole again. But sometimes, like today, like the night before, she inexplicably pushed him away. Shut him out. It seemed to come out of nowhere, and the whiplash was killing him. Almost as if she were two different people—

Oh.

He jerked to a stop on the sidewalk. Two people struggling to become one, or at a minimum to coexist in harmony with one another.

These last weeks, he'd spent a lot of time wanting her to be the person she'd once been. Then, gradually and almost without noticing, he'd fallen for the person she was now, never realizing the extent to which her past and her present were moving toward one another. Only it wasn't a smooth journey. How could it be?

*Wayfarer...*he smiled to himself. Had she intended the dual meaning for the name all along? More than one journey, more than one search for answers....

He was an imbecile, and a selfish one at that. She needed his support and understanding, not his petty resentment and eggshell ego. The anger and hurt evaporated, and now the greater weight of his soul cried out for him to turn around and race back to her.

But he was literal steps away from his meeting. He'd meet with Vance—quickly—then rush to the ship.

Resolve now propelled him forward. But before he took those final steps, he checked to confirm he had taken basic precautions. Heeding Nika's training, he'd worn a morph since leaving the ship. It made sense to do so; this being his hometown, the odds of him being seen and recognized were reasonably high.

But Vance wouldn't know who he was wearing this face, and he really didn't want to delve into the details of *why* he wore a different face. It would only lengthen a meeting he desperately wanted to keep short.

So once he spotted Vance leaning against the wrought-iron fence that bounded the park's centerpiece, an eight-thousand-year-old Kodai bonsai tree, he deactivated the morph.

Vance's expression brightened into a smile when he saw Dashiel approaching. "Sir, it's good to see you. You look...rested, actually. The sabbatical is treating you well."

"Eh." Dashiel brushed it off. He didn't intend to share how much having Nika beside him at night—not to mention being largely alcohol-and-dose-free—improved his sleep. "You look a little worn around the edges. I dropped a horrible burden on you, didn't I?"

"We're getting it done, sir, and it's not a burden. It's an opportunity and an honor. I expect you can't stay long, so what is it you need me to delve into?"

Dashiel's senses instantly spiked to high alert, and his body hummed from the surge of adrenaline released into the pathways of his body. Nika's training, plus a few tweaks to his routines she'd recommended, kicked in with impressive speed and efficiency, even if it was likely already too late.

His eyes scanned the park, despite the fact that his recent dalliances with invisibility made him doubt what he saw. "Your message said you had something you wanted to discuss with *me*."

Vance blinked. "No, I—" Abruptly his Manufacturing Director folded like an accordion and collapsed to the ground.

Dashiel knew he should run. But again, it was surely too late, so instead he knelt beside his fallen friend. "Vance, talk to me." He got no response. The man was breathing, but unconscious.

He froze at the press of cold metal against the base of his neck. His shoulders twitched.

"Don't even think about fighting back. At point-blank range on your port, an energy pulse will wipe all your programming and leave you a blank. I don't want that, and I'm certain you don't want it. Stand up slowly. Don't resist, and this won't be painful. Yet."

The voice sounded familiar, but he didn't risk glancing back to see the speaker. Instead, he did as instructed. Wrist restraints locked into place, pulling his arms tight across his back.

Nika!

A faint tingle passed over his skin, and his comms died.

"Now, now, no cheating. She's a smart woman, I'm sure she'll figure out what's happened to you soon enough. No need to give her a head start."

43

WAYFARER

MIRAI

*Y*our headquarters has been compromised.

For a nanosecond, time stopped. The words hung frozen in Nika's virtual vision, each letter painted in vivid prismatic strokes.

Then the clock of the world ticked forward.

Her combat routines activated, though she didn't yet have anything to strike out against. Her strategic ones began spinning out implications and next actions in branching diagrams.

She sent a response demanding more information, but didn't wait to hear an answer. Next she pinged Perrin while sprinting into the cockpit.

Get everyone out of The Chalet.

Nika? I'm not there right now. What's wrong?

Activated the in-atmosphere engine.

They know where it is, or how to access it. Justice, the Guides, someone. I'm on the way.

Oh, no! I'll meet you there.

Lifted off. Entered the destination coordinates.

No, don't go home. Start working on finding shelter for people. Is Joaquim at The Chalet?

Um...no.

At one kilometer altitude, engaged the emission dampener and cloaking device.

Ryan?

I think so.

I'll contact him and have him start moving people out all the doors.
What are you going to do?
Engaged the autopilot so she could think.
I'll have figured it out by the time I get there.

Flying horizontally in the atmosphere was a rougher ride than she'd expected. The skies were stormy today, and the hull shook as it pushed through turbulent air currents.

The thunderclouds acted out her churning thoughts in real time. Whether the enemy knew The Chalet's physical location and attacked from the street or came through the d-gate doors, she'd need to create an alternate exit—

Nika!

She jumped half out of the cockpit chair. A single word, a consequential word, the urgency it conveyed bleeding through the sterile transmission mechanism to choke off her breath.

Dashiel? What's happened?

No response arrived.

She'd never hated being right so deeply as she did at this moment.

Her hand hovered over the controls, and she almost turned the *Wayfarer* around. But where would she turn it toward? She had no idea where he was and no way to find out.

Everything was coming apart, everywhere and all at once. Now, as she sat there suspended in the sky, buffeted by terror and paralysis, it felt as if she were as well. Bit by quantum bit, disintegrating.

She held her hands out in front of her and stared at them with a sort of detached curiosity, expecting them to crumble to dust while she watched.

Was this even a fraction of what he'd felt when she'd disappeared five years ago? How did he survive it? The emotions that used her body as a playground all had names, catalogued and coded into algorithms to enable the fullness of sapient, living experience. *Hopelessness* to make her hands shake and her lips tremble. *Despair* to deny her air from her lungs and trigger a strong compulsion to hyperventilate. A wretched *melancholy* to narrow her vision into a walled tunnel, where all she perceived was the raging thundercloud ahead.

She could fly into it and never come out. End her fractured farce of a life and leave the world to its fate. To the Rasu—

Stop! She slapped herself across the cheek, then clung to the pain, the smarting sting left behind, letting it sharpen her focus.

She didn't want to let go of the emotions burying her, because they signified something deep and powerful and true. But for the sake of all the people she owed it to save, she must. So as a single tear carved a path down her cheek and fell to the floor, she shut off her emotion processes.

Breathed. Reasserted control. Analyzed the facts as they existed at this instant.

She couldn't save him. She didn't have the information or the tools required to do it. Not at present.

But if she was fast and smart and unrelenting, she could save everyone else.

ᴚᴇ

MIRAI

The Chalet was situated among a sea of factories that stretched across the eight hundred kilometers of grasslands between Mirai One and Mirai Two.

These weren't the sexy factories of the industrial sectors where Dashiel's assembly plants resided and the shiniest gadgets of a prosperous civilization were constructed. No, this was where the decidedly unsexy but necessary materials that supported such a civilization—piping, basic building materials, recyclers, linens and so on—were churned out by the millions of tonnes. The factories were almost entirely automated, and had been for so long that their existence and functionality was taken for granted by most people.

The Chalet had once been such a factory, owned by someone from Joaquim's former life whom he knew and trusted. To repay a debt Joaquim had never shared the nature of, the owner had agreed to fudge the numbers so it appeared the factory continued to operate. In return, they had a hidden place to live.

She was landing on the roof of The Chalet when two Justice transports materialized on the horizon from the direction of Mirai One. She had *no* time!

But the full cloaking system was engaged, and if the Rasu hadn't detected the ship, Justice transports weren't likely to, either. The roof should suffice as a staging area, for a time.

Ryan, you're going to have incoming in a few more seconds. I'm guessing their plan is to blow a hole in a wall and come through it.

Shit. We've still got about twenty people inside.

She opened the hatch and extended the ramp, then returned to the cockpit and fired up the laser. The tiniest bit of power, aimed at the roof.

A gaping hole opened up instantly, and she hastily shut the laser off before it tore through three levels and into the ground beneath the building.

Get everyone upstairs to the third floor dorm wing.

But the doors—

Will be taken out when Justice creates its own entrance any second now.

On it.

She unlocked the *Wayfarer's* grapnel and hurried outside. A torrential downpour greeted her, and in seconds the rain had soaked through her clothes and into her skin.

As she crouched beneath the hull, a shudder cascaded across the roof, bringing with it a rumbling noise so deep and low her bones vibrated to its cadence. Time was up.

She gripped the tensile fiber just above the grapnel's claw with both hands, then dragged it over to the hole in the roof she'd created. Designed as a last-resort tool to secure the ship to an object in space, usually one without either a dock or gravity, the fiber was twenty centimeters thick and the claw a meter wide. So not lightweight.

When she reached the hole, she heaved the claw through it, then looked back at the ship; the illusion of its nonexistence held, and the rain appeared to fall through where she knew it stood.

She leapt down after the claw to land on the floor below.

The sound of running preceded three people rounding the corner. She swung around, Glaser raised—

Dominic jumped. "Nika! Where the hells did you come from?"

She pointed at the hole and motioned them toward her. "Hurry. Up the cable. Where are the others?"

Dominic gave Josie a boost up into the opening. "Most everyone was right behind us, so I don't know. Ryan and Ava are trying to hold off the dynes at the base of the staircase to buy us time."

"Okay. You stay here and get people out as they arrive, but if the shooting moves too close, you head up, too. There's a cloaked ship on the roof. The ramp is extended, ten strides to the east. AEVs are patrolling the vicinity, so people need to get within the ship's cloaking field as soon as they reach the roof."

"Understood. Where are you going?"

But she was already sprinting down the stairs. She passed two groups of people on the way and motioned for them to keep heading up.

The discordant roar of an invasion grew deafening as she reached the final landing. Through the stairwell entry, crisscrossing laser fire shredded equipment, furniture and walls beneath billowing smoke.

She lobbed a projectile grenade over Ryan, Ava and IkeBot's heads and out onto The Floor as she slid in behind them. "Let's go."

"Stars, Nika! A little warning? And we can't go yet. Geoff and Lily are trapped on the second floor of the other wing, hiding in the tank room. Damned if we can get through to them."

"Who's Lily?" She might not be as plugged in to the hearts and minds of every NOIR member as Perrin was, but dammit, she knew their names.

Ryan leaned out to sweep a round of Glaser fire across the breadth of The Floor, then ducked back against the wall. "New girl. Ally who got injured at the transit hub explosion. Perrin let her stay here to get patched up."

"Noted." She checked her belt. Two grenades left.

She handed one to Ryan. "When I say, use this to take out the base of the opposite stairway, then get your asses to the third floor."

He nodded shakily and took the grenade.

She turned her kamero filter up to full, crouched low, and scrambled onto The Floor.

Hq (visual) | scan.infrared(240°:100°)

The energy signatures of the security dynes made them stand out like the gaudy billboards in the Southern Market. She counted six, spread out across the open space. WheatleyBot buzzed around them in a crazed, jagged non-pattern, harassing them with its lasers and so far evading theirs.

Three thermal signatures lay unmoving near where the doors had been before the gaping hole in the wall had consumed the entryway. Her muscles fought to move her toward the signatures while her brain forced them to move her toward the stairway. If she tried to save those people, she'd only share their fate and cause everyone else here to do the same.

Haphazard laser fire veered in her direction. She flattened onto the floor, but not fast enough, and pain lanced into her left shoulder. Just a graze, so she let the damage mitigation routines leap into action and crawled the remaining three meters to the stairway. Her left arm wasn't much help as she clambered up to the first landing and around the corner, then finally stood to vault up the remaining stairs to the second floor.

Now, Ryan.

Three seconds later the world quaked. Cracks exploded across the walls, ceiling and floor; racing clouds of debris chased her as she sprinted down the hall to the tank room—

—a streak of laser fire missed her other shoulder by barely a centimeter. "Friendly fire!"

Geoff and a woman with champagne hair were huddled in the corner behind the tank. "Come on, let's go."

"I'm sorry, Nika! I thought you were one of the Justice dynes."

"Clearly. Move!"

Geoff urged the woman—Lily, she assumed—out of hiding, and they scurried into the hall.

Nika didn't glance at the closed door to her room as they ran past it, though only through sheer force of will. Her home, and she'd never be seeing it again.

"Up the stairs." When they reached the third floor, she grabbed their arms to stop them. "Hold here, at the corner."

Dominic, get everybody away from the dividing wall.

Done.

She retrieved her last grenade, stepped into the hallway and studied the distance, then carefully sent it rolling down the floor toward the wall and ducked back around the corner.

It was overkill for an interior wall, but her Glaser wouldn't cut through it fast enough.

The explosion threw them into the air. Nika's injured shoulder slammed into the opposite wall. A chunk of ceiling landed on Lily's head, and she crumpled to the floor.

Perhaps a little too much overkill.

Dust clogged Nika's airways as she and Geoff picked Lily up. "Just a few more steps to go."

They picked their way across what remained of the dividing wall. Lily wasn't unconscious, but when she tried to make it to the other side under her own power, she tripped over a chunk of wall and landed face-first in the rubble.

Ryan appeared out of the dust-laden haze. "IkeBot, come here and help her!"

The dyne ambled over and lifted Lily into his arms to carry her to the hole in the roof, where two people leaned down into the hole and hoisted her up.

Nika grabbed Ryan's arm. "Is this everyone?"

"It's everyone who's functional."

Her gaze went to the still intact right stairway. "If only there'd been time to grab everyone's psyche backups...."

"Perrin moved them all off-site yesterday. Everything's safe."

"Fantastic. But why did she move them?"

Ryan winced and hunched over a little. "That's not my story to tell."

"Hey, are you injured—"

WheatleyBot screamed around the corner from the stairway, smoke pouring out of cracks in its frame, and circled Ryan in a cacophony of buzzes and chirps. He motioned for the little drone to fly up through the hole in the roof. "Time to go!"

Nika was the last to shimmy up the cable. When she reached the roof, she found it empty, which meant everyone had made it on board the *Wayfarer*.

Eighteen people was a tight fit in the small ship, and she squeezed her way past several of them to reach the cockpit, start up the engine and retract the ramp.

Ryan leaned heavily against the back of her chair. "I didn't have time to grab our hard files. Most of the server equipment got destroyed in the firefight, but I doubt all of it. There's a lot of valuable data stored inside."

She nodded resolutely as she lifted off. "I plan to take care of that."

"Of course you do...." His voice weakened with every syllable.

She looked back at him in concern. "Did you get hit?"

He grimaced and clutched the headrest with both hands. "Yeah, but so did you."

She'd forgotten all about her shoulder; it and much of her left arm were numb, and the material of her shirt was soaked through in blood. It could wait. "Dominic, Ava, get up here. Ryan needs help."

"No, I'll be...." His fingers slipped off the headrest as he collapsed to the cabin floor.

Dominic and Ava reached him almost immediately, and Nika forced herself to let them take care of him. The repair bench on the ship wasn't robust enough to take care of all these injuries; they were going to need access to more advanced benches, and likely a tank. She'd figure out where they might find that sort of help in a second, but first things first.

She continued their ascent until they hovered a hundred meters above The Chalet, where she set the laser to full strength and fired.

The laser cut into the roof like a lightning strike from the heavens. The roof tumbled into the third floor in broken chunks, then the roof and the floor below collapsed into the next floor. Then the remainder of the walls crumbled as the structure disintegrated to bury their home and the dynes who invaded it beneath a mountain of rubble.

44

MIRAI

Perrin approached the scene of the attack with growing dread, when she hadn't thought she retained any dread to summon.

Amid sirens and circling drones, a turbulent ocean of rubble loomed where The Chalet and half of the buildings surrounding it had once stood. All piled up in one location as the debris was, the destruction somehow seemed even more extensive than at the transit hub. Also because it was the signposts of her life buried underneath the rubble.

A sob welled up in her chest, and she covered her mouth to silence it. In the years she'd lived here, she'd rarely seen The Chalet from the outside; its façade held no sentimental value. Silly that its demolition would.

But it wasn't the sight, it was what it signified. Her home, gone. A place of camaraderie and friendship, gone. Everything she'd known for the last decade. The physicality of memories—the *places* where *this* and *that* had happened. Lives and trinkets.

On the other side of double barricades, she spotted Adlai giving instructions to a man, and possibly to the two mecha waiting off to the side.

When the man nodded and strode off toward the debris with the mecha in tow, Adlai's gaze swept across the scene, only to freeze on seeing her. A tentative smile crept onto his face—and quickly vanished, probably on account of her miserable appearance.

He started toward her, pausing to murmur something to a woman he passed before slipping through the barricade checkpoint and drawing near. "Perrin, I didn't—"

She closed the remaining distance between them and shoved him, hard. "You should have rescued him!"

He staggered backward, and she shoved him again. "We've lost our home. We've lost everything—and it's your fault! If you'd gone after Joaquim right away, this wouldn't have happened!"

He caught his footing, then stood his ground. When she tried to shove him yet again, he grasped her hands at the wrists. "I know. I'm so sorry."

Perrin struggled weakly for a second or two, but all the rage that had brimmed over abandoned her as swiftly as it had arrived. Adlai wrapped his arms around her, and she sank against his chest as the sniffles began. "We should have gone after him."

"We should have. I'm sorry." His hands stroked her back while he murmured condolences in a soft, comforting voice.

"They must have stolen his memories and our secrets and…what if there's nothing left of his mind?"

"I don't have an answer. I wish I did."

She squirmed anxiously until he loosened his grip on her, then retreated half a step. "Then what good are you?"

"That is an excellent question."

The devastated look on his face penetrated her misery like an arrow. How horrible of a person was she, to carelessly bury him in guilt and recriminations. "No, I didn't mean it." Her posture sagged, and it took all her effort to remain standing. "This is *my* fault. I should have forced you to get him out. I should have ordered everyone to abandon The Chalet the instant he was taken. I should have—"

"Hey, hey. We'll be here all night if we start tallying up all the blame on a scoreboard. I'm just…I'm glad you weren't here when this happened." He glanced behind him. "We haven't found many bodies yet. How many people…?"

Perrin wiped her cheeks with the back of her hand. They were sopping wet, though she didn't remember crying. "Almost everyone got out okay. Four, maybe five or six didn't. We're still trying to account for everyone."

"That's amazing. I mean how so many people were able to escape once the attack started."

"No—well, yes, but somebody warned Nika a few minutes ahead of time. I don't know the details. But whoever it was saved a lot of lives."

Adlai stared at the ground for a few seconds, seemingly lost in thought, before his attention returned to her. "I wonder who—but it doesn't matter for now. What can I do to help?"

She studied him, trying her hardest to be objective and discerning. He looked, as he always did, earnest and sincere. And compassionate. Damn him for that. "I need to know something. Are you all in? Are you willing to sacrifice your position and your power if it means ending this nightmare?"

"I've made a number of mistakes lately. I've let Dashiel down, let Nika down, let the people under my protection down, but most of all I've let you down. If I want to be able to face myself in the mirror in the morning, I've got to do everything I can to make things right. Yes, I am all in."

She tried not to act relieved, but she was so damn relieved. She reached out and took his hand. "Then you need to come with me right now."

AR

IkeBot carried his master inside the repair services building so swiftly yet with such gentleness Nika could swear the dyne was *worried*. But dynes possessed no emotion programming, which meant her oh-so-clever subconscious must be circumventing her blocked emotion processes to project repressed feelings onto the dyne.

Dominic and Geoff helped Lily inside, and the rest of the

wounded walked themselves off the *Wayfarer* and into the building.

They were in the sleaziest part of Mirai Four, which wasn't much of a city to begin with. The repair center of choice serviced the dregs of the city—black market merchants, smugglers, criminals and others who needed to keep their damage out of the official records. It wasn't ideal, but none of her options were. She only hoped the repair equipment worked.

Perrin came running out the door, against the flow of traffic, and grabbed Nika in a ferocious hug. "Thank the stars, you're okay. Were you really the one who destroyed The Chalet?" She drew back, eyes narrowed. "Wait, you're not okay. Get inside."

"Later." Nika hadn't had a chance to change shirts, but at least the blood had dried. Someone, she couldn't remember who, had stuck bonding tape over her wound during the flight, so there was no new blood, either.

She felt as numb as her arm. Chemicals and override routines had carried her through the attack and escape, but her body couldn't maintain them forever. She wasn't a machine, and her psyche wasn't built to go this long with no emotion processes guiding its responses. But she worried what might happen when she turned them back on.

Instead, she tried to focus on the next step, then the next. This wasn't over yet. "We need to find whatever safe harbor we can for the people who aren't injured. Let's spread people out. I think a lot of our allies will be willing to take in one or two people each."

"I've already been working on that for the people who weren't at The Chalet or managed to escape through the doors before the attack. I've used up most of our solid allies already, so we'll—"

Nika glanced around. "Where the hells is Joaquim?"

Perrin took a step back, away from Nika. "Someone took him. Kidnapped him."

"What? When?"

"Three nights ago."

Nika felt as though she'd been punched in the stomach. Emotions found their way through cracks in her system to form tiny rivulets. "Why didn't you *tell* me?"

"You would have abandoned your mission and rushed here to mount a rescue. He wouldn't want you to do that, not with so many lives at stake."

"Godsdammit, Perrin! It wasn't your call to make!"

"Yes, it was. It became my call to make when you left. Then Joaquim was taken, and it was up to me to lead. I've done the best I can." Her shoulders sagged; she looked as beat-up as the people who'd been caught in the attack. "Only, I don't know how to get him back. And now our home's gone. And I'm so tired."

Nika squeezed her eyes shut in frustration, then reached out and pulled Perrin into a hug. Rivulets became streams. "For the record, I'm angry at you for not telling me. But we have such bigger problems right now, and they're going to take you, me and a small army to solve."

"I know. And I actually did bring a small army—or someone who can bring one, anyway. But we can get to that in a minute." Perrin smiled weakly. "Did you find out what the Rasu Protocol is?"

"I found out where our people are being taken, and I have a good guess as to why the Guides are doing it. And it's all terrifying. But it also has to wait. We have to concentrate on keeping our people safe and getting Joaquim—" she groaned "—that's how they learned the location of The Chalet."

"I assume so. Do you think they've psyche-wiped him? Or stored him?"

"Hopefully not. They'll want to extract every iota of information he possesses first, and he has a lot." She swallowed, afraid to utter the words aloud. Then it would be real. "They have Dashiel, too."

"Oh, Nika...what are we going to do?"

I don't know what to do.

She dragged both hands through her tangled, bloody hair, struggling and failing to hold at bay a wave of anguish as the dam broke and streams became a flood.

Hit after hit after hit, they just kept coming. No matter how fast she ran or how hard she worked, they *just. kept. coming.* Dashiel gone. Joaquim gone. The Chalet gone. Parc gone. Maggie, Carson and Cair, gone. Tens of thousands gone, sacrificed on the altar of an enemy she did not know how to defeat.

She was only vaguely aware of sinking to her knees and dropping her head against the hull of the *Wayfarer*, or of the tears flowing down her cheeks. Memories new and very old flitted through her mind. Happier times. Victories. Moments when the world was hers to shape. Touches, caresses, smiles.

But the memories were swept aside by despair and hopelessness, returning a thousand fold stronger than before to savage her, exactly as she'd feared.

"Hey, Nika...gods, don't you cry, too. You can't give up. We'll figure something out, right?"

She had to find a pathway to a place where those moments were allowed to exist. She closed her eyes, searching for the calm at the center of the storm. She'd once lost a war and somehow built a civilization teeming with wonder and achievement atop the ashes. The strength to do it again had to be somewhere inside her. A light that remained lit when nothing else was left.

Diplomat. Rebel. Leader. Emissary. Beacon. People had called her many things over many lives, but the actions which made them true all came from the same place—within herself.

She breathed in. Stopped trying to hold the emotions at bay and let their full force sweep over and through her. Let them settle and find a balance. Let logic and rationality make their counterarguments. Began to consider how she could change an outcome that was *not* inevitable.

Breathed out.

She opened her eyes and met Perrin's desperate gaze. "Damn straight we will. We're going to get them both back. Then we're going to end this. So talk to me about how we get our small army."

45

MIRAI

The woman standing at the balcony atop the Justice Center wore a simple robe of deep jade with hints of amber threading at the cuffs. She didn't so much turn toward Nika as glide, as if she stood upon a pillow of air. Rich sepia skin accentuated gleaming copper eyes, lips the color of desert sand and bronze hair wound through with lustrous ribbons that matched her robe.

"Thank you for coming, Ms. Kirumase. I expect you do not remember me, but I am Guide Delacrai."

Nika stopped several meters back from the balcony and the woman. "I'm not Nika Kirumase—or not only. You saw to that five years ago."

"I did everything in my power to prevent your psyche-wipe, but I recognize this makes no difference to you. It shouldn't. Recently, possibly too late, I have come to accept the reality that my attempts to protect our people from within the Guides' inner circle will never be successful, and my sole remaining choice is to act beyond those bounds, despite the inevitable consequences."

"It doesn't have to be too late. Where are Dashiel and Joaquim being held?"

"The NOIR operative? He and Advisor Ridani are being interrogated in a secure wing of the Platform. Before leaving for this meeting, I paused the active interrogations and countermanded the eventual psyche-wipe orders, so they are safe for the time being. It will only be a matter of hours, however, before these actions are discovered by the other Guides and reversed."

Behind Delacrai, a twinkling light crossed the night sky far more swiftly than any star. Nika intended to be aboard it very soon. "I'll get them out before that happens."

Perrin and Advisor Weiss were both listening in to the conversation, but Nika pinged them nonetheless.

We've got a location. Start putting together a mission profile.

Already working on it.

"You will not be able to breach the location where they are being held without my assistance."

"Then you will give it."

A slight dip of the woman's chin served as assent.

Nika chuckled wryly to herself. Interesting. Was it possible she *could* be the diplomat as well as the rebel? What if diplomacy didn't have to mean weakness when it came from a position of strength?

She might never be truly whole, but perhaps she could be everything she needed to be.

She considered the woman opposite her anew. Delacrai would make good on her promise of assistance, or she wouldn't leave this rooftop. Still, they had a few minutes to spare while Perrin and Advisor Weiss pulled together resources. This opportunity may never come again, and Nika needed long-overdue answers.

"What did the Rasu offer the Guides in return for your willing surrender of tens of thousands of Asterion lives?"

"Nothing more and nothing less than the continued existence of the remaining millions. You have seen the Rasu? You have seen the power they wield?"

"You could say that."

"What you've seen is but a tiny glimpse of a tangential appendage of the monstrous weight of their true power. Their strongholds stretch across the Laniakea Supercluster like a spider's web, ensnaring all who become trapped within it. They can crush us out of existence with nary a thought, and they would have swiftly done so had they not realized we possessed something valuable to offer them."

"Which is?"

"Living bio-synthetic intelligences, powered by kyoseil and a uniquely innovative form of quantum programming. It is a combination rare in the universe."

"Says us, or them?"

Delacrai's lips quirked into the faintest hint of a smile. "Both."

"This doesn't explain what they're doing with the people you send them."

"I do not know what they are doing with our people."

Nika's jaw dropped, and for a second she had no response. The woman had answered in such a matter-of-fact, affectless tone, it had to be the truth. But how could the Guides have been so passive, so docile and compliant all these years?

"Have you tried to learn anything at all about what happens to them after you deliver them?"

"Of course. We've placed trackers in several of the bodies and stasis chambers. Without fail they are taken to one of the large platforms circling their star—the same one every time. Once there, one by one over the course of several weeks, they shut down. What is done to them in the interim, we cannot say."

Nika paced deliberately across the roof, relishing the feel of the cool night air on her skin, letting it quell her rage even as it reminded her how she was alive and she was fighting.

"Experiments. If the stasis chambers are kept in one central location and they cease functioning after a relatively short time, but not all at once, the Rasu are experimenting on them. And our people do not survive the experiments. Yet you *keep sending them*."

"To buy ourselves time. Time to find a way in which we can survive."

She gazed sideways at Delacrai, one eyebrow raised. "And how's that going so far?"

"I suspect you already know the answer."

"Humor me. Tell me all the reasons why we can't win."

"In ten thousand years we cannot build a military force to match the one they have stationed here, without considering what manner of reinforcements would soon arrive from other galaxies.

We cannot flee the way we did from the Anaden Empire. We are too many in number—tens of millions when before we were tens of thousands—and we must act under the assumption that the Rasu are watching us. If they are, they would be upon us like a hurricane the instant they detected any movements toward an exodus."

"So not well, then. You've had, what, eight years? Eight years you've wasted while more and more of our people die."

"Yes."

"At least you admit it."

"I no longer have the luxury of self-delusion. Still, I fear you do not fully appreciate the burden of protecting an entire species from the great evils the cosmos can send its way."

"You might be surprised." She had thousands more questions poised on the tip of her tongue...but the Platform passed overhead a second time to remind her that time was short and lives dear to her hung in the balance of it.

"We will deal with the Rasu tomorrow. Tonight, we're freeing Dashiel and Joaquim, and their psyches damn well better be intact when we do. We're calling off the inquisition against NOIR and its members. We're stopping the dispersal of all virutoxes through any medium, the kidnapping of people from outposts, and the shipment of people to Zaidam Bastille."

"All of that tonight?"

Nika had to give Delacrai credit; she hadn't expected such a mixture of blunt honesty and sharp tongue from the Guide. "I intend to get a solid start on all of it tonight, yes. By the way, when the fog clears, I've got a lengthy list of people needing new bodies and regens. Gratis, seeing as the Guides are responsible for their current lack thereof."

"I've no doubt you do, but the path from here to there is both lengthy and perilous. I will do what I can to help you free your friends, but the remainder of the Guides will not accede to the rest of your intentions. There is a chance Anavosa can be convinced— it will be difficult for you to believe given your psyche-wipe, but she was always fond of you. The other three will follow their chosen path to whatever end. They are beyond swaying."

"Then they can not be Guides any longer, because I'm not asking permission. Now, here's what I need from you."

46

MIRAI

Nika doubled-checked the contents of her weapons belt to confirm the new additions were secured. The visit to Justice's armory on the way to a lab in the basement—their temporary headquarters—had been a fruitful one.

As she did, she studied Adlai Weiss warily. "Perrin says you helped her, and Spencer vouches for you. You didn't come after Dashiel and I, and apparently you've pissed off the Guides something fierce. So I'll trust you for now, but if I see the first hint of you turning on us, you'll wake up in restraints."

"I believe you." He took the souped-up Glaser that Spencer offered him and checked it over. "You know, we used to be friends. You and I."

"I do know. It doesn't count for much, though, when you tried to arrest me and had your drones shoot me."

"I didn't...no, excuses fail me. It was a shitty move on my part. I'm sorry."

She laughed, but only briefly. His everyman schtick was fairly charming, but he had a long way to go to re-earn her trust. "What kind of force can you muster? I'm down a few people on account of a Justice hunter squad storming our home."

"Okay, that genuinely was not my doing. The Guides have taken every step available to them short of firing me, and I expect after tonight, that'll be a given, blackmail or not. In fact, I'm worried my access will have already been revoked, and I won't be able to get us onto the Platform."

"It won't be a problem. I've got special access codes for not only the Platform, but the secure wing where the Guides do their dirty work."

"Part of the data Delacrai gave you?"

"Yes. She's helping, for now. But if put on the spot in front of the other Guides, don't count on her to fall on her sword for us."

"I definitely will not. By the way, she was wrong earlier, when she said you didn't appreciate the burden of protecting an entire species."

"Why would you say that?"

"We used to call you 'The Voice of the Asterions.' Not to your face, not often. It made you squirm." He started to chuckle, then cleared his throat instead. "From where I stand, psyche-wipe or not, that title has never been more true than it is today. I mean, I used to think it referred to your role as an ambassador to other species, but what is NOIR if not you giving a voice to the people who have none?"

"I..." her heart swelled with inexplicable pride, but she couldn't get caught up in this right now, dammit "...thank you. But you didn't answer my question. What kind of force are you fielding tonight?"

"You've got me, Spencer and four combat-focused dynes borrowed from a hunter squad. But I'm going to have to reduce your number by one more."

"How?"

He glanced toward the door, where Perrin had just returned from checking on housing arrangements for some of the displaced NOIR members.

"Even if we succeed at rescuing Dashiel and Joaquim by ourselves, we will never succeed at overthrowing the Guides without the support of a large percentage of the Advisors. Now, Maris has a plan for making that support happen, but she needs Perrin's help tonight to pull it off—sorry, Advisor Maris Debray."

"I know who you meant."

"What?" Perrin stormed over and got in his face. "No. I have to help with the rescue mission." Her voice rose in pitch with each word, as it tended to do when she got worked up.

Weiss placed a hand on Perrin's shoulder. "She needs someone who can speak with authority for NOIR and who understands your tools and tricks—and someone who can blend in at a cocktail party. You're perfect for it."

Nika groaned. "Advisors and their asinine cocktail parties. How is a party going to unseat the Guides?"

"It's merely the ruse she'll use to get all the Advisors in one place and, conveniently, unable to interfere with our activities tonight." He returned his attention to Perrin. "Please? I can replace you on the infiltration team, but I'm not sure I can replace you for this job."

Perrin gazed uncertainly at Nika. "I want to go with you. But if you tell me to do this instead, I will."

Nika hesitated. She was highly skeptical about the usefulness of this 'cocktail party plan.' But in truth, while Perrin was competent in a firefight, Nika would feel better knowing she was elsewhere; if nothing else, if everything went south on the Platform, the *entirety* of NOIR leadership wouldn't be wiped out.

"And don't say you want to keep me safe. That's not a legitimate reason." Perrin spun back to Weiss. "Or you, either. You don't have the right to protect me."

"I know I don't, and I'm not."

Nika shrugged. "Honestly, we may be safer on the Platform than you will be surrounded by Advisors. But yes. Do it."

Perrin slouched, deflated, but she nodded. "Tell Joaquim—"

"You can tell him yourself when you see him. Later tonight."

"Okay." Perrin sighed in resignation and turned to Weiss. "Where do I need to go, and what do I need to take with me?"

ᚠ

After Perrin had departed, Spencer in tow as an escort out of the building, Nika paused running functionality checks on her internal defenses to eye Weiss suspiciously, again. "You're protecting her."

"I...maybe a little. I wasn't lying. Maris *does* need her help, and it's an important mission. But..." he shrugged "...can you blame me?"

"You like her."

"Doesn't everyone? I mean, I haven't known her long, but I assume everyone likes her."

"Of course they do. Not what I meant."

He ran a hand through his hair then grabbed a flak jacket from the stack by the door. "Maybe a little."

"If we survive tonight, you and I need to have a conversation."

"Now who's protecting her?"

"Me. But I've earned that right. Now, are we ready to move? My people will meet us on the way."

He considered the lab somewhat morosely, as if he were saying goodbye. "We're ready."

47

MIRAI

The door to the penthouse opened to reveal possibly the most beautiful woman Perrin had ever seen. Smooth ebony skin accentuated eyes like living orchids, perpetually blooming out from the pupil as white transmuted into violet. Behind a thick silver headband, a wild mane of obsidian curls exploded into the air around her.

The woman smiled, and the entire room brightened. "You must be Perrin! Adlai told me to expect you. It is such a pleasure to meet you—I don't care if the circumstances are dire. Please, come in. Rid yourself of that heavy bag and let me fix you a drink."

This wasn't the greeting Perrin had expected. She nodded hesitantly and followed Maris Debray into the expansive loft.

She was so hopelessly outclassed. She'd bought the nicest outfit she'd dared with Dashiel's money, a primrose and champagne cocktail dress with layered ruffles that swooshed around her knees, and styled her hair in a cascade of titian ringlets the way she'd seen in the latest vids from the upscale clubs. Even so, she couldn't feel more like a clumsy street urchin if she had a smudge of dirt on her nose and food between her teeth. What she'd said to Nika was true—no amount of silk and gems could infuse her persona with the level of elegance this woman displayed in her left pinky.

"What do you prefer, my dear? Sake? Bourbon? Or a glass of wine, perhaps?"

"Um, wine is fine, but you don't need to serve me."

"Nonsense. Now sit that bag down—anywhere works—and I'll give you a quick tour."

The bag slipped from Perrin's fingers as she accepted the glass of wine from Maris then followed her through the kitchen area and under an arch.

"This is my bedroom, and the lavatory is through this door. And...I suppose that concludes the tour. Everything else is out here in the open. Oh, and here's the door to reach the balcony. We should lock it down, lest someone decide to throw themselves to a temporary death once we tell them the truth in all its ghastliness."

Maris paused to study her. "Relax, please. Your dress is spectacular, your hair is magnificent, and tonight you and I are going to change the world."

Perrin blushed. "How did you know I was worried about my appearance?"

"Because you're clearly a person who expresses herself through her accoutrements. Your hair and your style are your creativity, your art. And I am the Dominion's foremost expert on such matters."

"I guess that's sort of true. I mean about me. I'm certain you're an expert."

Maris chuckled warmly. "Before we start setting everything up, tell me—how is Nika?"

"Oh, you knew Nika before? Of course you did, you're an Advisor, she was an Advisor...."

"True, and true. But I'll tell you a secret. Nika and I knew one another long before we were Advisors. I have known her for many thousands of years, and I've missed her so these last five. But I feel better now, knowing she's had you at her side."

ᴧᴿ

"The field on the door will act as a one-way barrier: people can come in without interference, but once inside, no one will be able to leave until you or I deactivate it. Except us. We're whitelisted."

"Perfect." Maris seemed to always be smiling, yet it always seemed to be genuine and infused anew with warmth. "What about communications?"

"I borrowed a device from Adlai. It's a portable version of what they use to block comms in the Justice Center detention wing. Let's conceal it…" Perrin gazed around the open room.

"In the flower arrangement, I think." Maris motioned to the vase of amethyst hyacinths decorating the dining table.

"Good choice. He also gave me a special bypass code, so you and I can remain in contact with the outside world. The code is apparently one of Justice's most closely held secrets, so we're supposed to guard it with our lives."

"Adlai can be such a drama queen."

Perrin burst out laughing.

"Don't tell him I said that, as I don't wish to hurt his feelings. He's far too self-conscious as it is."

"I won't." She placed the device in one palm and touched a fingertip from her other hand to it. "Also, I'm changing the code, since the other Justice Advisors likely know it."

"Excellent idea." Maris stared at Perrin curiously as she removed her fingertip and wedged the small device deep inside the vase. "So easily done? You must be the best slicer in NOIR."

"Oh, goodness, no. I'm not even the fourth or fifth best. But the worst slicer in NOIR is better at it than ninety-nine percent of Justice officers."

The woman seemed delighted at the notion. "Fascinating! Now, what if someone decides to shut discussion down by stunning everyone into unconsciousness?"

"Then they'll find they have a hard time leaving before we wake up, making it a pointless gesture." Perrin frowned. "Do Advisors routinely walk around armed?"

"Don't you?"

"Yes, but I'm a rebel."

"Indeed you are. No, most of us do not. But the Justice Advisors have been known to on occasion, and it's entirely possible Gemina will expect a trap and seek to protect herself."

Perrin went over to the bag she'd brought and dug around in it. "I don't have anything powerful enough to generate a nullation field as large as the main room here. But you and I can ensure we're impervious to anything less than a point-blank blast."

"Oh, won't Gemina be surprised. I so hope she tries to shoot me." Maris arched an eyebrow and ran opalescent fingernails along her jaw. "What if I need to shoot her?"

Perrin stood near the wall, full glass of wine in her hand, trying and she was certain failing miserably to look as if she belonged.

The loft was starting to fill up with strangers. Normally the first to greet and chat up every stranger she met, here she was a nervous wreck at a complete loss for words.

This was why Nika never let her go undercover.

Maris, though, was amazing. And after her initial awkwardness, Perrin had fallen under her spell, just like she imagined everyone did. They were fast friends, then they'd been friends positively forever. It wasn't true, but when in Maris' presence it was easy to believe the lie.

Speaking of, she tried to suppress any outward anxiety as Maris approached her, a brawny man with dark brown hair and a scowl etched upon his features in tow. "I want you to meet my friend, Perrin. She's a fabulously talented performance artist from Adjunct San. I'm trying to convince her to grace us here on Mirai with her work."

Perrin plastered on a smile and offered a hand. "It's nice to meet you...?"

"Blake Satair."

Her hand froze in midair; she locked down her facial muscles so her smile remained in place. This man had made Adlai's life a living hell, and odds were quite high he was responsible for orchestrating Joaquim's kidnapping.

She could retrieve the small stunner hidden in the inside of her waistband and put him on the floor in two seconds flat. Assuming his personal defenses were only good and not exceptional.

He accepted her hand for a perfunctory shake, then mercifully dropped it. "Maris does love her starlets." His gaze shifted to their host. "How long until you get to your big reveal? I do not have time to be here."

"It will be worth your time, Blake. Trust me."

"It had better be soon." He pivoted and strode off.

"You can unclench your spine now."

Perrin's false smile vanished. "I'm not sure I want to. Do you have any knives in your kitchen?"

"There's the spitfire I would expect from Nika's closest friend. Patience, my dear. We'll set the noose soon enough."

Maris placed a delicate hand on Perrin's elbow and leaned in while she nodded graciously to someone across the room. "It's time."

Perrin silently activated the communications shield. The encounter with Satair had swept away her nervousness and replaced it with focused purpose. She was a leader of NOIR, and she was here to advance a godsdamn rebellion. "We're now isolated. Or rather, they are."

Maris stepped away from her and toward the windows that overlooked the balcony and the city below, deflecting several attempts to snag her attention along the way. Once she reached the windows, she turned and faced the room.

"Everyone, thank you for coming tonight. I must admit a bit of deceit on my part in luring you here. This isn't a cocktail party—though I do hope you enjoy the cocktails in your hands—but instead a far more serious affair." She paused until the tension in the air became palpable. "I'm going to tell you all a story. Then you, each one of you, will have to make a choice."

END

OF

LINE

48

THE PLATFORM

MIRAI ORBIT

J oaquim's eyes popped open.

The soft glow of operational equipment created small areas of light in a dim room, but cast the remainder of it into deeper shadows.

He lay on a flat surface that was more slab than cot, and his wrists and ankles were clasped in restraints. The pressure of a coarse band against his forehead told him his head was restrained as well. The room appeared to be empty, though there were a few corners his confines prevented him from surveying. No sounds betrayed an external presence, however.

He checked his internal system clock, and his heart sank at the grim news it delivered. He'd been out for a little over three days. In a life that spanned millennia, those three days represented a veritable eternity. He didn't take the time to question why he'd awakened now; it only mattered that he had.

The last thing he remembered was walking down the street with Perrin as they returned from the meeting with Advisor Weiss....

Run.

Gods how he hoped she'd done so.

Dark thoughts latched onto his consciousness, but he forcibly set them aside. He needed to finish evaluating his situation, then respond to it.

Nothing was connected to his port, but he felt certain something had been until recently. The defensive tripwires in his OS had all been triggered, for all the good they'd done.

His captors had raped his mind. How much had they uncovered? His memories were intact, and on a cursory survey he saw no evidence of his programming being tampered with, but they could have derived *everything* and copied it out.

Well, not everything. Otherwise his MAD firewalls would have detonated, and he wouldn't be awake now. But surely too much.

He pinged Perrin, then Nika, then Ryan to warn them, but he didn't expect replies. Wherever he was being held, it was doubtless shielded to block communications.

So he needed to escape.

The restraints binding his wrists and ankles were metal, which meant even if he were able to maneuver his wrist blade to the correct angle, he wasn't going to be able to cut through one.

He closed his eyes and opened his sensory receptors. The subtle hum of electrons in motion danced across his skin. The restraints weren't mechanical. They were powered.

Armed with this knowledge, he ran a quick internal systems check. All his special routines and augments remained intact and functional. Whoever had kidnapped and interrogated him must have been in a hurry.

He steeled himself; this was going to hurt. With a silent command, he sent an electrical pulse surging out from his skin.

The natural conductivity of the restraints and slab material ricocheted a portion of it right back at him. His skin burned, and the odor of singed hair assaulted his nose. But his internal defenses warded off the indirect attack and kept it from frying crucial circuits.

More singeing, this time of circuits that didn't belong to him—

The burnt odor of charred circuitry still clogged the air in the apartment ten hours after the raid.

A breeze wafted through from an open window to move the air inside around a bit, and Joaquim tasted the more organic odor of singed hair on his tongue—

Dammit, he did not need memories of that horrific day driving him to distraction right now. Cassidy was dead but he was alive, and he intended to stay that way.

He tested the wrist restraints again...they moved a centimeter. He inhaled and put some muscle into it, and centimeter by centimeter they gave way.

Hands now free, he immediately brought both of them to his head. The restraint holding it in place was fabric, presumably to allow for precise control.

Using the blade embedded in his left wrist, he began cutting at it. Twice he cut himself instead, but after a few more slices the strap fell away. He slowly eased himself up, just in case some unseen equipment had locked his port down. But he was clear. He wrenched the ankle restraints up and away and climbed off the slab.

He swayed unsteadily for half a second, as he'd been lying there immobile for untold hours, but combat routines kicked in to heighten both his reflexes and his stability.

On the off chance that whatever data his captors had copied out from his mind was stored here in the room's server, he went over to the module, yanked a panel off, placed one hand inside and sent out another powerful pulse of electricity.

The skin covering his fingertips came back seared an ugly charcoal, but the satisfaction he gained from the act made a little charring worth it.

The door to his cell opened as he approached it. Not even locked? So his kidnappers were arrogant. If he had anything to say about it, their conceit would be their downfall.

A wide, curving hallway greeted him. Every twenty meters, a door. Additional cells?

If Perrin had been stupid and tried to save him instead of running, or had run but not fast enough, she could be in one of the cells. Escape was promptly put on hold.

He activated his kamero filter, again marveling at the arrogance evident in the lack of an interference field preventing him from doing so, and opened the first door down the hall to his right. Empty. And the next.

The sound of footfalls echoed from around the curve, so faintly he wouldn't have heard it if not for the tomb-like silence of the hallway. Kamero filter or not, he flattened himself against the inner wall of the empty room and waited.

A dyne made its way down the hall. It resembled a customized security dyne, sort of. He'd never seen a model like it.

As it passed the room, Joaquim spun out behind it, extended his blade and thrust it into the critical junction point above its torso, severing the operational signals to its limbs. The dyne collapsed to the floor, and he leapt on top of it and forced his blade under the casing that protected its primary neural core. When the casing finally bent up and out of the way, he ground the tip of the blade across the CPU housing.

Satisfied the dyne was permanently shut down, he retrieved its Glaser from the built-in holster and stuck it in the waist of his pants, as his kidnappers had confiscated his tactical belt.

The next cell was empty as well, but the door to the fourth opened to reveal a man restrained on a slab in a manner identical to his earlier circumstances.

The cell was otherwise empty, but he remained cautious as he stepped inside and approached the slab and its occupant—

"Oh, you have got to be fucking kidding me."

The man's eyes jerked open to dart around his limited field of vision. "What? Who's there?"

Joaquim deactivated the kamero filter and stepped up beside the slab. "How the fuck did you manage to get yourself strapped down in here?"

Recognition dawned in Dashiel Ridani's eyes. "The gallant but stupid way. You?"

"Was Nika captured? Is she all right?"

"She wasn't with me. The last time I saw her, she was on our ship. So, um…unfasten me?"

Joaquim's brow furrowed in contemplation.

"You're not seriously considering leaving me here. You're a first-class prick, but you're not sadistic or heartless or outright evil.

You can't be, or Nika would never have trusted you with NOIR."

He sighed audibly and went around to the module at the head of the slab. "For the record, I'm only rescuing you for her sake."

"Works for me."

The temptation to pulse the table with electricity and watch Ridani's hair and skin burn—just a touch—was strong, but he resisted. Quite noble of him, really. He disabled the slab's control system properly, then grabbed the closest wrist restraint with both hands and wrested it upward. Before he could reach for the other one, Ridani had yanked his arm out of it and was grasping at the head strap.

Joaquim happily stepped back and let the man get himself out of the rest of the restraints.

Ridani eased onto the floor, then frowned at Joaquim. "What happened to your fingers? And your hair?"

"I didn't have anyone to help *me* get free. I had to do it the hard way."

"Fair enough. What's the plan?"

"We need to check the other cells, in case more people are being held here. Then we need to find a way out of...wherever we are."

Ridani stepped toward the door until it slid open and peeked out. "The Platform, I think. I've never been in this section, but the architecture matches."

"So we're in space?"

"Seems so, in which case there's only one way out that offers breathable air on the other side: the d-gates to the towers on each Axis World."

"There could be a hangar bay, ships."

"As if the Guides would allow anyone to *dock* on the Platform. I highly doubt it."

"Whatever. D-gates work fine. I don't suppose you have a kamero filter installed?"

Ridani smirked. "Actually, I do. Nika's been teaching me a few tricks of your trade."

"Is shooting one of them?"

"Yes."

Joaquim sighed again and handed him the Glaser he'd confiscated from the dyne. "I have other weapons, so take this. Don't make me regret giving it to you."

"I won't." After surveying his clothes briefly, Ridani mimicked what Joaquim had done and stuck the Glaser in his waistband. "But I will..." he gestured to the hallway "...follow your lead."

49

MIRAI

"You're certain they'll follow your orders, even if it means firing on other Justice dynes?"

"They're machines. They obey their programming, and their programming tells them to obey me." Weiss tilted his head in Spencer's direction. "Or, in this case, Spencer."

Nika circled the four hunter dynes in an attempt at a critical assessment. They stood nearly three meters tall and were encased in thick, reinforced shells that supported multiple weapons. She'd never had the opportunity to examine one up close before. In every previous encounter, she'd have found herself flat on her back and likely in pieces if she'd tried to get within ten meters of one.

She ran a fingertip along the smooth metal of an appendage that appeared to be a dedicated rocket launcher; the dyne didn't flinch. "I don't suppose you can add me to the list of people who can give them orders?"

Weiss cringed and glanced at the street outside the small Justice depot station. "I *can*, but it will delay us another fifteen minutes."

"Nope. We've burned up too much time as it is. We need to move. Besides, I've never needed a dyne to do my shooting for me."

Behind her, Ava snorted. "You and me both. But be glad Ryan isn't here. You might have hurt his feelings saying that."

She wished Ryan *was* here. Not so much for his pets, though they would absolutely come in handy, but for his own slicing and combat skills. She'd taken twenty minutes to get her shoulder fixed earlier, but it was going to take another eight hours to fully patch up the damage Ryan had suffered during the attack on The Chalet, and they *definitely* couldn't wait that long.

As things were, she had Ava and Dominic. She hadn't been kidding when she'd said she was down people. Everyone else, other than Perrin, with reasonable combat experience had either taken significant damage in the attack...or was a corpse beneath the tonnes of rubble that had once been their home.

Justice wasn't doing much better, either. Spencer appeared to be the only field officer Weiss trusted, and thus the only field officer he was bringing. Between Ava and the four dynes, they were nevertheless packing plenty of firepower. As for manpower, the five of them would have to be enough.

ᴀʀ

Mirai Tower loomed above them like a shining obelisk in the night. A chill rippled across Nika's skin as she stared up at it; her last visit here hadn't gone so well. But this one would go better, because this time, she was prepared.

This time, her eyes were open.

Weiss indicated for them to hold outside the entrance while he and Spencer secured the lobby. She monitored the interaction on the mission channel.

"Justice Advisor Adlai Weiss. We have a security situation inside Mirai Tower. I'm bringing in a squad to address the situation. Once they are inside, I'm placing the Tower on lockdown. No one else is to be allowed inside until I lift the lockdown. Do you understand my orders?"

"Permission requested to alert Mirai Tower security squads and—"

"Negative. Mirai Tower security systems and squads may have been compromised. Lock all entrances and exits other than the Platform d-gate, but otherwise take no action. Do you understand my orders?"

"Affirmat—negative. Override issued."

Shit. "Get inside!"

She, Ava and Dominic sprinted past the hunter dynes, who continued to wait for proper orders, and through the doors.

"Unauthorized entry detected. Disarm and—"

The lobby security dynes were already on the ground by the time they arrived. Weiss' and Spencer's Glasers were raised as they swept the room for additional threats.

Ava scoffed. "Looks like we'll be doing this the hard way."

"We usually do." Nika gestured toward the entrance. "Might want to order your dynes to come along."

Spencer nodded. "I'll get them."

Weiss went over to the command console behind the security station, straddling one of the disabled dynes to reach it. His fingers flew across the panes for several seconds, then he stepped away and dragged a hand through his hair. "And I'm officially locked out. Dammit!"

A loud racket erupted from the entrance. Three of the hunter dynes had made it inside, but the doors slammed shut on the final one. It was made of tough material, as she'd earlier observed, and it struggled valiantly against the powered force of the doors.

"Squad One, keep those doors open."

The other three dynes responded instantly to Spencer's order, returning to the doors, grabbing the edges and dragging them open a few additional centimeters. The trapped dyne stumbled forward into the lobby. Other than two minor dents in its torso casing, it looked none the worse for wear.

"Release the doors."

The instant the dynes let go, the sliding doors slammed shut, sealing them all inside.

Nika gestured to the lift. "Nowhere to go but up."

"I'm working on it, but...."

"In a lockdown, the internal security squads have to be able to move through the building, don't they?"

"Yes."

She rolled her eyes at Weiss. "So stop trying to Advisor your way into the system and start impersonating internal Mirai Tower security."

"But—never mind. That makes sense." He tapped in a new code, and on the back wall of the lobby a panel slid open to reveal a spacious if unadorned lift. "Maintenance lift. Let's go."

Their four hunter dynes took up three-fourths of the space. The five of them squeezed into one corner, and they began ascending.

The shifting pitch of sirens whooshed by as they rose past floor after floor. Building security was now on high alert, which meant they would face armed opposition every step of the way.

Still, for these few moments of calm, Nika couldn't help but contemplate the history, the secrets, stored in the data vaults they sped past. The story of a civilization's achievements, and its sins. Somewhere, on one of the many floors, there was even an office she'd once called her own.

"We can expect resistance in the d-gate room, so we'll have to come out shooting."

"We can clear the way a bit first." Nika retrieved a stun grenade from her belt and adjusted the strength level. "On this setting, the grenade will pack enough of a punch to knock any dynes and drones out for a few seconds, but it shouldn't take out the power—because we need the power to be on to use the d-gate. Oh, and I assume it goes without saying to make sure your defensive shields are set to max so you don't get stunned as well."

Adlai arched an eyebrow. "Something tells me you've done this before."

She smiled. "Not in the d-gate room at the top of Mirai Tower, specifically."

He stared at her oddly. "For a second there, your expression...you looked exactly like...."

"Let me guess: Nika Kirumase." She shrugged. "It happens."

The lift began to slow, and all levity evaporated. "Get ready.

NOIR people take the left, Justice people and dynes, the right."

"But we—"

The lift passed the floor of the top level. "Now!"

Nika lobbed the grenade softly toward the center of the room.

The security dynes inside pivoted toward the lift, raising their weapons.

She leapt up the remaining half-meter onto the floor.

The grenade detonated, ionizing the air with a sharp hiss and scattered pops.

She crouched low and sprinted toward the left-most security dyne. She sensed Dominic veer to the right behind her; focused on her target as she was, she couldn't say where Ava, Spencer or Weiss had moved. The floor rumbled as all four of their hunter dynes advanced at once; subtle, they were not.

When she'd closed to a single meter away, her target jerked twice as it began to recover from the stun. Too late. She grabbed it by the neck and thrust one of her wrist blades into the base until her wrist met metal casing, then yanked it out and leapt away to let the dyne fall in a crumpled heap to the floor.

Next, she dropped low and checked the room. Amid a fair bit of chaos and the smoke of fried circuitry, a blaze of plasma energy melted four drones in a single pass.

From her position in front of the lift, weaponized arm extended, Ava cackled in delight. "New upgrades."

Their dynes had disabled the last two security units, and Weiss and Spencer were both staring at Ava, mouths agape. Weiss frowned. "Are those augments legal?"

Ava blinked at him incredulously, then glanced at Nika. "Is this fucker serious?"

"I'm honestly not sure—"

The windows on the west side of the room shattered beneath a barrage of laser fire. From *outside*.

Nika dove forward, knocking Dominic down beneath her. He

was somewhat new at this, and she expected a half-second delay in his response time.

Adlai: "AEVs on the west perimeter. Squad One, all firepower is authorized."

Nika and Dominic scrambled around the security station as the lasers swept across the circular room, trying to stay ahead of the fire. Her visual filters jolted and flickered as they tried to make sense of the scene in a useful way.

The outline of their hunter dynes stood tall as they tracked the source of the attack then fired four rockets from their mechanized appendages. The lasers honed in on them at the same instant.

The rockets found their targets. Every surface in the room convulsed as the shock wave from two explosions crashed through to hurtle spears of debris in their direction.

The silence that should have fallen in the aftermath was interrupted by the roar of distant crashes as the remains of the AEVs smashed into the ground far below.

Finally there was only smoke and the crackle of shorted electronics.

She crawled back to Dominic, who was leaning against the security station holding his left arm gingerly across his chest. "What's the damage? Let me see."

He nodded, and she carefully lifted his arm away from his chest. A gash seven centimeters long ran up from the crease of his elbow. Blood flowed freely from it, and the skin had been torn open all the way to the bone, exposing the soft glow of kyoseil-infused veins, including one vein that was sheared in two.

"Ouch. Okay, I'm not Perrin, but I can staunch the bleeding, I think."

"That would be a great start."

She dug around in the pack at her hip, where she'd stuffed a few minimal repair supplies, and retrieved some foam and a roll of flexmat. She quickly squeezed foam into the wound, then wrapped the flexmat around his arm. The 'skin' it formed would be minimal and have to be redone later, but it would seal the wound better than bonding tape.

Spencer came over as she was pressing the edges of the flexmat together. "How are we doing?"

Dominic straightened up slightly. "Don't ask me to dual wield, but otherwise I'm good."

Nika peered at him suspiciously. "I'd tell you to stay put, but it's too risky for you to stay here alone. I appreciate the spirit, but take it easy and let us weather the brunt of the opposition."

"Yes, ma'am."

She took his right hand and helped him up to standing, then surveyed the others. Ava was patrolling the perimeter of the room, eyes on the horizon for new arrivals. Weiss was bent over the primary control pane. She hadn't known him long this time around, but he didn't look happy.

"How bad is it?"

Spencer frowned. "We're down two dynes, and a third is down one weapon. A lot of the equipment in here is damaged. It's just a question of how badly."

Broken piles of metal were all that remained of the two fallen dynes. "I had my doubts, but the dynes got the job done. We'd have been toast without them." She exhaled and started picking her way through the debris toward Weiss. "But there's no reason to think more AEVs aren't incoming as we speak, so we need to get through the d-gate. Advisor?"

Weiss shook his head. "The controls are dead."

She walked up to the d-gate and studied it. It looked undamaged, but given how the devices wrent open the fabric of spacetime, they were not fragile creations; they couldn't be. "It's running on a separate power feed from the control equipment, so that's good." She felt along the rim of the frame, but found no interactive pad similar to the ones on the doors they used to access The Chalet.

Had used, because The Chalet was gone.

Nevertheless, it received an access code somehow. And she possessed that access code, a gift from Delacrai. She simply needed to get the code to the d-gate.

She strode back to the primary control pane and nudged Weiss out of the way, then crouched down and wrenched off the cover of the module beneath it. "Here's the problem. The power conduit feeding the signal generator overloaded and burnt out a length of fiber."

She took a deep breath and double-checked the state of her internal defenses. The power required to send snippets of code a few meters couldn't be that high, could it? She'd be fine. "Delacrai's access code is $\alpha\beta\alpha\theta$ $\beta\theta\alpha\alpha$ $\beta\alpha\beta\beta\beta$ $\theta\alpha$ $\alpha\theta$."

"Nika, what are you—?"

She reached in with both hands and pinched the conduit on either side of the short between her fingers.

Her teeth clattered together like banging cymbals. Her fingernails glowed white, and it felt as though her heart stuttered over two beats. "Input. It. *Now.*"

"Done!"

Let go, Nika. All you have to do is let go. She focused on her fingers, which seemed to be glued to the conduit, and directed every conscious process to willing them apart millimeter by—

—she flew backward across the room and slammed into what remained of a wall.

"Are you all right?" Weiss reached for her.

"Nobody touch me!" Her eyes darted around in a panicked search for anything she could use to ground herself—she crawled across the floor to the d-gate and flattened both palms against the rubberized frame that protected it from power surges.

Every muscle in her body unclenched as the overloaded nerve signals dissipated. Her legs had the consistency of jelly as she stumbled to her feet and met four stunned gazes. "So that's what being electrocuted feels like."

Weiss pursed his lips, then brought a hand to his jaw. "You, um...your eyes are still sparking a little."

She nodded unevenly and motioned to the now active d-gate. "Time's wasting. Let's move."

50

MIRAI

"Eight years ago, the Guides began a program of abducting people from minor outposts on fringe exploratory worlds. The program began small—one here, a few months later one there—but the pace has steadily increased. The companies responsible for the outposts were spun one of a variety of stories to cover up the kidnappings: a cosmic or mechanical accident, a government confiscation of the outpost's work, and so on."

"Hey, I've had two, no, three of those happen to companies under my jurisdiction in the last few years."

Maris nodded at Eamon Timoush, an Industry Advisor from Synra. "I suspect most of you have, even if you didn't recognize it as such at the time. Five years ago, Nika Kirumase identified a disturbing pattern in outpost disappearances and began investigating. For her trouble—" she shifted toward the entrance "—going somewhere, Gemina?"

Gemina Kail froze in the foyer, where she'd been creeping toward the door. "Something urgent has come up at the office. I need to see to it."

"That can't be. Or perhaps it can be, but if so, you would not know about it, given how this loft is currently shielded by a field that blocks all communications."

Exclamations and protests broke out among those gathered, but Maris smiled smoothly and gestured for calm. "It's a necessary and temporary precaution. Until you hear the whole story, you might do something foolish you will later regret. Also, Gemina, you're not getting out that door, so don't make a scene trying.

However, since you'll be staying, why don't you tell everyone what happened next? I believe you possess firsthand knowledge of this part of the story."

Gemina shot daggers of fury in her direction. "Fuck you."

"Fine. Then sit down and behave. For Nika's trouble, the Guides ordered her psyche-wiped—"

"What? No. She stepped down and underwent voluntary retirement and reinitialization." Selene Panetier, the Justice Advisor from Namino, leapt out of her chair for added emphasis.

Maris had always liked the woman better than the rest of the Justice Advisors, excepting Adlai. "No, Selene, she did not. Our dearest friend was psyche-wiped and—" she glanced over at Perrin "—how did it play out exactly?"

Perrin arched an eyebrow and twirled a chiffon ruffle with her hand. "Dumped in a side alley street in a rainstorm in the middle of the night."

"That's right." Maris turned back to the group, relieved to see an excess of horrified expressions. "Our Guides did this to one of our own. To the best one of us all. They did it to protect a secret. Gemina? Want to add anything?"

Renewed fury accompanied arms crossed tightly over the woman's chest. So petulant. "No? Ah well. I'd hoped this could become an interactive presentation, but, alas, Gemina doesn't want to play. Fast forward three more years. Outposts continue to be raided and the abductions concealed, but apparently it's no longer enough. The Guides arbitrarily make formerly innocent actions illegal. They increase the punishments for minor crimes. An insurgency named NOIR rises to protest these actions, and Justice gets busy. Right, Blake?"

Blake wore an inscrutable countenance, giving away nothing. "Self-evidently."

"Of course. But eventually even that wasn't enough—enough for what, you ask? We're almost there, don't worry. The Guides, it seems, needed *more* criminals. So they designed a virutox. You may have heard rumors about it recently. It alters an individual's core personality programming, destroying critical thinking algorithms, impulse control routines and emotional responses. The Guides arranged for 15,000 of Dashiel Ridani's limb augments to be stolen and the virutox implanted in them. Then they shipped the augments to merchants across the Dominion and unleashed the virutox upon our people."

She paused to take a sip of sake. "We're missing a few guests this evening. I assume everyone has heard about the tragic events at the Chosek Embassy involving Advisor Rowan. Cameron, did the Guides tell you that Iona's actions were the result of her being accidentally infected with this virutox they set loose?"

Cameron Breckel blinked. "No."

"Just an oversight, I'm sure. Yes, she fell victim to the virutox. I doubt the Guides intended this, but it turns out their creation works far better than they anticipated. It's filled up Justice's cells across every Dominion world. It's filled up Zaidam Bastille. So what a curious thing, then, that Zaidam Bastille is empty."

She let the gasps and confusion ripple around the room for several seconds before continuing. "Gemina, why is Zaidam Bastille empty?"

"You arrogant, self-righteous bitch. You're so proud of yourself, aren't you? But you've killed us all, you know. Everything we've done, we've done to save the Dominion. Now it will all be for nothing."

"*Why* is Zaidam Bastille empty?"

Gemina rolled her eyes. "It's fucked now, anyway, so it doesn't matter if I tell you. Eight years ago, the *Shorai* encountered an alien stronghold on the opposite edge of the galaxy from Kiyora. The crew was killed instantly, but the aliens recovered the bodies and studied them. When the *Shorai* stopped reporting in and failed to respond to communications, the Guides sent another ship to investigate. Its crew was captured and taken hostage so they could deliver a message back to the Guides.

"It consisted of the following: 'We are Rasu. We command hundreds of galaxies and millions of worlds. Our forces are legion, our power without peer. You will kneel before us, then you will die, unless you meet our demands. Your forms are useful to us. Deliver such number of your species to us as we require, alive but without conscious thought, when we require them, and we will not make your corner of this galaxy a priority. We might, in time, neglect it altogether. Refuse to comply, and your species will have seen its last sunrise.'"

Stunned silence fell...and the next second shattered in a cacophony of exclamations and questions. Maris understood full well the response—though she'd internalized what must have happened eight years earlier in the broadest strokes, the chilling, emotionless evil of the Rasu's message shook her deeply.

She cleared her throat and tried to regain control. "I understand. I feel the same as you, with as many questions. Please, give Gemina another moment." She gestured to Gemina. "Continue."

"The Guides agreed to the demand. What else could they do?"

Selene interjected. "They simply believed these Rasu when they said they were all-powerful?"

"Yes, they did. If you'd seen the stronghold the *Shorai* stumbled upon, you'd believe them, too. The sum total of our military and police forces are a gnat they can swat away without even noticing. So, yes, we've been taking people—criminals first, and those least likely to be missed. They are placed in stasis chambers and delivered to the Rasu every two to four months."

Gemina sighed. "But the Rasu's demands have continued to grow. With every delivery, they insist upon more bodies. The Guides have acted as they must, trying to manage the situation without causing a Dominion-wide panic. Trying to maintain order and calm, while working to find some way out of the trap. Some way to save our civilization. But now it's all going wrong, thanks to Nika Fucking Kirumase and her lap-dog Ridani."

Maris bristled at the casual insulting of her friends, but she kept her expression and stance professional, as she always did. Her voice rose forcibly above the growing uproar. "No, Gemina. It's all going wrong because the Guides have made bad decision after bad decision ever since the first Rasu demand. They should have told us, their most trusted Advisors. They should have asked for our help.

"In their isolation and their conceit, they have come to believe they are the only ones who are wise, and they've forgotten how clever and ingenious every Asterion can be. They've lost their consciences, and now their very souls. In their panicked attempts to prevent the citizens from panicking, they've lost their moral compass.

"Do you all know why Dashiel isn't here tonight telling this story himself? After all, he knows the details better than anyone save Nika herself. He's not here because the Guides had him kidnapped, and now he is being forcibly interrogated and tortured inside the Platform, after which he, too, will be psyche-wiped. We Advisors are as disposable to the Guides as a first-gen store clerk."

Selene again leapt up, this time with Cameron following suit. "We have to stop them."

"It's all right. It won't happen. As we speak, Adlai is rescuing Dashiel, with the help of Nika and our new friends in NOIR." She nodded in acknowledgement at Perrin.

"If Nika was psyche-wiped, how is she helping?"

"Wait, NOIR? How are they involved?"

Maris chuckled despite the direness of this night. "That, my friend, is a far longer story—"

"Oh, shit."

"Yes, Blake?"

"Lynch Gemina if you want to, but don't lynch me. I didn't know. The Guides have used me, like they've used all of us."

Gemina growled at him. "Spineless turncoat."

"You said it yourself, Gemina. You've lost."

"*I've* lost?"

Maris frowned. "Blake, what have you done?"

"On my way here, I received a report of a disturbance at Mirai Tower. The Guides sent me to Mirai to reestablish law and order, and that's what I've been trying to do. I ordered two hunter squads with AEVs to the Tower with instructions to subdue and contain the disturbance by any means necessary."

"You thoughtless *ass*."

"Remove the communications block. Let me call them off."

Maris hesitated—then spun around when someone grasped her arm.

Perrin shook her head. "No. He might be lying and intending to warn the Guides or even order a hunter squad *here*. Regardless, if he sent in the reinforcements before he arrived, it's too late to call them off. Either Nika and the others handled them, or they didn't. I don't trust any of these people, but I especially don't trust him. We can't risk him getting out a message, not when the wrong message can still turn the tide against our friends."

Maris smiled. "You are made of far tougher programming than you let on."

"No, I'm not."

"Yes, you *are*." She redirected her attention to Blake. "Let us hope you haven't caused irreparable losses tonight. Perrin is correct, however. No comms."

"It's your decision. I was merely trying to help." Blake stood, glass in hand. "I'm headed to the kitchen for a refill."

He walked half the length of the dinner table—and abruptly lunged for the flower arrangement at its center.

Perrin rushed forward, one arm extended, as streams of electricity leapt from her fingertips through the air. The vase shattered. Blake collapsed to the floor.

Gasps filled the air, and a couple of chairs were overturned as people scrambled backward.

"In my bag, there's a braid of cord. Get it and bring it to me."

Maris credited herself for the fact that her state of frozen shock lasted a scant two seconds. On the third she moved swiftly to Perrin's bag, which they'd tucked away in a corner behind a dracaena plant, and retrieved a bundle of flint-hued fiber.

By the time she returned, Selene was helping Perrin roll Blake onto his stomach while the others looked on uncertainly. Nobody seemed to know how to react. Frankly, this was a blessing.

"Everyone stay calm and let us handle our troublesome guest." No one argued, and her pointed gaze sought out Gemina.

The woman held her hands in the air and crossed one leg over the other. "He was willing to serve me up for a lynching. I'm happy to do the same for him."

No honor among thieves, as it were. Maris retrieved the communications blocker from where it had landed on the floor then picked her way through scattered glass shards to kneel beside Perrin and hand her the fiber.

"Thanks." Perrin held Blake's arms together behind his back and began winding the fiber around them in a crisscrossing pattern.

Meanwhile, Selene rummaged around in his pockets. She came up with a retracted blade and a device that looked similar to the small stunner Perrin had given Maris earlier in the evening.

"I appreciate the help." Perrin looped the fiber vertically a final time then held the two ends together. With a faint glow they fused together more completely than any lock. *Fascinating.*

Selene nodded curtly, then discreetly checked over the restraints. "I don't know what his game is, but I don't like how he's playing it. I'm Selene, by the way."

"I'm Perrin. It's so nice to meet you!"

"Um, you as well. You're with NOIR, I assume?"

Together, they hoisted Blake up onto his feet and dragged him back to the chair he'd occupied. "Why would you say that?"

"Give me a little credit. I *am* a Justice Advisor."

"Right. I...yes, I'm with NOIR. I'd appreciate it if you didn't try to arrest me."

"If I tried, you'd be arrested. But don't worry. So long as Maris is running this show, you're safe. Can I ask what you used to stun him? You didn't have a weapon in your hand."

Perrin grinned. "A defensive upgrade we developed recently, in light of Just—" she cut herself off "—in light of ongoing events." She studied the unconscious man for a few seconds before shifting around—her eyes widened in horror as they took in the wreckage of glass and flowers strewn across the table and the floor surrounding it. "Stars, I'm so sorry, Maris! Your beautiful vase...."

"It's nothing, and also entirely Blake's fault. He must have deep-scanned the room and spotted the device." She motioned over her shoulder, and her household dyne puttered out of its station to clean up the mess.

A groan warned them that Blake was coming to. Everyone took several steps back, and Maris noticed a Glaser had materialized in Selene's hand, which she held at her side.

He blinked groggily, then lifted his chin high. His shoulders flexed as he tested the restraints. They held, and a scowl settled onto his features as a suitably icy stare landed on her. "You will regret this, Maris Debray."

"I never regret anything. This, doubly so." She rolled her eyes at Perrin. "I don't suppose you have a muzzle in that magic bag of yours?"

"Oh, I bet I can fashion something suitable in a jiffy."

"Splendid. Now, where were we?"

51

THE PLATFORM

Dashiel had the opportunity to reflect on his generalized stupidity while they checked cell after cell and found them all empty. On the naive, idealistic notion he'd entertained that the Guides wouldn't dare come for *him*. That they retained a single algorithm capable of generating sympathy for others, never mind empathy. Or a sense of honor, respect, fair play. That they still *obeyed the rules*.

After Nika had disappeared five years ago, he'd obeyed the rules in his search for her. He'd *believed* in the rules, even when he stopped believing in the Guides. In the weeks since she'd resurfaced, he'd time and time again tried to nudge her back inside the lines the rules guarded.

But she had the right of it. When the enemy didn't accord the rules any respect, neither could they.

So this was what being an *actual* rebel felt like. He smiled to himself.

Lacese stopped ahead of him. "Hold up. I think we've reached the end of the interrogation wing."

Sure enough, a wall blocked the hallway ahead. A single wide doorway cut into it, with an access panel glowing placidly beside it.

He couldn't decide whether to be disappointed or relieved that Vance wasn't bolted down to a slab in one of the rooms. Hopefully the man had woken up on the grass in Kinsan Park with a headache and a short gap in his memory, and been allowed to go on his way.

"What are the odds your Advisor status will get us through this door?"

"Absurdly low. What are the odds you can slice it?"

"Higher than that, which isn't saying much." Lacese motioned ahead, and together they approached the door.

It slid open.

"That's odd."

Dashiel glanced at his companion. "Considering how this whole wing is deserted and no alarms are harassing our eardrums, I'd say we're getting help from somewhere. From someone."

"Color me skeptical, but I'll take it." Lacese moved deliberately through the open door, and Dashiel followed.

They were in a control room of some kind. Embedded hardware on both sides operated silently and without stewardship.

"Monitoring and control systems for the prisoners?"

"Probably."

Joaquim briefly studied a couple of displays. "We'll leave it alone for now. Let's keep moving."

At the far end of the room, another door waited, open.

Beyond it was a much larger chamber than any they'd encountered thus far. On the left, a series of archways bounded a central path that led to five d-gates. On the right, five similar archways led to individual rooms. The geometry of the chamber suggested they were much larger than the interrogation cells.

A long blade—longer than Nika's—extended out from Lacese's left wrist as he approached the first room.

Dashiel raised the borrowed Glaser and kept one eye on the d-gates.

"What the...?"

He hurried over to where Lacese had halted beneath one of the archways on the right.

As a first impression, the room resembled a sophisticated data vault. Servers stacked floor to ceiling lined two walls, except for an environmental control unit in one corner. In an alcove on the left side, an elaborate robe Dashiel had seen before hung beside a wig of long, straight black hair.

Photal fibers snaked out from the servers to connect into a curving glass frame encasing an Asterion body. A shell. Inky, dead eyes stared out unseeing. Naked, pale, hairless flesh radiated a waxy sheen. Where torso met legs, there were no sex organs, only more featureless flesh.

"What the bloody fuck am I looking at?"

Dashiel studied the robe and wig to make certain, then reluctantly returned to the shell. "Guide Luciene of Synra."

Silence clogged the air for several seconds.

"They're mannequins?"

Instinctively, Dashiel reached for an accommodating explanation. "Maybe his previous body failed, and the regen is still in progress. I imagine all bodies look creepily lifeless before we inhabit them."

"I'm pretty damn sure all my bodies came with a cock pre-installed."

"Yeah. If only to provide the necessary plumbing."

"Hey—"

"It wasn't an insult. I'm merely saying that sex is optional, but this body apparently isn't equipped for eating or drinking, either."

Lacese shot him a suspicious glare. "True. Which means it's not an Asterion body at all. It's just a doll controlled by a machine."

"Maybe. But it doesn't make him any less alive. I'm fairly certain we fought and lost a war over granting equal rights to sentient synthetic machines."

"Oh, I don't doubt it's alive. Nothing non-sentient could be so cruel and sadistic. But it's not Asterion, and it has no authority to rule us."

"Valid point." Dashiel felt nauseated. Luciene's body could rot on its frame for all he cared, but he really didn't want to see the contents of the other four rooms...though he was already visualizing what they held, so it hardly mattered now. "We should go."

"Not yet." Lacese took a step back and slowly turned his head from side to side. "I'm going to record all this and share it with the world. Everyone deserves to learn the truth."

He opened his mouth to protest, but it died in his throat. The man was right. It was time for the world to change. As an Advisor, he worried about what might replace the Guide-led system of government, but that wasn't a reason not to replace it. "You can record a vid and transmit it later, assuming we make it out alive. There's a comms block here."

"I know." Lacese nodded and backed out of the room, then gazed back the way they'd come. "I bet it's being generated in the control room we passed through. Head in there and try to shut it down."

"How am I supposed to do that?"

Lacese shrugged. "Shoot the hardware until everything short-circuits."

"And hope it's not the hardware that keeps the Platform in orbit? Okay. What are you going to do?"

"Take a quick look around."

He decided not to argue. Let the man stare at the dolls for a few minutes; Dashiel would just as soon be done with them.

When he reached the control room, he took a few seconds to try to determine what the equipment did, then promptly gave up. He'd need to tap into multiple signal flows to begin to diagnose the nature of the operating code, and they didn't have that kind of time.

So he stepped back into the entryway, raised the Glaser, held his breath and started firing into the hardware.

Sparks exploded into the air to the tune of overlapping crackles and pops. He shielded his eyes with his other arm and directed the energy stream across another section of the equipment—

"Halt and desist!"

Through the acrid smoke increasingly filling the room, the outline of a dyne appeared at the other entrance. It raised its own weapon—

Dashiel steadied the Glaser due ahead and fired. First at the appendage holding the weapon, until it clattered to the floor. Next at the 'head,' at a weak juncture where parts met, until the casing broke apart, pieces fell off and the central processing hardware burned.

The dyne joined its weapon on the floor, and Dashiel nearly joined them both as dizziness overtook him. It was the first time he'd shot something real. Not alive, granted, but at the moment the distinction seemed a minor one.

And he'd done a good job of it. Nika's training, instructions and custom routines had kicked in when he'd needed them, exactly how she'd said they would, and he'd gotten it done.

The aftermath was a kick in the head, though. He breathed in and ordered his racing heartbeat to slow, then swept the Glaser's energy stream over the equipment a few more times to complete his work.

He returned to the large chamber just as Lacese arrived on a lift from below. The man eyed him curiously. "Trouble?"

"Handled. What were you doing down there?"

"Like I said—taking a look around. I think the equipment keeping the Platform in orbit is down below, so we should be good." Lacese scowled. "The comms block is still up."

"Well, I can't shoot the equipment back there any more than I already did. The block's originating from somewhere else."

"Fine. I'll record now and transmit it as soon as we're clear." Lacese strode back into Luciene's space. "I am transmitting from a secret chamber within the Guides' Platform. What you see in front of you...."

Dashiel tuned out the spiel and pinched the bridge of his nose. He had a headache, presumably a gift left behind from being mind-probed for hours. He assumed they'd been searching for Nika's location, for starters, and he hoped she'd long since departed their landing site. Who had been assisting them in their investigation would have been next on the list, so the Guides could expand their dragnet sweep for traitors.

It was a short-sighted, doomed-to-fail approach to the problem. The Guides were running around stamping out brushfires while an inferno raged on every horizon. They should have consulted their Advisors eight years ago, but instead they imprisoned, psyche-wiped and sacrificed the people who most wanted to help.

He glanced at the row of storage rooms...but perhaps now he understood why everything had gone off the rails. How could the Guides properly value Asterion lives when they'd lost touch with what it meant to *be* an Asterion? Possibly forgotten entirely—

"Hey, one's missing."

Dashiel forced himself to check each of the rooms on the way to where Lacese stood at the entrance to the last one, even as his stomach roiled and churned in protest. By the time he reached it, he didn't need to peer inside. "Delacrai. She's out wandering the world somewhere."

Lacese shuddered visibly and gestured behind them, toward the d-gates. "I'm done, then. Is that the way out?"

"I believe they lead to the central chamber, which is close to out."

They mercifully left the dolls behind to approach the d-gates, and he stopped in front of the center one. "Here's hoping they aren't code-locked." He held his breath and stepped forward.

He emerged in the Guides' chamber, behind the dais. The expansive room was empty, dark and eerily quiet.

"So this is where you Advisors do your business?"

"Very little of it, trust me." He switched to infrared vision. "Those enormous doors on the other side are the way out, but something tells me they aren't going to open when we walk up to them."

"Why not?" Lacese jogged up to them ahead of Dashiel; his shoulders sagged when they remained closed.

"This is a public entrance. It's likely controlled by a different network than the private sanctum or the interrogation wing."

"I bet there's a control mechanism somewhere—"

From the other side of the door, muffled sounds grew louder. Thuds, the pounding of feet, a crash. Voices.

"One side of the fight has got to be friendly."

"You think they came for us?"

"I don't know about 'us'...." Lacese started banging on the door and shouting.

After several seconds the voices neared, though he couldn't make out what they were saying.

Lacese took two steps back and extended his blade. "In case the wrong side won."

"Good point." Dashiel retreated and aimed the Glaser at the center of the doors.

52

THE PLATFORM

Spencer confiscated the Glasers belonging to the disabled dynes that had assaulted them upon their arrival on the Platform. One of theirs had gone full-on melee with two of the attackers; it had ended in a pile of metal limbs, so they were now down to a single hunter dyne.

"Do we know where they're being held? This is a large facility."

"And it turns out I've never seen most of it." Adlai wiped blood of unknown origin off his forehead. "The interrogation wing should be about a third of the way around this outer ring to the right. Nika?"

She took in the expansive but dimly lit anteroom, wishing she could remember what must have been countless visits to it. "Delacrai gave me an access code for all the doors, so we should be able to reach it. Although, she also promised Platform security would be disabled, but the greeting from our welcoming party suggests otherwise."

"The other Guides might have discovered her countermeasures and are reversing them."

Nika adjusted her tactical belt and motioned for everyone to form up. "Then we need to hurry."

They had just passed two large, ornate doors on the left when the faint sound of movement and possibly voices echoed from the other side of the doors. "Hold up." She leaned in close and focused her aural receptors. Definitely voices, but she couldn't make out what was being said.

Adlai came up beside her. "What is it?"

She kept her own voice soft. "Someone's on the other side of these doors. It may be more security forces."

The doors began to shudder, almost as if someone or thing was pounding on them.

"If it was security, wouldn't they simply open the doors and attack? It sounds to me like whoever it is, they're trying to get out."

"Good point. Everyone, take up defensive positions ten meters back and be ready to shoot whatever comes through." She retrieved the multitool from her belt and began scanning the walls on either side of the doors. "I don't see anywhere to input an access code."

"There isn't anywhere that I'm aware of. The doors have always opened from the inside—wait, over here. I found a seam in the wall where one shouldn't be."

She joined Adlai on the left side of the doors, studied the area he indicated, then took several steps back and pointed her Glaser at it. "You might want to scoot to the side."

"Stars!" He jumped away as the laser met metal. "This is how you create the 'NOIR' graffiti, isn't it?"

"Yep." Her brow furrowed in concentration. A millimeter off the seam, and she risked frying the circuitry they were going to need to open the door.

A rectangular section of the wall fell away, revealing a small control panel. "See? There's always a method of emergency access." She went up to the panel and started to input the access code, then paused to motion Adlai back. "Weapon on the door."

He nodded and joined the others. She tapped in the code and quickly did the same.

The doors slid open with agonizing slowness, centimeter by centimeter revealing only darkness beyond—

"Would you *please* stop pointing a gun at me? It's still just as distracting as the first time."

All the air fled her lungs. Her Glaser clattered to the floor. "Dashiel?"

"Hey, I did find you again."

With a cackle she leapt forward into his embrace. A second Glaser joined hers on the floor as his arms wound around her and squeezed her close.

"You were right. Going to that meeting was a profoundly terrible idea."

She laughed as her lips found his ear. "I love you."

He was holding her so tightly she could feel his breath hitch in his chest. "Nika—"

"I'm fine, too. Thanks for asking."

"It's okay, darling. We can say all the words later." She reluctantly disentangled herself from Dashiel's embrace and turned to Joaquim. "Are you sure you're fine? You look like you took a detour through a crisper."

"You think you're funny, but you're not."

She reached out and hugged him. "I'm very, very glad you're fine."

"*Thank you.*" Joaquim rolled his eyes, then started peering behind her—his gaze locked on Adlai and turned to stone. "You asshole, you set me up!"

Nika scrambled in front of him, grabbing him by the shoulders before he was able to take a swing at Adlai. "No, he didn't. We think another Justice Advisor working for the Guides tracked him to the meeting and followed you when you left. The vaccine was legitimate. He's on our side."

Joaquim glared at Adlai for another beat before relaxing slightly. "You had better be right."

She stepped away to give him some space. "I am. We wouldn't have been able to rescue you without his help...though I guess the rescue is a bit abbreviated. How did you guys get free?"

"Talent and skill, obviously." Joaquim motioned a greeting at Ava and Dominic. "Where's Perrin? She wasn't in any of the cells—"

"She's safe. She badly wanted to come on this mission, but *her* talents were needed elsewhere."

"Hmm." Joaquim studied his left hand, where the fingertips had nearly been burnt off.

"We'll get you to a repair bench soon."

"Whenever. Listen, I don't know how much information they

succeeded in stealing from my mind. Passcodes, locations—" He cut himself off when Nika looked away. "What happened?"

She swallowed heavily and forced herself to meet his questioning stare. "They took out The Chalet. But almost everyone made it out safely."

"Motherfucking..." Joaquim sank against the wall and buried his face in his hands.

"It's not your fault."

"No shit." Abruptly he straightened up and made a show of shaking off the despair. "Luckily, I get to punish the bastards right fucking now. Oh, look, the comms block doesn't extend out to this anteroom. One second everyone. I've got a file to transmit." A long blink later, he gestured behind her. "Is this finally the actual way out?"

What had just happened? Nika studied him in concern for a few seconds before deciding now wasn't the time or place to push. They all had to compartmentalize a little despair if they wanted to get through this night. "Yes. Is anyone else being held back there in the bowels of this place?"

Joaquim smirked in Dashiel's' direction, which she guessed was an improvement over their earlier interactions. "Not any people."

Adlai nodded sharply. "Then let's vacate as well. Reinforcements will likely be moving in here or at the Tower any minute now."

Dashiel sidled up beside her as they moved toward the d-gate. "You met resistance getting here?"

"You could say that—"

"Get down!" Dashiel knocked her to the floor as laser fire streaked centimeters above their heads. Suddenly everyone was shouting and firing.

There was no cover beyond shadows to be found in the anteroom. She climbed to her knees to see a squad of hunter dynes advancing on them. She raised her Glaser as one fired on her—

—Joaquim slid in in front of her and manifested a force-field shield with one arm. The fire splattered off the shield.

Nika dove onto her stomach, stretched her Glaser out beneath the bottom of the shield and returned fire, if only to keep the dyne's attention on them. They caught a small break when their sole dyne defender waded into the line of fire to engage in a battle of energy and defenses.

This did nothing to address the other three attackers, however.

She unlatched a stun grenade from her belt with her other hand. "Ava, get ready on the right!"

"Roger that!"

She lobbed the grenade over the top of Joaquim's shield toward the right wall. Two seconds later it detonated, and in the periphery of her vision, Ava sprinted forward. She took a hit in the leg as she opened fire, but she held her aim. The powerful beam from her weaponized and upgraded arm slammed into the two dynes on the right, shredding them to pieces almost instantly.

Two down, two to go.

The dyne on the left continued to bear down on her and Joaquim. The other one shifted from Adlai and Spencer toward Ava, who was now semi-stranded in the middle of the room due to her leg wound. She trained her weaponized arm on it and fired, but without the benefit of the stun grenade distracting it, the dyne front-loaded its own defensive shield and rebuffed the considerable firepower, if temporarily.

Nika glanced behind her and was startled to see Dashiel flat on his stomach, firing on both dynes. A fleeting grin crossed her lips as she motioned him up beside her, fully behind the shield. "Thanks for the save. Cover me?"

He didn't hesitate in replacing her weapon beneath the lower edge of the shield with his.

She rose into a crouch. The second dyne was now fully focused on Ava, and also about to trample the woman.

Spencer rushed forward out of the shadows, grabbed Ava's non-weaponized arm and began dragging her backwards. A valiant move on his part, but it did little more than make him a target as well.

Nika launched herself forward into a sprint. When she had flanked the dyne, she pushed off the balls of her feet into the air, extended both blades from her wrists and drove them into the base of its neck on her way down.

The dyne jerked violently beneath her, but she hung on, throwing her weight around to encourage it to spin away from Ava and Spencer. It began to stumble unevenly, but continued to fire. So on the next spin she used one of her knees to shove the closest appendage up to dyne-chest height, causing it to fire directly on its partner. Unprepared for the friendly fire assault, the other dyne stumbled sideways and ceased firing on the others.

"Look out!"

The other dyne's upper body exploded. Someone had clocked it with a splinter grenade.

Before she could so much as wonder who, the legs of the dyne she'd attached herself to buckled and it collapsed to the floor, taking her with it.

She wrenched the blades around a couple of times to make certain it wasn't going to get back up, then retracted them and fell off the dyne's frame onto her ass with a winded laugh.

Dashiel was at her side the next second, and she let him help her up, only to frown in concern once she got a good look at him. "You took a hit."

"What?" She indicated his left shoulder, and he peered down at the ragged hole in his formerly white shirt and the blood soaking through it. "Damn. So that's what hurt."

She reached up and touched his cheek. "Welcome to the rebellion."

He winced, but wrapped a hand over hers. "Good to be here."

The growing din of recovery by the others intruded on the tender moment to remind her of their situation.

Ava was grumbling loudly as Spencer tried to wrap flexmat around her leg. "Godsdammit, not again. This was the new one, too."

"Hold still for one minute, please." Spencer appeared to have a fair share of blood on his person, but he was moving under his own power.

Dominic and Adlai leaned against the wall beside the tower d-gates, also covered in blood but upright. Their remaining hunter dyne stood in the center of the room, jagged pieces of metal hanging half off two of its appendages. It seemed everyone had taken damage, but they would all walk, or at least limp, away from the fight.

She felt over her torso and extremities and didn't find any holes. Of course, between the attack in the tower, one minor electrical overload and her tussle with the dyne, she sported enough cuts, bruises and scorch marks to add up to several holes worth of damage.

She reached in her pouch and retrieved some bonding tape, then carefully lifted Dashiel's shirt away from the wound. It looked like a through-and-through, thankfully, and she gave him a little smile while she sealed the entrance and exit wounds up. "This will stop the bleeding and let you move your arm, but don't push it."

"You won't have to tell me twice."

Satisfied with her work, she checked to make sure Spencer had succeeded in completing some level of triage on Ava, then shouted over the din. "All right, I know everybody's hurting, but we need to get out of here before we get overrun."

Everyone hobbled toward the Mirai d-gate, and Weiss took the lead. He readied his Glaser and stepped forward—

Nika's hand shot out and grabbed him by the arm. "Wait!"

53

MIRAI

"Surely the Guides tried to find another way."

"They never came to me asking for input or contingency plans. She's right. They're out of control."

Maris rubbed at her temples and doubled-down on patience. The problem with asking a room full of Advisors for their input was, they all gave it.

Perrin appeared at her side, a new urgency lighting her enchanting blue irises. "Yes, my dear? What is it?"

"Pull up the feed from the *@AltNex_2* channel. Everyone here needs to see what Joaquim's broadcasting from the Platform. You have the codes to shut off the communications block and door barrier when you're ready to do so. You've got everything well in hand. I'm sorry, Maris, but I have to go."

She immediately opened the channel.

"I am transmitting from a secret chamber within the Guides' Platform. What you see in front of you is the true face of your Guides."

A chill emanated from her most fundamental processes, and she instinctively recoiled from the image before her. This was going to change everything.

"The man narrating the vid—he's important to you?"

"Yes, he is."

She squeezed Perrin's hands. "Then go. Be safe. Be fierce."

Morph, mask, kamero filter, defensive shield—they all activated in a series of commands burned indelibly into Perrin's programming.

She ran, even though that drastically decreased the kamero filter's effectiveness. She likely resembled a blurry, wobbly blob to the pedestrians she bolted past on the street, but she didn't linger to ask them.

Maris' loft was in the heart of downtown, which meant Mirai Tower couldn't be more than five or six blocks away. But the buildings stretched tall in every direction, and there was no horizon upon which to find it.

She almost tripped over an unexpected shard of burnt metal lying in the middle of the sidewalk. Only then did she realize people weren't strolling casually as they normally did. Instead they were standing, pointing, scurrying away.

She rounded the corner at the next intersection and, for a heartbeat, stopped cold. Mirai Tower looked like ground zero of an all-out war zone. The windows of both the ground and top floors were blown out. A burning debris field littered the east lawn. An emergency response squad swarmed across the grounds, while two Justice squads guarded a gutted entrance.

Her pulse rocketed to liftoff velocity. Horrific images of Joaquim and Nika's burning bodies blasted fully formed into her mind...Adlai crawling toward them using his elbows, for his legs were burnt off....

She hunched over and vomited on the sidewalk. Curse her over-vivid imagination!

She shouldn't try to contact them; as Joaquim had drilled into her and everyone else countless times, surprise interruptions at the wrong time could ruin a mission's chance of success.

From within the labyrinth of downtown buildings, four AEVs cruised in and took up positions circling the apex of Mirai Tower. If the rescue team was already on the Platform, the AEVs were going to be waiting on them when they reemerged through the d-gate!

Was this the squad Advisor Satair had sent? No, that had to be the debris on the ground. But when the first squad was defeated, as it appeared it had been, reinforcements must have been automatically sent in. They wouldn't have required Satair's order to do so if the parameters were set ahead of time.

But they would respond to his order now.

She breathed out, commanding her OS to release every panic-countering chemical her body could produce. Until Joaquim and Nika returned, she was the leader of NOIR, and she had to be worthy of it. Time to make a battlefield decision.

Nika, if you're on the Platform, do not *come back through the d-gate to Mirai Tower. Four AEVs are waiting on you.*

Perrin? What—

Doesn't matter, no time, so on. I'll update you when it's clear.

Her gaze settled on the circling aircraft as she pinged Maris.

Maris, I need you to do something for me.

THE PLATFORM

Adlai jumped away from the d-gate at Nika's order. "What's wrong?"

"Perrin says there's another squad of AEVs waiting for us."

"Dammit—wait, how does she know? She's supposed to be at Maris' place."

Joaquim hurried up to them. "What about Perrin? Is she all right?"

Nika bit back her initial response in favor of a more diplomatic one. "Gentlemen, focus. The crucial information here is that a squad of AEVs is ready to atomize us if we go through the d-gate."

Dashiel leaned in over her shoulder, one hand resting on her waist. "Can't we go to one of the other towers instead? It will take us a while longer to get home, but we'll be off this orbital prison."

Adlai shook his head. "If Satair is behind this, or the Guides themselves, we have to assume AEVs are positioned outside every tower on every world."

"So what do we do?"

Dashiel was responding to the insanity currently engulfing them *far* better than she'd have expected. "Perrin said to hold on for a minute, and she'd contact me when we were in the clear."

Joaquim threw his hands in the air. "How is she going to get rid of a squad of AEVs?"

"I do not know. But she's done amazing work these last several days in both our absences. I say we have a little faith in her."

MIRAI

"We are the Advisors of the Asterion Dominion, and we shall never be helpless. Knowing all we now know, when dawn breaks on a new day, what are we going to do? I know what I plan to do, but what say you?"

Silence answered Maris for several portentous seconds. Everyone was tired, beaten down by too many revelations too fast. She sympathized; her bones and her soul felt weary, and she'd known most of the revelations ahead of time.

But Advisors were made of sterner stardust, and they had better fucking persevere. "Don't be shy now. Responsibility came with the honor of our posts."

"The Guides must be held accountable, to us and the people. I want to help Dashiel and, if it's truly her, Nika as well. And you, Maris, I expect."

She smiled gratefully. Often, a single voice was all it took to start the dominoes falling. "Thank you, Cameron. You're an honorable man."

Eamon nodded, seemingly to himself, and stepped forward—

Maris, I need you to do something for me.

Yes, Perrin? Anything.

An entire squad of AEVs has staked out Mirai Tower, waiting for

Nika and the others to return from the Platform. I need you to convince Advisor Satair to give you his signature and Justice authorization code. I'll use them to call off the AEVs.

She drew in a deep breath. Sterner stardust it was.

Give me three minutes.

She set her glass on the table. "Selene, as much as it saddens me to do it, can you please remove the gag from Blake's mouth? I have a question to ask him."

Selene checked the secureness of his restraints before unfastening the gag and stepping away.

"Thank you." She advanced several steps toward Blake. "Advisor Satair, I need your official signature and Justice authorization code."

"Why the hells should I give you anything?"

"Your AEVs are currently circling Mirai Tower, lying in wait for their prey to reappear. With your credentials, we will call them off."

Selene frowned. "I ought to be able to do it."

"I suspect Blake has locked all orders to himself alone, if only to prevent Adlai from countermanding them. But please, do try."

After a second, Selene sighed and shot Blake a scathing glare. "You really are a snake."

"I'll take that as a compliment." He shifted uncomfortably against his restraints. "Remove the comms block, and I'll recall them myself."

"Not a particularly shrewd snake, though, is he?" Maris arched an eyebrow at Selene, then removed the stunner Perrin had given her from the pocket of her pantsuit and closed the remaining distance to Blake's chair.

She leaned in close, her lips hovering at his ear, and pressed the stunner to the port at the base of his neck. "Give me the information I have asked for."

"Maris!"

She glanced up at Selene in question. "Would you like to do the honors?"

"No. I...that's one step too far for me to go, when there's still so much we don't know. But I won't stop you." The Justice Advisor gazed pointedly around the room. "And I will stop anyone who tries to interfere."

"Thank you, my friend." Maris returned her attention to Blake. His eyes burned with pure, poisonous hatred, as they should. "Now." She increased the pressure of the stunner on his port. "Tell me, or I will fry every last circuit in your duplicitous brain. Of course, you'll get regened eventually. Possibly. I suppose it depends on who wins."

"You wouldn't store me!"

"Sweetie, if you get my friends killed tonight, you had better hope storing is the worst I do to you."

∧R

Satair's signature is $\alpha\theta\beta\Psi\Xi\theta\Psi\Psi\alpha\Omega \forall$. His authorization code is $\theta\alpha\beta\alpha \ \theta\beta\theta\theta\alpha \ \alpha\beta\alpha\beta \ \theta\alpha \ \alpha\theta\theta\beta\alpha\theta$.

You're a lifesaver, literally. I'll take it from here.

A crowd had gathered along the barriers Justice squads had set up around Mirai Tower—barriers Perrin had slipped inside of while they were being formed. Now she lurked in the shadows, doing her best to evade the patrolling dynes.

She found the darkest, most deserted corner she could, then closed her eyes.

access nex.Mirai.MiraiOne
§ sysdir.NodeJC
handshaking
< $\Sigma \to \beta$
$\Phi \to$ kernel signature:
< $\alpha\theta\beta\Psi\Xi\theta\Psi\Psi\alpha\Omega \forall$
kernel signature $\to$ T
handshake complete
< command.M(n): Hг(Λ) = (parameters (location($41.22°$ N, $13.81°$ W +- 0.5km)))
T $\to$ nullOrder.all

Φ → passcode required:
< θαβα θβθθα αβαβ θα αθθβαθ
T → passcode accepted
< exec command.M(n)

She reopened her eyes in time to see the AEVs retreat from the Tower, pivot and fly off toward wherever they'd come from. On the ground, the squads surrounding the tower lowered their weapons and dispersed toward the perimeter. Several Justice officers glanced around in confusion and tried to order the dynes back to their posts, to no avail.

Blessed stars, it worked. Her knees nearly buckled beneath a wave of relief-driven adrenaline.

Nika, you're clear!

She ordered her limbs back into compliance, then took off running for the Tower entrance.

54

MIRAI

Nika was the last to traverse the d-gate connecting to Mirai Tower. A distinct and welcome lack of active chaos awaited her, but dear gods the room was wrecked.

Her eyes found everyone in turn, confirming no one had collapsed from their injuries. "We should get to the ground floor and out of the building. The AEVs are gone for now, but we don't have visibility into what manner of firepower might be headed our way next."

Joaquim held up a hand. "Actually, we need to step outside first. This place has a deck, doesn't it?"

The memory of the first time she met Dashiel blossomed in her mind. "It does, or did before earlier tonight. I can't guarantee the scaffolding is secure after the attack."

Adlai frowned. "Regardless, I'm not sure we have time."

"We have time for this." Joaquim looked around for the door, then strode outside.

She wanted to get moving, too, but when Joaquim was properly determined, there wasn't much anyone could do to dissuade him. She gave Adlai a resigned shrug and followed Joaquim. By the time she reached the door, Dashiel and Adlai had joined her.

A cool, clear night greeted them on the deck. The breeze washed over her like a cleansing wave, and she breathed in deeply as she joined Joaquim. "Okay, we're here. What's up?"

"Funny how you phrased it that way. The correct question is, 'what's not up any longer?'"

He pointed to the night sky and the bright light moving across it more swiftly than any star—

—an explosion ruptured the heavens, shooting out plumes of red and gold that for a moment consumed all the stars.

Adlai grabbed Joaquim by the shoulders. "Did you just *blow up the Platform?*"

"I did."

Beside her, Dashiel grimaced. "*That's* what he was doing down below."

"But the Guides!"

Joaquim squared off on Adlai. "The *Guides* took the love of my life from me. They took my freedom and raped my mind. They took my home. Now, they will never take another godsdamn thing from me."

"I should arrest you. What kind of Justice Advisor am I if I don't?"

Joaquim peered up at the sky, where debris from the shattered Platform had become flaming meteors streaking through the atmosphere. "Not sure any of you are Advisors any longer. No one left to advise."

He was enjoying this way too much, but after the day she'd had and everything that had led to this moment, Nika couldn't bring herself to be too angry at him.

"There's still a Justice Division, and I—"

Dashiel stepped up and placed a hand on Adlai's arm. "Let it go. Something had to give if we want to move forward. Better it be the Guides than us. Besides, they must have remote backups of remote backups. No way are they gone."

Joaquim groaned. "Probably not. But they've been exposed now. Their stronghold is gone, and the people have seen what they really are. They won't rule us ever again."

"True, and true. Still, you've kicked up a serious shitstorm now. The people will be afraid. They'll see the Platform destroyed and they'll think we're under attack. They'll think our government has fallen."

Nika took Dashiel's hand in hers. "We *are* under attack, and our government *has* fallen. It's up to us to save ourselves now."

ᴁ

A saffron dawn crept up the horizon to bathe the shadowy waters of Hataori Harbor in a warm glow, then spread across the city below until it touched Nika's skin. She drank in the light and the warmth in equal measure.

The last several hours had blurred into one another. The destruction of the Platform altered the calculus of their escape, and in the end they'd never left Mirai Tower. Once they controlled it, it became the safest place to huddle up and figure out how to face the chaos they'd played a large part in creating. Also, until order and a clear chain of command within the Justice Division was reestablished, the streets would remain dangerous for all of them.

Members of NOIR who had scattered during and after the attack on The Chalet arrived in groups to guard the entrance below and treat the injured. She didn't know if Joaquim or Perrin had asked them to come, or if they'd seen the Platform fall out of the sky and acted on their own initiative, but the sight of them here filled her with joy and fierce pride.

Dawn was becoming daylight when the door to the deck opened and Perrin peeked out. "Nika?"

The cocktail dress she'd arrived wearing, amid a tornado of hugs and exclamations minutes after the Platform's destruction, was gone. Someone must have brought her a change of clothes, and she now wore a pair of heather leggings and an oversized powder-blue sweater.

Nika waved her out onto the deck. "Is everything all right?"

"Stars if I know. No one's shot at us in at least an hour, so that's a positive. Though, I passed Joaquim and Dashiel on the way up, and they were standing there drinking juice and calmly *talking* to each other, so it's possible I bumped my head sometime during the night and this is all a hallucination."

"You and me both. Great work tonight, by the way."

"Me? I just went to a fancy cocktail party. You stormed the castle, rescued our boys and took down the Guides."

"Well, sort of. Dashiel and Joaquim basically rescued themselves. We merely cleared the escape route for them."

"I doubt 'merely' covers it. Listen, I realize you're going on stage in a few minutes, but first, there's someone here who badly wants to see you. And for the record, she's *wonderful*."

Before Nika could respond, Perrin spun around and hurried back to the door. A woman stepped out as Perrin reached it, and they shared a brief, murmured exchange before Perrin slipped inside.

The woman stared at her for several seconds wearing a strikingly poignant expression. Finally she approached the railing, only to stop a few meters away. "Nika, my goodness. I worried I would never see you again—I'm sorry, I realize you don't remember. I'm—"

Nika closed half the distance between them. "Maris. I do remember...some things. Bits and pieces." Another step, and she took the woman's hands in hers. "I remember that you were my friend, and for such a very long time. Longer than seems possible. I'm not quite the same person I was, but I hope we can be friends again."

Maris' lips parted. "I would like that so, so much. Though I would never dare try to take Perrin's place beside you. She's wonderful. An absolute delight."

"She is. Of course, she said the same thing about you. I suppose an ability to choose my friends well didn't get erased in the psyche-wipe."

"I hear it's not the only thing—"

Dashiel stuck his head out the door, a broad smile breaking across his face. "Now this is a welcome sight for my tired eyes. I hate to interrupt the reunion, but Adlai says we need to broadcast soon."

Maris gestured toward Dashiel. "Shall we, then?"

"You'll stand with us?"

"Oh, yes. And I brought some friends."

AR

Drone cams buzzed around everyone who had gathered in the conference room. Most of the people were strangers to Nika, but they all knew her...and she was starting to make her peace with that.

Those who had come here needed a leader and a beacon as much as those watching the drones' feed across the Dominion did. They needed a voice.

Rebel, diplomat, rebel once more and now both at once. Though too many pieces remained missing for her to fully understand the how and why, she was also starting to accept another truth: she had always been that voice. Time to step up and become it again.

"Live broadcast in 3...2...1...."

She faced the cams. "Good morning, afternoon and evening. Wherever you're located, the world looks a little different now than it did a few short hours ago. You have questions, and I'll try to answer them where I can. But many of the answers, we will have to find together.

"My name is Nika Tescarav. Or Kirumase if you prefer, it doesn't matter. What does matter is that I'm not alone, and neither are you. Standing here with me are the greater weight of your Advisors. Not the Guides' Advisors—*your* Advisors.

"We're reaching out to you today because our beloved Asterion Dominion is in grave danger, and we need your help to save it."

Don't Miss the Finale of the
Asterion Noir trilogy

THE
STARS
LIKE
GODS

Coming In 2019

***

SUBSCRIBE TO UPDATES

GSJENNSEN.COM/SUBSCRIBE

Get AURORA RISING Books 1 and 2 for FREE,
stay informed about ASTERION NOIR and new books,
and be the first to know about events and other news

Author's Note

I published my first novel, *Starshine*, in 2014. In the back of the book I put a short note asking readers to consider leaving a review or talking about the book with their friends. Since then I've had the unmitigated pleasure of watching my readers do that and so much more, and there's never been a more rewarding and humbling experience in my life.

So if you loved OF A DARKER VOID, tell someone. Leave a review, share your thoughts on social media, ask your library to get more copies, annoy your coworkers in the break room by talking about your favorite characters. Reviews are the backbone of a book's success, but there is no single act that will sell a book better than word-of-mouth.

My part of this deal is to write a book worth talking about—your part of the deal is to do the talking. If you keep doing your bit, I get to write a lot more books for you.

Of course, I can't write them overnight. While you're waiting for the next book, consider supporting other independent authors. Right now there are thousands of writers chasing the same dream you've enabled me to achieve. Take a small chance with a few dollars and a few hours of your time. In doing so, you may be changing an author's life.

Lastly, I want to hear from my readers. If you loved the book—or if you didn't—let me know. The beauty of independent publishing is its simplicity: there's the writer and the readers. Without any overhead, I can find out what I'm doing right and wrong directly from you, which is invaluable in making the next book better than this one. And the one after that. And the twenty after that.

Website: gsjennsen.com

Email: gs@gsjennsen.com
Twitter: @GSJennsen
Facebook: gsjennsen.author

Goodreads: G.S. Jennsen
Pinterest: gsjennsen
Instagram: gsjennsen

Find my books at a variety of retailers: gsj.space/book-retailers

ACKNOWLEDGEMENTS

Many thanks to my beta readers, editors and artists, who made everything about this book better, and to my family, who continue to put up with an egregious level of obsessive focus on my part for months at a time.

I also want to add a personal note of thanks to everyone who has read my books, left a review on Amazon, Goodreads or other sites, sent me a personal email expressing how the books have impacted you, or posted on social media to share how much you enjoyed them. You make this all worthwhile, every day.

About the Author

G. S. JENNSEN lives in Colorado with her husband and two dogs. She has written eleven novels and multiple short stories, all published by her imprint, Hypernova Publishing. She has become an internationally bestselling author since her first novel, *Starshine*, was published in March 2014. She has chosen to continue writing under an independent publishing model to ensure the integrity of her stories and her ability to execute on the vision she has for their telling.

While she has been a lawyer, a software engineer and an editor, she's found the life of a full-time author preferable by several orders of magnitude. When she isn't writing, she's gaming or working out or getting lost in the Colorado mountains that loom large outside the windows in her home. Or she's dealing with a flooded basement, or standing in a line at Walmart reading the tabloid headlines and wondering who all of those people are. Or sitting on her back porch with a glass of wine, looking up at the stars, trying to figure out what could be up there.

Made in the USA
Columbia, SC
04 June 2020

10220453R00238